Jessie's Heart

Wanonna Gray

Denise,
Thanks for your
support.
Much love
Noni 2007

Princess Press Publishing

Detroit, Michigan

Princess Press Publishing, LLC
P.O. BOX 04665,
Detroit, MI 48204-1232

Library of Congress Cataloging-in-Publication Data is available.

ISBN 978-0-9796157-0-2

Printed in the United States of America

Cover design by Wanonna Gray
Cover illustration by Marcus Margerum, MS Graphics

First Printing

ACKNOWLEDGEMENTS

Special thanks to my Lord and savior, Jesus Christ, first and foremost, who gave me this story and has allowed me to transform it into my first novel.

...To my husband Rob, who allowed time and space for me to create. Your patience and tolerance during the completion this book will always be appreciated - you keep me grounded.

...To my earthly angels, my sons, Alex, Robert, Ryan and Jalen, whose invaluable and uncompromising belief in me inspires me everyday and encourages me to be my best.

I also want to thank those others who were instrumental in extending love, support, and always ever ready to lend an ear. To Sherrhonda who pushed me, Sherry who encouraged me when I thought of giving up, and to my little sister Fran, whose confidence motivated me to continue on. To my parents who has always loved and supported me, and to all the members of my family with all my love.

DEDICATION

This book is written in loving memory of my grandparents, Eddie and Lula Mae Boswell who inspired a work that is close to my heart... You are loved and will never be forgotten.

INTRODUCTION

Whoever said the heart of a woman can be known is a certain fool. Untamable, unpredictable, and indiscernible, a woman's heart is at best mystifying, and at worst, unknowable. Within a woman's heart are thoughts, memories, feelings, emotions, and the secrets of life. Ah yes, secrets. Those deliciously dangerous hidden moments, forever tucked away in the inner sanctum of the soul, wherein lie magnificent magical memories, causing the lip to reflexively quiver into a smile when no one else is laughing. Secrets, causing the embarrassing flush scampered from cheek to cheek as, within an atom of time, one is transported back to a moment of sequestered bliss, trespassing touches, recalling the taste, touch, texture and smell of fully ripened passion fruit, swollen and bursting with the sweet nectar of the profane. Within these guarded reflections, one loses a sense of propriety and proximity, those close by not knowing the savor or flavor of succulent stolen kisses within seconds lasting an eternity, reminiscences echoing, reverberating and resounding within the corridors of the soul. The thump of the pulsating rhythm of fulfillments' promise thunders through the veins, pounding like native drums, desires' fire, quenched by nothing else but the thunderstorm of satisfaction. Gaze into the mirror of the past, and you will find secret's reflection, beckoning with the persistence of a siren's song. Timeless, exhilarating, forbidden and dangerous, the secrets of a woman's heart are often self-indulgent pleasures, life threateningly lethal decisions made for transient satisfaction of an eternal thirst. In the wrong company, these flights of fancy spell certain discovery and potential disaster.

Secrets simultaneously protect the innocent while preserving the guilty for the reckoning which surely must come... another day.

Some secrets we pray to forget, some we hold close to our hearts, others we regret. Then there are those, like an unseen ill-wind, blowing one adrift, an uncontrolled course change which can't be changed, but must be ridden to its conclusion. They creep down the dark and dank back steps of our consciousness, waiting their turn, even if it is not until the day of our last breath, they will find their voice, for no secret is kept forever. Taking on lives of their own, breathing and bemusing, breathless and amusing, secrets never die, and cannot lie; they languish in the vestibule of our lives, haunting waking thoughts, and disrupting peaceful sleep. Secrets too bold to believe, and too dangerous to conceive, are alive and well, kept in of the private vault....of Jessie's Heart.

Chapter 1

Tulah was only eighteen when she discovered she was pregnant once again, making her a mother for the third time. It wasn't until after she was expecting her second child that she married Louis Starks, the son of Kennedy Starks. Kennedy was a mullato man who passed for white before being found out, and ran out of Florida in the early 1900's. He moved from state to state before settling in Marietta, Georgia, where he met and married Sara James, a small framed, dignified woman, who was considered by all who knew her to be the consummate southern belle. Kennedy and Sarah started their family immediately, he working faithfully, she staying home to raise their family.

Kennedy made a living as a mortician at the Crest Funeral Home. Although he didn't have any formal training to perform in this position, he learned fast and worked hard, arriving at work before sun up, and not leaving until way after the sun had retreated into a restful slumber. Randolph Crest hired Kennedy because their policy not to embalm coloreds cost them money. After the reconstruction, many whites sold plantations and businesses and moved north, taking their businesses with them, forcing Crest to change his policy in order to stay afloat. He therefore hired, and then taught young Kennedy everything. Kennedy worked his way out of the back, to the position of Funeral Director, earning an astronomical twenty dollars a week, unheard of for a colored. Not that Crest wanted to pay it - he had no choice, given the lucrative business Kennedy brought in by being the black face of a white owned business. Kennedy's success firmly established the Starks name as one the leaders of

Marietta's small and exclusive black social registry. His two sons, Henry Lee and Louis James grew to be polite, educated and well-respected because they were considered a prosperous black family. No surprise his sons were earmarked to lead the second generation of black wealth in rural Georgia, and understood they were to insure wealth by marrying well.

Louis first saw Tulah Belle Armstrong at White's General Feed and Grain Store. He walked into the store and headed straight for the loose tobacco kept in the crystal humidor behind the counter. As he made his way to the counter, a faint flicker of movement, draped in a whisp of canary yellow and white flitted in the corner of his eye. As his turn caught up with his gaze, Louis' eyes rested upon a slender girl. He stood transfixed, watching the effortless grace of her movements, choreographed poetry gift wrapped in a sleeveless yellow cotton dress, white apron coverlet, a white slip hanging lazily beneath its hem, and on her feet, flat brown slippers with no socks. Her face was angular with a strong jaw, high cheekbones and prominent forehead. Her smoky hazel eyes, full-orbed with a slight Oriental upward slant, contained a mixture of adolescent innocence and premature development. Her skin, a dark brown, was as smooth as freshly spun silk, and her hair framed her face in tiny ringlets. Her delicate arms and graceful hands reached languidly into the candy bin, gingerly plucking lemon drops from the decanter and quickly dropping them into a brown paper bag for purchase. What got Louis' attention was that for every two lemon drops Tulah put in the bag, two would also go in her pocket. She looked right into the prying eyes of a bewildered Louis, flashed a knowing smile and went about her business of completing her purchase. Spellbound, Louis followed as she placed ten pennies on the counter and quickly headed for the door. As she started out of the door, she looked back at Louis and winked before exiting the market. Louis, intrigued by her cool and fearless behavior, quickly walked out after her. Removing his hat from his head, he apprehensively approached her.

"Excuse me ma'am. May I trouble you for a minute of yo' time?"

"Who me?" Tulah asked, as she straddled a worn bicycle.

"Yes ma'am. If that's alright with you."

"Well, you gone hafta follow me down here yonder, fo Mista White come out here and have my hide."

Not waiting for Louis' response, she took off on her bike, leaving a trail of dust billowing in its wake. Louis watched as the bike rocketed down the red dirt trail, disappearing from view. He smiled to himself, shaking his head as he put his hat back on, and entered the store.

"Mr. White, suh, how you be this day?"

"Just fine, Louis, just fine. How's your parent's?"

"They're fine, suh. Mr. White, do you know the young lady who just left here? The one buying lemon drops?"

"That little gal comes in here every day to buy lemon drops. Twice a day sometimes."

Mr. White answered, removing his glasses from his face and then retrieving an old and frequently used cotton handkerchief from his back pocket, wiping away the tiny beads of sweat above his eyebrows and on the back of his neck. Placing his bifocals so the bridge rested on the tip of his nose, he was a cherubic white man, whose stomach hung over his waist, supported by the folded white apron neatly folded and tightly tied around his waist like a girdle. He peered over his glasses and leaned toward Louis.

"Why you askin' bout that gal there, Louis? She got yo fancy?"

"Oh naw, suh. Just curious. I don't reckon I seen her round here b'fo is all."

"Well, come round here mo' often, she'll show up. I 'speck she loves her some lemon drops more'n anythin' else."

"Yes suh."

"Well, ain't you buying nothing, or you just come here to ask bout that gal?"

"Oh yes, suh. I come fo' a scoop a Cherry Deluxe tobacco."

Mr. White shook his head and chuckled beneath his breath as he measured out the portion of tobacco in the pewter scooper. Mr. White always gave Louis's a gentleman's portion, an extra third or so, because he was proud of his achievements as one of the "new coloreds," reminding himself he wasn't supposed to call them nigras anymore, though he never meant any harm. He placed the portion in the bag, pulled the drawstring, double knotted it, and handed it to Louis.

"15 cents."

Louis reached in his back pocket, placed the two dimes on the counter, and tucked the bag in his neatly pressed and crisply starched white shirt pocket.

"Keep the change." It always made Louis feel good to tip Mr. White. His father taught him to always give back more than you get, and don't ever owe anybody if you can help it – that's the way to get ahead in life. As Louis left the store, the image of Tulah's brilliant smile danced in his head. He decided to take Mr. White's suggestion and visit the store more often. Louis would be sure to make it his business to run into Tulah Belle Armstrong again.

Louis awakened to the song of country mornings, the solo of the rooster, nature's most effective alarm clock. Blossoming like a freshly watered summer rose, another deliciously hot Georgia day beamed down mightily where scarce slivers of shade was the only relief from the sun's pulsating gaze. The small town, beautifully adorned in the splendor of nature resembled a painter's canvas, displaying a panoramic view of rolling green hills blending into each other with seamless symmetry, and grandiose Georgia sycamores in their majestic posture reach far into heaven as if greeting God with open arms just waiting to be embraced. Long and winding roads meandered seemingly without end, leading everywhere and nowhere at once, while mockingbirds and kingfishers sang their sweet soliloquies hoping to entice and enchant capable suitors. Cows grazed lazily in the hazy morning pastures. Dew hung heavily off the edges of leaves and clung to the grass, dampening the earth with condensed moisture. The sweet smell of jasmine fragranced the air, with the vague scent of lilies and azaleas complementing the chorus of smells. All nature joined together each day, a morning symphony of thanksgiving for God's love, beckoning His embrace and favor. This was Louis' favorite time of day; the quiet and still time, when the earth stretches and shrugs off evening slumber, stirring and waking with the promise a new day always brings.

The long front porch was the pulpit to Louis's private sanctuary each morning, the quiet providing undisturbed opportunities to collect his thoughts, rehearse his dreams, and converse with God. Today there was an addition to those musings, the indelible image of Tulah's smile, wink, and knowing glance. Never in his twenty-two years had he been so struck. Louis was never brought up a learned man about religion, but he always felt close to God. Though he didn't always know what to say, the morning symphony always provided the melody to the song of love Louis felt for God. Louis often took the family Bible, three generations old, in his hands, rubbing the finely textured papers between his fingers while reading of God's sovereignty and great mercy towards all who loved and reverenced Him, bathing and cascading him in wholeness and peace. Once, Louis' Mama caught him reading the Bible and shamed him no end, telling him he didn't know what he was reading no how, and how that Bible was there to bless her table. Louis read it anyway, careful to return it to its exact spot before anyone could miss it.

The rickety storm door swung open and out came Henry, his older brother, holding two cups of coffee, passing one to Louis.

"Hey! What you doing here so early?" Louis took the cup, blowing then sipping the hot coffee.

"I was here late waiting for Etta and the kids and fell asleep in the back. Mama put a blanket over me and that was all she wrote." Henry laughed as he sat down beside Louis. "That little broken in sofa in the back cradles me like a baby."

"Etta ain't back from Memphis yet?"

"I was spectin' her last night, but she sent word sayin' that they'd be leaving first thing this morning. It got too late fo' them to travel at night. Besides, her Daddy wanna keep her there long as he can any how - still thinks she's his little girl."

Louis nodded and sipped from his cup.

"Good coffee."

"Etta learned me how to make it that way."

Louis was silent, still taking in the beauty of the new day.

"Whatcha doin' out here, man?"

"Enjoying the silence fo' it gets too loud, kids be running round, roosters and hens cluckin' n clackin', folks stirring up a fuss 'bout little uh nuthin'. So I gets up early fo' it all gets started."

"Since when ain't the country quiet enough?"

"Since dem Zachary's down yonda had all dem chillen." They laughed.

"I like it just like this – fo' a spell anyhow – I have a little peace and quiet first."

"I think I know what you mean."

Both Henry and Louis sat in silence enjoying their coffee when a young girl on a bike came riding past. Henry didn't even seem to notice her, but as she passed by, Louis stood and watched her till she was clear out of sight.

"You know her?"

"Can't say I do. She must be new round here." Louis answered still looking in the direction of where she rode by and disappeared into a thicket.

"I don't' recall nobody new in town, so I don't know where she comes from. Second time I've seen her though."

"Maybe she's visiting some of her people round here."

"I reckon thas' possible."

"Well, I'm a git going. Etta and the kids'll be home soon and I need to be back by day light, if ya know what I mean." Henry's gleam told Louis everything.

"Give her my best. And give my niece and nephews a big hug from their uncle."

"I'll do that. You done?"

"Naw, not yet. I'll take it in. Thanks."

Louis got his tripod, camera, and equipment and went into town, the beautiful day providing a great opportunity for business. Tinkering around with a camera when he was only twelve, his fascination for photography became an obsession. He learned all about the camera, how it worked, how to develop exposures into photographs, and hang them dry until they were transformed into a perfect, identical replica of the subject. Louis had an eye for beauty, and the camera was the perfect way to capture the essence of a subject and immortalize it forever. Photography was more than a hobby for Louis, it was therapeutic; it was what made him happy. He has since learned he could also make a decent living doing what he loves. He was the town photographer and that suited him just fine.

Louis had been saving to open his own studio, where patrons could come in and be photographed with different and fancy backdrops. That was the reason Louis still lived home with his parents at the age of twenty two, which was just fine with his Mama, who loved spoiling him. Louis could always count on his Mama to make him all kinds of home made cakes, pies and pastries. Almost to the point where he could purchase his own studio, no white man was willing to sell property to a colored. Louis had as tough a time finding a place to rent, which was the main reason he still took photographs on the street or in people's homes. Not being able to pursue his dreams just because he was black was one of the realities of life Louis just couldn't get used to. No matter how much white blood coursed through his veins, Louis was undeniably black. Other than the cold realities of life that held him back, Louis was a mild mannered, easy going, reasonably happy person. Among people of his own race, he was esteemed and well respected, but with the exception of a few, he was just another boy in the south who would never have a fair chance.

Louis set up in town under his favorite tree, an old elm tree, which just a few decades before bore the weight of many a runaway slaves who paid the price of their thirst for freedom with their lives. Nearly everyone in town passed by that old elm tree at some point throughout the day, which made it the perfect place to set up shop. It was just enough sunlight to cast the right kind of lighting needed, shady enough to block the glaring sun. Louis took photos of passersby and charged 25 cents for a developed photograph taking him two days to deliver. It was there, under the noonday shade of that old elm, Louis noticed Tulah Belle Armstrong for the third time in just two days. She was going into Mr. White's place of business, undoubtedly for more of her beloved lemon drops. Louis was intrigued and excited, wanting to run over and make the acquaintance of the young lady before she disappeared again. He couldn't leave his makeshift studio, but wasn't about to let opportunity to pass him by. Louis grabbed the first kid he saw and offered a whole 25 cents if he would stand there and watch his equipment while he ran over to the store. Once inside the store, he strolled over to Tulah and introduced himself.

"How do you do ma'am? My name is Louis Starks." Louis extended his hand to her. Tulah snickered at the thought of a gentleman calling her ma'am. She grabbed his hand and did a curtsy.

"And I'm Tulah Belle."

"Tulah Belle. That's a pretty name, for a pretty girl. Are you buying more lemon drops?" He asked and winked at her.

"I don't know what you mean, suh?"

"You know what I mean. Listen." Louis leaned in to her, "I could buy you all the lemon drops you want if you let me photograph you."

"Like I said, I don't know what you mean, suh."

"I mean I'd like to take your photograph. I got a shop right across the road, it's all set up and waiting just for you."

"Ain't no photo shop round these parts. I done rode my bicycle all round here and ain't no photo shops to be found."

"That's because I just set it up this morning, and it's right outside waiting for you. Now, what you say? Can I photograph you?"

"Well, that depends."

"On what?"

"How much is it gone cost me?"

"For you little lady, won't cost a thing. I'll even buy those lemon drops for you."

"What's yo angle?"

"My angle is that I get to keep yo' photo fo' myself and tell everyone it's a picture of my lady friend."

Tulah snickered again, this time covering her mouth. She was infatuated with the way Louis looked at her with those intense grey eyes of his, but continued with her rough edge approach.

"But I ain'tcha lady friend."

"You can be. That's up to you, of course."

"Well, I think I may let you if you throw in a coke cola."

"Alrighty then. It's a deal."

Louis had Tulah to sit on a stool just under the oak tree and smiled at her.

"This is gone be the best damned photo I ever took."

He noticed, as he positioned her on an old tree stump he covered with a clean cotton cloth and used for a stool, that Tulah had light brown eyes - hazel in fact. Such an unusual combination to have light eyes and dark skin, Louis thought to himself. Pretty round face, light eyes, a warm, inviting smile and dark brown hair. She was the prettiest girl Louis had ever seen, and he liked her energy - forceful and feisty with a sweetness he found irresistible.

As Louis prepared to take Tulah's photograph, she studied him from head to toe. She noticed how finely dressed and well-groomed he was. From the way his sandy brown colored hair was trimmed and brushed neatly to the back, to his finely pressed, crisp white shirt, and starched dark slacks, Louis was indeed a well-kept man. His lean, six foot tall frame, gave the appearance that he was much taller. His ivory complexion was sort of pale for her taste, but his skin was even and smooth, she yearned to reach out and touch it. Tulah even noticed that Louis' nails were neatly clipped and buffed to a dull shine, not dirty or grimy like most other men, or some women for that matter. She looked down at her own nails and took a mental note to manicure them once she got home. Tucking them under her apron so that they wouldn't show, she looked up at Louis and asked,

"How's this?" As she tilted her head to the side and smiled.

"That's perfect. Absolutely perfect - now don't move."

Louis put his entire head under the black cloth and held a small device in his hand. Each time he squeezed the device it caused a bright flash, startling Tulah.

"Ain't you never had yo' picture taken b'fo?"

"As a matta fack I have. Yo's ain't as fisticated as the ones I'm accustomed to is all." Louis laughed, knowing full well he had the most updated camera equipment in town.

"Is that right?"

"Yes, that's right."

"Well, I'm sorry to not be able to meet your standards. I reckon I need to get more up to date, so I can compete with the fancy, 'fisticated' cameras you're accustomed to. Hold that pose just like that." Louis said squeezing the device. He moved in close to Tulah, tucked a loose hair behind her ear, gently stroked her face, and then lifted her chin. As he turned to walk away, his after-shave loomed in the air behind him. Intoxicated by his fresh, clean scent, she closed her eyes and inhaled deeply to take in the full fragrance of his cologne. She opened her eyes, to see Louis smiling at her. Sobering herself, she stiffened and asked,

"Is we done?"

"Almost. So Tulah, are you new around here? I know just about everybody round these parts and I don't recall seeing you b'fo a couple of days ago."

"I came to stay wit my Aintie. I was living wit my Granny, but she got too old and senile to care fo me, so I'm wit my Aintie now."

"Who's yo Aintie?"

"Aint Cora."

"Ms. Cora Allen?"

"You know her?"

"Miss Cornbread Cora? Everybody knows her. She makes the best cornbread you ever did eat."

Tulah laughed at the thought of her Aunt Cora baking corn bread for the entire town, because she often suggested she should sell it for a nickel a slice.

"That's the one."

"Ain't this something? You Ms. Cora's niece, well I'll be. Where's yo Mama?"

"My Mama died when I was five," Tulah explained while casually sipping her coke.

"She got sick and got to coughin' real bad and didn't nobody know what to do. She went to sleep one night and nevva woke up. I guess she got tired of fightin.'"

"Well, where's yo pa?"

Tulah shrugged.

"I don't know. He run off after Mama died. That's when I went to live wit ma Granny. She just about grieved herself sick after Mama died. And you know what? Nobody even told me. I memba we had to get dressed up and folks was coming by bringing cakes and fried chicken, and was being especially nice to me that day, but I didn't understand why. After a few days I asked Granny when was Mama coming home and she told me that Mama was gone home to be wit da Lawd. I didn't know what she meant – not at the time anyway. My brother Aaron splained to me what happened better than anybody. But a course, he got tired of living wit Granny I guess, and after while he run off and got married."

"That's too bad, Tulah. I'm sorry you had such a hard life."

"My life aint' hard," She said emphatically. "My Granny was good to me and raised me like I was her very own chile. And Aint Cora, well, you know her, she as good as gold."

"I didn't mean nothing by it. I just meant that it's too bad you lost both your parents is all."

Tulah shrugged again, sipped her coke, and kept talking as though she and Louis were old friends reacquainting after a long separation. They talked way into evening, even as the sun began to set, leaving and amber glow across the sky and a musty smell from the stale heat rising from the parched ground. Day gave way to night and stars a billion miles away sparkled brightly through a blanket of darkness, offering ancient light to an otherwise somber evening. Hungry mosquitoes buzzed around looking for warm, moist skin to satisfy its long awaited cravings, and lightning bugs lit the path like a thousand tiny lanterns. A cool wind teased, with just enough of a breeze to offer a hint of relief that kept them anticipating more. Louis walked Tulah home, carrying his camera equipment over his shoulder, and she walked with her bike along side of her. As they approached her aunt's house, Tulah stopped him before reaching the gated fence.

"You betta stop right here. I don't wanta give Aint Cora the wrong idea bout me."

"I know your Aintie, she won't think nuttin' bad bout me."

Pressing her small palms into his chest, she insisted.

"It ain't you I'm worried bout. I'm just getting here good and I don't want her thinking I'm some fast gal who needs lookin afta. B'sides, you nearly twice my age." Tulah added tentatively."

Louis laughed. "I don't think I'm twice yo age, Tulah. How old is you anyway?"

"Fifteen. I'll be sixteen next May. How old is you, if I may ask?"

"I'm twenty two."

"Well, now you see. You're a third my age, but everyone says I'm pretty grown up for my age, so that makes us about even."

Louis laughed not knowing how to respond to her quick wit.

"Well, if you say so."

"Well, I do. So when is ma photographs gone be ready?"

"Uhn uhn. You mean my photographs," Louis corrected. "I bought a lot of lemon drops for these photos."

Tulah laughed.

"You shole did. I got enough to last me for two whole days."

She extended her hand to Louis.

"Well Mr. Starks, I had myself a good time today. I thank ya "

"My pleasure, Tulah. Uh, when can I see you again?"

"Don't worry - you will. I'll find you in town, or either I'll just come by your shop under that ole elm."

"Night Miss Tulah."

"Night Mr. Starks."

Louis stood in the shadow watching Tulah into the house. He walked home recounting the day and anticipating their next meeting. She was quite young, that part was true, but more tenacious, spirited and full of wisdom and spunk than any of the other women Louis had dated in the past. There was something special about Tulah, something special indeed; and Louis certainly intended to learn exactly what that something special was.

Chapter 2

Louis and Tulah started courting after their first meeting, seeing each other every day. Tulah came by his makeshift picture studio every evening just before dusk, and he would walk her home. Throughout the day she would come by and bring him a cool drink or help with his work. Louis loved her attention, and wanted everybody in town to know she was his girl. And although Tulah shared the same admiration, she was not as open with her feelings as was Louis. This kept Louis intrigued with Tulah. For her to be the youngest lady he's ever courted, she was certainly the most mysterious, and independent, not allowing him to do much for her, and not offering an account of parts of her day. There was a part of her that she kept reserved, and although Louis tried, he could never seem to penetrate through that part.

What Louis didn't know, was that Tulah was having trouble at home with Aint Cora. Cora had gotten after Tulah about seeing Louis, saying he was too old and experienced, and had forbidden Tulah to see him. Entering the house, Tulah saw Cora sitting at the kitchen table with a bowl of green beans. Cora snapped those beans with a quick rhythm.

"You ackin' like a tramp running round wit dat old man."

"Aint Cora, Louis ain't no old man. You know him and his parents. He come from a good family- a wealthy family. Thought you'd be happy for me is all."

"Dats what's turning yo head? His money? Little girl, don't be no fool. Dat man ain't thinking bout no little nappy head girl like you. He just think he can have his way witcha, like he do all dem other womens he runs wit."

"Aint Cora, Louis ain't seein' no other womens!"

Cora stopped snapping the beans to look Tulah squarely in the face.

"Don't you sass me gal. I will put you out of my house fo I let you come here sassin me." She rolled her eyes at Tulah and resumed the rhythmic snapping of her beans, tossing them into the bowl. "Sista Mabelle said she seed you and Louis out huggin and holdin hands lak yous married or something. Now you not gone come here and shame me. I got myself a good name round here and I ain't gone let you come here whorin around lak some hussy cause dat uppity half-breed got a little money and smiled in yo direction."

Cora paused for effect, letting her biting words penetrate Tulah's young, fragmented heart, as she kept snapping beans, now louder, with a heightened intensity and pace. Tulah felt a knot the size of a grapefruit grow in her throat, but she refused to cry. Tulah repressed her anger, though she felt like snapping Cora's neck as like one of those string beans. Composed, she cleared her throat, speaking in a low, deliberate tone, almost a whisper.

"Aint Cora, I aint gone shame you, or myself. And Louis ain't uppity and he ain't no half-breed."

The sound of the snapping beans stopped. Cora threw the handful of beans in her hand on the table, looked in Tulah's direction, and a laugh erupted out of her belly filling the house. Tulah, bewildered, grinned and started laughing too.

"Lil' girl is you blind? Now you jest shut yo mouth and listen here. I seed his momma in town and went to speak to er, and she ack lak she been suckin on lemons. Dats right, turned her mouth up lak I ain't good enough. And besides, I happen to know dat his Daddy was passin fo white fo he got hisself kicked outta Jacksonville. Dem white folks ain't goin fo no half white, black man, chasin afta dey womens. He almost got hisself kilt foolin round wit dem white folks down there. Now I know what I'm talkin' bout, Tulah, and you ain't ta see dat man no more."

"I's just thinkin' that maybe that uppity half-breed's got money to help is all." She said enticingly, knowing Cora's affection for money.

Cora leaned forward and looked at the young girl up and down with penetrating eyes, as if considering her words. She scooped up a handful of beans, picking up her rapid rhythm precisely where she left off.

"I said you ain't ta see him no more."

"But Aint Cora!"

"No more, Tulah!"

Tulah ran out of the house, the screen door slamming behind her. Hurt, angry and upset, Tulah ran down the hard, red, clay road with no destination. She thought about her mother, what she was like, and how she would be if she was still alive. The only times she ever wondered about her father were times she needed protection, representation, comfort and shelter. Times like this. She wondered if he were remarried or if he had other children. Tulah turned off those thoughts the moment they begin gripping her. She thought about running away to her brother's house, but he was too far away for traveling by foot. She even had herself a nephew. He would be just about five years old now, and Tulah had only seen him twice; the first time he was born, and again when Aaron, and Doris, his wife, came to town to visit for a few days and stayed with Tulah and her grandmother. Tulah knew she couldn't stay with her brother - Doris, her sister-in-law, wouldn't have it, and she wouldn't stay even if she could, because she was not about to leave Louis. He was kind to her, something she had experienced little of in her fifteen years. She wanted to commit to him, to let go and enjoy the intoxicating dizziness of love's freefall. He was that special, but she was afraid of committing. Tulah couldn't stand the thought of losing him; so many times she distanced herself from him attempting to protect her heart from being broken - again. Everyone around her who she really loved had left her in one way or the other. Granny, who loved her dearly stayed, but her mind left, which was the same thing in Tulah's mind. It nearly broke her heart when she had come in from school one day and granny didn't recognize her. She had been forgetful, losing things and repeating herself, but when she looked Tulah straight in her face and asked, "Who are you?" It crushed her in a way she had never known before. Only with granny had Tulah known what stability and unconditional love was.

Aint Cora, who she thought to be an upstanding, God-fearing woman, was showing her true self. Smiling, polite and righteous in front of all of her church friends, but at home, Cora was just plain old mean. She believed Cora loved her, but wanted to control her. As long as Tulah obeyed, everything was fine. But the moment she expressed thoughts or ideas of her own, Cora's temper quickly ignited, accusing Tulah of being disobedient, ungrateful and insolent. Tulah had enough of her unrelenting control. She could tolerate most things, but when she tried to drive a wedge between her and Louis, she knew it was time for her to go. It was one thing that she had to quell her impulsiveness, and keep her fast talking mouth shut, but to have Cora dictate how she should live her life was too much.

Tulah walked down to Critter's Creek, kicked off her slippers, and slipped her dainty feet into the cooling waters welcoming her with soothing caresses. As the sun was setting, she tossed rocks into the creek watching them sink into the deep down into the water, their impacts causing circular ripples to fan out across the water's surface like huge bull's-eyes, growing bigger and bigger. She tried to count how many circles would appear before disappearing, leaving the water calm and still. Tulah pulled her knees up to her chest, wrapped her arms around them and wondered if there was any truth to what Aint Cora said about Louis' parents being uppity and his father passing for white. She looked down at her chocolate covered skin and wondered if Louis could ever really want someone like her, or if he just wanted to have his way with her like Aint Cora said. Either way, Tulah wasn't going to stop seeing him because she had come to care for Louis and loved the way she felt when she was with him. No matter how uppity or half white he was, if he wanted her, he was going to have her. In that moment, Tulah decided she was going to give herself to Louis. And if sex was all he was after, she figured it was best to get it over with anyway.

The sun exchanged places with the full moon, a glistening illuminated silver platter in the night sky. The calm quietness of the southern summer night blanketed the countryside like Granny's home made quilt. A choir of crickets sang in unison commanding the attention of the humid summer's night. This was the time Tulah would normally be on her way to Louis so they could walk home together, but what reason could she give him as to why he couldn't? She thought to lie, but couldn't deceive him. Curled in a fetal position, Tulah felt Louis worrying. Not knowing what to do, where to go, or what to say to Louis,

Tulah was tossed in a raging sea of confusion. Tears welled up in her eyes like huge translucent orbs of light until her lids overflowed. The tears from the right eye fell across the bridge of her nose to the other cheek, joining with the tears of her left eye, coming to rest in the refuge of her ear. With a swipe of disgust, Tulah briskly dried her face with a quick hand motion, turned over on her back feeling the cool, damp earth and stared up at the sky. She connected the stars until the formation of the big dipper appeared, then searched for the little dipper as well. She fought back tears with clenched teeth and a determined will until she fell asleep.

Louis stayed at his makeshift studio well past quitting time, waiting for Tulah. Now completely dark, he wondered where she could be. Louis put away his camera equipment, glancing around every few seconds hoping to see her rounding Critter's Creek. By the time he packed his things away and Tulah was still not there, he became angry with her for her inconsiderateness, and for not being polite enough to come by and say that she wouldn't be requiring him to walk her home. As Louis left, he found himself headed not in the direction of home, but Ms. Cora's house. Once there, he hesitated before knocking on the door, remembering what Tulah said about not wanting her aunt to think that she was fast. Louis knew how upset Tulah had been when they ran into Miss Mabelle, Ms. Cora's busy body friend, in town one afternoon, which added to his reluctance. But since he had made the trip he figured he may as well knock on the door. Louis breathed a deep, soul cleansing breath, and knocked on the flimsy screen door. Cora opened the door, feigning surprise.

"Evenin' Mr. Starks. What brings you down these parts?"

Louis removed his hat from his head and stammered a greeting.

"Uh…Good evening Ms. Cora. Sorry to impose, but I came to call on Tulah."

"Well Tulah aint here. And b'sides it's rather late fo you ta be come callin on Tulah. I run a respectable home and I ain't tryin ta give folks the wrong idea about how I let my niece keep company. Menfolks can't just show up all times of da night. I know your folk raise you better'n dat."

"Tulah ain't home?" Cora looked through the screen door and narrowed her eyes in indignation.

"I mean, yes ma'am. Miss Cora, I really don't mean no harm, but if Tulah ain't home, where is she?"

Cora put her hands on her hips.

"Don't you take that high handed tone with me, boy."

"Yes ma'am. I apologize. Can I please leave a message fo' her?"

"I spose ta be yo' seckatary now, huh?"

"No ma'am." Louis reached in his pocket, pulled out two silver dollars, and extended his hand to Cora. Cora looked Louis up and down, gazed at the two coins glistening in his hand, reached around the half open screen door, and took the coins.

"Tell her I came by, please." Cora turned her back to Louis, placing the coins inside her bra then turned back around. "She go down to da water when she thow tantrums and get a spell on – might be down near Critter's Creek somewhere – I own't know." Her tone had changed. Funny what money will do, Louis thought to himself.

"Thank you, ma'am."

"Um hum." Cora said, still adjusting her clothes.

Louis picked up his equipment and started off the porch, but Cora stopped him.

"Mr. Starks."

"Yes ma'am"

"You ain't seen Tulah?"

"No ma'am. Not since early this morning. She was at Mr. White's store buying some mo of them lemon candies she likes, I reckon. But she was acting kind of odd."

"Whatcha mean by odd?"

"She wasn't doing much talking. That's odd for Tulah."

"Boy, you ain't knowed her long enough to tell if she can talk an chew gum at the same time. She a wile chile wit no home trainin'. Tulah Belle Armstrong ain't nuthin' but pure trouble. You better stick wit yo' own kind, dem prissy Atlanta gals yo' Mama be tryin' to fix you wit."

"Is everything alright, Ms. Cora? If I may ask."

"Tulah and I had a misunderstandin'. She off somewhere pouting is all."

"Thank you ma'am."

Louis said as the door pounded shut. He turned to walk away, but was disturbed by the fact that Tulah was missing and no one had seen or talked to her. Going home to wait for her to show up was not an option. Louis would never be able to rest his mind not knowing where his beloved was. He stopped by his brother's house, because it was along the way, and dropped off his equipment so he could begin his search for her. He had gotten himself so worked up about what could have happened to Tulah that he didn't bother to knock on his brother's door or explain what was going on, he just dumped the equipment on the porch and started on his way. Louis searched Marietta from end to end before Cora's words echoed in his ear. He headed for Critter's Creek.

Louis walked the creek's edge searching for Tulah in the luminescent moonlight. He attempted a prayer beneath his breath, asking God to look after Tulah, wherever she was. He thought about the sudden impact she had made on him. He couldn't imagine what his life would be like without that commanding, little, feisty woman with the mesmerizing brown eyes coming around telling him how to do his job. He then dared imagine life without her, and an emptiness gripped Louis' heart. He resisted the thought. Then he noticed a silhouette in the moonlight just at the creeks' edge. The closer he came, the faster his heart pounded, until he got close enough to make out her form – and there she lay asleep, curled in a tiny ball there on the ground with her spidery arms tucked insight her dress to keep her warm.

Louis thanked God for being so merciful. He fixed his eyes trying to trace her small, helpless body for injuries. Kneeling down beside her, Louis planted the gentlest, sweetest, most heartfelt kiss on her cheek. When she slowly opened her eyes and looked into his, he knew at that moment that he was in love with Tulah.

"Louis, I was just dreamin bout you."

Louis smiled at her and took her into his arms, grateful that no harm had come to her. Tulah held him back, not the reserved and guarded hugs she usually gives, but a warm and inviting embrace that welcomed his.

"Is I'm still dreamin?"

"If you are, I ain't 'bout to wake you up." She leaned forward to kiss Louis' cheek, but he turned his head to meet hers, her lips sliding across his face as they headed for their destination. Their lips fit together like two puzzle pieces cut to specifications, the long intoxicating kiss transporting them to a garden of delirious sensual pleasure. Then Tulah pulled back, squirming in his grip. Louis was puzzled by her sudden shift.

"Are you alright, girl?"

"I'm fine, Louis."

"Then what are you doing out here dis time a night by yo self? Yo aintie said yall had a spat and you took off outta there."

"She talks too much. Needs ta mind her own business."

Tulah straightened her dress.

"Whatever she did, what it enough of a reason for you to be out here alone in da dark?"

Tulah rubbed her arms, "Louis, I believe dees mosquitoes dun ate me up. I'm itching all over." Louis stretched out her arms to inspect them. Then he kissed her shoulder.

"Louis, stop that."

"Be right back." He veered off the path and temporarily disappeared into the darkness. He returned with a handful of leaves, crushing and rubbing them between his hands, then ran back to the creek and moistened them until they were a paste.

"Turn around." Louis applied the country remedy to her arms and back, Tulah enjoying the feel of his strong hands on her supple body. While he applied the liniment, he spoke.

"Don't ever do nothin' like that again. Like ta scared me to death. Come on, we need to be gettin' you back home. Your Aint Cora worried sick 'bout you."

"Hmph. I ain't nevva going back there – nevva. Did she say somethin' to you?"

"About what?"

Tulah searched his face for any indication Cora had said something negative. But all she saw was Louis' kind and loving face, replacing for a moment the memory of Cora's callous cruelty. Tulah knew then she would never give him up – at least not without a fight.

"Nevva mind Louis. I ain't goin' back is all."

"Well, where you goin' dis time a night?"

"I can stay here the night and head to ma brother's house in da moanin'."

"There ain't no way you staying out here tonight. You come on here, girl. You coming home wit me." He entoned forcefully.

Tulah breathed a sigh of relief, grateful to have someone in her life who, for once, was eager to give without wanting something in return first, but naturally she didn't want to show it.

"Louis, ain't no way I'm comin' ta yo house. Ain't yo house no how. Dat's yo Mama and Daddy's house."

"It's my house too and you coming. You ain't got nowhere else to go anyway," Louis said with finality.

"I aint nevva seen you so forceful Louis."

"I ain't never meant nothing so much before. And don't fight me on this Tulah, not this time. This time I'm right and you gone do it my way."

She'd never seen Louis so adamant. His power coursed through her like electric current, and she liked it, though she wouldn't show it. Tulah suppressed a smile and acquiesced.

Approaching Louis' house hand in hand was a surreal experience for Tulah. The large but modest antebellum white plantation style home sat far back off the winding road in the distance, with tiny incandescent lights in each window. Three huge trees framed the house on either side of the road, with a row of Georgia pines on each side of the path leading to the home. As Tulah got closer, she noted one was a pear tree, the others peach and walnut. A big lamp post stood guard in the front lawn, shedding light up the walk. On the porch was a wooden swing for two, and two wooden chairs with a small, round table between them. Walking up to this beautiful, expansive home with Louis was like a fairy tale. She had never felt so thrilled, excited and nervous in her whole life. At that moment, she didn't care if she ever saw Cora again. She knew Louis cared for her if he was willing to share his beautiful home with her. She knew her Aunt was an evil, bitter old woman trying to keep her from real beauty and real love. If Louis had awakened her here, instead of at the river, she would have sworn she had died and gone to heaven. Tulah was even willing to bet the mosquitoes here were not treacherous liked the ones where she lived. Walking up to the house with the man who she suddenly realized she loved overwhelmed her. She cupped Louis' huge hand in both of her small ones and stopped him.

"What's wrong?"

"Louis, I cain't go in there."

"Why not?"

"I don't belong here. Dis ain't my home and it's more than someone like me needs to be in."

"Oh Tulah, you belong here. You'll fit in just fine, honey."

"What's yo' Mama gone say when she see me in her fine house?"

"Don't you worry bout that. Just keep quiet when we going in. I'm gone hide you till morning and I'll explain it to Mama and Daddy later, okay?"

"You sho?"

"I'm sure. Now come along."

"Okay."

Louis reassuringly squeezed Tulah's hand and kissed the back of it. He winked at her, then put his index finger to his lips hushing her. He opened the unlocked door, and tiptoed through the living room, careful not to make noise. He held Tulah's hand leading her to a room in the back of the house, turning on a light and closing the door. Tulah glanced around the room taking in all of the beautiful pictures and trinkets decorating the green and gold wall papered room. There were pictures on every wall, and in the corner, a tall, oblong shaped full-length mirror standing on a brass stand that reflected the entire length of your body. There were matching hand towels and bath towels folded neatly on an antique blonde table. On the other matching table, slightly taller, was a suede and cloth tiffany lamp with gold fringes dangling off the ends of the shade. There were bottles of perfume in different sizes, shapes and colors on the same table. In the center of the room was a large, oval shaped porcelain tub on a huge green and gold rug.

"I'm gone get you a bath started. You feel free to use any one of those little perfume bottles to put in yo' bath water. Here's some fresh towels."

He said handing Tulah a bath towel and a face cloth.

"Here's some rubbin' alcohol for them mosquito bites. And when you get out the tub, I'll have you something ta sleep in. I'm gone go and get your water ready."

"Louis I ain't never seen nothin dis nice b'fo. Y'all shole got a nice place here."

Louis smiled at Tulah.

"I'm just happy ta have you here. I'm glad nothing bad happened to you."

"Louis, whose clothes am I gone sleep in? Not yo Mama's?"

"I'll have something for you. I told you not to worry about that."

After Tulah bathed and was sufficiently fragranced with perfumed oil, she felt exhausted. The events of the day, including the long walk and the hot bath, left her feeling quite fatigued. Louis took Tulah to the broken in sofa in the back room and had it prepared with clean cotton sheets and a feather stuffed pillow.

"I got this all made up fo' you. You gone rest real good on this sofa. It's nice and comfortable."

"Are you gone stay in here wit me? I mean suppose yo Mama or Daddy come in here and see a stranger sleeping on dey couch?"

"I'm gone stay right here wit ya. I'm gone make a pallet on the floor, right next to ya."

"Thank you Louis, fa being so nice ta me and makin' me feel special. Relaxin in dat tub a yorn with the perfumed bath water was like a dream. Septin it was better than any dream I ever had."

Louis chuckled a bit.

"Havin' you here is like a dream."

"I got a confession ta tell you. Me and Aint Cora got to fussin' cuz she don't wont me ta see you no mo, and I knew I wasn't goin to stop. Dats why I left."

"Why don't she want me to see you?"

"She say you too old and you got a lot of other womens and you don't really want nobody like me fo' nuthin' but...." Tulah stopped abruptly.

"Yo' Aintie wrong 'bout a lot a things. You'll see. But we'll work it all out tomorrow."

"Okay Louis."

Louis had never seen Tulah so agreeable, she is usually always ready to debate with him, proving herself right and him wrong. Not to be mean, it was just her way. She always pretended to know more than she did, and Louis quite enjoyed it. She had an uncanny way of making him laugh and acquiesce, letting her have the last say. But tonight, he saw a different side of Tulah. Tonight she let him into the guarded part that was always hidden away. She opened up to him and let him see her vulnerabilities, that she was not as experienced, worldly, or arrogant as she pretended to be. Typically, Tulah did most of the talking, but on this night, instead of her presumptuous boastings, she talked easily with a lazily deliberation about her uncertainties and insecurities, and Louis was careful not to interrupt. She spoke just above a whisper, careful not to be heard by anyone but him. Tulah quieted for a brief moment, obviously weighing what she was going to say next.

Laying on her side facing him, her velvet voice slightly husky from the mixture of the night air and the pampered treatment Louis had lavished on her, punctuated the stillness of the night.

"Louis, come rub my back - please."

A thousand thoughts ran through Louis' mind, of desire, passion, being discovered by his parents. Tulah spoke again.

"Dats okay... I know you probly tired from looking aft.." Louis interrupted her mid-sentence.

"Okay." Louis agreed excitedly, pushing past all his inner objections and good sense.

"Jus' my back now, you hear?"

"Okay."

Louis sat down on the sofa next to Tulah and began stroking her back in long fluid motions. His hands felt warm and strong, yet tender and careful. When Louis rubbed the small of her back through the satin nightgown he borrowed from his mother's vanity, Tulah released and involuntary sigh, and caught herself moving to the rhythm of his touch.

"You know Louis, I think it may be room enough on this sofa for da both of us."

Louis didn't respond right away.

"Dats if you care ta share the sofa wit me."

"Okay." Louis agreed.

"It's been a long day Louis and I'd just feel betta if you was up here wit me."

"Okay."

Louis stretched his long, lean body out on the sofa's edge behind her, their bodies fitly meshing as one. He placed his arm around her waist, as she nestled her body ever closer to his. Louis experienced a level of excitement, nervousness and pleasure like never before, even though he had been with several women in times past.

"Louis, is Aint Cora right?" You just want me for what you can git?"

Louis' mouth rested just behind her ear.

"First time I saw you in Mr. White's store, I knew you was special." His words penetrated her ear, traveling through her body and landing in that sweet spot every woman knows. He then kissed her in her ear, igniting a flood of sensory reactions setting off explosions in every area of her supple frame. Tulah moaned.

"If I could have the whole world, don't matter if I ain't got you. I'd just have to give the world back, das all." He raised himself, leaned over and kissed the corner of her mouth, she turning her head to meet his. He raised up again, this time enough so Tulah could shift her body to meet his. They kissed fully and deeply, exploring the depth of their mutual passion in a breathless embrace. Louis wrapped his arms around Tulah's small body, squeezed her tight, the smell of Tulah's sweet perfume filling Louis' head with intoxicating aromas, appealing to his senses. They kissed slower, softer, wetter, more deliberate, the hunger demanding full satisfaction. His body responded to hers as hers did his, their breathing turning to pants and gasps of air between kisses. Louis spoke.

"You ever been made love to, Tulah?"

"Naw, not yet. Why, is you gone make love ta me?"

"You want me to?"

"Yeah."

"You scared?"

"Should I be?"

"Naw, you shouldn't be scared. You gone like it."

"Ha you know?"

"Cause I like it."

"What I'm supposed ta do?"

Louis kissed her, his tongue playing with her lips, she suctioning his tongue deep into her mouth and returning the playful gesture with her own tongue. Louis' large hands traced the curves of her body, caressing her inner thigh. He positioned himself on top of her, slid his knee between hers, gently nudging her legs apart. Tulah followed his lead, letting her legs fall easily open. Louis, knowing this was her first time, took extra care to insure her body was sufficiently lubricated to receive his entry. While his manhood pulsed upon her thigh, his hand and gently unfolded the petals of her pouting flower until it began to give up its treasure trove of viscous nectar. She moaned, instinctively thrusting her pelvis toward his member. Louis took his other hand, sliding and guiding himself to her entrance. He inserted slowly and gradually, deliberately applying just enough force to cause continued penetration, until he was deep inside of her. She moved to meet his motion, occasionally jerking involuntarily.

He looked into her eyes to witness the wonder and awe of her delirium, her mouth gaping open at times gasping, her brow frowning in an expression conveying delight far from any she had known. His rhythm was constant, with beads of sweat falling from his brow like the slow drip of rain water from a full gutter, dropping and mixing with her own layer of moisture, a smooth glaze glistening in the candlelit room, the both of them entwined, their hot, wet bodies locked in a seamless unrehearsed yet choreographed ballet of writhing symmetry. They were one. His movements became less guarded as he moved skillfully and sinuously inside of her, kissing her lips, face, neck, and shoulders, hungrily. She met each of his thrusts with her own until she felt a tremor begin deep inside her, her body expressing the beginning of an involuntary chain reaction beyond her control. Louis looked into her eyes as they seemed to lose focus, and knew she was on her way. He quickened his rhythm, varying his angle of entry while penetrating to his full limit. Her mouth wide open, the tremors within now quickened into paroxysms of shuddering, bodying wrenching shaking and quaking, until her body erupted into a full explosion of pleasure. Tulah wrapped her arms around him, closed her eyes and let him have his way. When it was all over he kissed her on the lips rolled over onto his back. She noticed his eyes were closed.

"Mm mm mm. Louis Starks. You is a real man. I guess I'm a real woman now, huh?"

"You was a real woman b'fo tonight. Now let's get some sleep."

Tulah cuddled close to Louis, watching him fall into the otherworld of slumber. She closed her eyes and fell asleep with a big smile, having experienced the happiest night of her life. Louis snored loudly.

Chapter 3

The next morning, Tulah lay on the sofa with her eyes opened trying to discern her unfamiliar surroundings. It took a moment for her to remember she had gone to Louis' house and had slept there all night. She sat up, rubbed her eyes and looked around for Louis. She wanted to get up, but was too afraid of encountering his parents. She slowly got up, careful to not make any noise, and quickly dressed, hoping Louis would return soon. She gathered the sheets, folded them, and not knowing what else to do, she sat quietly on the sofa with her hands folded neatly in her lap.

The new day offered sunlight to the charming little room, showcasing its rich and elegant décor. The room was painted in an antique white, trimmed in camel's hair beige, with imported embossed French wallpaper. On one wall, pictures hung precisely in ornate and obviously expensive wooden frames - people she guessed were old relatives. She wondered if Louis had taken the photographs, as they displayed great detail, each telling its own story that was reflected in their sad eyes, and oppressed smiles. One photograph of an old woman captured Tulah's attention, she sitting in a rocking chair with a knitted blanket covering her legs. White hair pulled back in a bun, her thin skin was wrinkled, the color of ash. Her dark and deep socketed eyes told a story of generations of people who had suffered and survived. Creases bracketing the corners her mouth like two parentheses, they were a physical metaphor of concealment of secrets that she was forbade to tell, secrets held within so long until her mouth became fixed that way.

Tulah studied each of the pictures, their faces, their eyes, and wondered what each of their lives was like. She wondered if they accomplished the things they set out to do, dreamed of doing, and what they thought about. She wondered if one day, a photograph of her would be hanging on a wall somewhere, after she was dead and gone, and what some young girl who looked at her would think. Tulah had become so engrossed in the pictures she didn't hear Louis enter the room. When she looked up and saw him standing there, it was if a light had suddenly been turned on. She felt a euphoric rush sweep over her very soul like a gust of warm Georgia wind, leaving her feeling a deep tingle inside. The guarded exterior she usually projected had been burned away by the night's passion, but there was something more. A palpable presence filled the room. The ancestral spirits of those who occupied the walls gave her an inexplicable feeling of connection. Louis smiled at her, and she was bathed in the warmth of his smile, the feeling of love she had for him, with gratitude filling her heart.

"Mornin' Louis. Why you leave me in here alone?"

"I was out meditatin'. And you was sleepin' so sound, I didn't want to wake you."

"You was out doin' what?"

"Meditatin' - it's how I get my day started. Come here, I want to show you something."

Louis gently took Tulah by the arm and led her to the porch. She liked it when he touched her, took her, and possessed her, it gave her a feeling of belonging, of being wanted, and of being connected. He took a seat in the swinging chair and pulled Tulah down beside him. He wrapped his arms around her and pushed off with his legs, causing them to swing very slowly. Tulah rested her head on his shoulder and closed her eyes.

"You feel it?"

"What?"

"God. He's all around us. He's in the sky, the air, the breeze, the trees, he's everywhere. Listen to the birds. They singing to Him."

"Louis you so crazy. You cain't feel God in the trees and in the sky."

"Oh, but you can. He's everywhere. Every morning, God meets me here. He's always here, but in the morning before things get started good, is when you can really feel Him. I usually come out here by myself, but I wanna share this wit you. Nobody never be wit me in ma quiet time, 'til now," nodding his head with affirmative emphasis.

"Well, I'm sorry, but I cain't feel Him."

"He's here."

Louis looked up into the heavens with a content smile on his face.

"Louis, I gotta be getting outta here. Where's yo' Mama n Daddy?"

"Daddy already lef fo' work, and Mama, gone into town."

"So ain't nobody here but us?"

"Nope. Mama made some pastries fo' she left; they in the kitchen, maybe still warm. You hungry?"

"Yes indeed. I was so mad at Aint Cora yesday that I didn't even eat suppa' fo I left."

"Well come on, les' get you something ta eat."

They sat at the table eating home made apple and peach pastries with hand rolled crust and a glaze frosting drizzled over the top. As she jammed a piece in her mouth, Tulah looked up at Louis.

"Louis, I feel kinda embarrassed, but I gotta ask."

"What?"

"Is I'm supposed to feel sore - down there?"

Louis chuckled a bit, remembering that it was Tulah's first time. He took in a breath and let it go slowly.

"Well, I suppose you'll feel some sore, being your first time in all. Ain't real bad is it?"

"Not real bad. Hurts some, though."

"Well, you should be okay. Won't be bad the second time, and by the third time, it'll only be pleasure."

Tulah nodded in understanding.

"You want a glass of milk?"

Tulah nodded again.

"What you gone do about yo' Ain't Cora?"

"I ain't gone do nothing and I ain't going back there neither."

"Well, I can put you up fo' a day or two without bein' noticed."

"I ain't expect fa you ta take care a me. I can do dat on ma own."

"Listen Tulah, you know how I feel about you. If you can gimme a little time, I can get my own place. It's a little house not far from here that I been had my eye on for while. I can talk to the owner about lettin' me rent it. We can have our own place together. That way, ain't nothin yo aunt can say bout who you seein."

"Louis I can't just move in witcha. We ain't married and what yo' folks gone say about you being wit me?"

"What you mean, what they gone say?"

"Is dey gone like you seein' somebody like me? Livin wit somebody like me? I ain't got nothin. No Mama, no Daddy and no place ta go. I'm po, and you rich an everythang. Look at dis place. I ain't even know colored people live like dis." Louis took Tulah's hands in his and looked her in the eyes. She felt the power of his gaze penetrate her soul. Then he said the words she'd been waiting to hear.

"Tulah, I love you girl, I don't care what nobody says. That day in the store, when I first saw you, I believe I loved you then." Tulah looked down and smiled, twisting the silver band left to her from her mother, around her finger.

"Louis, I think Mama musta told God ta send me a angel. Cause aint nobody ever cared fa me lak yo do." Placing his index finger under her chin, and lifted her head and kissed her gently on the lips.

"I love you too, Louis. And I'll move in witcha, if you really want me to."

He knelt down next to her so that they were looking eye to eye. He whispered as if others were around,

"Since ain't nobody here, we can get in a little more practice playing house. This time I can take you ta ma room."

Louis and Tulah spent all morning in his room expressing the love they shared for one another, but Louis knew renting a house would be quite an expense. He had to get going to work. He asked Tulah if she would go with him like she does most days, but she declined, stating she didn't want to run into her aunt on the street and have a fall out. They decided it would be best she would go back to her aunt's house, explaining she had fallen asleep at the river and apologize for her insolence. This would buy them time to find the owner of the house, and get a few things in order before they could move in.

They both cleaned up and left the house just before noon. Tulah started in one direction and Louis in another. Louis had to go by Henry's house to get his equipment he'd left the night before, and Tulah reluctantly headed back to Cora's house. As she walked home she was elated thinking about the plans she and Louis made. She thought about the sacrifices Louis was willing to make for her, and wanted so badly to tell Cora how wrong she was about him. She wanted her to tell her Louis really does love her, and had made love to her last night and most of the morning just like a real, grown up woman. She wanted to tell her he loves her so much, he's getting a house for the two of them to live in.

Then suddenly, Tulah felt saddened. She thought about the sacrifices Louis was to make for her. Plans to save for his picture studio would have to be put on hold now. She knew the importance of his dream, it being all he ever talks about. With him having to pay rent and buy food, who knows how long it would be before he could get his studio. Tulah knew Louis really loved her if he was willing to give up so much. Then she concluded she couldn't let him do for her, which meant she would have to go back to Cora's house and tolerate her overbearing, hypocritical, and pernicious ways. But Tulah wasn't willing to endure Cora for another day. It was then Tulah knew she had to make a trip to her brother's house and hope for the best.

Tulah snuck into Cora's house after she had left for town. She gathered few of her clothes, enough to last for several days, some underwear and pair of stockings, and stuffed them in a knapsack. She went into the kitchen and got a tomato, a piece of bread, a slice of ham, a piece of cheese, and sliced a piece of aunt Cora's freshly made pecan pie. She packed everything neatly in a calfskin satchel, and went into Cora's room rummaging around for loose change. At the bottom of a purse Cora keeps in the back of her closet, Tulah found two quarters, three nickels, one dime, and seven pennies. She went around to the back of the house to retrieve her bicycle only to find Cora had hidden it. She checked the entire house, but the bike was nowhere to be found. Determined it wouldn't deter her, she started out of the door, suddenly stopping, she ran back to her room, took the picture of her Mama, and ran out of the house. She never looked back.

Tulah knew the money she had was not going to get her very

far, and her food supply wouldn't last very long. She figured if she could hitch a ride from someone to get closer to her brother, then she could walk the rest of the way. She wasn't exactly sure where Kingston was, but was determined to find it. Her heart ached each time she thought about leaving Louis, but she knew if she stopped to see him he would talk her out of leaving. She wouldn't allow him to give up his hopes and dreams for her. He might blame her later. She knew she was doing what was best.

Tulah walked for what seemed like miles under the blazing hot sun. The one essential ingredient she required, she didn't have, and would soon come to regret. Her full lips became cracked and parched, thirsting for just one drop of water. The back of her throat was so dry, it was difficult for her to swallow. Beads of sweat streamed down her face and neck and her dress had become completely soaked by the perspiration covering her back. Her shoes, worn and run over, were covered with dust, causing her hot feet to blister, making her feel as though they had been set ablaze. She wanted to stop, take cover from the searing, hot sun, find a place to rest and recover from the heat, but knew she couldn't. She had to make the most of her time and get as far as she could in the light of day. Her shoulders ached from toting a satchel on one side and a knapsack on the other, ever heavier with each torturous step.

After the sun had beaten down on her and taken its toll, Tulah began to feel faint. She had pushed herself as far as she could go, and knew she had to stop. Finding a shaded area under a tree, she decided to take refuge there. She opened her satchel and pulled out a tomato, now soft and bruised. Biting into it offered some relief to her dry throat, but not the kind she was hoping for. After eating the tomato, with her hands wet and sticky, Tulah suddenly felt sleepy. The sun had robbed her of her energy just as a thief would do a priceless jewel, leaving her with nothing but the hope of starting over. Tried as she might, to get up and get going, Tulah could not make her body cooperate. Her eyelids became heavy, as if coated with molasses. Giving in to her fatigue, she promised herself she would rest only for a moment, but careful not fall asleep.

Before long, Tulah was fast asleep and dreaming she was running through a meadow, happy, smiling at the sun as its warm glow massaged her face. Billowy clouds of white, like great mounds of unbundled cotton, were smeared against a soft, azure blue sky. The grass was tall, lush and green, and a landscape of flowers, red, purple, white and pink was on guard all about her. She ran as fast as could be to a nearby waterfall but could never seem to get to. The faster and harder she ran, the further away it was. In the distance there was a rainbow over the waterfall with luminously vibrant colors, brilliant blues, pretty purples, radiant reds, gorgeous greens and yellows and oranges so tantalizing it hurt her eyes to look upon. When finally she reached the falls, she gazed upward, to where the water fell from a tall peak, reaching far into the sky. The water in the pond beneath sparkled in the sun as if it were filled with thousands of crystallized diamonds. She fell to her knees, splashing water on her face, gulping hurriedly as if it would soon run out. The more she splashed, the more refreshed she felt. Then suddenly, the water became too much for her, filling her, overwhelming her, choking her. She fought feverishly to keep from drowning. She awoke out of the dream, startled as she re-oriented herself to reality, and opened her eyes.

Tulah realized that the rain had come and was smacking heavily against her face like tiny water balloons. She stood up and opened her mouth toward heaven in an effort to catch each sweet, cool, refreshing drop of rain to quench her ravenous thirst. Thunder rumbled across the sky, starting low and deep, culminating into a crescendo of light and sound that ripped through the heavens. Tulah didn't know where she was, or what she was going to do. She took cover under the tree, but it offered little refuge from the ominous thunderstorm. She reached in her knapsack, pulled out a sweater, and covered her head. Squatting under the tree, she remained there until the storm passed over.

Tulah packed her things and resumed her nebulous journey. Gathering the ends of her dress, she twisted and squeezed the remains of the rainstorm out of her clothing. Noticing something hard and round, like a rock, Tulah reached into the pocket of her dress retrieving a single sticky lemon drop. She peeled off lint that was stuck to it and promptly popped it into her mouth. Surely, this was a good omen, she thought, the single lemon drop offered hope to an otherwise menacing situation.

The day was fast coming to an end as the sun began to set, and Tulah was nowhere near the train station, the marker telling how far she was from her brother's house.

Now completely blanketed in darkness, the night had come. The evening humidity hung thick and heavy, making warm flesh irresistible to hungry mosquitoes. Tulah allowed thoughts she fought hard to keep at bay to finally hold sway in her mind. Perhaps she had made a mistake by leaving so hastily. She wondered if Aint Cora would be concerned, and couldn't bear the thought of what Louis must be going through. Never intentionally meaning to cause anyone worry, Tulah always tried to do the right thing, but no matter how altruistic her intentions, this was turning out all wrong.

Tears welled up in her eyes, rolled down her cheeks, fell heavy down her face, landing onto her dress. She wanted to turn back, but had come too far. Crying loudly and unabashed, Tulah wept helplessly.

"Hey dere gal. Whatchu makin' up all dat noise fo?"

Tulah squinted into the darkness, trying to connect the raspy, old voice with a face, but couldn't find one.

"You heh me gal?"

"Suh?"

"Don't you suh me. I'm a lady. Whatchu you makin' all dat ruckus about?"

"I believe I done lost my way."

"Where you headed?"

"To ma brother Aaron's house. He live in Kingston."

"Where? Come on up heh, I cain't heh so well."

Tulah slowly approached the house.

"Na whatcha say? You's headed where?"

"I's headed to ma brother's house, in Kingston."

"Gal, you know how fer Kingston is?"

"No ma'am."

"Well it's a long ways from heh, das how far. Ain't you got no place to stay fo da night?"

"No ma'am."

"You got a name?"

"Yes ma'am. Name Tulah Belle Armstrong."

"Armstrong?"

"Yes ma'am."

"Is you any kin to dem Armstrongs up in Cartersville?"

"Don't think so."

"Come on up heh, let me git a good look atcha."

Tulah walked up the stairs leading to the porch and stood before the old toothless woman. She starred at Tulah, jaws expanding and retracting as she chewed and spat into a glass slop jar sitting it down on the porch next to her.

"I reckon I can put cha up fa ta night. Help me up."

Tulah pulled the old woman by the arm and helped her to her feet. The woman stood about six inches shorter than Tulah and had a long, white braid down the middle of her back. She walked with a cane and took slow careful steps. Once inside, Tulah tried focusing her eyes to see in the dark room. The old woman lit a candle and handed it to Tulah.

"Follow me."

Tulah followed her lead through a dark cluttered room.

"You can sleep heh in the parlor."

The room, from what Tulah could tell had hard unfinished floors, and a lumpy sofa pushed against the wall.

"It's some covers over deh, but I don't reckon you be needin' em. I stays on da porch mosta da night bein so hot in heh. Is ya hungry?"

"I packed myself a lunch." Tulah said holding up the wet satchel.

"You been totin dat round all day?"

"Yes ma'am ."

"Lible ta be no good to ya na."

"It's still good."

"Well put tin da icebox. You be needin' it fo' later. I got some cornbread and beans in heh you can eat."

"I'm Lucy Mae Etter, folks round heh call me Mama Lou."

"Thanks Mama Lou. Ah be outcha way first thang in da mo'nin."

"Naw you won't. You gits ta earn yo keep. I got some chickens an pigs out yonda. Dey be needin tendin to. You gone git out deh and fetch me some eggs and slop dem pigs, then I'h gone fix us some brekfas. You can be on yo way afta dat if you want."

Tulah didn't answer right away. She was consumed with the thought of slopping pigs and fetching eggs. She had seen it done many times before, but had managed to keep away from it. And although appreciative of the hospitality, she wasn't sure she was the best person to ask of such a task.

"You heh me gal?"

"Uh, yes'um. I hear you."

"Alright. You come on in heh and lets git you sumptin ta eat."

Tulah watched as Mama Lou prepared her a meal of stringed beans and pan fried corn bread. If not for the fact Tulah was famished, the dimly lit, dingy little kitchen would have caused her to lose her appetite. Mama Lou sat across from Tulah watching her as she ate. To Tulah's great surprise the beans were quite tasty. The corn bread was fried in heavy lard, which made it greasy and heavy, but nonetheless, still tasty. After she had completed her meal, she cleaned up after herself and was looking forward to going to bed.

As Tulah lay on the lumpy sofa she thought of Louis, and how just the night before, she had lain on clean, fragranced sheets, a firm bed, and in the arms of the man she had grown to love. One night she was a princess living in a castle, the next night a pauper, living in poverty. How she wished she could have that night with Louis back once more. She thought about his eyes, his smile, and how she felt when he held her in his arms and rocked her lovingly on that swing. She remembered the tingles running up her spine when he kissed her gently on the forehead. She thought about his smell and breathed in deeply trying to remember his scent. Closing her eyes, she relived every moment they shared until she drifted off to sleep.

Chapter 4

Louis sat on his porch, swinging back and forth in the swing he had rocked Tulah in the night before. He had been there all night waiting for her return. He was there when a rousing thunderstorm lit up the sky and the rain fell hard and heavy onto the earth. He was there when the rain stopped and the sun spilled over dark, gray clouds, producing a silver lining around as a rainbow decorated the sky. He was there when the sun set, and dusky evening turned dark, and a blanket of darkness covered the night. And he was there through the midnight hours and into the early morning, still waiting for her return. The next morning, as the sun hung high at the dawning of a new day, the time Louis usually spends enjoying the beauty of the day and communing with God, the only thing he could manage as he looked up to heaven was: "God, please bring her back."

It could have been he had waited out all night in the cool, damp, night air, or he was love sick and missing Tulah; which ever was the case, Louis felt faint and stayed in bed all day. His Mama came in to check on him, offering tea with lemon and honey, his favorite when he wasn't feeling well, but he declined. She felt his forehead with the back of her hand, but he didn't feel warm. She offered to make him homemade chicken soup, which he refused as well, saying he didn't have an appetite. Concerned for Louis, she decided to stay home should he require her assistance. She let him have his rest and asked him to let her know if he needed anything. Louis lay in bed thinking about Tulah. He wondered what he could have done wrong she wouldn't come and talk to him. He knew Tulah was a feisty, independent and private person, but he thought he had conquered the barrier keeping her from him.

As angry as he was at Tulah, he also angry at himself for letting a "child" make him feel down. Louis called Tulah a child to dilute the pain of despair he felt, but he knew the "child" was more woman than any he had ever known. He tried to get comfortable, but no matter which way Louis turned his body he couldn't find a suitable position. Tossing and turning, Louis decided to get up and go for a walk. He hoped to see her along the way, but deep within he knew she was gone. Tulah, the woman child, with the mesmerizing eyes and warm personality, so spirited and full and life, the kind of person who makes your acquaintance, makes you feel like you are all that matters, and just when you are comfortable, she pulls back, distancing herself. Louis understood her though. He knew she had a problem committing herself to anyone. Everyone close to her, with the exception of her mother and grandmother, had abandoned her in one way or the other. Louis wanted to find Tulah to tell her his love was unconditional. He would never leave her. It was then he made God a promise - if He ever brought Tulah back, he would never ever leave her alone.

Tulah awakened to Mama Lou standing over. Tulah focused her eyes watching the blur standing before her slowly transform into a hunched over old lady.

"Chile, you best be getting up and tendin' to da chickens and hogs fo' da sun gits too hot."

Mama Lou told Tulah before spitting into her jar. Tulah was disgusted Mama Lou spitting into that nasty slop jar was the first sight of the day, but more than disgusted, she felt sick, nauseous even.

"Mama Lou, I think I'm gone be sick."

"You alright gal, just needs to git up and git started."

Tulah sat up, but felt light headed. She laid back down and grabbed her head.

"Mama Lou, I'm gone be sick fo sho."

Trying to rise, Tulah turned towards Mama Lou and regurgitated all over the floor.

"What's wrong witcha chile?"

Tulah didn't answer, she was hanging off the side of the bed still feeling dizzy, like she was going to get sick again.

"Well, don't move. I don't want you getting sick all over ma house."

Mama Lou slowly made her way into the kitchen and back to Tulah carrying an old rag in her hand.

"Heh chile, wipe yo mouth. We's got ta git dis mess cleaned up. Ooh it sho does smell bad."

Mama Lou said, looking at the regurgitated supper she had fed Tulah the night before.

"Um um um, all dem good beans gone ta waste."

Tulah looked at her with contempt, disgusted by the uncouth remark made about the wasted beans.

"Mama Lou, I just need a minute. Then I'm gone clean yo flo, tend ta yo chickens, slop your pigs and I'm gone be outta heh fo sun down."

"Naw you ain't. You ain't well. Prolly got heat stroke from all dat sun yestade. You take yo rest, then you got to git up and fetch dem eggs. You just need to eat is all."

Tulah wanted to lie back down but knew she needed to get up if she wanted to get out of Mama Lou's house as soon as possible. Willing herself to move, Tulah sat up straight, now able to get a good look at the dingy little house.

"My Lawd. How can she live in this dirty old shack?"

Tulah said, looking around the four room little house. Mama Lou had disappeared into the kitchen and was making her way back with a tiny, white, porcelain cup in her hand. She walked towards Tulah and held the cup in her direction.

"Here some tea fo ya. Tea always settles yo stomach."

Tulah accepted the cup and lifted it to her nose smelling the rich, distinctive aroma. She peeked inside the cup before taking a sip, noticing the cup had tiny lines and cracks through it. Wanting so badly to settle the queasiness, despite her apprehension, she took a sip from the cup. It was warm and soothing to her sore, empty stomach. Mama Lou stood over Tulah until the cup was almost empty. She took the cup by the handle before Tulah could finish, and swirled the remains around three times before walking back into the kitchen. She pointed Tulah towards a shed where she could find a bucket and some old rags to clean up the mess.

As Tulah cleaned, Mama Lou took the cup and drained the remaining tea. She stared into the cup and then looked towards the parlor where Tulah was cleaning the floor. Although Tulah was appreciative of the lumpy sofa, the warm meal, and the hot tea, she really wanted to be on her way to her brother's house. Once she had cleaned the floor and gathered eggs from the hen house, she turned her attention towards the pigs and despised Mama Lou for her unfairness. A born negotiator, Tulah had no leverage to barter with Mama Lou, and had to do as she was asked.

Tulah pulled the back end of her dress between her legs and tied it to the front. She tied a scarf around her head, removed her shoes, and climbed atop the wooden fence which contained three, fat little pigs belonging to Mama Lou. Easing herself down into the muck, she gathered mud in her hands and started for the closest pig. The closer she came, the more they scattered about, squealing and dodging her. She tried everything she knew, from darting after them as fast as she could, to playing possum, hoping they would settle down long enough for her to slop and feed them. Finally after she was able to get them settled, she slopped them and fed them corn husks. Fully disgusted and quite smelly, she tried to lift herself out of the pen. As she attempted to put one foot on the fence the other slid from under her, landing her right on her back. Tulah laid there with her eyes closed thinking this couldn't possibly be happening to her. She kept her eyes closed until she felt the snout of the pig sniffing her face and snorting in her ear.

When Tulah finally pulled herself out of the pig pen and made her way back towards the house Mama Lou was sitting on the porch waiting for her. When Mama Lou saw Tulah covered with mud, she smiled a toothless grin.

"I see you got yo'self quainted wit da pigs."

" I sho did. Those da stankiest, messiest creatures God evva made."

"Oh dem pigs ain't bad. I had some real big ones, bout 90 pounds each. Sold 'em off so's I could keep dis place. I kept one of 'em - had 'em cut up and sent to the smoke house. I got some sausages, and ham, neck bones and chitlins. Good eatin', dat one."

Tulah looked at her and shook her head.

"Mama Lou, I don't know how you do it."

"Heh? Gul, you know I cain't heh so well. Whatcha say?"

"I say I don't know how you do it - keep up dis place by yo self."

"Oh gul, you just gotta do whatcha gotta do. Sit on down right heh, I needs to talk to ya."

"I needs to be getting dis filth washed off me. I'm stankin' like dem nasty pigs."

"Sit on down heh, won't take but a minute."

Tulah reluctantly sat down on the porch and looked up and Mama Lou who was chewing again with her spit jar sitting close by. She looked Tulah square in the face and deep into her eyes.

"What is it, Mama Lou?"

"How long you been spectin?"

"Hmm? Spectin what?"

"Dat youngin' a yorn."

Tulah thought Mama Lou had lost her mind rambling about a youngin'. She tried to suppress a condescending laugh.

"Mama Lou, I ain't spectin no youngin'."

"Tea leaves, honey. I reads tea leaves, and dey don't lie." Mama Lou explained.

Tulah looked at her questionably, unclear of her meaning.

"Mama Lou, I don't thank I know whatcha mean."

"Chile, ain't you got sense enough to know you got a yougin' on da way?"

"Who me?"

Mama Lou responded to Tulah, by staring blankly at her.

"Sho nuff?"

"I read it in yo tea cup, clear as day I saw a chair. Dat means a new addition. I reckon dats why you was sick dis mo'nin."

"Is you sho?"

"Oh I's sho alright, I been readin' leaves for 30 years. I ain't nevva read em wrong."

"You mean I'm gone be somebody's Mama?"

Tulah said holding her stomach smiling.

"Where's dat youngin's Daddy?"

Tulah looked down suddenly feeling distraught about her situation. With prideful indignation she responded to her characteristically,

"Well didn't dem leaves a yorn tell you where he was at?"

"Chile, don't sass me."

"I'm sorry Mama Lou. Didn't mean no harm. I'm just sad cuz I knows I done messed up everything, I done messed it up real bad."

"Chile ain't nuttin dat bad. Anythang you done did wrong you can just undo it."

"It ain't dat easy."

Tulah said twisting the silver band around her finger.

"I done ran away from ma Aintie, and done ran out on da father uh ma chile. And wuhn't neither one of em deservin a dat. I was tryin ta do what was right, but look like da whole thang done gat all messed up. Now ma Aintie's mad I reckon, and I thank I may done broke my Louis' heart. What I'm gone do now?"

Tulah asked shaking her head.

"I hate myself fo what I done. I just do dumb thangs sometime."

"Chile, ain't need a hatin yo'self. We all done did sumptin dumb b'fo I reckon, God just made us ta be dat way. Is dat why you was runnin away las night?"

Tulah kept her head down and nodded.

"I was tryin ta git ta ma brother's house ta see if he'll let me stay wit him fo a while. Sept, I ain't know I was gone be a Mama. I thank I would a stayed home."

"Yo brotha don't know you coming?"

"No."

"Is he married?"

"Yeah."

"He got kids?"

Tulah nodded again.

"Well chile, how you know he got room an' food enough fo' ya?"

"I was jus' hopin I guess."

"Weh's yo folks at?"

"Mama died when I was only five and ma Daddy run off. Stayed wit my Granny fo' a while."

Tulah explained with her head down, looking up occasionally to gauge Mama Lou's reaction.

"Then I ended up wit ma Aintie, and that's how I met Louis."

"Well you cain't be doing all dat walkin in dis heat while you spectin. I reckon you gone have ta stay wit me fo a spell, til you feelin' stronger anyway. At least till ya outta da woods. First few monts can be hard on a woman."

It wasn't Tulah's first choice to stay in the dirty little house with a toothless old woman, but she had no choice. If not for the dirt, smell, and Mama Lou's slop jar making her nauseous at the sight and smell, she would be grateful for it. She surveyed the room wondering how long it's been since the last good cleaning. She knew if she stayed, she would have to give it a thorough cleaning in order to feel comfortable.

"Yes ma'am. Thank you for yo hospitality. I'll work real hard round here ta earn ma keep."

"Don't worry bout dat right now. I'h be glad fo' da company mo' dan anything. You gone round da back. I'h got a tin tub back dere, you can fetch you some water from the pump and take you a bath. I'h get brefas goin. Now help me up."

Mama Lou said reaching for Tulah's hand.

"You like catfish? I'h got a little corn meal left. I'h make you some catfish and cornbread and we can eat some eggs iffin' you ain't break em up."

"No ma'am, I ain't break none."

Tulah walked around to the back of the house and towards a big open field until she found the pump. She grabbed the handle and pumped forcefully until water ran freely onto her feet. The sun baked the stiff mud on her feet till it felt hard, like clay, and the water felt cool and refreshing, loosening the grime and cooling her toes. Filling a bucket with water, she walked back towards the house to pour it into the tub. It took several trips from the pump to the tub before it was full. Stepping into the tub, she slid under the water until she was completely submerged. The sun had climbed high into the sky and shone down hot and bright. She laid her head against the back of the tub and closed her eyes, letting the sun envelop her in its warmth. Rubbing her stomach, she thought about Louis and smiled at the thought of his baby growing inside of her. Tulah imagined she and Louis were married and had a house as grand as the one his parents live in. She imagined he would come home from a long days work and she would be waiting for him with his supper ready. Over dinner, he would tell her about his day and they would laugh and talk before settling on the porch, in the swing she loved so much, and Louis would rub her growing belly and tell her he loved her.

After Tulah bathed, she ate breakfast with Mama Lou and resolved to clean the house. The little four room house had a room in the front Mama Lou called the parlor. There was a small bedroom off to the left side of the parlor cluttered and smelled of mildew. The kitchen was toward the back and it contained a black, pot-bellied stove, an ice box and a table with two wooden chairs. There was another room off the back of the kitchen suitable for use as another bedroom, or as an indoor bathroom. The entire house was covered in dust and was the same color. The little shack was made of wood and had never been painted or finished, making everything look drab and gray; the walls, floors, furniture, all naked and gray from years of wear. The windows were covered with thick and heavy hand stitched curtains keeping the rooms dark. The lumpy old sofa, pushed against the wall, was moth eaten and stained. There was a rocking chair with a missing arm sitting in front of a fireplace Tulah guessed had never been used, except soot had been spilled onto the floor and was tracked through out the room.

There were no pictures on the walls, no rugs on the floor, no lamps or tables, or anything making the place look lived in, except for the mess in the kitchen. Tulah grabbed the bucket, the mop, several rags and some lye soap and naphtha and went to work cleaning the smelly old house. After several hours cleaning, sweeping, dusting and mopping, she pulled back the burlap curtains, and for the first time in recent history, the sun scampered through the shack like a rabbit on the hunt. Tulah was satisfied with her work, grateful the house was small, making her job less tedious. She decided she would pick some fresh flowers and look for some pictures to hang in order to give the shanty some identity and character. Mama Lou disappeared into the woods to gather herbs for her tea and had not returned, Tulah waiting anxiously to surprise her with a clean house. Tired from a long days work, she got a glass of water and sat on the creaky little porch to relax from her chores. A flurry of thoughts about Louis flooded her mind. She became even more grateful for the work around the house because it kept her mind occupied.

Tulah took the glass of water and touched her face and neck, cooling herself from the stifling heat. She drained the rest of the water, replenishing what she lost from exertion in the extreme heat. Mama Lou came out of the woods with a handful of twigs and weeds. Tulah stood when she saw Mama Lou slowly making her way back to the house, but Mama Lou held up her hand to stop her.

"Well, don't you need ma help?"

"Heh? Chile I'h done tole you I cain't heh so well."

"Mama Lou, do you need me to help you?"

Tulah said loudly and deliberately. Mama Lou didn't answer, but continued walking slowly towards the house.

"Naw chile. I's got to make it back and forf by myself. I cain't get to countin' on yo' li'l narrow behine ta help me git around, an' den when I gits used to it, you up an leave me. Den what I mo do?" Mama Lou answered breathlessly.

"I been doin thangs by myself for a long while."

"You tend to dem pigs by yo 'self too?"

"Naw. Na dat I cain't do. Dem boys up a yonda come round heh to help me do dat. As long as I make 'em some preserves an canned fruit, give 'em some eggs from time ta time dey keep comin back. Dey Mama git afta 'em too. She make 'em come help me."

Mama Lou made her way up the stairs and sat on an old wooden chair.

"Whatcha been doin chile?"

"I cleaned yo house fa ya. It's all fresh and clean now."

Tulah announced with pride, but Mama Lou looked straight ahead as if she didn't hear what she said.

"Mama Lou, is you alright?"

"I'm fine chile, jus' tired is all."

"Can you teach me to read leaves, like whatchu did wit ma tea cup?"

"It takes a practiced eye, and lots a patience. Young folks don't have patience."

"Mama Lou, where I got ta be? I ain't got no where ta go and nothin ta do all day. And I'm gone go crazy thinkin' bout Louis if I cain't find something to occupy ma mind."

"It ain't no crystal ball. You cain't be 'spectin ta learn what somebody doin' or what dey up to. Readin' tea leaves jus' help you understand thangs better, thangs dats confusin'. When problems come, dey help you to figure 'em cuz you sees 'em better."

"I wanta learn Mama Lou, please teach me."

"I guess I can show you if you willin' ta learn."

Over the next few months Mama Lou taught Tulah how to read tea leaves to the point where she was intuitive and skillful.

Mama Lou cooked and cared for Tulah, and in return she catered to Mama Lou by keeping her house clean, braiding her hair, and occasionally entertained her with stories of how she and Louis would live after they were married. The bond between the two of them was cemented, and they came to care for one another in a special kind of way. Because of Tulah's condition, Mama Lou had her fetch eggs, but no longer asked her to tend to the pigs.

Summer turned to autumn and the leaves once green and supple turned various colors, burnished red, taut orange and cinnamon brown before falling lifelessly to the ground. The sweet lullaby of birds quieted, and squirrels that once eagerly and playfully jumped from tree to tree to collect the fallen prizes from the pecan trees recoiled into hibernation to circumvent the cold and barren months of winter. The chirping of crickets hushed, and the glowing wings of lighting bugs ceased. The radiant heat emanated from the sun cooled, and the air, instead of dry and hot, became crisp, wispy, and harsh. The long days of summer once long and hot, was shortened, cooler, and the sky, instead of amber and orange, now turned a cerulean blue, indicative of the winter solstice that took place over the western hemisphere. Soon after, the winter months arrived and the wind blew stronger and harsher, bringing gloomy days, gray skies and blistery cold evenings, and with each successive winter day, Tulah's child grew strong and healthy within her.

Seven months along, Tulah's thin shapely figure had gradually been transformed into a wide outline of a figure. She turned Mama Lou's little shack into a warm and charming, comfortable home. The fireplace, now dusted and cleaned, glowed with a roaring fire from logs Tulah gathered and stacked to last throughout the winter. Sitting in front of the fireplace rocking in the chair she fixed from nailing sticks to it to replace the broken arm, she rubbed her belly and thought of her beloved Louis. She stared at the wall with distant eyes wondering where he was, what he was doing, and who he was with.

Mama Lou studied Tulah and recognized her pain. She felt sad for Tulah because she too had known great love and lost it. She knew what it was like to feel lonely and empty inside because the one true love of your life was no longer present. She wished there was something she could do to make everything alright, but Tulah would never let her in, always pretending being without her child's father didn't bother her. Mama Lou tried reading Tulah's tea leaves to understand her pain and to figure out a way to make things better for her, but she had become too personal with her and could no longer get a reading. She wanted to ask Tulah to talk about what she was feeling, so she could advise her and offer comfort, but she said nothing and worried instead. She walked over to Tulah, held her hand, kissed her on her forehead and said good night. Tulah didn't answer, but looked up at her and smiled with tears in her eyes.

"You alright chile?"

Tulah nodded, but didn't utter a word.

"You know thangs got a way a workin' dey self out. But den sometime you gotta do whatcha can ta help it out."

"Ma'am ?"

"I know whatcha feelin, but you ain't got da right ta depribe dat man a yorn of his youngin'. Dats his baby too. You doin' all dis sufferin when you really don't have ta."

"Mama Lou, I'm only suffering cause dis baby causin' me heartburn is all."

"Um hum. Dats whatcha say, but I know better. I watches you round here snifflin' and carryin' on, talking bout heartburn and backaches, but I know it's only cause you missin dat chile's Daddy. Whatchu need ta do is get in touch wit him for you git too far along and cain't turn around."

"Mama Lou, whatchu talking?"

"Heh me chile. I been round for a long time, and ain't nothing new ta me. I know what it like to be in love and I know what it like to lose yo love. But you carryin' his baby, and you keepin' it from him ain't right Tulah, just ain't right. Now I kin see you hurtin' and missin' him and he prolly feelin da same."

"But Mama Lou, I messed thangs up so bad."

"Shoot, dats alright. We all make mistakes. But when you keep makin' mistakes is what make thangs bad. You sposa learn from duh mistakes you done made, and not make em no mo."

"Well how am I spose ta contact him, what I'm gone say?"

"You know ha ta write don't cha? Send em a letter, and tellem da troof."

"You think he'll fagive me?"

"If he love you, he'll fagive you."

"I needs ta know dat you gone be alright fo I leave heh."

"Huh? Where you goin?"

"Neva mind dat chile. You contact him, soon as possible. Heh?"

"Yes ma'am. I'm gone send him a letter in da mornin."

Tulah tossed most of the night wondering what she would say to Louis in her letter; how she would tell him she is carrying his child. She worried because she knew her reading and writing skills were limited, and didn't want to embarrass herself with misspelled words. Louis used to think the world of her, but she doesn't know what he thinks of her now, and didn't want to make him feel any less of her because of her limited abilities. She wished she could hire a cart and have some one drive her back to his house; just show up and surprise him. She wondered how well he would receive her, if he would be as excited and happy to see her as she would be him, or if he would send her back where she came from because she left him without a saying a word. She hated herself for reacting so hastily and leaving, but she honestly felt it was the best thing to do. She pondered ways to express her thoughts and feelings in a way to make him understand her and not hate her. It drove her crazy thinking about it, and she wondered and worried until she fell asleep.

She dreamed she was in a hospital and everything was white. The walls, curtains, floors and ceilings, bed sheets and pillow cases, were all white, including the nurses and their uniforms. White dresses, white shoes and white masks over their faces. Tulah was sitting in the hospital bed looking around, but nobody looked or said anything to her. She tried to talk, to get their attention, but nobody noticed her. She moved her lips, but no sound came from them. Nurses were walking back and forth carrying newborn babies wrapped in white blankets. She tried to get out of bed, but couldn't make her body move; it was as if she had been tied down. She couldn't lift her arms from her sides, nor could she lift her legs. The only thing she could do was to shake her head back and forth.

She saw Louis come into the room; he looked so handsome wearing a white suit jacket and matching pants. He wore a white hat on his head and was holding a baby, but this baby was wrapped in a pink blanket. She tried to get his attention but he never looked in her direction. He was laughing and talking to the nurses as they passed and they all stopped to look at the babe in the pink blanket. Tulah wanted to get up to see the baby, but was restricted by the invisible ties keeping her bound to the bed. She wanted to scream, but couldn't. She saw Louis walk toward the door still cuddling the babe. She shook her head violently trying to get his attention, but he disappeared through white double doors.

Tulah was awakened by her reflexive jerking. She took a deep breath and pondered the meaning of her dream, concluding she was going to lose Louis and her baby because of her silence. She knew something must be done to change the course of her ill-fated dream, and decided she would contact Louis, but not by letter. Whatever the method, it had to be soon.

Chapter 5

Louis worked particularly hard this day, anxious to complete a project for the town's mayor. After reluctantly and finally accepting Tulah's leaving as final, Louis poured himself into his work. Forcing himself to go on without her, Louis was intent on pursuing his dream to purchase his own picture studio. Tulah was the fuel to his fire, igniting Louis to work fervently, determined to go on without her. He resolved that he didn't need her, and success would be the best way to make her regret leaving him. Louis' loss of Tulah was compounded when he learned he couldn't purchase the little storefront where he conducted business. He promised to never settle for renting when property ownership was the goal. But he would soon realize that whites weren't about to let that happen. He therefore had to concede his standards and accept what limited opportunities he had and take advantage of them. At least the façade out front bore the name of his business: LLT Picture Studio. The name didn't have any meaning, or so he told everyone that asked - just sounded catchy. In actuality, it was an acronym for the secret he held in his heart: Louis Loves Tulah.

Quite popular from peddling his services in front on the old elm hanging tree, Louis' photos were of good quality, which translated into more business. His grand opening brought in a flood of new customers. With a permanent location, Louis was no longer the source of snickering passersby, but was considered a *real* photographer, his popularity spreading to nearby counties. It was not unusual for up-and-coming blacks to travel hundreds of miles just to sit with Louis for their family portraits. The fact that he was the son of the town's only black funeral director worked greatly in his favor as well. There had been some talk around town of a lover that jilted him and left town hurriedly, but young women only found that news to be an invitation to comfort him from his time of grief. Young girls and older women alike threw themselves at Louis, bringing packed lunches and dinners to the studio. Often they claimed having prepared too much food and wished not to see it go to waste. Home baked cookies, warm cornbread, and pecan pies were a regular aroma at Louis's studio. He was the town's best catch, women relentlessly vying to be in his company, dressing in their Sunday best and going to the studio to be photographed. Louis accepted their business, knowing they'd never be able to buy his heart – just his photos.

Smitten, his heart had been stolen by a woman-child who swept into his life like a mid-summer storm, loved him deeply, fully, completely, and then abruptly left him aching, empty and alone. He kept the picture of Tulah in his back pocket, taking it out and gazing at her beautiful visage from time to time. Her eyes, full of fire and wonder, seized his heart each time he looked at them. He wanted to frame the picture and sit it out for everyone to see, declaring his love for her to the world, but he knew he would only be called a fool. So instead, he kept the picture in his wallet and took it out when he had a private moment to reminisce and relive the time they spent together. Although he was hurt, angry and lonely, he found it difficult to let her go.

The job of working on a project for Huxley Ambrose, Marietta's mayor, came shortly after Louis opened his studio. He photographed Ambrose's wife, Sybil, and their two young children, when he spotted them going into Mr. White's general store. He asked to photograph her, adding that if she was not completely satisfied, she would not have to pay and could keep the photos. Sybil Ambrose's reluctance to have a black man photograph her was quelled by the fact that he was fair skinned, good looking, polite and finely dressed. At least he looked professional, she mused. Sybil followed Louis to his makeshift studio with her two unruly straplings, and the three of them posed for their portrait. Louis took a plethora of shots from every conceivable angle, stretching his considerable skills to limits he had not aspired to before. He captured the essence of her plain and unremarkable profile, transforming and enhancing her few attributes into a photogenic masterpiece, his gift working to its fullest potential. He had toys on hand for the children to pose with, to put them at ease and make the photos look more natural. Quite satisfied with his work, he completed the shoot and promised to have the pictures back in two days. He asked how he should deliver the pictures, and Sybil said she would have someone to come by and pick them up. As they prepared to leave, Louis attempted to take the stuffed toy from her young son, and the boy fell into a tantrum. Mrs. Ambrose superciliously told Louis the child would just have to keep the toy to keep him appeased.

After two days, Sybil Ambrose had someone to come by and collect the photos just as she had promised, and a week after that, Louis still had not heard anything decisive. He was tempted to go to their mansion, but knowing his boundaries, he didn't chance it. He would just have to wait. Several weeks went by before Louis saw Mrs. Ambrose again. While looking out of his studio window, he saw her ornate black lacquer imported horse drawn carriage, the accordion top pulled back to let the Georgia sun in. Dressed in a full bodice yellow taffeta dress, matching wide brimmed hat with a white satin bow in front, and coordinating parasol extended above her head, Mrs. Ambrose came in town to see her physician. Louis bolted out the door and ran alongside the carriage, grabbing the harness as he jogged alongside.

"Mrs. Ambrose?"

"Young man, you gave me a start! Now you unhand my carriage immediately, before I call the law!" Louis, half out of breath, let go of the harness as he continued to jog alongside the carriage.

"The photos... were you pleased with the photos ma'am?" Sybil looked him up and down.

"Are you actually speaking to me, boy? Such gumption you have." Sybil looked straight ahead, not acknowledging his presence. Louis took his hat off and continued jogging.

"I'm sorry, ma'am," he puffed between breaths. "Forgot my manners. Louis Starks, ma'am. I took the photographs of you and yo' youngin's few weeks ago, remember? Messenger came by and picked 'em up. Didn't you get them?"

Sybil motioned for her driver to stop the carriage. She stared Louis up and down with a look of disapproval.

"Oh yes, I expect I remember you now." The dust from the carriage's wake washed over Louis like ash from a volcano. He coughed, cleared his throat, then spoke.

"How'd you like the pictures?" Louis managed a dust covered smile, anticipating a positive response. He took his hat and attempted to beat the dust off his clothes.

"Oh yes. You. Well, if you must know, I didn't like them at all, actually. The quality was grainy and dark, the lighting was poor, and you didn't photograph my best side, like the New York photographer who took pictures of Huxley and me when he became mayor. I didn't look like myself – not at all."

Louis scratched his head, perplexed as to what could have happened because he was superbly confident that those photos were some of his best work. He knew the business that would come from the mayor's endorsement would generate a high volume of business. Bad mouthing his work, however, could very well put him out of business. Careful about how he proceeded, Louis spoke.

"Ma'am, I took a lot of time and care to capture your beauty, if you don't mind me saying so, ma'am. And yo youngins', with the stuffed toys an' all – y'all looked like ya shoulda been posin' for a magazine cover. Y'all looked fine to me. I was real pleased with myself for those photos." Louis spoke subserviently.

"Well, I'm glad you were so pleased, but I on the other hand was not. And if memory serves correct, you said I was not obligated to pay if I was not satisfied. Did you not?"

"Why yes ma'am, that's what I said, but I…"

"Well, that concludes our business then, now doesn't it Mr.?"

"Starks, ma'am, Louis Starks."

"Right. Have a fine day, Mr. Starks." She motioned for her driver to continue on, he tapping the black stallions lightly with the riding crop, and off they went.

Louis was out done with her condescending and aloof behavior towards him. He knew that those photos were of excellent quality and professionally done. Not to mention that she let her children waltz away with the toys he uses for props. It's not like she couldn't afford to buy them there own toys, no, that wasn't good enough, she had to go and take his. But he knew there was no one to blame but himself. Standing there in the middle of the street watching the beautiful carriage makes its way through town, Louis knew he'd given away the pictures with his eagerness to get her business by offering his services with a one way guarantee. As he dejectedly turned and walked back to his studio, patting the dust from his clothes, Louis gathered himself. He knew his work was excellent, and made up his mind right then and there to never put the prestige of a client above the sale. He had invested nearly sixty dollars in materials, using the highest quality paper to develop the pictures, spending a week in time and effort to deliver a superior product to an inferior client who because of color sat in the seat of advantage. Louis knew Sybil lied. She loved those pictures, but took advantage of his naivety. There was no other way he could justify her actions, besides being just plain old mean, high and mighty, and prejudice towards a black man for having his own business. Louis was livid, but what made matters worse was that there wasn't a single thing he could do about it. Like his Daddy always said, "First time, shame on you – second time, shame on me." It was a lesson he bought and paid for – the best kind, his Daddy always said.

A week later, Mayor and Mrs. Ambrose paid Louis a visit. His heart skipped a beat when he saw them both standing there looking important and bothered. He couldn't imagine what they could have wanted that they would come all the way in town to his shop. Louis replayed the incident with Sybil while calculating the benefit of not ruffling Mayor Ambrose's feathers. His Mama's words spoke to him, "Make your self useful to your enemy until you are strong enough to overtake them." Louis straightened his tie and his back, and walked briskly toward them with his right hand outstretched to the Mayor.

"Good afternoon, Mayor Ambrose sir, Mrs. Ambrose. How can I help you, sir?" Mayor Ambrose took the gold chained spectacle from his right eye, and pointed at Louis. Louis braced himself for the worst.

"My wife tells me you photographed her and my boys some weeks ago. Is that correct?" Ambrose placed the spectacle in his vest pocket, the gold chain dangling impressively. "Yes sir, that's right. It was a pleasure serving your family." Louis said, swallowing hard. Sybil refused to look Louis in the eye, making him even more nervous. Ambrose paused, walked to the window and looked out at the city he was responsible for. Then he turned, walked toward Louis, and, with his hand again grabbing the spectacle, he pointed at Louis.

"Well, I saw those photos and I tell you I ain't never seen anything like em."

"Sir?"

"Those are the best damned photos I've ever seen."

Louis didn't realize he was holding his breath until he exhaled a sigh of relief. Sybil's body language signaled disapproval as she fidgeted with her parasol.

"Thank you, sir!"

Ambrose bellowed. "Ha! To get my two children to sit still long enough to pose for a photograph was miracle enough, but you made them rascals look like angels. Saw the stuffed toys you gave 'em. Real professional, boy."

"Thank you, sir."

"Got a project for ya."

Louis was hesitant to do any more favors after the fiasco that took place with his wife and the way she cheated him out of his pay. He was careful in the way he answered.

"Well sir, business has been picking up around here."

"Oh, never mind that. This project will put you on the map. This is just the kind of publicity you want."

"My pleasure, sir." Louis reluctantly acquiesced. "How can I serve you?" Louis measured his words. Louis' father drilled in his boys the power of silence, and the pregnant pause. Huxley spoke.

"You know it's almost re-election time, and I need to show myself as the family man's candidate. So I want you to come to my home and photograph me sitting in my parlor with Sybil standing over my shoulder, and the kids standing in front of me. I'm going to plaster these pictures all over town..." The Mayor framed his hands and extended his arms. "...Ambrose Huxley – The Family Man's Mayor."

Louis got excited at the thought, but held his ground. His prolonged silence punctuated the business proposition. Louis took a deep breath, and then spoke.

"Well sir, that sounds good... as one possible idea. The posin' and creative part is what I do best. If you'll leave that to me, I guarantee you and your family will look as good, if not better, as your lovely wife and children did in the photos I gave you." Louis glanced at Sybil, who furtively looked out of the corner of her eye at Louis.

"You say you gave 'em?" Huxley looked at his wife, puzzled, then back at Louis.

"How much they cost?" Louis knew he had him, resisting the urge to up sell him, he gave the Mayor the accurate price.

"Well sir, sittin' and processin' and materials an' labor come up to – fifty five dollars." Mayor Huxley reached into his pocket inside his morning coat, pulled out his wallet, and retrieved a crisp one hundred dollar bill.

"That's your money, plus an advance you so you can get what you'll need to get started." Louis accepted the cash, fighting the urge to yell, scream and jump with joy.

"Thank you Mr. Mayor, sir. I'm gone get started right away," Louis said while reaching out to shake the mayor's hand. Louis looked over at Mrs. Ambrose and noticed a gritted teeth smile on her tart little face. Sensing Louis' apprehension, she attempted an explanation.

"I'm always a little skeptical at first. It takes thangs a while to grow on me, but Huxley got me to seeing your photos in a different kind of way, and I must say… they are rather good."

Louis accepted her feeble apology, inasmuch as it no longer mattered what Sybil thought. His work with her brought in both the Mayor's business and endorsement, all the approval Louis needed. From that day forward, Louis was so busy he had to hire two assistants. With Election Day fast approaching, Louis and his crew worked around the clock to finish the photos, bringing in Louis' biggest payday - $250. The response to the photos were so favorable, Mayor Ambrose ordered an additional $100 worth more. The town's people lined up to have their photos taken by "The Mayor's Photographer."

Louis stayed at the shop working all night, sunrise beckoning him to go home. Taking off his apron and putting on his jacket, he noticed a letter lying on the desk by the cash register. It was addressed to him with a return address he did not readily identify.

"Ortonville?"

He flipped the letter and found an address, but no name. He slid the letter into his breast pocket, placed his fedora neatly on his head, locked the store and headed home. Louis climbed into bed, closed his eyes and started drifting off to sleep, but was suddenly jolted awake at the thought of the anonymous letter. Louis lay in bed wondering who he knew in Ortonville. The faint possibility of the letter coming from Tulah excited him, but he contained his enthusiasm for fear of disappointment. Wide awake now, Louis finally decided he would not be able to rest until the mysterious letter was at last read. He sat up and stretched before rising.

Louis walked over to the dresser, studying the address. He felt a tinge of excitement coursing through his veins. He returned to the bed, fingering the ends of the envelope, questioning if the letter was from Tulah, and if so, why now? Had she gotten married? Was she telling him it was over, and she never wanted to see him again? These thoughts and more passed through Louis' head. He had seen Cora, Tulah's aunt, in town from time to time, but she never mentioned anything regarding Tulah. He peeled the flap open, pulled out the letter and began reading.

My Dearest Louis,

Louis' heart danced, his hands trembling slightly. He quickly looked at the closing of the letter to see the name of the sender and at the bottom and it was signed, *Love Always, Tulah.* Louis smiled, took a deep breath, let it go slowly, and started again from the top.

My Dearest Louis,

There is so much I want to say to you I barely know where to start. I'll begin by saying how sorry I am for leaving you with no word or explanation. The time we spent together was the happiest time of my life, and holding on to that was the single thing that has kept me sane while being apart from you. When you said you were willing to get us a place to live together and take care of me I was overjoyed at the thought, but then I realized how much you would have to give up to make that happen, and I couldn't let you do that for me. Your dreams and your happiness mean more to me than having to endure Aunt Cora's selfish ways. But after spending such a glorious time with you I couldn't accept anything less than what we shared and decided it was best that I leave. I thought leaving would be the best thing, but then I realized what a horrible mistake it was. I have never regretted anything more. I love you Louis. I still love you more than anything in this world. I have been staying with Lucy Mae Etter, folks round here call her Mama Lou, and she has been taking care of me in my delicate condition. Louis I need you to come for me. I didn't put my name on the outside of the letter because I didn't want it to end up in the wrong hands and have the wrong folks looking for me. I will explain everything when I see you. I hope you still care for me because I love you so much. Please come in a hurry Louis, because my time is almost come.

Love always,

Tulah

"Her delicate condition? What in the world does that mean?"

Louis thought she was dying. He jumped up off the side of the bed and nervously paced the floor. Then grabbing the letter, he read it again, *"...in my delicate condition...come in a hurry Louis, because my time is almost come."*

"Dear Lord, is my Tulah dyin'?"

Louis wanted to confirm what it meant by asking his father, but decided better of involving his father. He decided instead to ask his mother in a way that would keep his business with Tulah private. He strolled casually into the kitchen where his mother was preparing dough for home made biscuits, planted a kiss on her cheek, and took a seat at the table.

"Whatcha doin' Mama?"

"I thought you were supposed to be sleeping. I heard you come in this morning, were you at that shop all night, Louis?"

"Yeah, I'm trying to get the rest of this work done for the mayor."

"You just like yo' Daddy, two of the most ambitious people I know," she said while flipping the dough over and rolling it out with a rolling pin.

"I'm doing what I love most, so that makes it alright."

"Who told you that?"

"Told me what?"

"That doing what you love takes the place of proper rest?"

"Nobody told me, it just feels right. Don't even feel like I'm working most times."

Louis's mother looked up from rolling the dough and smiled at Louis.

"Now if that don't sound like yo' Daddy."

Louis chuckled. He liked being compared to his father, because he held him in high esteem. He was the hardest working, most honorable man Louis knew, full of character, principle and pride. Louis always thought if he could be half the man his father is, then he would be alright.

"You really think I sound like Daddy?"

"Um hum, you a lot like yo' Daddy."

She said smiling at Louis while rolling the dough into small, fist-sized balls.

"Hey ma, what it mean when a lady says she's in delicate condition?"

Turning her attention to Louis, she stopped rolling the dough and looked at him with stern consternation.

"Who said that?"

"What's wrong with saying that? What's it mean?"

"Depends on who said it."

"Why does it depend on who said it?"

"Well, who was it?"

"Tell me why, Mama. Why does it depend on who said it?"

"Did somebody say that because they wanted you to know, or did they just say it?"

"Mama, you gone drive me crazy."

Louis's mother continued to stare at him apprehensively.

"Okay, I saw two ladies talking and I heard one tell the other she was in delicate condition. I didn't know what she meant by it."

"She wasn't telling *you* she was in delicate condition, was she?"

"No Mama, I don't even think she meant for me ta hear it."

"You sure about that?"

"Yes Mama."

Louis lied. He never kept anything from his Mama, but under the circumstances he couldn't tell her anything until he had gotten the story straight for himself.

"Well, if you say so. It usually means a woman is expecting a baby. That's why I asked who said it. I hope who ever this lady is, she got herself a husband."

Louis was reeling by this time. The thought of having a baby was overwhelming him. He momentarily felt light headed and he almost lost his balance. If true, he thought, he had to get to Tulah right away.

"And what if she says my time is almost come?"

"I guess she means the child will be here more sooner than later."

Louis jumped out of his chair and leapt into the air with excitement. He grabbed his Mama and squeezed her tight planting a big kiss on her cheek.

"Whew!" Louis screamed with excitement.

"What the devil is wrong with you?"

"Nothing Mama, everything is alright now. Everything is just fine." He said hurrying out of the kitchen.

Louis went back into his room and re-read the letter. The thought of him being a Daddy was as incredible as Tulah saying she still loved him. This was by far the best news he'd heard in a long time, and it couldn't have come at a better time. He had established himself as a successful business man, he landed a major project with the mayor, and had begun saving money. The only thing missing now was Tulah, and now he would have her and a new baby. He knew God had heard his prayers and he thanked him for being so faithful. Louis packed a small suitcase and decided to figure out the rest along the way, because nothing was going to hold him back from Tulah.

"I'm coming Tulah baby. I'm coming for ya."

Chapter 6

Tulah was on edge from the day she sent the letter to Louis. Eight days had passed and Tulah worried constantly, afraid that Louis wouldn't respond to her favorably, if at all. There was so much she wanted to say, hoping he'd come so she could say it face to face. She thanked God for Cassie, the young girl down the road, who wrote the letter for her and keeping everything in confidence, but couldn't stand Cassie asking everyday if she had heard back yet. Tulah knew Cassie meant well and was only excited for her, but each time she asked, and Tulah had to tell her 'no word yet', it was a painful reminder of the possibility Louis may not be coming at all. Mama Lou was just as bad, even though she didn't utter a word, her questioning eyes spoke volumes. She was careful not to over step her boundaries by prying, but Tulah knew what she wanted to say.

Tulah spared Mama Lou the burden of asking if she contacted her child's father when she told her that little Cassie down the road had helped her to prepare a letter and send it off. Mama Lou seemed relieved when Tulah gave her the news. She knew Mama Lou loved her and she was welcome to live with her for as long as she wanted, so she couldn't figure out why it meant so much to her that she contact Louis. She could only imagine Mama Lou didn't want her to experience the same kind of pain in her and Louis's relationship she herself had endured. When Tulah told Mama Lou she sent a letter, she asked her what she should do next.

"Wait on 'em, honey. That's all you can do now is wait."

"Mama Lou, do you think he'll come?"

"He'll be here honey, don't you worry. He's coming."

"I wish I was as confident as you is about this."

"Time is the healer of all thangs. Time has a way uh workin' thangs out, puttin' thangs in day riteful place, an' all you can do is wait."

"I feel so nervous I could throw up right here on dis here floor."

"Oh gul, drank you some tea. Ain't no need a you getting' dat baby all nervous. It'll come here wit da colic."

"With da what?"

"Sumptin' you don't wanna wish on yo youngin'."

"Oh Mama Lou, what I'm gone say to him? I'm so excited – ooh. This baby just kicked the fool outta me."

"Dat's cause you too excited, getting' it all nervous. Go on and have a seat ova there on da couch."

Tulah walked toward the sofa holding her stomach and carefully lowered herself to take a seat.

"I ain't evva felt dis chile kick so hard."

"Probly just like you wit da same feisty attitude. It's his way a sayin' sit yo behind still."

Tulah laughed at the thought.

"Mama Lou, how you know it's a boy?"

"You betta hope it's a boy. You don't want no fast talkin' little gal like you."

They both laughed.

"You don't mean dat Mama Lou."

"Chile I'll be happy for a healthy baby, no matta iffin' it's a boy or a gul."

"Now dat's what I like to hear."

"You want some tea?"

"Yeah, tea will be mighty nice. But I'll get it Mama Lou, you been looking right tired here lately. You feelin' alright?"

"I's just ole is all. I used ta watch ma Daddy sit on a chair and be sleep in thirty seconds. I use ta wonda why he would fall asleep so fast, soon as he sit down, he sleep. I thought it was cause he work so hard in da fields, now I reckon I understand, ain't just workin hard, its cause you gets ole."

"Mama Lou, ain't nothing ole about you. You sharper'n most folk I know – sept you just move slower is all."

Tulah laughed, teasing Mama Lou. She laughed easily and

wasn't as uptight as she had been of late. Mama Lou was relieved as well. She couldn't bear the thought of leaving Tulah alone with a newborn on the way. She knew Tulah wasn't ready to handle the responsibility of being a new mother, running a household and handling her funeral arrangements by herself. Mama Lou knew she was dying. She had known for quite sometime but had hoped for more time after Tulah came into her life, giving her so much joy and laughter. She was looking forward to going home to be with the Lord, anxious to see her husband on the other side, but since Tulah came, she found herself hoping to stay.

That's why Mama Lou pushed Tulah so hard to contact Louis. She didn't want her to have to face hardships on her own, and besides, all children need to have their father. Mama Lou had grown to love Tulah and the new babe growing within her, and she wanted them both happy. She had willed her house, her farm and all her farm animals to Tulah. She figured since Tulah turned her little shack into a warm and loving home, it would be a sufficient home for her, Louis and the baby. She was at peace now, knowing Louis was coming. She didn't have to fight for another day here on earth, she could slip away during the night and meet her Maker. However, there was just one other thing that compelled her to stay – the new baby. If she could see that little face, smell the freshness of its breath and cuddle it in her arms just once, then she would be ready to go. Mama Lou had been working on a quilt for the little one. She was almost finished and wanted to surprise Tulah with it hoping to make her feel better, since she had been so down lately. But since Tulah had hopes of Louis coming for her, she had been elated with anticipation. Tulah tried to hide her excitement at first, but after a while could no longer mask it, and finally just gave up trying. She laughed and giggled, and was so happy Mama Lou couldn't help but feel excited as well.

After they had a supper of smoked neck bones, black eyed peas, rice and Tulah's attempt at her aunt's famous corn bread, they settled in front of the fireplace.

"You know, I been working on sumptin' fo' da baby. I was gone wait till it got heh, but I guess now is a good a time as any."

"What is it Mama Lou?"

"Hep me outta dis chair. Betta yet, go look in da room under da bed. You gone see sumptin wrapped in brown paper, fetch it ta me."

Tulah obediently rose from her chair and wobbled into the room. When she realized she couldn't get down low enough to look under the bed, she tried fishing it out with her foot. She was able to feel it, but couldn't get a good enough grip on it to drag it out. She squatted down, steadying herself by holding on to the bed post, she slid her right foot under the bed. She felt the package with her foot and pulled it with all the force she could muster. Suddenly, Tulah felt a pain on the side of her stomach ripping through her groin area, traveling to her back and promptly down her spine. The pain was so intense it cut off her breath. She held her stomach as her knees buckled from under her. Falling to her knees, she screamed a gut wrenching cry. She fell over on her side and balled herself into a fetal position, holding her stomach, hoping the pain would quickly subside.

Mama Lou's blood ran cold when she heard Tulah scream. She was so afraid of what could have happened to Tulah she was frozen in place with fear. She wanted to get out of her chair, but her mind was racing, filling her head with all kinds of chilling thoughts, so all she could do is cup her hands towards heaven and cry. Tulah's pain was so great, that she rocked herself as she cried out for help.

"MAMA LOU!!!! HELP ME, HELP ME, GOD HELP ME. SOMEBODY HELP ME PLEASE!!!"

Mama Lou managed to rise from her chair and started slowly, hesitantly, towards the room.

"I'm comin' chile, hold on."

Mama Lou made it to the room, but didn't see Tulah. She walked further into the room and saw her feet sticking out by the bed. As she got closer, she could hear Tulah moaning and whimpering in pain. She was on the floor holding her stomach and rocking as tears streamed down her face.

"What happened?"

Tulah didn't answer, she kept moaning and crying.

"Dear God, what she done did ta herself? Baby, you gots ta tell Mama what happened, where it hurt?"

Tulah tried to speak, but the pain stabbed through her like a knife. She shook her head trying to tell Mama Lou she couldn't talk. Mama Lou wanted to help her, but she couldn't get down far enough to sooth her, and couldn't get Tulah to tell her what happened. Unable to lift her, she sat on the edge of the bed crying, watching as Tulah writhed in pain. Finally the pain subsided, Tulah's body uncoiling from the grip of agony, and stretching her legs out. Still holding her stomach, Tulah turned to Mama Lou.

"I don't know what happened, but I had a sharp pain in my stomach, back and in my vagina. Is dat a labor pain?"

"I don't know chile, you might be in labor, cause it shole hurt just like dat. But you too early ta be in labor."

"I know. But if dats what it feel like, God help me."

"You thank you kin git up off of da floor?"

"I thank so."

"Go slow chile, just move slow."

Tulah tried to rise, but again felt a pain in her stomach, not as intense as before, but still there. She sat up and braced herself on the edge of the bed where Mama Lou sat. Once she realized it was too painful to rise from a sitting position, she let her legs fall over to one side, and pushed into a kneeling position. Holding tightly to the bed post, she put one foot on the floor and slowly lifted herself with her other leg until she was able to stand. Mama Lou helplessly watched Tulah, and prayed God would give her strength enough to get up on her own. Once Tulah was up, she felt pressure in her vaginal area and had to quickly take a seat.

"Mama Lou, I don't know what I done done ta ma'self, but I don't thank labor is suppose to feel like dis. I thank I done hurt ma'self bad. I think I need a doctor."

"Chile I know. But ain't nothing I kin do till da mornin' when dem kids come heh to feed da chickens. I kin ask them to fetch a doctor then, but ain't nothing I kin do ta night."

"I needs to lay down. I don't thank I needs to be movin' too much. It just hurt too much when I try ta move."

"Alright chile. Go on and lay down. I get you some help in da mornin'."

Tulah rested through the night, and Mama Lou stayed in the room with her mostly watching and praying. First thing the next morning, Cassie and the other children from down the road came just as expected, and Mama Lou was on the porch anxiously awaiting them. She waited outside so they wouldn't disturb Tulah with their loud talking and laughing. She instructed them to run home and tell their mother to send for a doctor right away. When the doctor arrived, he examined Tulah and was able to determine she had sprained her groin and dilated 3 centimeters. It was no real concern since she was 36 weeks pregnant, but was ordered to bed rest.

Tulah's jubilation subsided after almost two weeks of sending the letter to Louis and he had not responded. She had hoped he would have been there by now. In her letter, she did not come right out and say she was expecting a baby, but she thought she had said as much as necessary to at least entice him enough to come and see about her. Tulah concluded since he hadn't come, he really did hate her and didn't want anything more to do with her. The thought of Louis hating her coupled with the fact she was bedridden and more than likely would be delivering their child alone pushed Tulah in a deep depression.

The doctor wouldn't be coming back to check on Tulah, he only did it as a one time favor for Cassie's mom, who worked for him as a maid and part time midwife. Cassie's mom came to check in on Tulah once a week to make sure she was resting comfortably until the baby was due. After the second week, when she came to check on Tulah she noticed the bedding and her night gown were wet.

"I think your water broke."

"What dat mean?"

"It means the sac the baby lives in done broke and it's ready to come. You having any pain?"

"No more than usual back pain."

"Girl, if your water done broke you gotta have dis baby. You don't wanna have no dry labor."

"I don't understand whatcha tryin' ta say. Is my baby gone be alright?"

"Yo baby gone be fine, Lord willin', we just gotta get yo contractions started."

"How you gone do dat?"

"Laxatives."

"Huh? You gone make me take a laxative?"

"Dats right, and we gotta move fast."

Tulah was afraid, but felt everything would be okay. Cassie was instructed to run home and fetch the laxatives from their medicine chest and to get some fresh towels. Cassie's mother, Dorothy, had worked for the doctor and his wife for many years and had learned a few medical techniques from him prompting her into the role of the town's unofficial nurse. She knew just what to do for colds, headaches, fever, and how to deliver babies. She gave Tulah the laxatives and made her drink lots of water. She waited in the parlor with Mama Lou until the laxatives had time to work. Cassie, who was not much younger than Tulah, did all the chores around the house and kept the other children quiet.

When it came time for Tulah to deliver, she experienced gripping labor pains and an overwhelming urge use the bathroom. She kept telling Dorothy she needed to get up so she could use it, but Dorothy made Tulah lay still. She told her if she had an urge to push then to just do it. Several hours and three bed sheets later, Tulah delivered a baby girl. She was a tiny little thing. Light skinned, dark curly hair, and the cutest little heart shaped, pink lips. Tulah held the new born in her arms and kissed her tiny little face. Cuddling her close, she rocked her and whispered she loved her in her ear. Mama Lou waited patiently outside the bedroom door until Dorothy came out and told her everything was alright and Tulah had delivered a baby girl.

The next morning Tulah awakened to the gentle cry of her new born. Mama Lou had fallen asleep in the chair across from the bed and continued to sleep through the growing wails of the hungry babe. Tulah sat up and looked around for her baby and found her wrapped in a blankets lying in a dresser drawer. She gingerly swung her legs off the side of the bed and headed towards the crying baby. Still moving a little slow from the intense delivery, she lifted the baby into her arms and kissed her little pink lips.

She made her way back to the bed, adjusted the baby in her left arm and began to feed her from her milk filled breast. Mama Lou opened her eyes to the sight of Tulah nursing the baby.

"My my, ain't dat a sight."

"Mornin' Mama Lou."

"Just look at dat little gul guzzling up all dat milk. She shole is a pretty little thang, ain't she?"

"Mama Lou, can you believe I gots me a baby? I just cain't get used to da thought of me bein' somebody's Mama."

"I know chile, seems like a miracle don't it?"

"As close to a miracle as I'm ever gone get."

"Whatchu gone name her?"

"I don't know yet. I thought her Daddy would be here ta help me thank of a name. But I reckon I'm gone have ta do it ma'self now."

"Well dats what we gone have ta do. Whatcha come up wit so fur?"

"I don't know. I keep looking at her tryin ta see what she look like. I think she look like a Priscilla. You like dat?"

"Naw, I don't like no Priscilla. I like Beatrice. I knew a lady name Beatrice when I was a girl. She was a nice lady."

"Um um Mama Lou, I don't like Beatrice. Sounds too old for a little baby."

"Chile, how is a name gone sound too old?"

"I don't know. I guess I just don't like it. Mama Lou, Is my breast gone stay big like dey is?"

"Long as you got milk in em."

"I don't mind em being big, cause dey ain't nevva been big, but dey hurt."

"Yea but she gone empty em out. When ever dey git too full you gone have ta feed her to give you some relief."

"Seem like a lot for her to drink."

"It might be right na, but she gone git bigger and she gone eat more and more."

"Well, I hope she get big real soon, or got a big appetite one. Cause these big ole thangs hurt." Tulah laughed. "I got da blanket you made fo'me. It shole is pretty Mama Lou, thank you."

"Huh? You know I cain't heh so well. Whatchu say?"

"I said thank you fo'the blanket you made."

"You welcome chile. Dem patches of cloth come from a blanket my Mammie made fo'me. I mixed it wit some other cloth I had but nevva used."

"When you find time to make a blanket?"

"Mostly late at night, when you was sleepin'. I knew da baby gone be needin' somethin' to be wrapped in, and by God's grace heh she is. "

"Dats what I'm gone call her. Grace. Just like God's grace."

"Now I likes dat. Little baby Grace."

"You wanna hold her?"

"She so little."

"It's okay, Mama Lou."

Mama Lou looked at Grace, unsure if her feeble hands would

hold her. Tulah got up and gently placed Grace in her arms. She sat back on the bed and watched Mama Lou hold little Grace and make faces at her, trying to get her to smile. Tulah was happy at the thought of being a mother, but her joy quickly waned as her thoughts traveled back home to Louis. She never expected things to turn out the way they had, and felt afraid of being a parent alone. Mama Lou saw Tulah's countenance change and knew the source of her sadness. She reassured her things would work out, that babies bring blessings, and to be excited about her future.

Later that evening, Dorothy brought dinner for Tulah and Mama Lou, with Cassie in tow to clean the dishes and help tidy up. After dinner Dorothy showed Tulah how to fold cotton cloths into diapers by pinning them at the sides. She promised to return early in the morning to bring breakfast before leaving for work. That evening, Tulah felt especially down. Having gotten little Grace to sleep early she climbed into bed, cuddled her pillow, and fell off to sleep.

Tulah dreamed of Critter's Creek where Louis found her the night she ran away from Cora's house. She was sitting peacefully on the shore, watching the beauty of the sunset paint a smoky orange glaze on the water's surface, its shimmering effervescence sparkling in the twilight. Tulah shielded the brilliant sun with her hand above her eyes, in an effort to make out a sailboat in the distance. The vessel's canvas sails filled with wind, and the silhouette of a person on board. Tulah untied her shoes, removing them as she walked to the mouth of the creek for a better look. The cool water licked her toes as she waded in knee deep. She made out the figure on board – it was Mama Lou. Tulah waved and called out to her, but the sails became even fuller with the breeze, carrying the sailboat and Mama Lou further away. Tulah noticed the sky had filled with ominous, foreboding clouds of charcoal gray. Tulah was afraid. She looked from the sky to the boat, which by now could barely be made out, a tiny pinpoint of light separating the smoky orange glaze on the water's surface from the ashen sky of gray.

The sailboat had drifted to the horizon, where land and sea meet sky. Readily identifiable to the eye but impossible to touch, the horizon is an optical illusion existing only in the dimension of the mind. Mama Lou had drifted to another dimension.

Chapter 7

The next morning, Tulah got up to feed little Grace. She went into the parlor and found Mama Lou sleeping in the chair. Her slop jar was on the floor beneath her, and her head slightly to the side, her hands folded neatly on her lap. Tulah, disturbed by the dream, became fearful. She walked over and gently nudged her shoulder. Mama Lou's hands fell gently open. Tulah called her name. Mama Lou didn't respond. Tulah knew, but nonetheless touched Mama Lou's face with the back of her hand and felt cold and pasty flesh. At that moment, she knew Mama Lou had made her transition. Tulah sat on the floor directly in front on Mama Lou, put her head down as uncoaxed, silent tears fell heavily down her face. Her body rocked with the rhythm of her mourning, her chest convulsing as she attempted to manage her inconsolable grief. She shook her head in disbelief, placed both hands over her aching heart, and gently rocked back and forth. She heard Grace crying from the other room, but couldn't move. Heavier now, she cried vociferously, as grief gave birth to even deeper pain. Tulah felt nauseous. Grace cried louder and Tulah cried harder, both feeling matriarchal abandonment for entirely different reasons.

Tulah loved Mama Lou, but did not realize how much until now. Mama Lou was the mother she never had, her closest and dearest friend, one who loved her unconditionally and had her best interests at heart – and now she was gone. Tulah decided she couldn't go on, not wanting to endure any more pain or suffering. She'd been through enough, lost enough. Tulah wished she could die too. She looked over at Mama Lou's slop jar on the floor, and amazingly, it didn't look repulsive to her like it normally did. Now it was only a jar Mama used to rid her mouth of the disgusting taste of gall from her toothless gums. She felt bad she would cringe and shiver every time Mama would spit in the jar. She felt bad she felt anything negative about the woman who took her in and opened her home and heart to her with no questions asked, and no expectations.

Tulah heard a knock at the door, but again, couldn't make herself move. Grief rendered her paralyzed, unable to move from her spot on the floor, she ignored the sound. The knocking continued, until finally Dorothy pushed the door open.

"Helloo, where is everybody?"

She came in and saw Tulah sitting on the floor in front of Mama Lou. At first glance Dorothy knew the seriousness of the situation.

"Tulah, baby, I'm sorry."

Tulah shook her head unable to speak. When she heard the compassion in Dorothy's voice, she covered her face with her hands and cried even harder. Dorothy went over and touched Mama Lou's face, and then turning her attention to Tulah she tried to lift her off the floor. After helping her to her feet, she gave her a warm and sympathetic embrace. Trying to find the right words to comfort her, she held her hands and looked her in the eye.

"She's in a better place now Tulah, and you *will* be okay."

Tulah shook her head, rejecting Dorothy's words.

"Yes, yes you will. You will be okay. I know it hurts now, but it'll get betta, life goes on. You've got a baby to look after, a baby needs you, and you jus gotta be strong, honey."

"I don't wanna be strong! I'm tied of being strong. I been strong all my life and I'm jus tied, Dorothy. I cain't do it no mo. I ain't got nobody, and no shoulder ta cry on. Ma Mama died, ma Daddy left me, ma brotha gone. Ma man don't even wont me no mo, I gotta a baby ta raise by ma'self and na Mama Lou done died. What I got ta live for?"

"Don't you talk like dat, don't you evva talk like dat, you hear me? God don't want you to think it, and I don't want ta hear it. You got every thang in da worl ta live fa. Especially dat baby."

It was then that Dorothy noticed Grace's wails from the other room. She looked at Tulah then headed in the back to retrieve the crying baby. When she reached Grace, she was covered in sweat and sucking hungrily at her tiny fist. She coddled her and spoke gently in her ear trying to sooth her.

"You need ta feed dis baby. You got to pull yo'self tagetha and take care yo baby. Na here, feed her." Dorothy said handing Grace to Tulah.

"I'll take care of Mama Lou, and you take care of dis baby. She needs her Mama. Don't make dis baby suffa, Tulah. You take care of her like Mama Lou would've wanted you to."

Tulah received Grace and began to feed her. She leaned back on the couch, closed her eyes and tears streamed down her face.

"I'm gone hafta leave you here fo a minute, but I'm gone be right back. I gotta go an get some help. Tulah, baby, you gone be alright?"

Tulah nodded, but refused to open her eyes, not wanting to look at Mama Lou. Dorothy left and closed the door quietly behind her. Tulah opened her eyes and looked at Grace who was so contented with her feeding she was grunting with pleasure. When she looked down at her, Grace looked back into her mother's eyes, and Tulah felt comforted by the little soul feeding off of her own body. She suddenly felt connected to Grace and felt surprisingly soothed by her touch. She grabbed her little hand and Grace responded by wrapping her tiny fingers around Tulah's. Tulah lifted her hand to her mouth and kissed her soft, chubby knuckles and managed a smile. She looked over at Mama Lou and felt a flush of sorrow, so she quickly averted her eyes in the opposite direction. Dorothy came back a short while after and had her brother Milledge with her. She knocked on the door twice before entering. Tulah had just finished feeding Grace and had her lying over her shoulder.

"Tulah? I'm back baby. I brought ma brotha Milledge wit me, he gone help us get Mama Lou laid to rest."

"How you ma'am? Sorry bout yo lost."

Tulah nodded her head, but didn't speak.

"Na I cain't get her outta here by ma'self but I'm gone get her prepared so when the undertaker come she'll be ready," Milledge explained.

"Tulah, you wanna go in da back room, so Milledge can get her ready?" Dorothy asked.

Tulah didn't answer, but shrugged her shoulders.

"Come on honey, let him do what he gotta do, okay? I'll stay witchu. Come on now." Dorothy instructed while guiding Tulah into the back room. She closed the door behind them and offered to clean Grace and change her diaper. After she bathed Grace, and laid her down for a nap, she sat next to Tulah on the bed and brushed her hair. Tulah, who is always so full of chatter, remained silent while Dorothy did most of the talking.

"You know honey, you need to get yo'self tagetha too. Why don't you go on and get yo'self a bath, I'll tend to da baby if she wake up."

Tulah went around to the back and prepared to bathe. As she sat in the big, tin tub, she thought back to the day she met Mama Lou, how she was distraught and alone, not knowing where she was going or what she would do, until Mama Lou took her in. And after feeling her life was finally back in order, and things would start looking up, life plays this cruel joke, taking Mama Lou from her, landing her right back in a place of despair and isolation - Tulah's lifelong companions. After her mother died, it was a downward spiral of losing those closest to her. She could handle a loss after her Daddy took off, or so she thought, but then her brother ran off, leaving her with her grandmother. Then her grandmother went senile, Cora deceived her, Louis got over her, and now Mama Lou had died. It was just too much for one person to handle.

Tulah sat in the tub and wrapped her arms around her shoulders trying to comfort herself. She wanted to think optimistically, and concentrate on the positive things in her life, but besides baby Grace, she couldn't find one. Even the thought of her new baby was spoiled by the notion of having to provide for her on her own with no means of support. Getting out of the tub, Tulah mechanically dressed herself and went back into the room, where Dorothy was with Grace. When she came into the room, Dorothy told her Milledge had removed Mama Lou and was taking her to the funeral home down on Ruepart Street. She informed Tulah she was going to have to go down to the funeral home to give Mr. Dawson instructions on how she wanted to lay Mama Lou to rest. Tulah was weakened by the thought of having to complete such a task. Dorothy also advised Tulah that Grace was sleeping and she would have to leave to get dinner started for Cassie, but would bring her a plate if she got hungry.

Tulah went into the parlor and stared at the chair where Mama Lou sat only hours ago. The house was quiet and cold. Tulah felt utterly alone. She took a seat on the couch, lifted her knees to her chest, and wrapped her arms around her legs. She sat that way for what seemed like hours, motionless and emotionally drained. Tulah was startled by a knock on the door. Lifting her head and looking in the direction of the door she waited for Dorothy to come in. But when no one came in, she figured it was some of the town's people coming to pay respects after hearing about Mama Lou. Not wanting to be bothered, Tulah ignored it, hoping who ever it was would go away. But when the knocking persisted, Tulah yelled out.

"Who is it?"

"I'm looking for Tulah Belle Armstrong." Tulah knew that voice. Louis. Tulah leaped from the couch and ran to the door, flinging it open. There stood Louis, wearing a white suit jacket, matching pants, and a white fedora, just like in her dream. Tulah took one look at Louis and fell into his arms crying. Louis squeezed her tightly against his chest, and kissed her forehead.

"Tulah, baby, what's wrong?"

"Come on in here Louis, it's cold out there."

Louis came in, took off his hat, and closed the door behind him. Tulah looked at him lovingly; she had almost forgotten how handsome he was. She was so overwhelmed by his presence she stood on her toes and wrapped her arms around his neck. He hugged her around her waist, lifting her off the floor, and kissing her on the lips. When he eased her back onto the floor, she laid her head on his chest, trying to take refuge from the hurt she had endured for the last few months, and the loss experienced earlier in the day.

"Hey, are you alright?"

Tulah was suddenly angered by his delay.

"What took you so long to get here?"

"Tulah I came as soon as I could…"

"No you didn't." She interrupted. "You made me wait for you. You did it on purpose. It was yo way of punishin' me!" Tulah lunged at him, swinging wildly, knocking his white fedora off his head and onto the floor. Louis grappled with her, catching her flailing arms and pulling her into his massive frame. Tulah sobbed deeply, her face buried in Louis' chest. He caressed her, rocking gently back and forth. Tulah quickly remembered how good it felt to be in his arms again.

"I wasn't tryin'ta punish you. You da one run off and left me with no word as to why. I'm the one who was bein' punished. And I don't even know what I did ta deserve it. But here I am anyway."

The combination of his soothing touch and sensible words brought Tulah back to reality. "You right Louis. Iss ma fault. I'm sorry. So much dun gone wrong. I messed every thang up, I'm jus glad you come fo'me."

"Ain't nuthin' never gone separate us again - nevva. You hear me?"

"Mama Lou died dis mornin'."

Louis wrinkled his brow and looked at her, "The lady that took you in, the one that lives here?"

Tulah nodded as tears slid down her face.

"Oh baby, I'm so sorry. What happened?"

Tulah shrugged her shoulders.

"I don't know. I came in here dis morning and she was already dead. I wish you coulda met her."

"Come here baby." Louis continued to rock her, just as he did when they were back home. She let herself fall completely and totally into the security of Louis' kind, gentle arms and patient, caring spirit. She closed her eyes and leaned into him, feeling the full length of his lean, powerful body. It was the comfort she missed, hungered and longed for. From the bedroom, Grace began cooing. Tulah looked as Louis' eyes became as big as quarters, his faced filled with wonder and anticipation.

"Louis, we got ourself a baby."

Louis pulled back and looked her into her eyes, but she quickly looked away, feeling ashamed of keeping this from him and trying to avoid his intense stare seemed to cut right through her.

"I know I was wrong to keep this from you, but I was scared. I didn't even know until after I got here." Louis looked toward the sound of the baby.

"Tulah, where's the baby? What is it?"

"It's a girl." Tulah smiled sheepishly.

"Where is she? Is she healthy?"

"She fine Louis, she in na back."

"I want ta see her."

"Alright Louis, but I need ta explain some thangs to ya first."

"Why didn't you tell me when you found out you was pregnant?"

"Stupid, I guess. I didn't know what you thought by the way I left. You get ma letta?"

"Yeah, I got it." Louis said reaching into his breast pocket to retrieve the letter.

"I tried to explain it in da letta. I didn't want you to give up all your dreams fo'me."

Louis interrupted her.

"Tulah, we can talk about this later, I want ta see ma baby."

Tulah nodded and stood.

"Okay."

She walked towards the back of the house and slowly opened the door. Grace was in a dresser drawer being used as a crib. Louis looked at the baby and smiled.

"Ma baby. Can I hold her?"

Tulah reached inside of the drawer and gently lifted Grace. She kissed her tiny forehead, and handed her to Louis.

"What's her name?"

"I named her Grace. Like God's grace. I wanted to wait fo' you, but I…"

"Shhh. I like it. Hi, Grace." Louis said to the sleeping baby. "I'm yo Daddy."

He looked at the drawer being used for her bed and the humble little house. It was clean, but not nearly good enough for his baby, or Tulah. He rocked Grace in his arms and kissed the top of her head. Without moving his eyes from Grace he told Tulah,

"We gone have ta get married."

"What?"

"Tulah, I love you girl. I ain't never loved nobody else like I do you. And now you got ma baby. It's the right thang ta do. Do you love me?"

"Yeah Louis, I love you. I love you so much it hurt."

"Well, do you wanna marry me?"

"Yeah, I'll marry you." She said laughing.

Louis looked at her and he laughed too. He bent down and kissed her and she reciprocated.

Chapter 8

Louis came in and took charge of the situation. He took care of Mama Lou's remains by sending word back home to his father to do all the arrangements. Mama Lou had been saving a little money here and there to settle her funeral costs, but Louis took care of that so Tulah could keep the extra money. They stayed at Mama Lou's for a few weeks before going back home. Tulah wanted to stay longer, but Louis had to get back to the business, which was the reason he couldn't leave as early as he wanted to, and Tulah was impressed with his news about the mayor.

Dorothy looked after the house in their absence, Tulah's first sole material possession, along with the farm and animals. Louis and Tulah got married at the city's courthouse and Dorothy, Milledge, Cassie and some of the other town's folk showed up as witnesses. They planned a big wedding, but Tulah learned that she was expecting her second child, so they pushed up the wedding date so she could say they were married before seeing Aunt Cora. Prior to leaving for home, Louis took Tulah shopping, so Mrs. Louis Starks would look her very best. She wore a tan and red dress with a matching red hat, white hand gloves, and a brand new string of real pearls. She had a gold band around her finger, replacing the silver one she inherited from her Mama, and little Grace rode in a store bought stroller, not a hand me down like most other folks had.

Tulah now knew what it felt like to be Mrs. Starks, wife of an affluent business owner, and it felt good. She walked with her head held high and her shoulders back, proud of her husband and the fine name he created for himself. Louis hired a horse and carriage to come by drive them back home to Marietta. As Tulah boarded the carriage, she was proud to be Louis' wife, and couldn't wait to get home to tell Aunt Cora that the little nappy head she said Louis would never want was now married to him, has his baby, and another on the way, and is showering her with love she never knew existed. Once inside the coach, she watched Louis as he held Grace and nuzzled her little neck, knowing he would be the best father anyone could ever hope for. He noticed her smiling at him and grabbed her hand, giving her a reassuring squeeze. Tulah smiled back and wondered what she had done to deserve to be so happy. Mama Lou must have put in a good word to God on her behalf.

"How you feeling, honey?"

"Nervous."

"Ain't no need ta be nervous. You look beautiful, like a lady. And I done made an honest woman of you, so there ain't nothing to be worried about."

"I know, but I ain't been there in so long, and I don't know what Aint Cora gone say."

"Well, that's the last thing you gotta be worried about. Ain't nothing she can say about you that aint good. You ma wife now, and you and me and Grace gone stay at Mama and Daddy's till we get us a place of our own."

"I know Louis, but…"

"But what? You're a Starks now. You ain't even gotta go by Cora's if you don't want to."

"Oh, I'm goin', I want her ta know that we married and I want her ta see da baby."

Louis laughed.

"What you think yo' Mama and Daddy gone say?"

"I kinda got the idea Mama might already know."

"How she know?"

"I was asking her to explain ta me what it mean to be expectin'."

"Louis, I know you ain't ask her dat. You know what dat mean."

"I didn't know what it meant. When you said your time is come, I thought you was dying, girl."

"Louis, you so crazy."

They both laughed easily. Tulah laid her head on Louis' shoulder and enjoyed the rest of the ride. When they arrived in Marietta, people gathered and whispered to see Louis driving in with Tulah and a new baby, while others waved and spoke friendly greetings. Tulah held possessively onto Louis' arm, letting everyone know she was his wife.

She knew what a catch Louis was, and since she had not been around, lonely women hoping for a husband had been circling Louis like vultures over a carcass. Tulah intended to let them all know the dream of having Louis Starks was over, because she was back to stay.

Louis was as proud to have Tulah as she was to have him. Tulah was the most beautiful girl he had ever seen, a masterpiece dipped in chocolate with light brown eyes. She was short, small framed, and very shapely, with dark brown, finely textured and wavy hair. He loved every inch of her.

Louis had the driver take Tulah by the picture studio before they went to his parent's house. When she rode by the little shop with a façade out front that read: LLT Picture Studio, she beamed with pride. It was a charming little red brick studio, white shutters on either side of the windows, and a white door with big, square windows. There was a flower bed underneath the window, empty due to the cold winter weather. Tulah envisioned planting beautiful flowers next spring, then asked Louis what the LLT stood for. Louis, for the first time, uttered the secret he'd kept from the world - *Louis Loves Tulah*. She smiled, snuggled close to him and gave him a kiss. As they drove by, she noticed the shop was open and patrons were inside.

"Louis, how is yo' shop open fo' business when you ain't there?"

"Oh, I got ma'self two employees," he proudly said.

"Naw you don't!"

"Yes I do! I had to get some help in there. The Lord shole is good."

"Louis, is we rich?"

"Not yet. I'm working to make that happen. I'm gone give y'all everything, Tulah. And if thangs keep working like they is, we gone be alright."

"I nevva dreamed of all dis. 'Specially afta Mama Lou died. I nevva thought I'd be happy agin. Then you showed up and everythang changed. I jus' caint believe how happy I am."

"God works in mysterious ways."

"Humph. You can say dat agin."

Before long, the coach pulled up in front of Louis' parent's home, which was even more beautiful than Tulah remembered. As they slowed to a stop, Louis' Mama came to the door and stood on the porch waiting for them. Louis handed Grace to Tulah, and jumped down to greet his Mama. He kissed her on the cheek, held her hand and led her to the horse drawn coach.

"Mama, I want you ta meet Tulah Belle Starks, and little Grace. This here is yo' new daughter-in-law, and your new grandbaby. Come on, honey, let me help you down."

He took little Grace back from Tulah, then grabbed her hand helping her out of the carriage.

"My Lord, Louis. Did you say your wife and baby?"

"That's right Mama. This here is my wife."

Tulah stood before Louis' mother and for the first time was at a loss for words. Finally, she said,

"Should I call you Mama, or Mrs. Starks?" Tulah inquired.

Louis' mother responded by giving Tulah a big hug. She held her back at arms length to get a good look at her and then embraced her once again. Tears formed in her eyes, causing them to look like they were floating in pool of water. She turned to Louis and reached for the baby.

"Let me see my grandbaby. I wanna hold her."

Holding Grace in her arms, her tears were released and fell to her face in big drops.

"My Lord, I got a new daughter-in-law and a new grandbaby. Louis, how come you kept this from me all this time? Is this what you was talking about that day in the kitchen?"

"Yes ma'am. I hated havin' to keep it from you, but I didn't have all the details ma'self."

"Whatchu mean you didn't have all the details? Details about what?"

"I'll explain everythang to you, Mama. But we gotta get Grace outta this cold weather."

Louis' mother turned to Tulah and then back to Louis.

"She's pretty Louis. What is your name again, honey?"

"Tulah."

"Well Tulah, I'd like it if you called me Mama."

"Yes ma'am."

"Come on, let's get y'all inside. Yo' Daddy gone be surprised when he gits home. I can't believe it ma'self. Louis, you is always full of surprises."

Once inside Grace started to whimper, but Louis' mother held on to her tighter, rocking her and walking back and forth trying to quiet her. Tulah wanted to take her, but was so happy about being accepted by Louis' mother, that she didn't want to say anything to ruin it. As if on queue, Louis noticed Tulah's tension and told his Mama to give her back to Tulah.

"She's probably hungry Mama. It was a long ride."

"I can feed her. Tulah do you have a bottle for her?"

"No ma'am, I breast feed."

"Oh, well in that case, I guess I can't feed her." She laughed lightly. "Here you go." She said handing Grace back to Tulah.

"Well how about some tea? I want to get to know Tulah, and know all the details Louis seemed to have left out. Do you like tea?"

"Yes ma'am, sounds real nice."

"Tea for you, Louis?" Louis nodded.

"Thanks Mama."

"Alrighty, then excuse me while I get it started."

Louis took a seat on the couch next to Tulah, while she unbuttoned her dress, exposing her full breast. She positioned Grace on her lap and put a blanket over her breast to cover herself, just like Dorothy had shown her. Grace began to suckle and smack hungrily, and Louis pulled the blanket back to get a peek. Tulah smacked his hand.

"Yo' Mama is in the other room – stop it now."

"Tulah, we married, girl. You my wife now. What you think married folks do? We don't have to hide or be shame to love each other in front of other folk. 'Sides, it what they expect from newlyweds."

"I just gotta get used to it I guess."

"Whatcha think of Mama? She's great, isn't she?"

"Yeah. A lot nicer than I 'spected. Folks in town used ta say she uppity. She ain't like that at all."

"Mama ain't never been uppity. It's what folks expect cause we doin' alright is all. Won't be long, fo' day sayin' it about you too."

"Well, why don't day say it about you?"

"'Cause I'm a man. Men is different than women. People don't expect men to be funny actin'. If a man does alright fo' himself, then he gets respected. Women do alright, she get respect, but she'll also get talked about behind her back. I seen ma Mama go through it all her life. And she is the best Christian woman you ever wanna know."

"Well, I don't care what day say bout me. I been talked about all my life too, and I don't spect it to change na. Only difference is I can look good and live good with ma husband and ma baby, while day doin' dey talkin'."

"You gone like Daddy too, and ma brother Henry and his wife Etta. Once they here the news, you can bet they'll be on they way here to welcome you to the family."

"Louis, this all just so much at one time. I feel like ma head is spinnin'. Is they as nice as yo' Mama? I mean, I just wonda if dey gone like me. Not cause I'm yo wife, you know, like dey hafta be nice ta me. But if dey gone really like me."

"Of course they gone like you, Tulah. We are all the same. We family. And family takes care of each other, looks out fo'one another, and protect each other. You a part of this family now, and they gone love you just like I do. Besides, what's not to love?"

"Thank you, Louis. Fa' bein so nice ta me and makin' me feel so special. You nevva know how much dat means ta me." Louis lifted Tulah's hand and kissed it, just as his mother was returning from the kitchen with a serving of tea on a silver tray.

"My my, look at the newly weds." She said sitting the tray on the table in front of Tulah. "You know Tulah, you've got to be a special lady to snag this one over here. I was beginning to think he'd settle down and get married. So tell me about yourself. Where are you from?" She asked, handing Louis a tea cup.

Tulah looked at Louis before answering.

"Well, I was born in Marietta. Ma Mama died when I was five, so me and ma brotha went to live wit ma granny in Decatur. When granny went senile, I had to come here ta live wit my Aint Cora, and dats when I met Louis."

"Cora Allen?"

"Yes ma'am."

"I know her. Well, we haven't formally met, but I've seen around town before."

Tulah felt embarrassed because she knew what Cora thought about Louis' Mama, and didn't know how she treated her in passing.

"She told me she seen you around too."

"Well, now that we're family, I guess I'll have to make it a point to stop and get better acquainted with her."

"Yes ma'am."

"And I'm sorry to hear about yo' Mama. But thank God for aunties and grannies." She smiled at Tulah.

"And I'm gonna spoil ma little grandbaby rotten. Is she still eating?"

Tulah peeked under the blanket and saw Grace had fallen asleep.

"Naw, she's sleeping now."

"Give her to me, I'm gonna lay her on my bed in the back. And don't worry; I'll put plenty of pillows around her so she won't fall." Sarah told her as she walked towards the back with Grace.

Over the next few hours, Tulah and Sarah, Louis' Mama, talked and got acquainted with one another. They talked most of the morning and well into the afternoon. Sarah listened intently as Tulah spoke of Aunt Cora's betrayal and not wanting Louis to sacrifice his dreams for her. She told her about Mama Lou taking her in and her unexpected death, and the house and land Mama Lou left Tulah in Ortonville. Happy to be accepted by Sarah, Tulah spoke openly and honestly about her vulnerabilities and insecurities, not masking or covering them as she use to. She sensed sincerity in Sarah, a warm and calm spirit she gravitated to. She did not, however, tell her she was expecting again. Louis stepped out to let them get to know each other on their own and Tulah decided she didn't want to tell that part of the story without Louis being there.

Louis returned with Henry, both carrying large pieces of lumber. Tulah and Sarah were seated in the living room sipping tea.

"What's all the ruckus?" Sarah asked.

"Got a crib for little Gracie we gone put together."

Henry sat the large pieces of wood on the floor and turned his attention to Tulah. He smiled a big, hearty smile and lumbered over to her. Tulah stood to greet him and Henry's six foot two, two hundred sixty pound frame towered over her. She extended her hand to him, but instead of him shaking her hand, he wrapped his arms around her and lifted her off the floor, laughing. Tulah laughed too, taken aback by his overly friendly and unexpected behavior. Henry lowered Tulah back to earth, smacked Louis on the back and laughed again.

"This the same little girl who was ridin' her bike that morning I spent the night over here."

"That's right. That's the one."

Henry extended his hand to Tulah and she reciprocated.

"Well it's good to finally meet you. Now maybe my little brother can get some meat on his bones like me," he said, rubbing his round belly.

"I was just as skinny as he is when I first got married," he said laughing.

"Good to meet you too." Tulah said, straightening her dress.

"Tulah, I got Gracie a crib we can set up in the back 'til we get a place of our own. You see our room yet?" He winked at Tulah, who suppressed a smile before answering.

"No, me and Mama been talkin' since you left."

"That's right, and I've got to get dinner started before yo' Daddy gets home. Tulah, Louis gone show you around. I got to get my dinner goin'."

"Thank you," Tulah said with a smile.

"Honey, you're more than welcome. Welcome to the family."

Turning her attention to Henry, she asked, "You staying for dinner?"

"Naw, Etta already got dinner goin', but we comin' for dessert. She wanna meet Tulah. But I wanna see the baby - where she at?"

"Yo' Mama laid her on her bed in the back." Tulah answered.

"She's sleeping Henry - you'll see her later on this evening." Sarah told him.

"Alright Mama."

"Thanks Henry. I'm gone get this crib put together for Grace - I'll see you later."

Kennedy, Louis' dad arrived later that evening. He noticed, aside from the smell of fried chicken and biscuits, the luggage sitting by the front door. He walked into the kitchen where Sarah was setting the table for four.

"Louis back?"

"Show is, and does he have a surprise for you."

"Where is he?" Looking at the place settings, he asked, "Who is the other setting for?"

"That's part of your surprise."

Just then Louis came in with Grace in tow.

"Hey Daddy."

"Hey son, whose baby is that?"

"Mine." Louis beamed.

"Yours?"

Tulah heard Louis talking to his Dad from the other room and came out to meet him.

"This here is little Grace." He said walking over to his dad and placing Grace in his arms. Kennedy took Grace and stared into her little face.

"Well, ain't no question about her being yours." He said taking a seat at the table.

Tulah walked in and Kennedy looked up at her. Louis positioned Tulah in front on him and wrapped his arms around her small waist.

"This here's my wife, Tulah. Tulah, this here's ma Daddy. Mr. Kennedy Starks."

Kennedy's eyes widened when he heard Louis say wife. He looked at Sarah, who raised her eyebrows and smiled.

"I told you, you would be surprised."

"Son, when did all this take place?"

"Well, when I went to Ortonville, my business was not just to take pictures and handle them funeral arrangements I contacted you about. I went to go see 'bout Tulah. We been together for sometime. She left for Ortonville because she thought she was a burden to me." Kennedy turned his attention to Tulah.

"I'm sorry young lady - how do you do?" He said reaching for her hand.

"I'm fine, thank you." Tulah answered, curtsying and reaching to meet Kennedy's hand. Tulah was amazed at the man who stood before her. He had the same grey eyes as Louis, but looking into his face was like looking into the face of a white man. His skin was thin and pale, like Mr. White's at the general merchandise store. His hair was fine and oily and laid to his head like it was wet. He was tall and lean, like Louis, but had a wide midsection that gave the appearance of one who is comfortable, settled. He wore a long sleeved shirt monogrammed with KAS, on the ends of his sleeves, and his hands were as white as ivory. As he took Tulah's hand in his own, she felt the strength of a man who was very confident, but with skin so soft, you would think he had never known a hard days work. Shaking his hand, Tulah observed the contrast between his hand and hers. His were big, strong, soft, and pale, while hers were small, fragile, coarse and dark. She wondered if the contrast in their hands would be indicative of how he viewed her, smaller, weaker, and less significant. Tulah has always been sure of herself, confident and even arrogant, but in Louis' parent's presence, she felt deficient, which made her irritable and defensive. Her desire to fit in and be accepted soon replaced her feelings of inadequacy.

"You left 'cause you was pregnant?"

"Well sir, didn't know I was pregnant until after I left."

"Then why did you leave?"

"Daddy, we'll talk after dinner, we just went through this with Mama. Let's just eat now. We had a long ride and we both starving."

Chapter 9

After dinner, Henry, Etta, and their children came to have dessert with Louis, Tulah and the family. They sat at the dining room table, Sarah serving home made pound cake with lemon icing and a fresh pot of coffee. Tulah was awed at the beautiful antique china Sarah served dinner and dessert on. The high glossed, rich cherry wood table was only to be found in the finest of homes. The place settings were real linen with laced edges, and the silverware was trimmed in an 18 karat gold plate. There was a 3 tier crystal chandelier over the table, with porcelain salt and pepper shakers standing like sentinels on the dining room table. Tulah never knew black folk lived like this.

Tulah sat next to Louis, who sat across from Etta. As they talked, Tulah noticed how Etta kept batting her eyes flirtatiously and smiling - a little too friendly for her comfort - at Louis. Whenever Etta said anything, it was directed at Louis. Etta would pull a locket of her hair and twist it around her fingertip as she spoke, always maintaining eye contact with Louis. When she spoke to everyone else, it was in a normal tone, not friendly or giggly like when she spoke to Louis. Etta did, however, speak to everyone else; everyone else except for Tulah, who she ignored the entire evening.

Tulah studied how polished and poised Etta was, and felt threatened by her good looks. She was a brown skinned, buxom beauty, with long black hair that cascaded down her back in thick locks, with amazingly long thick, dark lashes. She wore colored powder on her eyelids making her wild, flirty eyes appear bigger. She wore a soft pink chiffon dress with a matching pink ribbon in her hair, her pierced ears adorned with tiny silver stud earrings. Her nails were neatly manicured and when she smiled, she revealed a beautiful set of pearly white teeth. Etta was indeed a southern belle.

"I was beginning to think it was impossible for any body to grab hold of Louis," she said as she twisted her hair looking at Louis.

"It was impossible- for anybody besides Tulah, that is." Louis said, placing his hand on Tulah's thigh.

Etta ignored his unreceptive response and proceeded with her advances toward him, which the rest of the family seemed to overlook. Tulah didn't want to appear rude, but was not about to stand by and be disrespected. She removed Louis' hand off of her knee, then stood and excused herself. Without waiting for a reply, Tulah walked away in a huff. Moments later Louis excused himself and followed her into their room.

"Tulah, what's wrong?"

"What is it with you and Etta? Y'all spose ta be likin' each other or something?" Tulah asked indignantly with her hand on her hip demanding an answer.

"Etta? Ain't nothing going on. She's my brother's wife, honey."

"Louis, I ain't crazy, and don't ack like you is either, cause I know you ain't. Dat woman in there done made it clear what she's afta, and it ain't Henry."

"I know she a little flirty, but she don't mean no harm. She's like that with everybody."

"Not wit ma husband she ain't. Na you gone tella something or I will."

"Don't be like dat, baby. Just ignore her."

"Like da rest a y'all doin? Uh uh, dats why she ackin' like dat. B'sides, she ain't said two words ta me since she been here, and when she looked at me she cut her eyes at me. I don't like her. And why ain't Henry sayin' nothin' bout it?"

"I don't know. Dey understand each other I guess. She always flirtin', and he just ignore it. So I guess dats why we do too."

"Well you married now. Somebody gone hafta tell dat heffa to cool her heels."

"Ooh, look at you acting jealous." Louis said grabbing Tulah around her waist.

"Uhn uhn - I ain't playin', Louis. You betta fix dat, fo' I do." Tulah responded, pushing Louis' hands away. Etta knocked on the half cracked door, pushing it open.

"Sorry to interrupt, but I wanna get a look at dat youngin' fo we gets ready ta leave. You gone bring her out here, Louis, or do I need to come in?"

Tulah looked at Louis and narrowed her eyes into slits. Louis took that as a warning and walked over to the door, now more than half open.

"Excuse us." He said closing the door in Etta's face. "See? She means nothing."

"Not good enough. I mean I know you makin' a point an' all, but she don't strike me as one to take a hint. You gone hafta tella yo' wife don't like da way she carryin' on, and *you* don't either."

"I'll talk to her, but I'm telling you, it don't mean nothing."

"I know it don't mean nuthin' ta you, but I cain't say da same fo' her."

"Alright, I'll take care of it. Now come on back out, let's not be rude."

Louis and Tulah came out of the room with Grace. They introduced their newest addition to the family, passing her around so everyone could get a look. Grace looked more like Louis than she did Tulah. Her doe-like eyes were a soft brown, not hazel like her mother's, or grey like her father's. Her almost bald head had thin wisps of light brown hair laid flat to her head. Her pasty complexion could be compared to cream, and she had a long keen nose, like Louis'. Her little lips were pink and heart shaped. Louis told everyone her lips were formed like a heart because she is he and Tulah's love child. Henry teased Tulah about learning how to cook to fatten Louis up like him, but Etta interrupted, telling Henry Tulah wouldn't want Louis to be fat like him.

When it came time for Henry and Etta to leave, Etta finally acknowledged Tulah and shook her hand. However, when she said goodbye to Louis, she hugged him and gave him a lingering kiss on the cheek, so close to his mouth she caught the corner of his lips. Tulah was infuriated, especially because Louis didn't resist. Try as she might, Tulah could barely keep her composure. Louis and Kennedy walked out on the porch to see Henry and Etta off. Sarah sensed Tulah's tension and walked over to her and touched her arm.

"Honey, don't let her get to ya. It took me a while to get used to the way she is, but Henry don't seem to mind, so we overlook her. She don't mean nothin' by it. She really is harmless."

It took every ounce of energy for Tulah to muster a smile.

"Well, I don't know dat I kin get used to it. We family now, and I don't want ta start no trouble, but I don't like it."

"I know, honey. But Louis loves you. I'm his Mama and I know. Trust me on this, okay?"

"Okay."

"Okay." Sarah said rubbing Tulah's arm.

Kennedy and Louis came in from seeing Henry and Etta off.

"Well ain't we just one big happy family?" Kennedy said kissing little Grace on the cheek.

"I've got to get up early, so I'm turning in. You all got everything you need?"

"Yeah Daddy, we gone be fine." Louis said placing his arm around Tulah.

"Good. Well, good night."

"Good night Daddy."

"Good night Mr. Starks."

"I'm gone get these dishes cleaned up and I'll be right on." Sarah explained.

"I'll be happy ta help you clean. You been cookin' all day," Tulah offered.

"Uhn uhn. You go right on to bed with your husband. I'll be fine."

"But I insist."

"So do I, now go on to bed. Go on. Good night."

"Thank you, Mrs. Starks. I mean Mama."

"Thanks Mama. Well, you heard her. Let's get some shut eye," Louis told her.

Louis took Grace from Tulah and headed back into the bedroom. Once in the room, he told Tulah to close the door as he laid Grace in her crib. When he turned around to face Tulah, she was staring at him contemptuously.

"What's wrong now?"

"I saw you kiss her."

Louis took in a deep breath and folded his arms.

"Tulah, I know it's hard fo' you ta understand, cause you don't know Etta. But she is the last thang you got ta worry about."

"Why is she always hangin' on you and trying to smile up in yo' face? Did you have something with her, Louis? Just tell da truth."

"Baby, I ain't never had nothing going on with Etta, I don't want her, and I want you. I came for you didn't I? I married you, the mother of my baby. Come here." Louis said sitting on the bed and pulling Tulah down on his lap.

"What do I have ta do you make you believe me? What can I do to make you know you da only one I'm in love wit?" He lifted her hand to his mouth and kissed it. Then he kissed her on the lips. Tulah closed her eyes and kissed him with all the love and passion she felt for him.

"I get scared Louis. I ain't nevva had nobody to love me like you do and I don't want nobody trying to take that away from me."

"Baby, you ain't ever gotta worry about nobody takin' me from you."

Louis kissed her again and rubbed her back with his large, strong hand, and she melted at his touch. Giving herself fully to him, they made love all night, and fell asleep in each others arms.

The next morning, Tulah awakened to a screaming Grace. For the last few weeks she and Louis slept at Mama Lou's in a lumpy old bed with springs sticking out of it. Now that they have the luxury of sleeping on a thick, padded, firm mattress, they slept most of the morning away. Tulah sat up in the bed, stretched, and rubbed her eyes. She couldn't make her way to Grace because Louis was still stretched out sleeping in front of her, separating her from the crib. She rubbed his stomach trying to get him to wake up.

"Louis, I gotta get Gracie. Wake up."

"Huh?"

"Wake up, Louis. You in my way."

Louis shifted and pulled the covers up over his shoulders and turned away from Tulah.

"Louis!"

"Huh?"

"Move, boy. I gotta get Gracie."

"Oh."

Louis rolled over and Tulah crawled over him. She reached into the crib and retrieved Grace. She sat back on the bed and unlaced her gown to feed her, but suddenly felt queasy. She held her stomach, but by then it was too late. She laid Grace on the bed next to Louis.

"Louis! I'm gone be sick, get da baby."

She dashed out of the room, ran down the hall, pushed the door open, fell to her knees, wrapped her arms around the toilet, and vomited right into the bowl, continuing until her stomach cramped and there was nothing left but the taste of bile. When she finished, she laid her head on her arms and sat motionless, weak and drained of energy.

"Um hum. I know what that means."

Tulah didn't have enough energy to turn her head in the direction of the voice.

"I thought you looked a little bloated, then I figured it was baby fat from Grace, but I guess I know better now. You alright?"

Tulah couldn't answer, but shook her head no.

"Come on, baby, let me help you up. You don't want to be laying yo' face so close to that toilet bowl. I keep a clean house, but that ain't no place to rest."

Sarah walked over and helped Tulah to her feet. In the distance they could hear the muffled cries of Grace.

"She's sounds hungry to me. You know Tulah if you're expecting another baby, you might want to think about bottle feeding Grace. She'll be pulling all your nutrients, and you won't have anything left for the new baby."

Tulah nodded, trying to pull herself together enough to answer.

"I know you right, but I gotta feed 'er."

"How far along are you?"

"Not far, maybe just a few weeks. About the time when Louis came fo' me."

"Well, we gone hafta find you a doctor and get Grace some bottled milk."

"Yes ma'am."

Louis came out of the room bare footed, wearing pajama pants and holding Grace. He looked at Sarah helping Tulah to the sofa and inquired of what had happened.

"What happened was that youngin' of yorn is letting the whole world know of his or her presence."

"Who Gracie?" Louis asked bewildered.

"No, not Gracie. Didn't you hear me say him or her? I'm talking about your new baby. And yes, I know. The cats out the bag now. This poor girl ain't got nothing left in her the way she got sick. Babies will sure do you bad in the beginning."

Louis walked over to where Tulah was sitting on the sofa.

"Is it normal for her ta be sick like dat?" He asked touching Tulah on the shoulder.

"It's normal. It's called morning sickness, and believe me, I know all about it."

"Tulah you alright?" Louis asked.

"Um um. I feel terrible. I feel like I kin' lay down right here on dis' floor I feel so bad."

"She needs something to eat. She'll be alright after a while." Sarah told him.

"How'd you get Gracie to stop cryin'?" Tulah asked him.

"I stuck her thumb in her mouth."

"Louis, you didn't."

"I did too. She stopped cryin' didn't she?"

"Louis, you so crazy." Tulah said weakly.

Sarah prepared a meal of scrambled eggs, grits, and ham slices with left over biscuits from the night before. Tulah ate while feeding Grace at the same time. After breakfast, Sarah sent Louis down to Mr. White's for some bottles and powdered milk for Grace. With Louis out of the house, Tulah decided to ask Sarah about Etta.

"Mama Starks, can I ask you a question?"

"Sure, honey, what is it?"

"What you think about Etta?"

Sarah sipped her coffee, looked at Tulah and smiled, as if she was expecting her question. "Why do you ask?"

Tulah took a deep breath and let it go slowly. She was careful to weigh her words so that they didn't offend.

"Well, I think she kinda friendly, you know what I mean?"

Sarah snickered a bit, knowing full well what Tulah meant.

"I know she takes some getting used to, but all in all she's alright. She loves Henry, and takes good care of the children, which is what's most important." Sarah took another sip of her coffee, set her cup on the table, and continued.

"She is 'friendly', as you say, but I think she just likes attention. I don't see her as no real threat. She knows how close Henry and Louis are, and she knows how important family is, so I don't think she would do anything to come between them, or with the family." Tulah nodded her head, contemplating her words.

"Louis loves you, honey. So don't let nothing or nobody so frivolous come between the two of you. You hear me?"

"Yes ma'am."

"Good girl. Now what are you're plans for today?"

"We going ta see ma Ainty. I ain't really lookin' forward ta dat. I mean I am, but da last time I saw Aint Cora we had a bad fallin' out."

"I know how complicated family can be, but things have a way of working themselves out, you know?" Tulah looked at Sarah with admiration and smiled warmly at her. Sarah noticed the long pause and asked Tulah what was on her mind.

"It's jus dat Mama Lou would always say dat same thang. And when I heard you say it again, make me see how much thangs already work don' worked out. It make me think about how right she was." Tulah teared up. Sarah took her handkerchief, dabbing the moisture from Tulah's eyes. Sarah smiled at Tulah, who sheepishly returned the smile. They embraced. Tulah mused about God having replaced Mama Lou with yet another kind spirit in her life, giving her a secure feeling deeper than any she'd ever known.

Chapter 10

Tulah was smartly dressed in a grey wool suit, matching grey hat, and white gloves, which she complimented with the strand of pearls Louis purchased for her in Ortonville. Looking in the mirror at her reflection, she was satisfied with what she saw- a lady, just as Louis had said. She vacillated on if she would wear the gloves or not, because she wanted Aunt Cora to see the shiny, gold band on the third finger of her left hand, a tangible testament to the commitment of love and loyalty she and Louis shared. She decided to wear the gloves, then slip them off just before giving Cora the news of her marriage to Louis. Etta had done similarly at Sarah's house, a subtle yet effective gesture showcasing her own gold band of matrimony. She didn't care for Etta, but couldn't help but admire her polished air, flaunting white folk's etiquette with seamless ease. Tulah decided, despite her dislike for Etta, she could stand to adopt some of her flatulent ways.

Tulah convinced an unwilling Louis to go to the studio while she visited Cora, since he'd been gone close to a month. Tulah's real reason for not wanting Louis to go was so she could face Cora alone, woman to woman for the first time in her life, as well keep Louis from her disrespectful and contentious manner. Whatever malicious venom Cora had to spew, Tulah would bear the brunt of it, cushioning the blow for Louis later. She rehearsed her words over and over again as she walked to Cora's, pushing Gracie in the new stroller, and speaking to the rhythm of the squeaking wheels until the words dripped off her lips like fresh creamed butter.

Tulah stood on Aunt Cora's porch before knocking. Breathing in deeply, the cool, crisp air cleansed her lungs as she inhaled, then exhaling, she released a column of warm condensed air out of her mouth. She did this several times trying to calm her nerves before rapidly knocking on the door. She straightened her skirt, fingered her pearls, arched her back, took another deep breath, and knocked again, harder this time. The span of time from when she knocked to when Cora opened the door seemed an eternity. Tulah's heart pounded against her chest, and she felt slightly light-headed. She couldn't tell if it was nervousness, or symptoms accompanied from her first trimester. She looked down into the face of her beautiful, sleeping baby, and drew strength from her. Gracie was a reminder for Tulah that she is loved and has a home aside of this one, where her presence is welcomed and wanted. She hated herself for getting so worked up over seeing Aunt Cora. She questioned herself as to why she felt so nervous and apprehensive, only coming up with that being with Louis feels so good, and that seeing Cora may actually wake her from the virtual dream that she's been living in. She feared that Cora would remind her that she's not worthy of happiness or acceptance, her cruelty was the last remnant of Tulah's sense of worthlessness.

Tulah decided seeing Cora isn't worth the torture or anguish that she was putting herself through and prepared to leave. Tulah bundled Grace and just as headed down the stairs to leave, the door swung open. There stood Cora.

"Tulah, is that you?"

"Yes ma'am, me and my baby girl, Grace."

"Your what? Lord, you got yo'self a baby?" Cora opened the door wider and stepped out onto the porch.

"My Lord, you got a baby!" she said, looking at Tulah and the fancy clothes she wore. Cora looked from Grace to Tulah, back to Grace, and for the first time Tulah could remember, Cora was at a lost for words. She shook her head in disbelief, reflexively inviting Tulah and Grace in.

"Where you been chile? You had me worried."

"Livin' in Ortonville for a while... fo' I got married."

"Fo' you got married? Ta who?"

"Louis Starks is who. He ma husband now."

"Louis Starks is yo' husband?"

"Yes ma'am." Tulah removed the glove on her left hand in the same grandiose manner as Etta had done the day before, pulling the baby finger first, then each finger successively, finally removing completely, revealing the gold band. Cora grabbed her hand and pulled it to her face to get a closer look, and shook her head again.

"An dis y'all youngin'?"

"Yes ma'am. Dis here is Grace."

Cora bent down and pulled the covers off of Grace to get a better look at the sleeping child. She stood up, put her hands on her hips, and looked at Tulah, surveying her from head to toe, and then busted out in a big, hearty laugh.

"Girl, come gimme a hug!" Cora told her, hugging her around the neck. Tulah met her embrace, but quickly let go, familiar with Cora's normally stingy hugs. To Tulah's surprise, Cora held her with genuine warmth as never before. She tried to release Cora, but was locked firmly in a bear hug, Cora rocking Tulah in her arms as tears streamed freely. Finally, Cora pulled back and looked at Tulah again.

"I was so worried 'bout chu. I prayed and prayed and asked the Lord to look after you. God shole is good, thank you Jesus."

Cora raised waved her hands towards heaven, waving them in the air.

"I din't know what happen to you. I wrote Aaron, and he said he ain't seent chu. I didn't know what to think." Cora's words were getting caught in her throat, her emotions causing her to continue crying.

"I was so sad and depressed. My sister's baby girl was gone. Folks at da church was praying wit me, den finally da Lord gave me a peace. He just lifted da burden so I wouldn't have to cry no mo'. It was like he was letting me know dat you was okay. But my, my, my, how God will work thangs out. Look at chu. Lookin' good, married and got yo'self a baby!"

"Yes ma'am." Tulah responded. She found herself in a quandary because she was prepared to defend herself, letting Cora know that she was no longer a child but a woman who no longer had to answer to her. She practiced her speech of how she would give Cora a piece of her mind and leave, letting her know that she didn't intend on crawling back to her for a place to live, because she had a much finer home to live in. However, Cora's response was much different from what she expected or planned for. Therefore, she didn't know how to react, and it took her a while to adjust to this caring, compassionate and warmer version of Cora.

"Well, come on in. Let me get a look at da baby."

Tulah took a seat on the sofa, pulled the blankets back and lifted Grace out of the stroller. Tulah gave Cora a lightweight blanket, then handed Grace to her. Cora took Grace and gently bounced her in her arms as she walked back and forth throughout the living room.

"How old is she?"

"She almost 4 weeks old."

"She's a pretty baby, Tulah. Pale, like her Daddy. How you like being a Mama?"

"Alright, 'cept the little bit a sleep I get feedin' her through da night."

"Dat's cause you ain't got enough up there to feed her." Cora told her, referring to her small breasts. "You need more, so she can eat more."

"Louis got her some bottles. So from now on I'm gone be bottle feedin' her."

"Bottle feedin'? Dat ain't no good fo' her. How cow's milk gone be better than Mama's milk? Cow's milk is fo' cows," Cora said with finality.

"When you get married?"

"February 25th."

"And when was Grace born?"

As the flurry of questions continued, Tulah knew the kinder, gentler version of Cora was quickly fading. She knew Cora's congeniality was too good to be true, but she indulged her through the inquisition.

"Gracie was born on February 11th."

"Why y'all wait till afta da baby was born? You know I saw Louis in town, and he ain't said nothin' 'bout all dis."

"Everythang happen so fast."

"Why y'all wait to get married? If you gone get married, you shoulda done it befo' she was born. I guess its alright since don't nobody know, but you know what dey call babies born fo' dey parents get married." Tulah was agitated.

"Let somebody call my baby a name and see what happens."

"Whatchu gone do? What can you do? Beat up da world?"

"See what happens, is all I hafta say."

"See what happens, humph. Ain't a thang you can do."

"Aint Cora, you always gotta get somethin' started, always tryin' ta find da worse in everythang. Why cain't chu jus' be happy fo' me?"

Tulah's questions sobered Cora, and she softened her approach.

"It ain't dat I'm not happy fo' you. I jus know how mean people can be."

"Well ain't nobody gotta know my business. At least I got a husband, and Aint Cora he so good ta me. I didn't know mens could love lak dat."

"Treat chu real nice does he?" Cora asked smiling.

"Real real nice."

"What about his Mama?"

"She nice too, and his Daddy. I met his brother and his wife and kids last night."

Tulah didn't tell Cora about Etta and her flirtatious nature, not providing Cora with any more negative ammunition, though she really wanted someone else's opinion besides Louis' mother's. She respected Louis' mother, but after all, she was Louis' mother, who would naturally water the situation down for Louis' sake.

"Ain't she funny actin'?"

"Um um, not at all. Nothin' like I thought she would be. She real nice."

"Um hum, don't trust dat. All dat glitter ain't gold."

"What? Aint Cora, what dat mean?"

"Jus 'cause she ackin' nice don't mean nothin'. She could be fakin' you know."

Tulah shook her head, but decided not to challenge Cora, so she stayed silent.

"What?"

"Dere you go agin. I knew I shouldna come over here. I jus wanted you to know I'm all right."

"Where was you all dis time?"

Tulah tweaked the truth, telling Cora she stayed with Lucy Mae Etter, a friend of Louis' family, and they chose to wait before marrying, until his business took off. Tulah steered the conversation away from their marriage, bringing up Louis' work with the mayor. Now that Louis was a part of her family, Cora was eager to use her newfound bragging rights at church and around town.

Tulah lied effortlessly, deceiving Cora, and it felt good. She told Cora about Lucy dying, omitting the part about the estate, knowing Cora would steal it if she could.

As dusk approached, Tulah gathered her things, wrapped up a sleeping Gracie, and lovingly tucked her in the stroller. Tulah cleared her throat, and prepared to speak the words she rehearsed.

"Aint Cora, I came to say thank ya fo' takin' me in an all. You din't have to, I know dat. But I never deserved how you treated me. I know you thank I was unruly and disrespeckful, but you aint never tried to help me. You jus talk about me- make me feel worser den what I already did. Use ta hurt." Cora listened attentively while Tulah spoke. "That day fo I left, I put my feet in Critter's Creek, went to sleep, then woke up – das when it stopped hurtin', Aint Cora - I woke up. Das when I realize, you cain't hurt me no more. Das what I came ta tell you. You cain't hurt me no mo', 'cause I'm awake now and won't be goin' back ta sleep no mo'." As Tulah gathered her things, she took an envelope out of her bag, and handed it to Cora. Once Tulah and Gracie were well down the road, Cora opened the envelope, to find a twenty dollar bill, which she quickly folded and stuffed into her bra.

A liberated Tulah leisurely strolled up the front walk of Louis' parent's home with Gracie. Just a month ago she thought her life was over. Now, as she walked up to the most beautiful home she had ever seen, with her husband waiting inside to receive her, Tulah gave thanks. As she struggled to carry the stroller up the stairs, the front door opened. Louis bounded out the door, down the stairs, lifted the stroller up the stairs in one swift motion, and set Grace gently in the foyer. He then darted back, and just as deftly whisked Tulah off her feet, carrying her up the stairs and into the house. Louis sat her on her feet, hugged her, and kissed her deeply. He helped take her coat off, laid it on a nearby chair, then pointed to a small brown bag on the table. Tulah opened the bag, and was overjoyed at what was inside - lemon drops. She beamed a toothy smile and hugged Louis.

"And I gotta another surprise for in the morning. You gone really love it."

"What is it, Louis? Tell me."

"You gotta wait. How's Cora?" He lifted Grace out of the stroller.

"Lot betta than I expected. She cain't wait to meet yo' parents."

"I was wonderin' how she would take it."

"I know - me too. I told her Lucy was a friend of yo' family's and we made arrangements fo' me ta live there while I was pregnant."

"What you tell her that fo'?"

"I don't know. She start askin' me a lotta questions an' I ain't feel like hearin' her mouth."

"Tulah, you don't owe her nothing. Don't let nobody make you feel like you gotta lie just to please them. Ain't nothing worth lying about."

"Louis, you just better than me about those kinda thangs. I always had to explain myself ta people and try an' please 'em. I'm jus' used ta doin' it is all."

"Well baby, you just gotta work on changin' that."

"I know, and I will. Now tell me, what's my surprise?"

"Okay, I'll give you part of it. I went to see about dat place down yonder, the one by the lake, and I rented it this morning."

"Louis, we got our own place?"

"Shole do, but it won't be ready fo' a week. So we can take dat time ta go and pick some furniture fo' it. Mama can go witchu when I'm working."

Tulah hugged him around his neck, jumping him up and down.

"Louis you make me so happy. Is you gone always be dis' good ta me?"

"Course I am."

"You betta be, cause I'm gettin' used to it. Don't go changin' on me."

"I ain't ."

"Now what's the other surprise?"

"Cain't tell you I said, so don't try ta make me."

"Is it as good as the one 'bout the house?"

"You'll see."

Tulah awoke the next morning reaching across the bed for Louis, only to find he was not there. She sat up, looked around the room, got out of the bed, peeked in at Grace, and went down the hall. She looked in the bathroom, the kitchen and in the living room. Louis was nowhere to be found. Tulah sat on the sofa, wondering where Louis could be, when she heard a faint squeaking noise coming from the porch. She looked out of the window and saw Louis sitting on the swinging chair with the Bible in his lap. Tulah gently tapped on the window to get his attention. He looked up, smiled, and gestured for her to come out. Tulah went to the closet and grabbed her coat, put it around her shoulders and went out on the porch with Louis.

She sat next to him as he put his arm around her. It was just like when they had sat there the first night she spent with Louis, only this time it was better, because now she was his wife. She laid her head on his chest and he started humming a tune. She felt Louis' voice vibrating through his chest and in her ears. She smiled while trying to figure out the tune, but the vibrating was so loud it drowned out the melody.

"What's dat tune, Louis?"

"Oh, you wouldn't know it. It's a tune Mama used to sing ta me when I was a boy. I don't even remember the words - that's why I hum it."

"Got a nice tune."

"Uh huh."

"Whatcha doin' out here so early?"

"This is da time I spend wit God. 'Member?" He took her hand, interlacing his fingers between hers.

"I remember now. You still do dat?"

"Every morning. I cain't get ma day started right wit out giving God His time first."

"Is you gone be a preacher or something?"

"I thought about it. Because I feel so strong about it in here, you know?" Louis pointed to his chest. Tulah didn't answer, considering the thought of being a preacher's wife. She pictured herself on the front pew, wearing a fancy dress, nice hat and gloves, and a big, wide hand fan to cool herself with while Louis preached in the pulpit. Holding their new born son in her arms, with Grace sitting next to her, neatly dressed in a pretty pink dress with white knee socks and shiny white shoes, Tulah saw it all as clear as day. Tulah returned from her daydream.

"That's a nice thought, Louis. You want yo' own church?"

"I ain't got that far. I just want to do it because I love God and want to do right by people. Teaching people the word of God is the only way folk can ever do right. I don't mind preaching if it'll help folk."

"You is amazing ta me, Louis. Ain't ever met nobody like you."

"I'm glad you think so, cause you gone be stuck wit me fo a long time." He laughed and squeezed her hand tighter. Louis quickly sobered. "Feeling sick this morning?"

"Naw. Feel pretty good."

"Grace still sleepin'?"

"Yeah, dem bottles helping her sleep longer, she get mo' full I thank."

"That's good. I'm going to bring ma camera home tonight so I can take some pictures of you and Grace. I need a new picture of you anyway 'cause I'm still carrying that worn out picture I had when I shot you in front of Mr. White's store."

"Naw you don't? Lemme see."

Louis pulled his wallet out, retrieved the small tattered piece of photo paper with her image on it. She flashed a wide grin, flattered he still carried her picture with him, yet another affirmation of his love.

"Is dat da surprise?"

"Naw! This surprise is way bigger. You gone pass right out when you see."

"Oooh - I cain't wait. Please tell me, Louis."

"Nope. Not 'til later." He kissed her on the cheek.

"I gotta get outta here, lot to do today, so I'm gone see you later this evening. I love you."

Chapter 11

Louis had been gone a few hours, the same as usual, but for Tulah, it was an eternity. She likened the experience to Christmas Eve's, which Tulah hadn't celebrated since she was six or seven years old. Tulah hadn't celebrated Christmas with presents since she was maybe years old, but she could remember being so excited that she couldn't sleep, her stomach would be tied in knots, and she fidgeted constantly, not being able to keep still. This experience was like the anticipation of opening Christmas gifts, she was as giddy as a five year old. She pestered and probed Louis' Mama for clues every chance she got.

"Is it somethin' for me or for Gracie?"

"I don't know, Tulah."

"Is it somethin' I can wear?"

"Can't say."

"Is it big or small?"

"Not sure."

"Can I hold it in ma hand?"

"It's possible."

"Is it somethin I can eat?"

"Could be."

"What color is it?"

"Tulah, you gone drive me crazy, girl. I really don't know what it is. He didn't tell me. I was just messin' witcha to have some fun, but you bout to run me ragged."

"I'm jus so excited."

"I know you are. I'm excited for you. But no more questions, please. Here, take these beans and pick 'em for me.

That'll take your mind off of it, I hope."

Tulah laughed and took the bowl of beans from Sarah. She sat at the table, but she unconsciously shook her legs in anticipation.

"Tulah!"

"Huh?"

"Is it possible for you to stop that fidgeting?"

"I'm sorry."

Just then, they were interrupted by what sounded like a horn blowing. They exchanged bewildered looks and got up to start towards the front door. The blowing persistently continued as they made their way to the front. Sarah opened the front door, and there sat a shiny new car, with a driver wearing a chauffeur's cap sitting behind the wheel, blowing the horn as if trying to wake the dead. Sarah and Tulah stepped out on the porch to get a closer look. It was Louis.

"Oh my Lord, he done bought an automobile!"

Tulah stood on the porch with wide eyes and her mouth hanging open. She was transfixed. Sarah ran off the porch to see the automobile while Tulah remained stock still, covering her mouth with her hands.

"Come on out here, girl. Take a look at our new automobile."

Tulah couldn't believe what she was seeing. She expected something simple, a new dress for a new photo, or perhaps some earrings to match the string of pearls Louis had given her, but never an automobile. It was beyond the scope of her imagination. She walked slowly to the steps, but could make herself go no further. Sarah looked back at Tulah and then walked over and took her by the hand.

"I think she's in shock, Louis."

Tulah walked over to the automobile and ran her hand along the shiny panel of the door, over the handle, and the side view mirror. Louis grinned and blew the horn again, startling Tulah.

"You bought dis fo' us?"

"Yeah I bought it. It's ours!"

"We got us a automobile?"

"Yeah girl. Ths here is a Phaeton, a Graham Paige DC Phaeton. Brand new off the line, and it's modern, too. It's got a 'lectric self-starter, 'lectric headlights and balloon tires - look at em."

"Oooh, your Daddy gone be shocked." Sarah told Louis. "I told him, you are full of surprises these days."

"I got a family Mama. We need us a car. I can't have Tulah walking wit Gracie and pregnant too."

Tulah could no longer contain her excitement. She screamed and jumped up and down.

"Let me in!"

Louis held the door open to let her inside.

"Come on in. Mama you can get in too."

Tulah got in on Louis' side and sat on his lap. She touched every gadget on the front panel and blew the horn. She squealed in pure delight at the noise of horn sounding with just a moderate touch.

"Wanna go for a ride?"

"Yes!"

"Come on, get in so I can close the door."

"Y'all go on."

"Naw, come on Mama. You ain't never been in an automobile like this one before. Don't you want go for a ride?"

"Yeah, but I'll go later, or did you all forget, you have a baby in the house?"

"Oh shoot. I done forgot bout ma baby." Tulah said.

"It's okay, you all go ahead. I'll look after Gracie. You can take me for a ride later."

"Thanks Mama. We won't be gone long."

Louis and Tulah took off down the road in their brand new Phaeton. Louis was happy and proud, well on the road to being an accomplished man, just like his father. They drove around town and waved to passersby, even the ones they didn't know. Louis suggested they stop by Cora's house. The suggestion made Tulah excited and nervous. She agreed. They pulled into Cora's yard and Louis tapped on the wheel to sound the horn. Tulah wanted to jump out and run to the door, but contained herself, choosing to wait for Cora to come out. Louis blew and blew, but no one came to the door. Tulah remembered Cora was probably at Wednesday night Bible class and suggested they go by the church. That way they could show off the car to most of the town people and offer Cora a ride home.

Driving up the path led to the church Louis spotted Henry, Etta, and their children. They were just about to board their horse and buggy when Louis drove up blowing the horn. They both stopped, but Henry walked towards the car, not knowing who was inside. Louis tipped the chauffeur's cap.

"Can I offer you a lift?"

"Heeey man! Who's automobile is this?"

"Ours."

"You bought a car?"

"Yeah, I just picked it up this evening. Come on, let's take it for a ride."

When Etta realized the driver of the vehicle was Louis, she came over to get a better look. Tulah's excitement turned to angst as Etta sauntered up to the vehicle, tossing her shiny long hair and pursing her painted lips into a seductive grin.

"Oooh this shole is nice, Louis."

"Thank you."

"Hello Tulah." Etta said. "I know you is enjoying this fine car."

"I certainly am." She said cuddling closer to Louis and clutching his arm. "We been driving all over town, too. This little town shole look different when you seein' it from a car. Everythang just whiz right by you so fast."

Henry, Etta and their children circled around the car, touching it randomly with the same reserved caution one would have when sticking a toe in water to test the temperature.

"How you start it?" Henry asked.

"'Lectric." Louis answered with a smile.

"This shole is nice, man."

"What's this do?" One of the children asked while standing on his toes pointing to a gadget inside of the car.

"I don't know, but don't touch it." Henry told the boy.

"Y'all wanna ride?" Louis asked again.

"You cain't fit all us in you car. Besides, I cain't leave my rig. Come on by the house tomorrow, we can go riding then."

"I gotta be at the studio for most of tomorrow, got a real busy day. But I'll come by and pick you up in the evening, about six or seven, fo' dark."

As Louis and Henry conversed about the car, Tulah and Etta engaged in strained but polite conversation, during which Tulah noticed Etta's attention was only slightly on their conversation, but was more focused on what Louis and Henry were saying, her eyes darting from Tulah to them. Henry boarded his family in the buggy, and Louis tooted the horn as they departed. Shortly after, Tulah saw Cora come out of church with some of her friends.

"Aint Cora! Aint Cora, over here!" Tulah shouted, waving her hand to get Cora's attention. Cora looked in Tulah's direction, but was perplexed because she didn't recall knowing anyone who drove a car.

"Aint Cora, it's me." Louis stepped out and stood in front of the car with a big smile on his face. When Cora realized it was Louis and Tulah in the car she smiled and invited her friends over to meet her niece Tulah, and her husband Louis Starks. Cora and her friends gathered around the car while she made introductions. Cora took pride in showing off to her friends how prosperous and well off Tulah and Louis were. Louis' name, and his picture studio, was already enough to turn the heads and raise the brows of the stern and disparaging church women, but Cora continued with her boastings to further impress them. Louis nor Tulah said much, but their eyes met several times to confirm they were thinking the same thoughts about Cora as she bragged about their accomplishments.

When Louis dropped Cora off at home, he saw her inside. When they got to the front door, Cora thanked Louis and told him she would be fine, but Louis insisted on coming in. Once inside, Louis took five dollars out of his pocket and handed it to Cora.

"What's this?"

"Well, I know before Tulah left she took a little change from you, and I wanted to get it back to you."

Cora looked at Louis, studying his face. Obviously Tulah hadn't discussed the twenty dollar gift she'd given Cora with him.

"She didn't take that much from me."

"I know, but I wanted ta make sure you got it all back. It might be a little extra, but it's alright."

"Naw, its okay, Louis. I ain't mad about it no mo', and besides, y'all got a family and you gone need yo' money."

"Yeah, but God is blessing us, and I want to do the right thing. It would make me feel better if you'll accept this."

Cora stared into his face and paused before accepting the money.

"I told you it was alright, but if you insist, I'll take it."

"I insist."

"You know, Louis, I feel real proud of you." She said crumpling the dollar bills and stuffing them in her purse. "I didn't know what ta think of you at first, but Tulah look like she real happy and y'all look like you love each other. So that makes me happy. You a good man."

Louis chuckled. "Thanks Aunt Cora. We do love each other and we are happy. I appreciate you saying such kind things."

"Well, I wouldn't say it if it wasn't true."

"Thank you."

"I'm glad you in the family." She told him before embracing him.

The next morning was sunny, bright, and cold. Louis observed how the barren land had changed from the fertile and fragrant version of its former self, and how the earth was now cold and hard, void of grass or flowers. A few birds remained during wintry weather, their melodic symphonies hushed by the cold, harsh months of winter. The trees still stood tall and strong, however, they were devoid of leaves, fruit and even squirrels. The tranquility and silence of early morning was replaced by frigid temperatures, nature's deterrent for noisy and over-active children. Louis sat on the porch holding the Bible on his lap reflecting on the goodness of God. The crisp air blew its cold breath, but it didn't keep Louis from his meeting with God on the front porch. He was faithful, having met God everyday over the past few years. He wore gloves, a hat and a muffler wrapped around his neck. His warm exhalations cascaded out of his mouth into the cold air, creating a thin stream of smoke which vaporized within seconds. This morning he thanked God for the life bestowed him, the happiness and love for his family. His time of meditation and thanksgiving was interrupted when his father came outside and asked if he could join him.

"We can go inside, Daddy. I don't expect you to sit out here in the cold cause I am."

"It's okay. It's a private matter I want to discuss with you, and this is the best place to have it." Louis looked at his father with concern.

"Everything alright?"

"I have some - concerns."

"Concerns about what? What is it Daddy?"

"Son, I don't know how else to say it, so I'm just gone get it out."

"Alright."

"It's Tulah. She comes from a family who doesn't have anything. It's too bad about her mother and father, she can't help that. But from what I understand, she was passed from one relative to the other with very little or no education at all. I had this talk with your mother and she forbade me to mention it to you, but son, we've always been close, so I know I can reason with you."

"Reason with me about what?"

Kennedy paused in his usual manner, gathering his thoughts to insure a balance of precision and compassion.

"Son, you know how hard we've worked to give you and your brother a comfortable way of life. We have a responsibility to maintain that lifestyle for those coming after us. You have to make the kind of decisions you can live with, as opposed to hasty ones you'll end up regretting." Louis' countenance began to fall, his shoulders slightly slumping as his father continued.

"She's not right for you."

"How can you say that?"

"Son, she doesn't even know how to speak good English. How is she going to raise your children? Can she encourage their curiosities? Can she develop their intellect? Look at you, already with one baby and another one on the way. Son, can't you see that all this is going way too fast and headed for disaster? She's going to corner you in with a bunch of children and have you broke and busted with no way to provide for them."

"Daddy! You are wrong about this." Louis said rising to his feet. "I can't even believe that you are saying this."

"I'm saying it because I know better."

"No you don't Daddy. Not this time. This time you're wrong. Tulah is a good girl. Okay, she may not have a good education, but that's not her fault. She's smart though. She's quick, think on her feet. School can't teach that no how. And she takes good care of Gracie." Louis stressfully ran his hand over his head and continued.

"Daddy, you know I respect you. But I don't appreciate you talkin' 'bout Tulah dat way. You steppin' way outta line."

Louis rose to his feet, walking toward the window. "You liked

Tulah. Where is all dis comin' from… you talk to Cora?"

"No. It came from me, no one else."

"I know Tulah - she a good wife to me and a good mother to our daughter."

"What's to feeding, changing and dressing a baby? Little girls do that with baby dolls all day. Louis, she's a child herself." Louis controlled his anger. He'd never disrespected his father, and wasn't going to be drawn over that line, but saw himself edging ever closer.

"Daddy she got a good heart, and smart as a whip."

"Louis. Look at you. You bought a car, rented a house, and you're paying rent on a studio."

"I can handle it."

"You're not thinking rationally. You're spending your whole life savings."

"She's my wife, Daddy." Louis said almost pleadingly. "What do you suggest I do? Never mind. I don't want to know. I'm not backing down on this."

"You had no right to go off and pull something like this without talking to me first!"

"Daddy, I'm a grown man. I didn't need to talk to you about this. It was my decision."

"No it wasn't! As hard as I've worked to provide you with a good life? You don't make those kinds of decisions as you're living in my house."

Louis turned to look at his father, not believing what he'd just heard.

"Your house? You know what Daddy? You can have yo' house. Me and wife and baby will be outta yo house come night fall."

"Son, you misunderstand."

"Naw, you taught me to listen real good, Daddy. Real good."

"I don't want *you* to leave. Now we'll take care of the children, but she can go back and stay with her aunt. We can get your marriage annulled. It'll be like it never happened."

"Daddy?" Louis' pitch raised considerably.

"Boy, who you raisin' your voice at? I'm still your father." Louis wanted to ask his father to reconsider and give himself some time to get to know Tulah, but knew that it would have been pointless. His father was relentless in his rancor and was not willing to concede. Louis responded.

"Nothing else to talk about then."

Louis got up and stormed into the house. Tulah was stirring about in their bedroom, and he wasn't ready to face her. He was very angry and didn't want her to ask him why, so he went into the bathroom and closed the door behind him. Louis was outraged, hurt and disappointed. He always thought his father was the most objective, reasonable and intelligent man living. But this night Louis saw a different side of his father, a side he didn't know existed. What could make his father say those things? He began to pray immediately because he didn't want to feel contempt for his father or think objectionable thoughts about him. After composing himself, he went to Tulah, kissed her on the forehead and quickly left, trying to avoid any questions.

Chapter 12

Louis had been at work only a few hours when Etta walked in. She was impeccably dressed wearing a green dress with tiny blue and white flowers on it, and a blue sash around her slim waist. She wore a blue head band on her head, had her lips painted bright red, and smelled of sweet perfume. She smiled coquettishly and batted her eyes when she saw Louis standing behind the counter.

"Hey Louis."

"Hey Etta. What you doing here?"

"I wanted to get photographed as a surprise for Henry."

"Oh that's thoughtful of you Etta, but I can't fit you in today. My schedule is much too full."

"Ain't nobody here now." Etta surmised, looking around the empty studio.

"I know. I got a small break in between customers, but it won't be enough time to do a sitting for you."

"Well how much time you got?"

"Not much, about thirty minutes. Why?"

"Well, I was thinking since I'm here you can show me that fine automobile of yours."

"Oh yeah, it is a fine piece of machinery. You wanna see it?"

"Course I do." She said flirtatiously.

Under normal circumstances, Louis would have brushed Etta off, but he was alone in the studio, and haunted by thoughts of the conversation he had with his father earlier that morning, so he welcomed the invitation to help get things off his mind.

"Hold on, let me get the keys." He told her.

By the time he retrieved them, a customer walked into the studio and asked for information about getting photographed. He hurriedly gave Etta the keys, his attention now focused on the potential customer. Meanwhile, Tulah had taken Gracie for a walk and decided to stop by the studio to check on Louis, concerned that he seemed agitated before leaving for work that morning. As she turned the corner, she could see the back of their shiny new automobile sitting out on the street, right in front of the studio. She smiled inside, feeling good about their new car. As she got closer, she saw a figure inside the vehicle. She narrowed her eyes to be sure they were not deceiving her, but knew they weren't when she recognized the long, black hair. Tulah parked Gracie's stroller next to the building, marched over to the car and snatched the door open. Etta looked up smiling, but it quickly faded when she saw Tulah standing over her breathing heavily.

"Heeeey Tulah." Etta said nervously. Tulah grabbed a handful of Etta's hair and dragged her out of the car on and onto the street. Etta screamed and tried to get up, but before she could Tulah hit her, knocking her back down to the ground. Each time Etta tried to get up, Tulah would whack her again, sending her back onto the pavement. Inside the studio, Louis thought he heard screams, but when he looked outside the window he didn't see anyone because it was then Tulah had knocked Etta back to the ground. It wasn't until the customer opened the door to leave Louis heard the cries for help. He ran over to the door in just enough time to witness Tulah knocking Etta to the ground. He ran outside and wrapped his arms around Tulah, lifting her off the ground, to stop her from further assaulting Etta.

"Let me go, Louis. Take your hands offa me." Tulah tried to break free from Louis' hold.

The customer ran over and helped Etta to her feet.

"Should I call the police, Mr. Starks?"

"Naw, don't call the police, that won't be necessary. I can handle it. Thank you, sir. I can handle it from here."

"I kin stick around and help you Mr. Starks."

"No thank you. You go on now. I got it from here. Go on now." Louis told him. He wanted to get rid of the man before he figured out it was his wife and sister-in-law fighting like frivolous school girls, and then his business would be all over town. The customer reluctantly walked away, obedient to what he was told, but kept looking back wondering why he was being shooed away.

"Get in here." Louis demanded. "What are you two doing out here fighting like this? And Tulah you're pregnant. What are you trying to do?"

Etta got up dusting herself off and crying. Tulah was breathing fast and hard and felt a pain in her lower stomach that made her double over. Louis grabbed her by the arm but she snatched away from him.

"Tulah you alright?"

She didn't answer, but took in long exaggerated breaths and let them go slowly trying to calm herself.

"Come inside and sit down till you feel better." He told her. Tulah looked up at Louis and despite the pain she was in, mustered up enough energy to ask him why Etta was in the car.

"What was she doin' in your car?"

"She wanted to see it, so I gave her the keys. Why are you out here fighting?" But before she could answer, he turned his attention to Etta.

"Why are you fighting, don't you know Tulah is pregnant?"

"No I didn't know, how am I supposed to know? Besides, she attacked me!"

"You stay away from my husband, you understand me?"

"Get inside, the both of you. You can't be carryin' on like this in public. Let me help you Tulah."

"I'm okay, just get Gracie."

Louis turned to see Gracie's stroller parked on the road next to the building. He ran over to make sure she was unharmed.

"I cain't believe you all are out here fightin' while my baby out here all alone. Get in here now!" Louis demanded.

Both Tulah and Etta came inside the studio and Louis pulled out a chair for Tulah to have a seat. He rubbed her on the back and scolded her at the same time.

"You cain't be fighting nobody in your condition, Tulah. You know better than to do something like that. Etta, are you alright?"

"Naw, I ain't alright. How am I supposed to be alright when she come pulling me by my hair like some caveman."

"Who you callin' a caveman?"

"Tulah, cut it out. I hope you're alright Etta, but you best be getting on home."

"What? Look at my dress - and my hair!" Etta screamed at him pulling twigs out of her hair.

"I know, and I'm sorry about that. But you are going to have to…"

"Girl, I know you heard my husband. Now you best be getting on outta here." Tulah interrupted. "And I bet not evva catch you in my husband's car again." Etta grabbed her purse off the counter and stormed out of the studio, slamming the door behind her. Louis stooped down in front of Tulah, looking her eye to eye.

"Tulah, don't ever pull nothing like that again, you understand me? You pregnant and you my wife. You cain't be picking fights in the street."

"Me?"

"I'm not done yet," Louis snapped. "You left Gracie on the side of the road, pushed against a building like yesterday's trash. What you thinkin' 'bout?" Do you know how embarrassing it is to have to break up a fight my wife is in, in front of my studio, a place of business I am trying to build for us?"

Louis stood, and stressfully ran his hand over the back of his head, took a deep breath and let it go slowly. Walking over to the counter, he got a cigarette and lit it. He took a long drag and blew smoke through his nose and mouth before he continued. Tulah was angered, but dared not say a word because she realized how upset Louis was. She didn't feel sorry for pulling Etta's hair, dragging her onto the ground, or slugging her. She did however, regret embarrassing Louis and for putting Gracie in harms' way.

"Louis, can I say something?"

"What?" Louis answered grimly.

Tulah was taken aback by the way he answered her so coldly. Louis was upset by Tulah's actions, Etta didn't deserve what had happened to her, but what really had him upset was what his father had said about Tulah, and how she, unknowingly, was proving him right. The last thing he wanted was for his father to find out what happened.

"You don't have to be so mean ta me, Louis. All I wanted ta say was I'm sorry. I didn't mean fo' it ta happen dat way. I just got angry when I saw her sitting in yo' car like she had some rights ta be there."

"Tulah, baby, how many times do I have ta tell you Etta ain't nobody fo' you to be worried about? She came to get photographed for Henry. I told her I couldn't fit her in, then she asked to see the car. I had a customer, so I gave her the keys and told her to go on a have a look by herself." Louis said stooping down in front of Tulah and grabbing her hands in his. "Ain't nothing to it."

"Yes it is. She come down here ta see you. She knew what she was doin."

Louis shook his head, but Tulah stopped him.

"Not ahn, Louis. Don't do dat, cause I know what I'm talking about. Now I know I was wrong ta pick a fight, but dat heffa knows what she's doin'. She's afta you."

"Tulah, do you trust me?"

"What?"

"Do you trust me?"

"Yeah, but I know womens, and she a snake. It's her who I don't trust."

"Enough about her. Do you trust me?"

"I said yeah."

"Then that's all that matters. Listen, all I'm saying is you my wife Tulah Belle Starks, and whether you like it or not, you have an important role to play in this family. My father worked hard to create opportunities for us, and because you are my wife, that includes you and our children. I don't ever want to see you carrying on like that again. You have to carry yourself like a Starks at all times, no matter who makes you mad or push your buttons, you have to always stay in control. People like Etta are jealous, and will say some mean things tryin' to get to you so she can run back and blow it up. You understand me?"

Tulah shook her head.

"Yes. Yes Louis, I understand."

"Good. Now I want you to go home and pack a few things for us so we can stay at the new house. Are you feeling alright?"

"Yeah, I'm okay. And Louis, I'm real sorry fo'ackin' like dat."

"I know baby, it's okay. Now I want you to go on home and pack up a few things."

"Why we gotta stay at the new house? I thought it wasn't ready yet."

Louis didn't want to tell her he told his father they would be leaving his house. "I just want to try to make it livable. Get a head start. And since I won't be getting off until late, I figured we could just spend the night."

"Alright." Tulah said excitedly. "You sure you ain't mad at me?"

"Naw baby, I'm not mad. Just go on home and pack enough for all of us to stay over night."

"Okay Louis." Tulah rose to her feet.

"You gone be alright walkin' home?"

"Shoot, I feel fine."

"That's real good. I'll be home around five thirty. Be ready when I get there."

"Alright." Tulah walked over and put her arms around Louis' waist. She apologized again and kissed him before leaving the studio. As she walked home, she replayed the events with Etta over in her mind and laughed to herself. She was willing to bet Etta would no longer be a problem to her or Louis again.

When Tulah got home she opened the door to the aroma of smothered pork chops and home made biscuits. She parked Gracie's stroller by the front door and lifted her out. She gathered the rest of her bottles to store in the ice box when she heard voices coming from the kitchen. Tulah tiptoed quietly towards the voices, getting just bits and pieces of the conversation. When she was close enough to hear what was being said, she realized it was about her.

"Then she yanked me by the hair and dragged me out of the car."

"By your hair?"

"Yeah, by my hair. My neck is sore and stiff."

Hearing the conversation made Tulah angry all over again. She thought she had handled Etta, but Etta trumped her by going to Sarah and telling her how badly she had behaved at Louis' studio. But Tulah wasn't about to let Etta have the upper hand, or let her know she was bothered by her tattling. She took a deep breath to compose herself, arched her back and stoically walked into the kitchen. The conversation came to a halt.

"Hey Mama, whatchall doin? Ooh wee it smell good in here." She said walking over to the stove to get a whiff of the simmering pork chops. "Gracie shole enjoyed her walk. Dat fresh air done plum tired her out. I'm gone go and lay her down."

Tulah walked out of the kitchen before either one of them

had a chance to speak. As she walked by Etta she narrowed her eyes into slits and tightened her lips. Etta glared at Tulah, but dared not utter a word.

"That's a good idea, Tulah. And once you lay Gracie down, you come on back in here so I can have a word with you," Sarah called.

"Alright."

As soon as Tulah was out of sight the conversation started back up again, but she couldn't make out what was being said. She wanted to stand by and listen, but thought it best to lay Gracie down and return to defend herself. She put Gracie in her crib and took another deep breath before joining the Sarah and Etta in the kitchen. She walked over to the kitchen table and pulled out a chair, taking a seat. Sarah turned her attention to Tulah, and the way she her pursed mouth let Tulah know she was displeased at what she had been told.

"Tulah, Etta told me about what happened this afternoon down at the studio. But in all fairness, I think I need to hear your side of the story."

"Well, I don't know what she been telling you. But she carried herself down to Louis' studio and hopped in his car like she had some rights to be there. And I didn't like it." Tulah said turning to face Etta.

"Go on."

"So I went over and snatched her outta the car."

"Just like that?"

"Yeah."

"You didn't ask her why she was there, or what was going on?"

"I knew what was goin' on. She always smilin' up on Louis, twistin' her hair around her finger when she talkin' ta him. I knew what was goin' on."

"You didn't know nothing, you little..," Etta started.

"Uh uh, stop that." Sarah interjected. "I'm not going to have that in my house. I heard your side, Etta. Now I want to hear from Tulah." Etta stopped talking and started impatiently tapping her fingers on the table.

"What did you think was going on, Tulah?"

"She afta Louis. I ain't crazy." She said looking directly at Etta. "I don't know what she doin' at home or why she ain't happy, but Louis is my husband now. And I ain't gone let no womens come smilin' and twistin' dey hair all in his face."

"She's insecure." Etta said pompously.

"You insecure! Dat's why you gotta be smilin' and grinnin' up in my husband's face. I done seen yo' kind befoe. You lookin fo'validation." Tulah shot back at her.

Etta turned and looked at Tulah, shocked by what she just heard.

"I'm leaving. I don't hafta say here and listen to this." She got up to leave.

"Bye." Tulah said, waving her hand at Etta.

"Stop it, Tulah. Etta you don't have to leave."

"Yes I do Mama. I'm not staying as long as she's here."

"I wish you all wouldn't carry on like this. Etta sit down."

"I need to be getting home anyway. My dress is torn with a hole in it, and I need to get home and changed. Will you talk to Dad for me?"

"Of course I will, but can I at least get you girls to talking?"

"Mama, I ain't got nothin' to say to her. She's barbaric and immature." Etta said of Tulah.

"Well in dat case, I ain't got nothin' ta say neither. I made my point."

"You're so childish."

"And you so full of it."

"Okay, okay, that's enough." Sarah said interrupting them.

"Bye Mama, make sure you speak to Dad."

"I will Etta."

After Etta left, Sarah reprimanded Tulah about her lack of control and public display of imprudence. She also scolded her about being so physical in her condition, and how important it is she conducts herself as a respectable young lady and mother. She told Tulah her anger was justified, but she couldn't act on it. She also promised she wouldn't tell Kennedy about what happened as long as Tulah promised to never let it happen again. Tulah did, and then told Sarah she had to pack so she and Louis could spend the night at the new house. When Sarah inquired why, Tulah explained Louis wanted to get a head start on getting the place livable. Sarah observed Tulah's excitement, knowing she was unaware of the real reason they were leaving. Kennedy told Sarah about the conversation he had with Louis, so she knew

Louis was angry and wanted to protect his wife from his father's closed minded and objectionable views of her.

It was for this reason she promised Tulah she wouldn't tell Kennedy about what happened earlier day. She knew once he heard about Tulah acting so vulgar and violent that he would use it to continue to build a case against her. Sarah wasn't concerned about his views of Tulah, knowing he would come around eventually. Her concern was if he continued to pontificate his negative views of Tulah, he would drive an irreparable wedge between himself and Louis. Sarah would have picked a more suitable wife for Louis, if it were up to her. However, Louis loved Tulah, and his happiness was most important. Besides, she knew Tulah was a good girl. She knew if she took Tulah under her tutelage, she could be groomed into a fine young woman, and for the sake of family, she was going to make every effort.

Chapter 13

Louis and Tulah moved into their new place and got it to feeling like home right away. In just a few days, they had all the comforts of home. Louis sent Tulah shopping, and she decorated each room however she saw fit. Because he was established in the community as a successful business man, he was extended a new innovation by the Federal Reserve called credit. People could make purchases now and pay later, allowing them to hold on to their cash longer. The purpose of credit was so consumers would buy, and hopefully stimulate the slumping economy. With this new innovation, Tulah was able to go on a spending frenzy and decorate their small but comfortable house into an elegant and elaborate home. They bought new living room furniture with a cocktail table and matching end tables, a dining room set, bedroom furniture for themselves and a new bedroom set for Gracie, and a brand new crib for the new baby. Tulah had a beautiful new wardrobe with matching hats for each dress. They even had a radio on the kitchen table. She was living a life she never knew she could have and was enjoying every minute of it. Before long, it was time for Tulah to have the new baby and she was able to go to a hospital to deliver the child. On November 21, 1929, Tulah had a baby girl, and named her Lucille, after Louis and Mama Lou. Louis was so proud of his wife and two girls; there was nothing he would withhold from them. He accommodated Tulah with anything she wanted.

What he did not tell her was he had fallen upon hard times. Business had dropped off significantly and the money was not coming in as steadily as in times past. Louis had to solicit business in the streets. However, the most unfortunate turn of fate was that hard times seemed to be hitting everyone at the same time and people did not view getting photographed as a priority. It became difficult for Louis to pay his bills on time and he had to let go of the assistant he hired. Accordingly, he abandoned what had become traditional values to him, such as saving and investing his money. The rapid decline in sales caused him to postpone pleasure purchases, buying only what was needed. Initially, Louis used credit to make leisurely purchases, but before long, he was using credit to pay his monthly bills. He had gone through his life savings in under a year trying to keep a handle on his growing debt. Under normal circumstances, Louis would have consulted with his father about what to do, but because of their differences, he struggled through the difficult times on his own. He went to his brother Henry, for a loan, but Henry had lost his job and was losing his home as well. Consequently, Henry, Etta and their children had to move in with his parents.

It was a very difficult time for Louis. He knew if business didn't pick up he would also have suffer a loss. He went to the mayor to try and get business from him, but the mayor didn't have any work to offer him. Not being able to meet the bills on time, or pay his creditors, it became clear what needed to be done. After much deliberation, and careful consideration, Louis reluctantly closed the doors to his beloved studio. It broke his heart and wounded his pride, but under the dire circumstances, there was no other recourse. He continued to take photographs out of his home for a while, but soon after, his clientele dropped off.

Tulah was very supportive of Louis during this difficult period and encouraged him to keep his spirits high, but after he closed the studio Louis fell into a depression. He kept to himself and didn't have much to say to anyone. He wouldn't eat, only picking at his food and becoming thinner than he already was. Waking up in the morning and getting dressed with no place to go was especially hard for him. But he would still get dressed in his nice slacks and dress shirt and tie and go for a walk around town. The only thing remaining the same about Louis was his daily ritual of sitting on the porch early in the morning to commune with God - which he would do without fail. Tulah sat with out on the porch with him one morning, offering solace, but

Louis didn't respond. He acknowledged she was there by holding her hand, but still didn't utter a word.

Tulah begged Louis to go back to Ortonville so they could live in the house Mama Lou left them, but Louis' pride wouldn't allow it. Having to leave his home after closing his studio was humiliating. He was a self-sufficient businessman and breadwinner. He insisted things would get better and business would pick up, but the year of 1930 was a different. Business was on the decline for everyone. After the stock market crash, the already sluggish economy continued on a downward spiral. The newspapers were full of news about banks closing, businesses failing, and people out of work. With little consumer demand for products because people couldn't afford to buy, hundreds of factories and mills closed, leaving thousands without jobs. One afternoon, while going on a stroll to occupy his time, he walked past the bank where a small, angry mob had gathered outside. He looked into the frustrated faces of the people in the crowd with their fists clinched and knew something had gone dreadfully wrong.

"What is it, what's happened?"

"This damnable bank has closed its doors and took my money with 'em." One man answered.

"What do you mean they've closed their doors?"

"They say they've gone broke. My whole life savings in there! I've lost everything." Louis could relate to the man's tears. He reached out to touch his shoulder, to offer some consolation, but he was pushed to the side by an irate man beating on the door and yelling hysterically. The crowd had gotten out of control and refused to leave, so some of the workers inside called the police. Shortly after, a police car pulled up to disperse the crowd making them all leave. Louis wearily walked home after witnessing the desperate and frightened people agonize over losing everything they owned. He was burdened by what he saw and felt helpless to change any of it.

Louis stayed at his comfortable little home for as long as he could, but after his rent got three months behind, his landlord could not extend him another month's stay and asked him to leave the premises. Tulah and Louis sold off their furniture piece by piece to buy food and gas to travel back to Ortonville. At least there, they wouldn't have to worry about paying rent. The house there was small and shabby, but it was theirs and it was rent free. Tulah went to the store to make a purchase with what they earned from their sells to eat along the way and stock their home with food for a while. Gas was five gallons for a dollar, so they filled up their Phaeton and prepared for the long ride.

Stopping at his parent's house before leaving was a sad and humbling experience for Louis. Tulah tried to console him, but words couldn't comfort his pain. Tulah felt sad about losing the nice things, but was content to have Louis and her children. Louis, on the other hand, was devastated. He worked and saved for over five years, building his business and clientele from nothing and turning it into a thriving business, just to stand by and helplessly watch it become defunct. She also knew there was friction between Louis and his Dad, mostly because of her, but Louis never once blamed her for their differences. There were times when she knew Louis would have gone to his father for a loan or for advice, but he never did, choosing to protect Tulah from his father's myopic views of her and to avoid the 'I told you so' speech. Truth was, Tulah had nothing to with his misfortune. It was what the newspapers called The Great Depression, and it hit the entire world the same way at the same time.

Bidding his family goodbye was both painful and distressing. It was one thing to lose his business and his home, but now he had to bid his family goodbye as well. The strained look in Louis' eyes was more than Tulah could bear. Sarah took Tulah and Gracie in the kitchen where Etta was preparing homemade cookies for their road trip. Sarah handed Gracie a cookie while she bounced Lucille on her knee to keep her quiet. Tulah and Etta had not quite made peace, but would tolerate one another for the sake of peace. Tulah took a seat at the kitchen table and put her head down.

"Keep your chin up, Tulah. You have no reason to put your head down."

"I know, Mama. I just feel so bad fo' Louis. He work so hard ta keep thangs together and he feel like it was all fo' nothin'. I keep tellin 'em dat he shouldn't feel dat way, but he won't listen ta me. I wish I could take his pain away." Tears filled Tulah's eyes, but she wiped them with the palm of her hand before they could fall.

"I know baby. Men have so much pride, and when they fail,

they take it personal. Louis is so much like his father, so I know what you going through. It's okay to cry, I understand. So you just go on and get it outta your system, cause you gone hafta be strong for Louis. Men think they are the backbone of a family, but it's really the women who hold everything together. We have to care for everybody else's needs before we can tend to our own. So you just keep on loving him and supporting him, and let him know you're there for him. Even though it doesn't feel like it, he's listening to you and it makes a difference for him to know you still love him. The whole world can come down on him, but as long as the woman he loves still sees him as her hero, that's enough incentive for him to get up and keep going. You understand?"

Tulah nodded her head.

"You know Tulah, we ain't had the best relationship, but I am sorry for what you going through and I do understand." Etta offered. "We went through the same thang. It was just as hard for Henry when he lost his job and then our house. Henry was so ashamed he didn't even tell me. I didn't find out he had lost his job until we was packing to move out of our house."

Tulah looked puzzled.

"You didn't know he lost his job?"

"No. He was getting dressed and leaving the house everyday. So I didn't have time to grieve one thing for grieving two. I told him it wasn't his fault, but men just feel like it is."

"It's that dat blasted Hoover's fault." Sarah exclaimed. She felt the president and his antics were the cause of the poor economy. "People are losing their jobs, savings, mortgages and farms are being foreclosed on left and right."

"I know, right down on Dirthmeyer Street people are building shacks out of old crates and got their whole family living out of them. They're calling it Hooverville."

"Hooverville? Why dey call it dat? Tulah asked.

"Because they're saying it's Hoover's fault we're in this predicament, and he's refusing government aid to people." Sarah explained. "Just be grateful to the good Lord you all have a place to go, that's already paid for."

"I know, I keep telling Louis dat. But he keep sayin' dat a self-made man cain't count on what somebody else left him."

"It's that pride of his." His mother contended. "Pride is good to have, but the kind he has is to his detriment."

Louis, Kennedy and Henry talked quietly among themselves in the living room. When Louis came in, Kennedy grabbed him by the shoulders, looked him square in the eyes, then embraced him tightly and whispered in his ear.

"I love you, son. And I'm proud of the man you've turned out to be."

Louis' hard exterior became undone when his father spoke those words in his ear. He had tried so hard to be strong and to take his losses in stride, all the while longing to speak with his father and to get his advice. He felt he failed his family, his father and the community of black people who supported him and took pride in his success as if it were their own. He held on to the hurt, refusing to give in to the disappointment he endured when his business closed, and the shame in losing his house. Tulah tried comforting him, offering him her body, but he couldn't even make love to her due to the stress he was under. Louis wanted to be Tulah's savior, providing her with unconditional love and material gain; to give her everything, and was disheartened things had not worked out the way he had planned. He hid all these feelings deep within, and had become sullen and withdrawn. When Kennedy spoke those words to him, however, his hard exterior came crashing down, and for the first time Louis cried. He took a seat on the sofa dropped his head and shook it in defeat.

"I don't know what I could have done differently. I've gone over it in my head again and again, and I just don't know."

"Son, there was nothing you could have done. Everybody's feeling the pinch. The only reason I keep working is because people keep dying, and as of late, they are dying much faster, either from starvation, or because they've worried themselves to death. We are going through hard times, and from what I understand, they are going to get worse before they get better. But I've raised you to be a strong and self-sufficient, God-fearing man, you'll find your way. It won't be easy, but you'll get through it." He said, taking a seat on the sofa and placing his hand on Louis' shoulder.

"Thanks Daddy, that means a lot to me to hear you say that. Look, I know we've had some differences."

"Don't worry about that, none of that matters now. I was wrong. I stepped outta line. You have to live your life for you, just like I had to live mine for me. I made some mistakes when I was young and I just didn't want to see you make the same ones."

Louis nodded and reached out to shake his father's hand. Sarah, Tulah and Etta came out of the kitchen carrying sandwiches and chocolate chip cookies.

"You ready, Louis?" Tulah asked.

"Just about." He answered reaching for Lucille. "Look Daddy, she's got red hair, just like grandma."

Kennedy reached out to touch the tiny, but furry head of Lucille. There were tiny wisps of reddish, blond hair growing out of the scalp of the toddler.

"Yeah, I guess she does."

"How can you tell? She's just as bald as an eagle." Henry laughed.

"That means she gone have good hair, like her Daddy." Tulah added.

"This boy ain't got no good hair, that's a conk." Henry said rubbing his hair over Louis' hair, messing it up. "Now she might have good hair if she takes after her uncle. ain't dat right?" He asked Lucille kissing the top of her head.

Kennedy looked down at Gracie, who was still holding on to her cookie.

"Come here, baby." He said to her. "Do you know who I am?"

Without answering, Gracie nodded.

"What's my name?" He asked.

"Grandpa."

"That's right." He said lifting her off the floor and into the air. "Don't you ever forget your grandpa, alright?"

Gracie nodded again. Kennedy turned his attention to Louis.

"How long of a drive is it, son?"

"Couple hours by car. We gotta be getting a move on, too. We told Dorothy we'd be there before dark. And we still gotta stop by Cora's, so we gone be getting on."

Louis, Tulah and the girls said there goodbyes, and even Etta wished them well and shook Tulah's hand before they took off. They made a stop at Cora's house, where they picked up fried chicken, cornbread and a sweet potato pie. Cora had also fallen upon hard times, but she took in borders to help keep her mortgage paid. She wanted to offer Louis and Tulah the extra room, but was getting by relatively well with the extra she picked up from her borders. Louis would never have accepted a hand out anyway. It was close to three o'clock before they started on their way. Louis was quiet for most of the ride, but held firmly to Tulah's hand. When she told him she loved him and everything would work out, he lifted her hand to his mouth and kissed it.

Louis and Tulah pulled into Mama Lou's old house just after six o'clock and Dorothy was there waiting to receive them.

"Heeey! Y'all made it!" She shouted to them as they pulled in. She looked at the fancy car they drove up in and raised her eye brows. When Louis pulled the car in and parked, Tulah jumped out and ran towards Dorothy.

"Hey girl, come hug my neck." She told her. "How y'all been doin?"

"We doin' fine Dorothy. You remember Louis?"

"Course I do. Hey Louis, how you?" She said reaching to shake his hand. Louis met Dorothy's hand with his own and shook it.

"How you doing Dorothy? Good to see you again." Louis smiled, but felt displeased to have to live in the dusty little shack he had just drove up to.

"I need ta talk ta y'all about something." She said, suddenly looking serious.

"What is it?" Tulah asked.

Dorothy looked inside the car and saw the girls and screamed.

"These y'all girls? Oooh weee, Grace done got big. And dis her sister? Y'all is so blessed. God shole is smilin' down on y'all." She said changing the subject.

Louis and Tulah exchanged looks before inquiring of Dorothy what was wrong.

"Dorothy, is everything alright?"

"Uh, yeah. Just one little problem, but we gone have it worked out real soon."

"Well, what is it?" Tulah asked.

Dorothy walked up to Tulah and gestured for Louis to join her.

"It's Milledge."

"What about him?"

"Well he been stayin' here to keep a eye on thangs and to

keep up wit da farm animals. But since he been here, he lost his place and he kinda don't have nowhere to go."

"Why cain't he stay at yo' place?" Tulah questioned.

"Cassie and her husband living wit me, as well as my other chillen, and I just don't have no mo room."

"Cassie married?"

Dorothy flashed a bright smile. "Yeah, uh huh, she pregnant, too."

"I don't believe it. She done growed up."

"Yup. She got a couple mo' monts to go."

Tulah looked at Louis to get his reaction, but couldn't read his thoughts.

"We all hittin' it hard." Louis answered. "It's a small place, but we'll work it out. He can stay, but he'll have to earn his keep."

"Oh thank you, Mr. Starks."

"Dorothy, call me Louis. I appreciate you and Milledge keeping up the place while we were gone."

"Well you was sendin' money to keep it up."

"I appreciate you anyhow. How's everything else?"

"Everythang else is fine. You know. Well as can be expected anyhow."

Louis nodded and reached into his breast pocket to retrieve a pack of cigarettes.

"I'm tired, I just want to get inside and get settled so I can get some sleep. Tell Milledge he can stay. We'll work out the details later." He said before grabbing the bags out of the car and taking them into the house.

Chapter 14

As time moved forward, the times became harder. Louis would leave early in the morning and drive into town looking for work, but by the end of the day, he would always return with the same results - no work to be found. Some days when Louis was out for looking for work, Tulah would become bored and restless. She would sometimes take the girls for a walk into town and down to the pond. Walking along the road, she noticed a huge billboard had been erected advertising Coca Cola. There was a beautiful woman holding a coke in her hand smiling. Tulah couldn't stand looking at the sign, because it always made her want a Coke. She would close her eyes, hold her head back and smile, just like the woman on the billboard, imagining she had a nice, cold Coca Cola to quench her dry throat from the blazing hot sun. Once, when she was walking with the girls, they witnessed a horrible fight between two men who had a disagreement about politics. The two dirty and grungy old men fought furiously while calling each other obscene names. Tulah hurried past them and headed straight home. Not feeling safe walking with the girls, she decided to do something safe and constructive - plant a garden out in the yard. Besides needing something to busy herself with, she figured it was a way to have fresh vegetables without buying them from the market. She dug a hole deep in the ground, while the girls followed behind her dropping seeds in the earth and covering it with rich, fertile dirt.

Early one morning, Louis was up at the crack of dawn seeking God for direction. He stood out on the porch and took in a clean breath of fresh air. Looking up into the sky, he noticed a bird soaring high in the sky, almost touching the clouds, dipping and gliding, enjoying its flight. He wished his life could be so care free. He walked out in the yard and towards the thicket and into the area where the pigs and chickens were kept neatly in a pen. Milledge was already out slopping the pigs. Louis walked towards him observing how methodical he was in the way he feed them. Humming a spiritual, he systematically cared for each animal, throwing feed to each and watering them down. Louis stepped up on the fence and leaned forward suddenly inspired with what he thought to be an ingenious idea.

"Hey there, Milledge."

"Mornin' Louis."

"How long you been out here?"

"I get up early in da mornin', ta try an beat this heat."

"Hey man, how many chickens we got?"

"Twelve."

"And these three pigs here?"

"Dats right."

"Good work, Milledge. I'll be talkin' to ya."

Louis walked back towards the house with a little more energy than when he went out. He felt encouraged from the idea he got by watching Milledge. He went in the house and into the bedroom. Walking over to the bed where Tulah was still sleeping with Lucille snuggled up under her, he shook his head, despising the dismal little house. He took a seat on the edge of the bed and gently shook her.

"Tulah. Baby wake up. I need ta talk to you."

"What's wrong, Louis?"

"Nothing's wrong. I think I know a way ta make some money."

Tulah wiped her eyes, stretched and sat up, yawing.

"How?"

"We got twelve pigs out there, and three pigs."

"Yeah."

"Well you gotta trust me on this."

"I trust you, Louis. Whatcha thankin' bout doin?"

"You know everybody's catchin' hard times these days living, working, even feeding their families."

"I know."

"Well Tulah, if we sold a few of them chickens and bought

turkeys we can start a turkey farm. Because we'll be raising them here, we can charge less than what the store would charge. We can raise chickens and turkeys up enough to sell them, and then we could sell the eggs too."

"A turkey farm?"

"Yeah. Everybody loves turkey."

"Why would we sell for less than the store?"

"Stores have to sell a certain amount for overhead, you know, rent needs to be paid, utilities, and employees. We won't have no overhead. We'll let Millege do most of the work, because he knows a lot about farming, you should have seen him out in the field. Anyway, he needs a place to live, so we'll let him earn his keep by tending them. We'll still pay him, of course, for taking care of them, but it won't have to be as much because he owes us. We'll keep most of the profit ourselves."

"A turkey raising business, huh?"

"Yeah Tulah, what you think?"

"I don't know nothing bout dat stuff. But if you think you could pull it off, then I'm witchu. How many chickens you gone sell?"

"Well, I still got some credit left. I can go and buy some chicken coops and cages to separate the chickens from the turkeys. I can maybe buy some full grown turkeys to breed, so that way we can keep most of the chickens, but it depends on how many I can get on credit. I'll start feeding them and getting them plump and healthy, come Thanksgiving time, we'll sell them off and we'll be in good shape."

"Louis you is so smart. I nevva would've thought of nothin' like dat. You is truly a business man."

Louis smiled.

"I'm happy to see you smile again."

"Well now I have something to look forward to. So I can take care of my family like I want to. Go on back to sleep, I'm going to talk to Milledge and see what we can come up with by putting our heads together."

When Louis left, Tulah laid back down, but was too excited to sleep. She lay there thinking about how successful they would be, because she completely trusted Louis' judgment. She thought how good it would feel to live in a beautiful home once again like they had in Marietta. Then she thought when things got a little better and money started coming in like before, perhaps they could add another room onto the small home they occupied. That way, it would be spacious enough for all of them, but already paid for which would make it perfect, because they wouldn't have to pack up and leave their home again.

Louis was so elated about his new business venture he felt like celebrating. Later that day, he took Tulah for a walk through the woods to a nearby lake. He carried fishing poles, an old bucket, and a jar full of worms, so he could teach Tulah how to fish. During their walk, he pointed out to her the beauty of nature, how autumn had decorated the earth in a magnificent display of radiant hues. The trees glowed in awesome splendor showcasing leaves of red, yellow, rust and orange. The warm breeze caressed their skin as gently as a mother cradling the face of her adored child before kissing it. They sat on the river bed with the sun on their backs, facing a breathtaking view of the lake that was comparable to a masterful portrait. The lake was surrounded by an audience of lush green trees that seemingly assembled themselves to spy the affection shared between the two. The water, calm and relaxing, reflected the beauty of the trees. The manifestation of the sun illuminating a brilliant blue sky resembled the color of melon, while birds dipped and glided, stretching their wings in the fragranced air. Louis attempted to show Tulah how to hook a worm on the line, but it squirmed and wiggled until it set itself free. Once he achieved a loaded line, he stood behind her showing her how to pull back, and cast the rod forward, releasing the button once she finds the spot where she wanted to drop the line. They stayed at the lake most of the afternoon, fishing, laughing, talking, and making plans for their future. They only caught five small fish, but the quality time they spent was much needed, for they had not had any in several months. They walked home hand in hand and Tulah was happier than she had been in a long time. She missed seeing Louis this way, calm, relaxed, happy and hopeful. This was the same Louis she fell in love with, the man he was when he was excited about getting his studio going. She realized how important it was for Louis to be productive and to provide for his family, and Tulah admired him even more for that trait.

Early the next morning, Louis was up and out before sun up. He and Milledge drove into town to make a purchase of coops, feed, and other things necessary to raise turkeys. Tulah suggested he should go to other turkey farms to get an idea on how they raise them, feed them, breed them, and so on, but Louis was in too much of a hurry, and far too excited to wait. Besides, he figured Milledge knew enough about farming to get them going. They left at 7:30 in the morning and didn't return until after 9:00 that evening. According to Louis, they had driven over 100 miles in search of turkeys healthy and strong enough to endure the taxing ride home. He said they found a turkey farm right outside Decatur and talked to the owner, getting all kinds of useful and important information. After he took Louis and Milledge around showing them how farming is done, Louis bought 150 full-grown turkeys, and 50 baby turkeys, which were called poults. Poults are essential to the business because it's when they are young they can be nurtured into a uniform and superior flock. He also purchased over 500lbs of grains and feeds.

The turkey farmer was having all of Louis' purchases delivered the next day, because he had trucks big enough to accommodate the large purchase. Louis did, however, manage to bring a cute and furry little poult home for Gracie and Lucille. Tulah had already put them down for bed, but Louis was so excited he had awakened them with the over-active poult. Louis and Tulah took joy in watching Gracie chase the helpless poult all over the house, while Lucille stood back, uncertain if she liked it or not.

"Hey Gracie, what you gone name it?" Tulah asked of the small, flailing turkey.

"I'm gonna call her Daisy."

"Daisy? That shole is a pretty name. But how you know it's a girl."

"She's a girl, I can tell by her eyes." Tulah and Louis busted up laughing.

That night as Louis and Tulah lay in bed he confessed his fears.

"Tulah, I hope I'm doing the right thing."

"Why you say dat?"

"I don't know. I just hope I'm not moving too fast on this. I mean, what if something went wrong? What if Milledge doesn't know enough about farming turkey's to make this a success? What if nobody wants to buy turkeys and we left with 150 turkeys running round here we have to keep feeding and caring for? Then what would we do? I can't fail another venture, Tulah. I can't live through that again."

Tulah rolled over so she was facing Louis.

"You not gone fail, Louis. You just gotta keep thinkin' how successful you gone be. Everything'll work out. You smart. And you know how ta do business and how to talk ta people. Besides, everybody like you. All da people around here think you real smart and dey like you."

"Yeah Tulah, but that's not enough."

"Yes it is. They'll buy from you cause dey like you."

"That's not enough of a reason. I need them to have money to buy. Sometimes when people like you, it causes more of a problem. They think cause your'e nice you'll extend them credit. You know, like what I have? Buy now and pay later. But I'm not a manufacturer; I can't afford to extend them credit. We need them to have money to buy right now. What do you think will happen when I tell them no, I can't give them turkeys or eggs on credit? They'll think I'm mean and then won't want to do business with me. Having a business is hard work, Tulah. Hard work."

Tulah didn't know what to say to Louis. She wanted to assure him everything would be okay, but from what she could tell, he had already convinced himself it wouldn't be. She thought about what Sarah told her about making a man feel he is a hero and she knew she had to say something to make him feel better.

"Louis, no matter what happens, good or bad, I'll still love you and I'll stay by yo side fo'evva. I think you da smartest man I'll evva know. You my hero, come what may."

Louis chuckled under his breath then turned to take Tulah in his arms.

"Thanks baby. You always know what to say."

"I don't always know what ta say, but I know I mean wit all ma heart."

"I know things have been rough, and you had to let go of a lot of nice things, pretty little things I know you like, but are you happy you married me?"

"It's the best thing I evva did. Next ta ma girls, it's the only thing I'm proud of."

The following morning, Louis and Milledge was up early ready to receive their delivery. Louis was so excited Tulah couldn't get him to eat, but he smoked incessantly. A big truck pulled up with cages, coops, turkeys, poults, feed and grain. When the truck came to a stop, a short, but stout man with a bandana tied around his head jumped out. He extended his hand to Louis and introduced himself. They walked around to the back of the truck and he let the door down revealing numerous stacked cages with turkeys inside. The funky smell of turkeys hit them in the face before the turkeys could be seen. Throwing Louis a pair of work gloves, he gestured for him to assist him in getting the cages down.

"You gonna get your boy to help?" The man asked, speaking of Milledge.

"What boy?" Louis asked, perplexed by his meaning.

"Your boy. Ain't he your work hand?"

Louis finally understood what he was getting at. It wasn't the first time Louis had been mistaken for a white man. He didn't mind the mistaken identity so much, but when ever it happened, there was always something derogatory implied towards blacks, such as referring to a full grown man as a boy. But he handled it tactfully, as he always does, not letting the ignorance of others get to him.

"No, Milledge isn't my workhand." He explained. "He's my business partner." He told him with a smile. The man nodded, realizing his mistake and worked quickly without saying a word. Once all of the cages had been removed from the truck, Louis noticed a great deal of the turkeys had died during the transport.

"What's wrong with these turkeys? Some of 'em are dead."

"Not uncommon for turkeys to expire en route."

"Maybe it's common for you, but not for me it isn't."

"Well, you should have transported them yourself."

"I paid to have these turkeys transported, and I was assured they would be fine. How do I know these weren't healthy birds to begin with? How do I know you didn't bring me all the sick or already dead birds?"

"I guess there ain't no way of telling, now is it?" The man answered sarcastically. "Look, we ain't got no reason to sell you bad birds, okay? This is our business, we been farming turkeys for 20 years. You don't make it in this business that long by cheating people."

"I don't mean to accuse you falsely; I just wasn't expecting anything like this. There has got to be 15, 20 dead turkeys. How am I suppose to sustain a loss like this?"

"Look, I'll talk to my boss, see what he's willing to do. I can't make any promises, but I'll talk to him."

"I'd appreciate that." Louis told him reaching to shake his hand. He met Louis' hand with his own and jumped back inside the truck and drove off. Louis and Milledge looked at all of the loud, clucking turkeys and then at each other.

"Where do we start?" Louis asked him.

"I guess we can start by getting these coops set up and out of this heat. We can water the turkeys down to keep 'em cool, and then get 'em situated. We'll put the adult turkeys together and then the poults."

"Alrighty, let's get to it."

Louis and Milledge worked all morning, through the afternoon and late into the evening. Stacking, nailing, measuring and separating. Tulah and Dorothy came out to bring them sandwiches after calling for them to come and eat and they wouldn't. Gracie came along carrying her poult, and Lucille followed close behind. Tulah got one whiff of the smelly turkeys and her stomach became a queasy, turning and churning like batter being mixed for bread. She ran to the bushes in just enough time to regurgitate her supper. Louis ran over to see about her, but shook his head knowingly as he turned a bucket over so she could take a seat. When her stomach finally settled, she looked at him.

"Whatchu lookin' at me like dat fo?"

Louis smiled and shook his head.

"What?"

"You know what. For as long as I been with you, I only known you to get sick for one reason."

"Uh uh . I was careful not to let that happen."

"What you talking about, you was careful? You can't stop what God wants to happen."

"What's wrong with mommy?" Gracie asked.

"Mommy sick." Lucille answered.

"Mommy is gone have y'all a little sister or brother." Louis announced.

"Louis don't tell them dat. Its dem stanky turkeys. They stank so bad, dey made me feel sick to ma stomach."

"Mommy, are you gonna have a baby?"

"Naw chile, don't listen to yo Daddy. He just being silly."

Dorothy made her way over to Tulah and Louis.

"Do you want to know my opinion? Cause I shole dreamt about fish."

"I know what you gone say wit yo fish dreams. So when I want yo opinion, I'll ask for it."

"Okay, I know how ta mind my business. But if you not feeling well, I can take the girls back to my house so you can get some rest."

"I think that'll be a good idea Dorothy. We just about finished, and it's getting dark anyway. Come on baby, let me help you home." Louis told her, helping her to her feet.

Over the next few months Louis and Milledge toiled to get the turkeys acclimated to their new environment. After some died off and others he found to be no good but for eggs, he had 68 adult, female turkeys, and 43 males. The poults grew to be strong and healthy and had begun mating. His turkey population was growing rapidly and feeding them had become expensive because they were growing, multiplying and eating so fast. He had to use the last of his credit line to purchase more feed. He knew it was not a good idea to overextend himself, but he found himself in a predicament had little control of. By Thanksgiving, Louis had 300 young turkeys and was expecting the winter season to ignite his business into a thriving enterprise. But the failing economy was taking its toll, hitting harder than he expected. Unemployment was becoming more and more prevalent and businesses continued to close. People had no money to buy and therefore, Louis could not sell the turkeys. He found himself in debt with no way out. Louis and Tulah was able to manage relatively well, since their house was paid for and they were raising their own food, but Louis couldn't afford to pay his lenders the money was extended to him on credit, and he stressed over his quandary because now he had another baby on the way.

This pregnancy was a difficult one for Tulah. Despite her loss of appetite, she gained a lot of weight and her feet were always swollen. She didn't have much energy and could barely care for the girls. Louis was always trying to get her to eat, but she refused to eat yet another turkey. Living on a turkey farm, she had become an expert at finding new and innovative ways to prepare them. She baked them, smoked them, broiled them and fried them. She made turkey hash, turkey stew, turkey pot pie and turkey soup. Tulah had more than her share of turkey and couldn't stomach another bite. However, the mystery of her weight gain was hidden in the fact she would consume Cokes and eat corn starch by the box. When no one was around, she would get a clump of corn starch and spoon it into her mouth, crunching down on the starch until it got wet and thick. Tulah couldn't get enough of the thick, starchy substance that turned pasty in her mouth. Once, Louis came in when she was eating some. She tried to hide it, but the white, crusty corners of her mouth gave her away. He told her corn starch was not a nourishing meal for the new baby, so she promised she would stop with the starch and eat healthier meals. As time grew closer for her to deliver, she slept more and more throughout the day. Dorothy would stop by to check on things, but Cassie had recently delivered her new baby, and Dorothy was torn between caring for her while still trying to work. Louis did all he could, but his time was consumed with tending to his failing turkey farm and trying to find odd jobs to run it. Even though he was not able to sell his turkeys, they became a great commodity to barter with. He would therefore, spend his days driving around looking for a sell or a trade off. Worried about Tulah, and not being able to care for her like he wanted, he sent word to Aunt Cora. Upon the news about Tulah, Cora was there before the week was out.

Chapter 15

"Push chile! This ain't yo first youngin', you gone kill dis baby if you don't push it outta there!" The midwife scolded.

"Aughhh!" Tulah screamed. "Just bear down chile. Take the pain and push! It's almost here, now."

Tulah took a deep breath, closed her eyes tight and pushed with all her might. When she ran out of air, she took another deep breath and gave it all she had. She grabbed hold of the bed sheet and stuffed it in her mouth biting down feverishly and hysterically shaking her head. With no more energy and wrecked with pain, Tulah passed out from exhaustion.

"She's here. Your little girl is here!"

The midwife held a screaming baby girl up to Tulah, but she was slumped over on the bed unconscious and oblivious to her new bundle of joy. She wrapped the new baby in a sterile cloth and laid her on Tulah's stomach as she rubbed her arm and put cool cloths on her head.

"You gone be alright gal. You just hold on, dis here chile needs her Mama. You hold on, here?"

She rubbed Tulah's arms and legs frantically trying to revive her. When Tulah didn't respond, she called Cora in the room.

"Cora! Cora! You'd better git in here, right now!"

Cora ran to the aid of the midwife and covered her mouth in sheer fright at the sight of Tulah slumped over on the bed.

"She ain't dead is she?"

"Naw she ain't dead. Grab dis baby."

She handed the newborn to Cora and went to work trying to revive Tulah. She gingerly placed her head in her lap and fanned her while replacing the old cloths with fresh new ones.

"Come on here gal. Don't you give up on me. Don't you give up on dat chile of yorn. You fight gal, you hear me? Fight!"

Cora rocked the baby and paced the floor in tears.

"Dear Lord, please don't take her. Not now sweet Jesus, not now."

The midwife rocked Tulah's limp body and spoke gently in her ear.

"You come on back to us, chile. Everything's alright. You come on back here."

"Oh dear God, please don't carry her away from here." Cora prayed, while rocking the baby.

Louis peeked inside the room,

"What's wrong? What's going on?"

"Oh the Lawd done took my Tulah way from here!"

"Now he ain't. She still breathin', but she weak. Lawd she so weak." The midwife told him.

Louis ran over to the side of the bed and kneeled by Tulah's side.

"Tulah! Tulah, wake up girl! You hear me girl. Wake up!"

Tulah didn't respond to Louis's pleas, nor did she respond to the midwife's coaxing. Louis grabbed a glass of water from the nightstand and threw it in Tulah's face. Tulah took in a short, quick breath and started coughing.

"You alright Tulah?"

Tulah nodded her head, coughing.

"You gone choke me ta deaf, Louis. You tryin' ta drown me?"

Louis was relieved to see the feistiness he loved about Tulah was still there. He hugged his wife and kissed her on the cheek.

"Girl you gave us a fright." He said, patting her on the back. "I'm sorry honey, you alright now?"

Tulah nodded. "I'm alright. Where's my baby, what did I have?"

"You got yo'self a little girl." The midwife told her.

"Another little girl, the Lawd shole is good." Cora said handing her the baby. "She shole is heavy."

"She is heavy, and you still weak, Tulah. So don't be tryin to hold her just yet. You just give her to her Daddy."

Louis took the baby from Tulah, seeing her for the first time.

"She's got to be 8 pounds or more."

Louis said weighing her in his hands and smiling with great pride. He peeled the blanket back examining every inch of her. He felt her smooth, wrinkled, apricot colored skin, lifted her to his face and breathed in deeply, taking in the smell of his newborn. When he looked into her bright, wondering eyes, she looked back at him with an understanding that startled him. Louis knew right at that moment she would be something special. He checked her fingers and toes and gently kissed the crown of her head.

"Well it's no wonder the poor girl passed out. You alright, Tulah?"

"Yes Aint Cora, I feel just fine, now it's over. I want ta see my baby."

Louis walked over to Tulah and sat on the edge of the bed still cradling the newest edition to their family.

"What we gone call her?

Tulah recalled seeing an advertisement in town with the prettiest white woman she'd ever seen holding a coke in her hand and smiling. Each time she'd pass that advertisement, she'd stop to look at the beautiful smiling woman and imagine what her life was like. At the bottom of the picture in small captions it said, "Join Jessie in her favorite soft drink, Coca Cola." The billboard would make Tulah want a coke every time she saw it. The thought of the smiling woman stayed with her long after she would pass it by. She would think about her late in the evenings sometimes and wonder if they were drinking Cokes at the same time. She even thought of changing her hair color the same light brown like Jessie's. Once, while she was enjoying a Coke, a thought occurred to her that perhaps if she had a girl and named her Jessie she would have a nice life just like the lady on the billboard.

"Jessie. I'm gone call her Jessie. Let me hold her Louis." Tulah said reaching for the new born. Once she held her securely in her arms, she kissed her forehead, smiled down at her and spoke gently.

"I'm gone call you Jessie, and you gone have yo'self a real nice life. Mo better then anybody else in these parts, ain't dat right?" She said, kissing Jessie's forehead.

Chapter 16

Hopelessness and despair increased, as people lacked adequate food, clothing and shelter. Living conditions deteriorated. The great depression, as it was called, reeked havoc on the lives of the American people. Soup kitchens were set up to serve warm bread and hot soup to people, but it was never enough to fill the empty bellies of those who depended solely on them for food. It became more common than not to see people rummaging through garbage dumps for food. Louis and Tulah's experience was no different than any one else's after their turkey business went defunct. Being in debt with no way out and no money coming in to pay his bills, lenders came and repossessed Louis' car. For as long as he had the car, he was able to drive around and try to pick up odd jobs. But now that his car was gone, the effects, as far as Louis was concerned, was equivalent to cutting off his legs. He knew he had to do something, but was short on ideas and less on alternatives.

Dorothy recently lost her house because she could no longer afford it. She, Milledge, Cassie and Cassie's new husband, packed up and was moving up north with relatives in Chicago. Dorothy told Louis and Tulah that opportunities were better up north, and a cousin already had work lined up for Milledge. She asked them to consider relocating up north where the auto industry was still thriving and in need of workers. It was tempting to Louis, but he had limited means and couldn't afford to pack up his family and move them to a city he had never been to before. He did however, discuss the idea of moving with Tulah, and to his surprise, she was receptive.

"Aint Cora used ta always say, nothin' ventured, nothin' gained. I reckon dats her way a sayin' dat if you don't try somethin' out, you nevva gone know what you capable a doin."

"That's a good point, Tulah. But we gone have ta figure out how we can get enough money to go up there and find a place ta live. Dorothy and Milledge got family they can stay with until they get settled. We don't know anybody up there."

"Well Louis, you know I been holdin' on ta dat money Mama Lou left fa me. I ain't spent a dolla of it."

"If you let me use it, I promise, baby, I'll pay back every penny."

"You don't hafta pay me back. Dat ain't my money, it's our money."

"You know how I feel about takin' hand outs, Tulah."

"Well, you shouldn't feel like dat bout yo' wife. You been takin' care of me and da girls all dis time. Na it's ma turn ta help. Let me help, Louis. I want to."

Louis reached out and pulled Tulah's hand to his mouth, and then kissed it.

"How much we got?"

"One hundred twenty three dollars." She announced proudly.

Louis shook his head.

"What?"

"That's not nearly enough to move our family out of state. We gone need money to get us a place ta stay and pay rent for a couple of months, just in case I can't find a job right away."

"How much is dat gone be?"

"I don't know. It depends on how high the cost of living is up north."

"Well, how you gone fine out?"

Louis took in a long breath and let it out slowly. Pulling a pack of cigarettes out of his breast pocket, he tapped the bottom of the pack freeing a single cigarette before placing it between his lips. He struck a match to light it and then took a long drag. Standing, he contemplatively paced the floor, blew out a cloud of thick smoke and ran his hand over the back of his head. He walked back over to where Tulah was sitting, and took a seat on the sofa right next to her.

"The only way I'm gone know for sure, is to go up there and check things out. You know, poke around a bit. See if I can find a job, maybe a place for us ta live, and then I can send for you and the girls once I get things set up for us."

"Sound like you already been thinking bout it."

"Well, I have, sort of. I mean, every since Dorothy mentioned it I can't help but think about it. The thought of working these days sounds like a dream to me. "

"How long you think it's gone take? To find us a place ta live? Cause I can't take care of the house, the farm and da girls wit out you."

"I don't know baby, for as long as it takes. The way I see it, we don't have much choice. Cause if we stay down here, we ain't gone make it for much longer."

Tulah closed her eyes, clasped her hands together and raised them to her forehead as if in prayer.

"What Tulah?" Louis asked, but she didn't answer. He reached out and placed his hand on her knee, but she only shook her head.

"What baby? If you don't want me to go, I won't."

Tulah let her hands down and opened her eyes. A single tear fell down her cheek and she put her hand over Louis' hand.

"I know you gotta go, and I want you to, but I'm gone miss you so much. I caint help but think about da time when we was separated, when I was pregnant wit Gracie, and dat was bad enough, but now dat I got all da girls I don't know what I'm gone do. I want you ta go and fine somethin' better than what's down here, but I'm so scared, Louis. How am I gone make it by myself? Dorothy and Milledge gone be gone, how am I gone make it wit deez girls on my own?"

"Tulah, it'll only be for a while. And it ain't much left to the farm, I don't even know if it's fair to call it that." Louis put his cigarette out and turned back to Tulah. "You a strong woman, more'n any other woman I've ever known. That's why I feel in love with you, because of your strength and independence."

"Louis I ain't dat strong, I just ack lak it because I be scared. It's all a ack." Tulah said crying.

"Tulah, you want me to stay?"

"Noooo," She whined.

"Then what do you want me to do?"

"I want you to go, I mean I don't want you to, but I know you have to. I just… I don't know Louis. I ain't nevva been by myself wit da girls. What if I'm not strong enough to make it on my own?"

"Girl, you walked all the way here when you was pregnant wit Gracie. You strong enough alright."

"Da kinda strong you talkin' bout is physical strength."

"No I'm not. You got a will to survive. Dat takes a strong mind. But if you want, I can contact momma, she won't mind if y'all stay with her. She always saying she want to spend more time with the girls anyway."

Tulah pondered his words, then decisively told him,

"Uhn uhn. Dats okay. I don't wanna put yo' momma out. It ain't just me and Gracie no mo, we got a house full now."

"All shoot, dat won't matter."

"And you know yo' Daddy been sick. I wouldn't do dat ta them. I reckon we just gone hafta stick it out here."

"Alright. Now all we gotta do is get up enough money."

"Louis, why don't you just take da money I got and by a bus ticket, or a train ticket? When you get up there, you can fine a job, save some money and send some home. I know you wanna get up enough money, but I think da first thang you need ta do is ta get there."

"That's not a bad idea, but I cain't leave you all with nothing. You all are gonna need some money to get by while I'm gone. Don't worry, baby, I'll think of something."

Over the next few weeks, Louis worked as many odd jobs as he could find, saving money for his trip, and putting some aside for Tulah and the girls in his absence. The money he managed to save was but a fraction of what Mama Lou left for Tulah. Louis felt hopeless. He looked to God for direction, but didn't feel quite the same about God's grace and mercy as he had before all of his troubles. He felt forgotten, isolated and forsaken by God, and the closeness he once felt waned considerably. He concluded that God had turned his back on him when he needed him most. Louis ceased his morning communions with God, no more quiet time to meditate on his goodness, and no more faith that God would bring him through. Reluctantly, he decided to take a walk through the woods where he conversed with God in times past, to have a talk man to Man, and ask God why He had abandoned him. He didn't know what to expect from God anymore. He didn't know if he would hear a voice shout down from heaven, or if he should listen for a small, still voice down in his spirit. Kneeling on a rock, he cried and prayed, asking guidance. After praying for direction and having none to come, Louis took matters into his own hands.

He went home and told Tulah to pack their things, because they were moving in with his parents. Not leaving any room for discussion, Louis packed all their things and had them back at his parent's house within two weeks. Once they arrived, Louis learned that Kennedy was gravely ill. Breathing the formaldehyde fumes he'd worked with for decades had taken its toll, with violent coughing spells, hallucinations, and convulsions. Though some days were better than others, his condition was worsening, exacerbated by a lack of sleep with most days filled with the discomfort of coughing his lungs raw. Kennedy was a shell of the man once was. Louis was taken aback at site of his once strong and vital father, now weak and debilitated. Sarah sent word to Louis and told him Kennedy wasn't doing well, but Louis never expected his condition to be this bad. After seeing his father, he found solitude in the bathroom, and wept sore.

He explained to Kennedy that he had plans to move his family up north, but after seeing him in such a fragile state, he reconsidered, not willing to leave his father like this. Kennedy pleaded with Louis not to change his plans, assuring him he would be fine, now that he could breathe in the fresh air of home as opposed to being in the tomb of the funeral home basement, breathing toxic fumes all day. The way Sarah fussed over him and attended to his every need, Kennedy had no choice but to get better. He told Louis he shouldn't change his plans and promised him he would get better.

Bright and early on Monday morning, Louis was all packed with a one way ticket to Ohio. He hated leaving his family, but was comforted by the fact they were staying with his parents. Even though he and his father had their differences concerning Louis' decision to marry Tulah, he knew his father had finally accepted her, and they were in good hands. Louis wouldn't allow Tulah to bring the girls down to the train station to see him off, and she didn't want to leave them with his parent's, so they said their goodbyes at the house before he left. He hugged Tulah around her waist and lifted her off the ground. Holding her suspended in the air, he kissed her and whispered in her ear that he loved her and would send for them as soon as he could. When he put Tulah down, he reached into his pocket and pulled out a wad of money. Tulah's eyes widened when she got a look at all the money Louis had. She never asked, but guessed Kennedy must have given him the extra cash he needed for the trip.

Louis peeled back three twenties and pressed them in the palm of Tulah's hand. Closing his hand over hers, he told her with extreme caution she should spend the money wisely and only when necessary. Henry and his family were still living at his parent's house and he knew that Tulah and Etta living in the same house would be a challenge. But Tulah assured him he didn't have anything to worry about, because not only was she completely secure in their relationship, but she has three daughters now, two of which were very observant, and she had to be on her best behavior for their sake. Tulah fought the urge to cry as Louis started down the road. She and the girls waved to him as he walked off into the distance. Henry went to the train station to see Louis off, Louis asking him to look after his family and keep him posted on their father's progress.

Louis boarded the train, checked his bag, found his row, and settled back into his seat. He removed his hat from his head and put his head down as the train started to move forward. He always imagined traveling, not alone, but with his family, to show them the country, the world. How his life had taken a turn, coming so close to the goals he'd planned for his whole life- an economic, social and political standing that garnered the respect of family and community. Foolish goals, he thought. What a fool he had been to think that God would allow those things to happen for him. God abandoned him, left him out on a limb with no way back. Everything he wanted and desired, he had to get it on his own, alone, without God. It was up to him and him alone. He had to make it happen.

Louis' thoughts were interrupted when the porter asked to see his ticket. He lifted his head and placed his hat back on his head before retrieving the ticket from his breast pocket and handing it to the porter. The porter checked the ticket and handed it back to Louis.

"Suh, yo' ticket say you in da right seat, but I think somebody made a mistake."

"Excuse me?"

"Suh, dey got you in da wrong section. If you give me a minute, I'll check the front and have you in first class in just a jiffy."

Louis chuckled to himself understanding the mistake.

"No, you are the one that's mistaken. I'm in the right seat."

"Suh?"

"I'm a black man. No different from you, okay?"

The porter took a good look at Louis, then nodded and tipped his hat.

"Yes suh." He said before walking away.

As the train traversed the country side, Louis looked out the window and saw both beauty and oppression in the town that had been home to him for so many years. He reclined and closed his eyes. Louis was tired of things not working out for him. He didn't want to think anymore, dream about his future, or reflect on his past. As the train chugged its way relentlessly forward, rocking and jerking about, it rocked Louis to sleep. He was awakened by a sturdy hand shaking him. As Louis opened his eyes, the porter was standing over him with a smile on his face.

"Sorry to disturb you, but we had some sandwiches left over from first class, and I thought you might like one."

Louis sat up, wiped his eyes, and returned the smile.

"What kind you got?"

"It's a pastrami sandwich. You ever had pastrami?"

"No, I don't think I have."

"It's good, man. I'll bring you a cup of coffee if you can wait a minute. I gotta wait till the kitchen is clear before I can sneak one out."

"Why do you have to sneak it out?"

"Man, are you serious? I'm ain't supposed to be bringing food out to no coloreds."

"Then why are you?"

"Well, we don't get too many coloreds on the train, so I look out for 'em when we do."

"Won't you get in trouble if you're caught?"

"Shoot yeah. But I'll just tell 'em I didn't know you was a colored dude. They can't blame me for that." He said laughing. "Enjoy your sandwich, suh. I'll get coffee out to you soon as I can."

"Thanks man."

Louis didn't realize how hungry he was until he took his first bite. The sandwich was different, kind of fatty and salty, but very tasty. He made a mental note to remember the name so he could order one once he got up north. Just as he was taking his last bite, the porter returned with a cup of hot coffee and a slice of lemon meringue pie. Louis thoroughly enjoyed his lunch. Sitting back in his seat with a full stomach, he looked out of the window and wondered how far he'd traveled. The royal treatment he was getting from porter made him realize how good the life of the privileged must be.

Louis settled back into his seat, closed his eyes, and hoped the opportunities up north he had heard so much about would be attainable to him and his family.

Chapter 17

With limited living quarters and having to help care for Kennedy, Tulah and Etta were forced to engage in polite conversation. Sarah did most of the cooking to assure healthy and wholesome meals, essential for Kennedy's recovery, were provided daily. However, Tulah and Etta took turns with chores, shopping, laundry, looking after the children and keeping them quiet so that they wouldn't disturb Kennedy. Having to rotate roles and responsibilities, the two women collaborated, consulted, and on occasion, would manage a smile. Tulah, ever observant to her children, noticed how kind and patient Etta was while interacting with the girls, treating them no differently than how she treated her own. It was because of that, Tulah'se reserved and cautioned exchange she set aside for Etta slowly began to fade.

"You know Etta, I just have to say I do appreciate da way you look afta my girls and treat dem so kind."

"Humph" Etta chuckled, "Never mind our differences, I love those girls."

"I know you do, and dey love you, too. I just gotta say dat I'm really sorry about how we got off to such a bad start - and the fight and all."

Etta laughed.

"The fight? That was years ago. Why you bringing that up now?"

"I guess cause I hated you so much back then and now you just seem different."

Etta smiled at her and continued to fold clothes, placing them neatly on the folding table.

"Hey, I found these earrings I had from a long time ago. I think they would look nice on you. You want em?"

"I caint wear no earrings, I don't have pierced ears." Tulah answered, pulling on her naked earlobes.

"I can pierce em for you." Etta said excitedly. It's really easy. All we need is some ice and a needle."

"A needle?"

"Yeah."

"Uhn uhn, no thanks. Dat sounds painful."

"It's not. That's what the ice is for. You freeze your earlobe, and when it's numb, you stick the needle through it."

"Is dat how you did yours?"

"My sister did mine when I was twelve. Oh come on, it won't be that bad. It'll look pretty. What do you say?" The girls jumped up and down eagerly and urged Tulah to let Etta pierce her ears.

Tulah agreed while the girls gathered around to watch. Etta had Tulah to hold an ice cube on her earlobe until it was numb, and sticking a threaded sewing needle straight through it, Tulah had pierced ears. Then tying the end of the thread, she greased her lobes with ointment.

"It's important to keep your lobes lubricated and pull the string every day to keep your holes open, or else your earlobes will start to heal and the thread will grow right into your skin." Etta advised.

"When can I put earrings in?"

"You won't be able to wear earrings for a couple weeks. First, you gotta make sure your holes stay open without the string. Just keep em lubricated, and keep pulling those strings, you'll be in earrings before you know it."

With each passing day, Tulah and Etta's relationship budded into a blossoming comradeship. Tulah felt good having developed a friendship with Etta after all the years of bitterness and old resentments. Having relaxed and easy conversation with her sure felt better than the strained and forced effort she had practiced for so many years. Talking and laughing with Etta helped to pass time and made time away from Louis a little more bearable. He had been gone for three weeks already and Tulah heard from him only twice. Because he had not set up a permanent residence, she had to wait to hear from him. Louis drifted from one place to another urgently trying to find a place to call home. Within three weeks, he'd been to four different cities in Ohio looking for work. When nothing materialized, he continued further north until he reached Michigan, settling in Detroit. He took up residence at an apartment on the east side of Detroit, where rent was due at the end of every week. Now that he had an address, Tulah and the girls could write back to him. They wanted to know what was the city was like, if there were lots of people there, if jobs were plenteous, and when he would be sending for them.

Louis tried to answer all their questions and keep them updated on his progress each time he wrote. He told Tulah that he was going to see about a job with an automotive company and to keep her fingers crossed, because if he gets this job, he would make enough to get them a place of their own and could save enough to send for them real soon. Before he closed his letter, he asked Tulah to ask his momma about getting a telephone. That way, they could talk when ever they wanted. However, the real reason he wanted a phone, although he would never mention it to Tulah, was that he had a difficult time understanding her writing, and many times couldn't even finish her letters.

Meanwhile, Kennedy's health continued to decline. He would have hallucinations and random outbursts. He'd developed bronchitis and his lungs were severly damaged. No one said anything, but they all knew that his health most likely would not be restored. Sarah always worried and in a few short weeks, had aged considerably. She was always cooking, cleaning, washing, baking, and gardening; anything that would help her to keep her mind off of Kennedy's failing health. Kennedy's illness took its toll on the entire family in ways more detrimental than anyone imagined. Sarah lost weight and became forgetful, always misplacing things and repeating herself. Henry started drinking and stayed gone most of the day. Etta found consolation in food, constantly eating to calm her nerves, and their two boys were always in the streets getting into things they had no business. When Louis would write asking how everyone was doing, Tulah would tell him that everything was just fine. She didn't want to alarm him by telling that his family was falling apart and that his father was slowy dying, therefore, she told him that all was well.

Ten weeks after Louis left, Kennedy died at home in his bed with Sarah right by his side. It was a cold and rainy afternoon and the family sat quietly in the living room waiting for the coroner to come and take Kennedy's remains. Irony would have it that the place where Kennedy worked for so many years, preparing the deceaced for their burial, would come to do the same for him. Henry had been gone the entire day and no one knew where to find him. Sarah sat solemnly on the sofa, broken in spirit, tired in body, troubled in mind, yet relieved that Kennedy no longer had to endure the pain and suffering caused by his illness.

"Tulah, you're going to have to contact Louis. Let him know that his Daddy is gone on to rest, and he needs to be getting back here as soon as he can." Sarah said, in a small, strained voice. She tried to keep her composure by being rigid and direct, but her voice betrayed her, revealing the broken syncopation in her cadence. "Etta, I know you do the best you can, but I want you to keep your boys in check, at least until this is over. Get a handle on them running these streets and getting into trouble. Tell them to do it out of respect for their grandfather if nothing else."

"Yes ma'am."

Tulah's heart skipped a beat at the thought of writing to Louis, and telling him that his father was dead. She had misled him, telling him that he was fine, and now she would have to face her worse fears and tell him that Kennedy is gone. Lucille came and put her arms around Tulah's neck.

"Don't be sad mommy."

Tulah looked into the sweet and innocent face of Lucille and smiled, embracing her, she drew strength from her ingenuous concern. Suddenly there was a loud thump that came from the porch. Everyone exchanged bewildered looks before jumping up and running to the door. Henry's two boys were sent to find him after Kennedy died. They found him at a local bar slumped over on the counter talking to the bar keep. When they delivered the news that his father had passed, he fell out of the chair on onto the floor writhing hysterically. His boys, embarrassed by his irratic behavior nervously exchanged looks before Joe ran out of the bar, leaving Josh alone to care for Henry. Leroy, the bartender, and some others in the bar helped Henry to his feet and asked Josh if he needed help getting him home. But before Josh could answer, Henry collected himself and said he could make it on his own. As soon as they left the bar, Henry drunk and distraught ran home and stumbled up the stairs.

"Mama! Tell me it aint so!" Henry cried.

Sarah stood to embrace him, but his knees buckled beneath him, falling to his knees, he wrapped his arms around Sarah's waist and cried.

Etta ran over to Henry, held him, rocked him and spoke gently in his ear, trying to calm him. Because of Henry's stature, Tulah always believed that he was the stronger of the two brothers. However, living in the same house with Henry for the last ten weeks, and watching how he conducted himself and his family from day to day, she learned that Louis was the strong one. Louis is enterprising and resourceful. He's a fighter, as was his father, always willing to try new things, and never give up.When adverse situations would arise, Louise would kick into high gear, and give it all he's got, working diligently to accomplish a desired goal. Henry, on the other hand is sensitive and easily discouraged. When he lost his job, he didn't have enough courage to tell Etta for fear of what she would do. When he lost his house, he moved his family into his parents' house, and has been there every since. When Kennedy got sick, he was too emotionally fragile to deal with it, so he comforted himself by drinking; and when his boys ran the streets and got into trouble, he yelled at them, but did'nt enforce any real discipline. Tulah respected Louis, but watching how Henry handled adversities as opposed to how Louis does, she reverenced him even more.

As Tulah observed Henry fall to the floor and cry like a baby, her heart ached at the thought of how Louis would take the news, knowing how deeply he cared for his father. Henry knelt on the floor crying, and his family crowded around him, embracing him and mourning the lost of their patriarch. Tulah stood back with tears falling heavily off the ends of her face, while her girls imulated the scene they witnessed by crowding around her and hugging her tightly. She never cared for Kennedy in the same way that the rest of the family did, however, she sympathized with them, being all too familiar with the pain they were experiencing. She gathered the girls and took them into her room leaving the rest of the family in the living room to grieve.

After several attempts, and many crumpled papers thrown carelessly to the floor, Tulah composed a carefully written letter to Louis, and sent it by express mail to ensure an expediant delivery. To her great surprise, when Louis responded, he said that he would not be at the funeral. He started a new job, and his boss told him that he could leave to attend the funeral, but couldn not guarantee that his job would be there when he returned. Louis did not get in with the automotive company as he had hoped, but landed a job in a steel factory that produced parts for the automotive company. The pay was not as good, but would sufficiently provide enough to secure a home and send for his family. Being so close to having enough, Louis could just not afford to lose this job. He vascilated many times before accepting the fact that there was absolutely nothing he could do at this juncture. He wanted to go home to see to his mother's comfort, but she said that she understood how important it is that he keeps his job and told him to stay and work so he can secure a home for his family.

Louis grieved of course, losing the greatest influence in his life and the person he admired most. He spent his entire life trying to imulate his father and achieve, despite the obstacles he had to face, the same accomplishments that his father had. However, he grieved mostly because he lost his best friend, and felt that his world would never be the same now that his father was gone. He wanted so badly to make his father proud. He worked so hard to make that happen, and had almost achieved it before things got bad. Louis felt good that they had a heart to heart before he left town and had made ammends concerning his decision about his wife. The only regret Louis had was that he was not there during the rough times and did not have a chance to say goodbye.

The day of the funeral came, and people from all walks of life came to pay their last respect. After the reverend delivered the ulogy about what a good, Christian, self-made man Kennedy was, they served dinner at the church. People who attended ranged from the mayor himself, to impoverished country folk, who Kennedy didn't know personally, but had serviced when they lost a loved one. It seemed as though every one who came in brought cakes, pies, home made rolls, fried chicken, greens, candied yams, ham, or potato salad. During rough times, black folks tend to comfort themselves with food. Bringing a food dish was a way to express feelings of compassion and support when finding the right words to say would escape them. Kennedy's funeral was the biggest social event that Tulah had ever seen in her life. She was dressed in an all black dress with silver buttons that fastened from behind, and wore a black hat with a veil that covered her eyes. She completed her ensemble with a pair of white gloves and a small pair of silver stud earrings that Etta lent her. Being one of Kennedy's daughter-in-laws, she was obligated to greet guests, smile, serve, and answer questions about where Louis was.

"Louis got a good job up in Detroit. He would've been here sept his boss need him so much. He's making real good money and will be sending for us real soon." She told all who asked. Cora grabbed her by the arm, pulled her to the side, to ask her why she was being so brash in the way she responded to the guest.

"Girl, what is wrong witchu talking to these folks lak dat? Dees some important, rich folk, you caint be talkin to dem lak dat."

"I'm sick a people askin me bout ma business."

"Tulah, dey just asking. Course they wanna know where Louis is. Dat's a understandable question seein dat his Daddy just died."

"Yeah I know it is. I'm just sicka feeling lak I gotta explain to people bout where he is and why he aint here." Tulah adjusted Jessie on her slender hip and continued. "I just don't understand Louis, him and his Daddy had a good relationship. If mine was like there's…" She stopped and fidgeted with the laces on Jessie's pink dress. Cora studied Tulah, noticing a sadness she had never seen before. She was careful not to interrupt.

"Go on. If yorn was like dere's what?"

I wouldn't let nobody stop me from coming." Tulah confided. She stared out of the window contemplatively, wishing she could have experienced the same with her father. She noticed how dark and gloomy it was outside, indicative of her sullen mood. Realizing she had exposed a vulnerable side, she snapped back.

"You know maybe I should just make an announcement, dat way everybody could just stop asking."

"Tulah, if you love your husband like you say you do, then you gone hafta represent him properly. Show yourself as a good wife. You know how Louis is, and you his wife, do thangs like you know he would want."

"Yes ma'am." Tulah acquiesced.

"Here, hand me da baby and you go an see if Sarah can use a hand in da kitchen."

Tulah handed Jessie to Cora and made her way into the kitchen. She came in on the tail end of a conversation that Sarah had all her guests engaged in. She told of how Kennedy had taken Henry and Louis to the lake to teach them to swim. Henry was six, and Louis was only four. It was a beautiful summer's day and Sarah was sitting on the beach watching Kennedy and the boys splash about, playing in the water. Louis was sitting in the middle of an old tire that was being used as a life preserver, while Kennedy practiced the breast stroke with Henry. A group of teen aged boys came along and dove into the water splashing water in Louis' face and knocking him off of the rubber tire. When Louis jumped, the tire flipped over and he fell into the water. Kennedy was keeping Henry afloat by supporting him with his arms underneath his torso while he practiced his strokes. When he saw Louis' tire flip over, and his young son going under the water he panicked. He dropped Henry to run to Louis' aid, and then realizing that he had dropped Henry in the water, he dropped Louis to run to Henry's aid. Sarah stood on the side screaming to Kennedy to get her baby, and when he did, she would scream for him to get Henry. The small crowd that gathered around Sarah laughed and gasped in horror as she gave the details of the panicked situation.

"What happened next?" One man asked. "One of the boys who started all of the commotion caught on to what was happening and went in after Henry while Kennedy rescued Louis."

"Why didn't you jump in to save em?" Another asked. "I didn't know how to swim. If I had jumped in Kennedy would have lost us all." She laughed. "It was the most terrifying ten seconds of my life." She told them.

"That's how I wanna remember Kennedy." One of his friends said solemnly. "Laughing and enjoying his boys. I don't want to remember him like he was a few weeks ago." The man said referring to the violent outburst Kennedy had when he came to visit him. He cut his visit short and told Sarah that he understood, but clearly the visit had unnerved him.

"Yes, I know. His boys were the joy of his life." Sarah said reminiscently.

"And so were you." Another guest added.

"Thank you Johnny Mae. That's sweet of you to say."

"I'm not trying to be sweet, I'm being honest. Kennedy was able to make it as far as he did because of you. You always loved him and supported him no matter what he decided to do. I remember when yall first got married and he wanted to be a mechanic. You remember that?"

Thinking back on the early days of their marriage, Sarah became full of emotion and couldn't answer for fear of crying, so she nodded to avoid speaking and letting her feelings escape.

"Kennedy was always trying something new, and Sarah you stood by him and believed in him and wouldn't let him give up. You'll never know how much that meant to him. He loved you so much, and the reason he was able to be as successful as he was, is because of you."

Sarah nodded again, but was suddenly overcome by the earthshattering realization that Kennedy was no more. It pierced her heart and released an emotional tidal wave of fear and pain that gripped her soul, causing her to writhe and shake while tears streamed down her face. The ingenuous remarks made by their good friend Johnny Mae, opened a wound in Sarahs heart that she knew she would never be able to heal. Johnny Mae reached out and held Sarah and rubbed her back while she cried. Listening in on the conversation helped Tulah to understand what is expected of her as Louis' wife. She was now able to comprehend that being a wife was more than cooking, cleaning and supplying plenty of good loving, but to also encourage, nurture, support and trust. However, trust stood out more than anything else. She felt bad that she was so stern to the guests when they inquired of Louis' whereabouts, but from here on out , she intended to make up for her short comings and be the best wife that Louis could ever have.

Chapter 18

Early one crisp September morning, Tulah, Gracie, Lucille, and Jessie boarded a lackluster Greyhound bus northward bound for the city of Detroit. Tulah choked from inhaling thick plumes of carbon monoxide that was emitted from the bus' exhaust. She covered her nose and mouth with a hanky as she boarded the bus and situated the girls in their seats. After getting them settled, she looked out of the window and waved goodbye to a teary eyed Sarah, who was accompanied by Henry, Etta and their children. Tulah was elated at the thought of going to a big city like Detroit, but she was also fearful because she was leaving the only home she'd ever known. Gracie now 5, Lucille 4, and Jessie only a year old, was headed for a new life and a new home, but for Tulah is was a whole new world. As the bus started out, the big engine hummed as the bus sputtered and jerked before down shifting into a steady pace.

Starting out on the road, they were amazed by the mountains that peaked way into the heavens and the trees that surrounded the two-laned highway. Cars on the other side of the road whizzed by them with a sound that crescendoed then fell as they disappeared down the road. Gracie and Lucille were thrilled by the experience of riding on the large bus with a picture of a dog plastered on the side. They looked out of the window in awe and pointed and waved to every vehicle they passed. After they grew tired of that, they entertained themselves by keeping company with the other passengers. Lucille peeked over her chair then ducked down, in a one-sided game of peek-a-boo with an elderly woman who sat behind them, while Gracie colored in her picture book. Tulah sat across the isle holding Jessie on her lap, thrilled and excited and looking forward to living in the big city.

Moving along the highway she watched the sun climb high into the sky, feeding the earth and its inhabitants with life and energy, then slowly slide to the west, creating shadows that grew and shrunk as the bus traversed along the side of the road. Tulah became sleepy, partly from the steady hum of the bus' engine droning constantly in her ears, and partly from waking early that morning to prepare for her trip. She looked over at the girls who were now sound asleep, Lucille resting her head on Gracie's small shoulder. Tulah reached into ther bag and pulled out a pen and paper to make a list of things she wanted to do when she made it to Detroit. First on the list was to go back to school. She knew that if she wanted her girls to finish school and get a college education that she had to at least have a high school diploma. Louis was already educated and she didn't want her girls to think more highly of him because of it. Next on the list was to become a better wife to Louis, even if that meant finding a job so he didn't have to work as hard.

She laid her head back against the seat, closed her eyes and drifted off to sleep. Tulah shifted in her seat to find a comfortable position, after which, she started to dream. She dreamed that she had arrived in Detroit, and everything was shiny, new and clean. The trees and the grass were clean and well kept, and the sheen that emmited from it was so bright, she had to place her hand above her brow to deflect the glare. There was a row of tiny white houses neatly allligned on either side of the street. The people there were finely dressed in fancy clothes and matching hats and smiled and waved, welcoming her to Detroit. Louis took her by the hand, led her to a big house and handed her a shiny, gold key. She walked up the stairs and right up to the front door to try and open it, only the key didn't fit. She became frustrated and threw the key to the ground shattering it in thousands of pieces.

Tulah was awakened by the hissing of the brakes screeching to a stop and the driver announcing that they had arrived. She woke the girls and took inventory of their things before gathering them to leave. She led them from the back of the bus towards the exiting doors. Looking out of the window and spotted Louis standing by the bus terminal talking to a slick-headed gentleman.

She felt a surge rip down the center of her spine catching just a glance at her beloved.

"There's yo Daddy!" She said excitedly.

"Where, where?" Gracie asked.

"Come on, hold yo sista's hand." Tulah told her as she headed for the door.

"Wait mommy, you're going too fast." Tulah ran down the bus stairs and bolted out of the doors.

"Louis, Louis, over here!"

"Hey baby, you made it." Louis ran over to the bus, wrapped his arms around her waist and kissed her longingly. He took Jessie from Tulah, holding her in one arm, he reached down and picked Gracie and Lucille up in the other. Holding all three girls in his arms he bounced them up and down, kissed them and told them how much he missed them.

"Where are your bags, Tulah?"

"Dey on the bus in da back. Dey wouldn't let me keep em in wit me. It wussn't dat much room."

"Well let's get em so we can get outta here."

"So dis is da city? Louis, how you likin' it up here?"

"I'm gone like it much better now that my family's here with me. Come on baby, I want you to meet a friend of mine." Louis told her leading her to a tall, thin, dark skinned, chain-smoking man. "This is Martin Walker, he's one of my co-worker's and a real good friend. Martin's gone give us a lift home. Martin, this here is my wife Tulah and my baby girls. This is Gracie, Lucille and this little sleepy one is Jessie." Louis said introducing Martin to his family. Tulah tentatively reached out her hand to Martin and he grabbed it and lifted it to his mouth.

"My pleasure." He said, before kissing Tulah's hand.

"Don't get fresh with my wife, man, stay cool." Louis told him.

"Oh man, I'm just happy to finally meet her. I'm not gone try nothing with your wife, Louis. You my main man." Then tipping his hat he told Tulah, "Forgive me if I come across too forward. I don't mean to offend you."

"Dat's okay." Tulah told him.

"Come on man, let's get them out of the cold." Louis added.

"Right this way." Martin said leading the way to his car. Louis piled the girls in the back and stepped aside to let Tulah in. When she sat down he handed Jessie to her and shut the door. He took a seat in the front with Martin and they took off.

"Baby, I know it's dark, but I told Martin to give you the scenic route."

"What dat mean?" Tulah asked, offended that she was in the back and Louis was up front with Martin.

"I told him to drive the way you can see some of the pretty sites."

"We got a long way to drive?"

"No, not too far. Why, what's wrong?"

"Nothing's wrong, sept I gotta pee."

"Well we'll just go home, I can take you out tomorrow after I get home from work. It's a lot of pretty places I know you gone like."

Tulah looked out of the window into the streets of the city. The most obvious difference from the city and the country were the lights. There were lights everywhere, and it lit up the night making it as visible as in the day. There were lots of cars out on the streets, and the streets were all paved. No dirt roads anywhere and the houses were all lined up in a row on either side of the street, unlike the houses in Marietta where there were lots of space between one house to the next. Tulah was elated to be there, but was even more excited about seeing Louis. There was so much she wanted to say to him. She wanted to be next to him, snuggle up under him and breathe in deeply to get the smell of his aftershave that she loved so much. She wanted to tell him about Henry's drinking, and his boy's running the streets getting into trouble. She wanted to tell him that his Mama needs to be checked on periodically because she had lost so much weight and couldn't sit still. But she opted to wait until they were in the privacy of there own home, where she could express her thoughts and feelings without Martin being there.

They pulled up to a house that was made of red brick and had two doors in the front of the house and two porches, one down and a smaller up top.

"This is it. This is home, Tulah."

"What kind of house is this?" Tulah asked stretching her neck out of the window to get a better look.

"I know it's different from the houses back home. It's a two family house."

"Two family?"

"Yeah, that means that two familys can live in it, but with separate quarters."

Martin laughed.

"What's funny?" Louis asked him.

"You got yo'self a certified bunkin." He said laughing again.

"It's just different from the houses back home. Of course she wants to know, because we didn't have houses like this." Louis defended.

"Who is he calling a bunkin?"

"I guess I'm getting off to a bad start with your wife, man." Turning to face Tulah he offered an explaination for his brashness.

"I know you don't know me, but that's just my sense of humor. Not everybody can appreciate it. I just take some getting used to. Louis'll tell you. Tell her, man."

"It's okay baby, he don't mean nothing by it."

Tulah turned her attention back to the house and inspected how tall it was.

"It shole is big."

"I know, that's because one family lives up and the other lives down."

"You mean dey stacked on toppa each other?"

"Yeah, I guess you can say that."

"Ooh wee, I caint wait to see what it look like on da inside. Which one we live in, upstairs or down?"

"We live upstairs."

"Is dat our porch?" Tulah asked, referring to the little porch on top.

"Yup, shole is. Come on let's go inside."

Tulah walked up to the house and noticed that besides two doors, the face of the house also had two addresses and two mail boxes. Louis retrieved the key and opened the door which led to a narrow hallway with a tall flight of stairs. The walls were a dingy yellow, and grimy from what looked like years of greasy and dirty hands touching the walls. The stairs were hard wood, soiled and scuffed from people dragging furniture over the once smooth surface. There was a light bulb at the top of the stairs that offered light to the constricted, little hallway. Broken glass could be heard crunching under their feet as they walked up the stairs onto the landing. Tulah looked at Louis and he explained that there was a once a globe that hung in the place of the light bulb, but that he broke it while changing the bulb.

When they reached the top of the stairs, Louis opened another door that led to the living room. It was a small 10 x 13 foot room with a large window on one side that covered most of the wall. There was no furniture in the empty room, only boxes filled with camera equipment, old photos, and some filled with clothes. There were two brown doors almost side by side that was painted dark brown with a glossy finish. One door opened to a small closet, and the other led to the porch that over looked the entire neighborhood. There was a smaller room off of the living room which was just enough room for a small table and four chairs. In the tiny kitchen, there was one window and the walls were painted a pale blue; it was just enough room to accommodate for a stove and small refrigerator. There were two small bedrooms and a tiny bathroom. Louis walked to the back room where a mattress was laid out on a floor with a sheet stretched over it.

"I know it's not much, but it's a start. This is the girl's room."

"How they gone all fit on one mattress?"

"We can make a pallet on the floor with some blankets for Gracie, and let the babies sleep on the mattress."

"We got enough blanket to make it feel soft?"

"I don't know, we just gone have to use what we got."

Martin dragged the rest of Tulah's bags inside and yelled to them from the living room.

"Aye Louis! You all set, man?" Louis put up one finger to Tulah and asked her to give him a minute.

"Yeah man, thanks. I appreciate you." He told him, reaching in his pocket to retrieve a small wad of cash and handing Martin a few bills. Martin accepted the cash, stuffed them in his pocket and shook Louis' hand.

"Tulah, it was nice meeting you." He yelled loud enough for her to hear him from the other room. Tulah walked in the room holding Jessie.

"Nice ta meet you too. Thanks for the lift."

"Anytime." He told her before leaving. Louis walked back down stairs with Martin to see him out and to lock the door on the front of the house. He ran back up the stairs to Tulah waiting for him at the top of the landing. She had laid Jessie on the down, so when Louis came in she wrapped her arms around his neck and squeezed him tight.

"I missed you so much." She whispered in his ear. He responded by kissing her.

"Are the girls sleep?"

"Not yet, I don't think. But I caint wait, Louis."

"Hold on." He told her, tipping back in the room to peek in at the girls. They were sleeping soundly, tuckered out from the long bus ride.

"Come here." He said taking her hand and leading her to the other room. The room had a mattress and box spring that set on a metal frame. Louis pulled her in and gently closed the door. He backed her onto the bed and began to seductively undress her.

Louis was up early the next morning. He had to be at work by seven o'clock, and was running late from a long night of catching up with Tulah. Tulah awakened to Louis frantically rushing around the room trying to get dressed.

"Mornin' baby, I didn't mean to wake you. I'm running late. Food's in the fridge, and I left you a couple of dollars in the kitchen on the counter." He walked over and kissed her on the lips. "I'll see you when I get in this evening."

"How long you gone be gone?"

"I'm off at four thirty. I'll see you this evening." He said, rushing out the door still buttoning his shirt.

Tulah lay in bed looking around the room. Then remembering she was in the city, she jumped out of bed and ran to the living room. She ran to the door that led to the front porch and opened it. Tentivlely, she walked out on the porch to get a better look at the view that the porch offered in the light of day. She walked over to the railing and looked down, making mental note to never let the girls play out on the porch. Tulah crossed her arms and rubbed them with her hands trying to warm herself from the morning breeze, causing chill bumps to rise on her cool skin. The high-spirited, little country girl had finally made it to the big city. Looking down at the neighborhood, she saw people hurrying about. One lady wearing a red coat and hat looked up at her and waved. Tulah waved back and smiled.

"You made it huh?" She yelled up at her.

Tulah looked around before answering, "You talking ta me?"

"Yeah, I'm Mabelle. Me and my husband Earl live right over here." She said ponting to a large brick house with brown shutters. "We been looking after your husband for you. I couldn't hardly wait for you to come, I've been waiting to meet you." She shouted.

"Oh, thank you Mabelle, I'm Tulah."

"I know, sweetie. I gotta get to work, but we'll be over later. Good to meet you." She said waving again before walking briskly down the street. Tulah stood out on the porch watching Mabelle walk away until she turned the corner.

"Mommy, where's Daddy?" Tulah turned to see Gracie standing at the threshold rubbing her eyes.

"He's gone to work baby. Go on back in. I don't want you out here, you here me?" Gracie nodded and went back inside. Tulah took another quick look at the neighborhood before going back inside the house. Shutting the door, she surveyed the room trying to decipher what she could do to make the tiny flat look and feel more like home.

"I'm hungry." Gracie told Tulah. "I know. Let's go in here and see what we got." Tulah walked into the kitchen opened the fridge to find a bottle of milk, a carton of eggs, and a few slices of bologna wrapped in white paper. Tulah fried the bologna in a large, cast-iron skillet, and scrambled eggs from the grease left in the pan from the bologna. After feeding the girls, she made Gracie help her unpack their luggage and clean the house, while Lucille looked after Jessie. By eleven o'clock, the entire house was clean, the bed was made, the clothes were all put away, all of Louis' shirts were ironed, and the boxes were stacked neatly on one side of the room. By noon, the girls were bathed, their hair was combed, and Tulah was bored and restless. There was nothing else for her to do. She went over to the door cracked it open and looked down on the street. On the corner she saw a tall pole with a blue sign at the top of it. She leaned over the banister trying to read what it said, 'St. Albertis' was spelled out in large, white letters, on a blue background.

"I guess that's the name of the street we live on." Gracie walked over to Tulah and asked,

"What cha doin Mama?"

"Come here." She told her, grabbing her hand and pulling her out on the porch. "Look out here. See all these houses? You ain't never seen nothing like dis down south."

Gracie stood on the tip of her toes looking over the rail and at the houses all lined up in a row.

"It's somethin' ain't it?" Gracie didn't answer, busy looking at all the houses on the block. "It's gotta be twenty houses on dis block. And look at how big dey is."

"Want me to count em, Mama?"

"Naw baby, you ain't gotta count em, we'll get a better look at em when yo Daddy get here." Tulah looked at Gracie and saw how amazed and curious she was by their new surroundings. "I'm letting you out here now cuz you wit me, but I don't want you out here by yo'self. It could be dangerous, and if you fall, you might die. Understand?"

"Yes mommy."

"Come on, let's go back in. Where's Lucille and Jessie?"

"In the room sleeping."

"Well you need ta go lie down too. I'm sleepy myself, I think I might go and take a nap."

"Can I come in your room and lie down with you."

"Alright, come on."

Chapter 19

When Louis got home, he found Tulah and Gracie sleeping in one room, while the Lucille and Jessie slept in the other room on a mattress. He walked over and rubbed his hand along Tulah's hip and gently shook her. She rolled over and looked up at him, a smile spreading across her face.

"What time is it?" She whispered.

"Five o'clock."

"Ooh, I gotta get up, dees girls gone be hungry when dey wake up."

"Don't worry about that, we've been invited to dinner."

"Wit who?"

"With Mabelle and Earl. She told me she met you this morning."

"Oh yeah, I saw her when I was standing out on da porch dis morning. The one live downa street?"

"That's the one. She wants us to come to dinner. She insists that we come to dinner."

"All of us?"

"Yeah, she wants to meet you all."

"She work?" Tulah asked sitting up, scratching her head.

"Yeah. Why?"

"She was shole in a hurry dis morning, saying she got to get ta work. I wonder where she work at. You know?"

"No, I sure don't."

"Dey got enough work up north fa womens to work?"

"I guess some places do. Come on let's get the girls ready."

"Okay, but Louis what kind a work do you do at the steel factory?"

"I have to melt steel down and mold it into car parts."

"You have ta melt steel?"

"Um hum. It's gets hot in there too. Temperatures get over 120 degrees."

"120 degrees? My Lord, Louis. Dey give you plenty of cold water ta drink?" Louis chuckled a bit before answering. "I wish. People get so hot in there they pass out from the heat. They give you lots of breaks though, but no cold water."

Louis, Tulah and the girls walked a few houses down before reaching Earl and Mabelle's place. They stayed in the bottom flat of their two family house. When they reached the front door Tulah could smell fish frying and hear loud music playing. She looked apprehensively at Louis and he winked at her and smiled, assuring her that it was okay. Voices could be heard yelling back and forth at each other before the large wooden door swung open.

"Hey, they're here! Come on in yall and make yo'self at home."

Louis held the door open for Tulah and the girls as he followed right behind them.

"Hi Mabelle, thanks for having us over." Tulah told her.

"You welcome, baby. Now introduce me to these pretty little girls."

"This is Gracie, our oldest." Louis chimed in, touching each child on the top of the head as he introduced them. "This is Lucille, and this little one is Jessie."

"Well, aint that something? All girls, huh?"

"Yes ma'am." Tulah answered.

"Yes ma'am? Girl, who you talking to? Save the ma'ams for the mammys. You can call me Mabelle." She answered, laughing. "Come on in and have a seat. Louis you got yo'self a nice family, and your wife is so pretty and petite."

Tulah took a seat on the sofa with Jessie on her lap while the other girls sat next to her.

"Yall gone hafta excuse me. I'm gone finish up in the kitchen, dinner will be ready shortly."

Mabelle walked out of the room, heading back into the kitchen. Tulah watched her as she turned and walked away noticing her large backside that swayed from side to side with each step. Mabelle isn't a fat woman, as much as she is big boned.

She has a fair complexion, and stood about 5'4, with thick arms, stout legs, and the biggest backside on this side of the Mason Dixon line. She has a pretty round face surrounded by locks of curly brown hair. She talked loud and laughed a lot, frequently making jokes and laughing at them, many times when no one else found them funny. Beads of perspiration would form on the bridge of her nose that she constantly wiped away with the palm of her hand. From just the brief introduction, Tulah could tell that Mabelle was different from any other woman that she had known before. Earl came in to meet Tulah and was surprisingly quite the opposite of Mabelle. Where she was boisterous and brash, he was soft spoken and placid. Where she gregarious, he was reserved, offering only a lighthearted chuckle, and where she was big boned, he was small-framed and wirey. The only similarity they had was that they both stood at about the same height.

Mabelle prepared a dinner of fried catfish, French fries and cole slaw. She had soda pop for the girls, and served cheap red wine to the adults. Tulah had never had wine before and didn't care for the taste, but she didn't want to appear rude or unappreciative, so she gulped it down quickly to get it over with. It left a bitter taste in her mouth that became keener when she burped. When Mabelle noticed her glass was empty, she politely refilled her glass. Unbeknownst to Tulah, the fatique she thought she was feeling from being tired was actually a buzz from the wine. Louis also had a glass, but sipped his slowly while smoking a cigarette. After they finished dinner, Tulah was ready to go home."I think we need to get going, Louis. It's getting late and I need ta get da girls in the bed."

"It ain't late!" Mabelle butted in. "It's only seven thirty."

"I know, but dats late fa us. We used ta gettin ready fa bed by dis time."

"Girl, you aint in the county no more. You in the city, and we be just getting started dis time a night. Ain't that right, Earl?"

"She said she gotta go, Mabelle. She gotta get her kids to bed." He responded.

"Well, I guess I ain't think about it since I aint got no kids. But seven thirty is late? Humph. You can take the girl out the county, but you can't take the county out the girl." Mabelle said, laughing at her own quip.

"Be nice, Mabelle." Louis told her.

"I am being nice. I like your wife. Why you think I'm trying to get her to stay?"

"Well, she's here now, and we aint going nowhere."

"That's right, we here na, and I like you too, Mabelle. Thanks fa havin us over. Everything was delicious."

"You welcome, baby. Now listen. I want yall back here Friday night. I'll cook dinner and we can play some cards. You ever play bid whiz, Tulah?"

"No."

"Alright then, it's settled. Back here Friday night."

"Alright Mabelle, you got it. Let me get my family home. Thanks again." Louis told her then turning to shake Earl's hand.

As they walked home, Gracie ran ahead of them and Lucille followed.

"Hey, slow down! Where are you going?"

"I know the way home, Daddy. It's four houses away."

"Alright, but be careful."

Tulah dragged along leaning against Louis and laying her head on his shoulder.

"I don't know why I feel so sleepy after taking dat long nap earlier today."

"You're not sleepy, you're tipsy." He told her.

"I'm what?"

"Tipsy. From the wine. I saw you gulping it down. That's why you feel like that. You're supposed to sip it slowly."

"You mean I done got drunk?"

"I didn't say drunk, but you might be a little high."

"I was trying to drank it down fast ta get it over wit, like you know how you do with castor oil?"

"Well, that wasn't castor oil. And the reason you feel like that is because it went straight to your head."

"Why did'nt you tell me I'm supposed to drink it slow?"

"I am telling you. I wasn't going to say nothing in front of them. But it's okay, because now you know what it feels like to have a buzz. Just as long as you do it when you're with me, so just enjoy it."

"Enjoy feelin like I'm movin in slow motion and sleepy? No thanks."

"That's the reason people drink, to mellow you out, slow you down, you know like after a hard day."

"Well yo brother done seen a lot a hard days, cause he don't just get mellow, he get stone cold drunk." Tulah blurted out without thinking. Then realizing what she said, she stopped, put her hand over her mouth, and then bursted out laughing. She caught herself and tried to be serious, attempting an apology to Louis, but before she could get through it she started laughing again. Louis stood there looking at her, piecing together what he had just been told. He wasn't upset with Tulah, he understood her behavior, but what had him concerned is what he had just learned about his brother. He looked her square in the face hoping that his seriousness would sober her, but when Tulah saw that Louis was making an effort to look stern, she laughed even harder. She was angry with herself for her uncouth remark and outlandish behavior, but she didn't seem to have any control. She felt numb, but tingly and warm at the same time. Everytime she tried to calm herself and hold back her laugh, it would grow bigger with uncontrollable exuberance, forcing its way out. Her sides ached and her head spinned. Louis shook his head and walked away leaving Tulah standing there laughing. Gracie and Lucille ran back hearing their mother laughing hysterically.

"What's so funny, Daddy? Why is mommy laughing so much?"

"She just remembered a funny joke."

"What is it? Tell me the joke so I can laugh."

"It's a grown up joke, little kids wouldn't understand. Go on and help mommy home, go grab her hand." Louis told Gracie. "Mommy what's so funny?" Lucille asked. "Nothin baby, mommy got a big mouth." Tulah answered still laughing. "Louis, Louis, wait for me." Tulah yelled after him. Louis continued walking away from her, up the stairs and into the house. He turned the lights on so Tulah could find her way up the stairs safely, and went and laid Jessie down in the back room. He went back to the stairs to make sure Tulah and the girls made it in.

"Okay girls, go and get dressed for bed, I'll take care of mommy."

"We need our bath." Gracie told him.

"You'll get it in the morning, go on and do like I say now, go ahead."

Gracie obediently took Lucille by the hand and led her to the back room. Tulah came in and stood against the wall. She looked at Louis and smiled.

"You mad at me, Louis?"

"No, I'm not mad. You just don't need to drink wine."

"I know, an I'm sorry. I wanted ta tell you about Henry, but not like this. Just please don't be mad at me, I can't take it when you mad at me."

"I'm not mad, Tulah. I'm disappointed is all."

"I know, Louis, but I'm sorry."

"No baby, not at you. I'm disappointed in Henry. I was hoping he could stay strong and hold the family together, not get drunk."

"He just weak, Louis. He ain't lak you. I been watchin ha he handle thangs and he let thangs gets to be too much for him. He caint take much."

"How you mean?"

"When yo Daddy got sick, he couldn't take it. He couldn't even look at him fo tears wellin up in his eyes. He was hurtin real bad and didn't know ha to deal wit it, so he started drinkin, and Louis he was drinkin a lot."

"How's Mama doin?"

"She was goin though a rough time too. She just kept sayin she lost her best friend. She kept moving around, couldn't keep still. She lost a lot a weight too; we couldn't get her to eat nothing."

Louis put both his hand on his head and slid them to the back.

"I shoulda been there." He said shakin his head.

"Wasn't nothing you coulda did, Louis. Me and Etta got to be friends and we did all we could to keep thangs goin round there. Henry just couldn't take it, I don't thank he woulda did no betta if you was there. We did help yo Mama though, and she was happy she had us to get her through it."

Louis balled his fist and hit it against the palm of his hand. "I shoulda been there."

"Louis, I'm sorry."

"I'm goin to bed." He said walking away.

As they lay in bed Tulah tried to comfort Louis. She held him in her arms and rocked him back and forth while rubbing his head. Louis was unresponsive, and gently, subtely pulled away.

"I love you Louis, and when you hurt, I hurt. Please let me take care of you."

"I love you too, Tulah. It's just that I never let myself grieve, you know? When I heard about Daddy I just kept working, staying busy, hoping the hurt would go away, but hearing about Henry and Mama tonight stirred up old wounds I been tryin to keep closed."

"Its cuz a ma big mouth, ain't it?"

"Naw Tulah, it's just something that gotta come out."

"Well, you know God works all thangs out." She said, hoping that her words would sooth him. Tulah knew how much Louis loved God, and had heard people repeat that phrase over and over again at the funeral. She was trying to say something clever and comforting, but to her surprise, when she said it, Louis turned cold, jerking away from her and stiffening.

"What's wrong witchu?"

"I don't wanna hear nothinn about God. You hear me?"

"Whachu talking about, Louis?"

"I don't wanna hear nothing about God. God don't care about me or you."

"Louis, don't say that."

"It's true. I been praying to God all my life, trusting in him, believing in him, and everytime God let me down. First, my shop closed down. Do you know how long and hard I worked for that? I prayed everyday asking God to help me get it and keep it, and Tulah, you'll never know how bad it hurt when I had to close the doors to that studio. I spent my whole life's savings trying to keep that studio going, and what I didn't lose at the studio I lost at the bank when they closed their doors."

"Oh baby." Tulah answered sympathetically.

"Naw, it's okay. I've moved past it. But after I got through that, we had to move back to the house Mama Lou left you. I had no pride as a man moving back into that house, Tulah. I know it was free, but it left me with no pride. Then the turkey business failed, my Daddy died and I didn't even have enough money to go back home and see him put to rest. God don't care about me, because if he did he wouldn't let me, a man who always tried to do the right thing, and put him first, suffer like I have."

Tulah didn't know or care that much about religion, God, or Christianity, but she hated seeing Louis' faith fail. She admired the relationship he shared with God and loved that he spoke about God like they were two old friends. Although she didn't have a personal relationship with God, she felt comforted knowing that Louis did- like she would have special favors of some kind with God because of him. But now that he was speaking so indifferently about God, it frightened her.

"I know you hurtin baby, but do you thank that is God responsible for this? All the thangs you been through, do you think God is deliberate and doing this to be mean?" Louis took his time before answering, and when he did he remained fixed in his opinion.

"Maybe not to be mean, but he shole aint making much effort to be nice either."

"I don't like hearing you talk like dat, Louis."

"Well, get used to it."

"Ever since I been knowin you all you talk about is trustin God, doing the right thang and believin' on him. And now dat I be tryin ta do like you say, here you go changing on me."

"It's just the way thangs are, Tulah. Ain't nothing out here free, we gotta work hard and make it for ourselves."

"Well, that's what I been sayin all along, then you told me how wrong I was."

"You wasn't the one wrong, Tulah. I was."

Louis turned over and pulled the covers up over his shoulders, and tossed a goodnight at Tulah. But she was persistent, trying to make Louis open up to her.

"Louis don't say dat. You was right about God all along. It was me who didn't know."

"Goodnight Tulah." He said with finality, shortly after, Louis was snoring.

Chapter 20

The next morning when Louis got up and left for work, Tulah got the girls dressed and left the house to get Gracie registered for school. The local school, Campbell Elementary, was just a few blocks up the street, but walking with two little girls and carrying one on her hip was a cumbersome job for Tulah. She was apprehensive to have to go to the school and get Gracie registered by herself, because she did'nt know what would be expected of her, and it made her feel nervous. Outside the school, small school-aged childred cried and laughed, ran and skipped, offered greetings and said goodbyes while bustling parents strived to get them there on time. Once Tulah arrived, she walked in looking all around the large building with tall ceilings and shiny floors. There were colorful pictures painted on the walls and lots of white people standing around who would smile and nod as she passed by. She walked up to one of them and told them that she was there to get her daughter registered for school, and she told Tulah she would be happy to help.

Once Gracie was all registered and placed in a classroom, Tulah gave her a big hug, told her to be on her best behavior before leaving her in the care of her new teacher. Gracie was excited to be going to school; she sat down at a table and immediately started a conversation with a little girl who sat at her table. Tulah was uncomfortable leaving Gracie at school all day, but watching her interact with the other child made Tulah feel at ease. Lucille, however, was a different story. She was upset when it came time to leave her sister at school. She cried and fell out on the floor saying that they couldn't leave without Gracie.

Everytime Tulah tried to pull Lucille up from the floor, she would stiffen her body to resist her and cry even louder. A short, stout white man wearing a navy blue suit came over to see what the commotion was about. He had a smug look on his face and was obviously agitated by Lucille's behavior.

"What's seems to be the problem?" He asked in an upight voice.

"She just upset dat she gotta leave her sista at school. Dey used to being together all day."

The man nodded in understanding, then bent down to get closer to Lucille.

"You've got to stop with all that noise, do you understand me? There are other children that are here to learn, and you're disrupting them with all that crying."

Lucille stopped crying and looked at the strange man who reprimanded her. Understanding that she was being scolded, she started crying again, this time because her feelings were hurt. He looked at Tulah and became even more agitated.

"Okay, that's enough. You shut your mouth right now or you'll be sorry."

"Uhn uhn, wait a minute. You aint gone talk ta her lak dat. You don't tell ma baby ta shut up. Me or her Daddy don't talk ta her lak dat and you aint gone do it neither. I don't know who you thank you is talking ta somebody lak dat. She a little girl."

"Okay ma'am." The man answered nervously. "That's fine."

"Don't you tell me it's fine. It ain't fine when you thank you can talk ta a little girl lak dat. I betchu don't talk to da white kids lak dat."

"Ma'am I'm going to have to ask you to leave."

"You ain't gotta ask me ta leave, I was leaving anyway till you came buttin in my business."

As Tulah's voice escalated, people who were in the front office came out to see what all the noise was about. The principle came out of his office and asked what was going on.

"Mr. Philborn, what's going on out here?"

"I was just asking her to leave." Mr. Philborn answered, but that only angered Tulah more.

"I'll tell you what's goin on. My daughter is upset cause she hafta leave her sista, so he gone come out here and tell her to shut up or she'll be sorry."

"Is that what happened Mr. Philborn?"

"No."

"Yes it is an you know it."

"It didn't happen quite like that."

"It happened just like dat." Tulah retorted.

Mr. Philborn became flustered and turned red in the face. The principal introduced himself to Tulah and asked if she wanted to come in his office and have a seat until she was able to settle Lucille down. Tulah refused telling him that she and Lucille would be fine. She grabbed Lucille's hand, adjusted Jessie on her hip, and left the building so angry that tears formed in her eyes. She walked so fast, that Lucille had to skip just to keep up with her. Lucille didn't offer a word, understanding that her malfeasance was mostly to blame for the commotion. Walking down the long street, almost a full block away, Tulah allowed her tears to fall.

"What's wrong Mama?"

"White people think dey can talk ta us lak we ain't nothin'. He ain't have no right talkin ta you lak dat. And let me tell you something little girl." She said stopping to scold Lucille. "Don't you evva in yo life carry on lak dat again, you hear me? I aint nevva had to whup you, but I'll shole do it if you evva show out on me lak dat again." She said jerking Lucille's arm as she scolded her. "You understand me?"

"Yes." Lucille let silent tears fall from her face, not willing to contest the warning she had just received. Driven by her anger, Tulah marched down the street practically dragging Lucille behind her. She remembered when she herself had been scolded by a teacher at school when she was only eight. The teacher had written a complex problem on the board and asked if there was anyone who could solve it. Tulah anxiously waved her hand in the air trying to get the teacher's attention so that she could make an attempt at solving the problem. She was confident that she knew the answer because her brother, Aaron, used that same example out of the book when helping her with her homework the night before. Her teacher looked around the room and asked again if there was anyone who was brave enough to try. But his inquiry was not directed at her. This became clearer to Tulah when she looked around the room and realized that there was no one else in the room with their hand raised. Seeing that there was no competition, she vigorously waved her hand in the air and grunted.

"No one wants to try?" He asked. "It's not that difficult. Paulette... James?" He went down the row calling out her white classmate's names and skipping over the colored children. When no one responded, he walked back to the board and began writing out the answer. Tulah became frustrated and her sharp tongue went to work.

"He know he saw me. He ack lak coloreds aint smart enough to answer a question." Tulah blurted out to no one in particular.

"What did you say young lady?" He asked, obviously agitated by her candor. He walked over to her desk, stood over her and asked again, "What did you say to me?" Tulah opened her mouth to answer and but before she could utter a sound, he smacked her right across the face. The room momentarily went dark, and when the light came back, Tulah could feel her face stinging from his open hand across her cheek. Involuntary tears tried to push their way out, but Tulah stopped them before they could fall. She refused to give him the satisfaction of seeing her cry. She had to sit in the corner for the rest of the day with her chair facing the wall, away from the rest of the class. Tulah was embarrassed and angry. She wanted to scream at him for humiliating her in front of the entire class. All she wanted to do was to answer a question, show him that she had been studying, and make him feel proud of her for doing her work. But it had all gone wrong and she was helpless against his callousness. Powerless to challenge him, and unable to defend herself, she sat quietly in the corner and silently wept. Tulah lost interest in school that day. She no longer studied, feeling that it was pointless if no one would take the time to notice anyway. As she got older, she realized that her presence in school was not required, and when she was certain that no one missed her she eventually stopped going.

When Tulah returned home with a repentant Lucille in tow, she was badly in need of a cup of coffee. Searching the empty cabinets, her craving would have to go unsatisfied. She walked around the small house and felt utterly bored. Stepping out on the small porch, she took a seat and looked over the balcony. The waking city was alive with sound. So different from how it was in the south. Car horns blarring, engines roaring, and in the distance a faint churning of factory machines. Most of the days to come would follow the pattern of this one- getting the girls dressed and fed, walking Gracie to school and walking back home to an empty and quiet house. The highlight of the day would be to take other routes home, walking down unfamiliar streets, and learning the names of them. Every Friday, when Louis got paid, she could look forward to going to the market to buy groceries for the week, and then going over to Mabelle and Earl's house for cards that night. After a while, Louis stopped joining Tulah for card night and Mabelle's, growing less tolerant of Mabelle's belligerence that was exacerbated when she drank from her unyielding supply of cheap wine. On the nights that Tulah would go to Mabelle's house, Louis would stay home with the girls and cook dinner for them letting Gracie and Lucille assist him, while Gracie kept them entertained with her adventures of what happened in school.

Since the first time Tulah had wine at Mabelle's, she had come to enjoy the taste of the sweet, red wine. Many times she would drink with Mabelle until her speech became slurred and she would stagger when she tried to walk. On the nights she drank heavily, she would stay out longer to be sure that Louis and the girls were asleep, and then she would tip in the house way after midnight. Louis disapproved of the time she spent at Mabelle's, but kept his opinions to himself, allowing her to make her own decisions. It wasn't until she came in late one night, and stumbling around in the dark she stubbed her toe on the foot of the bed and swore so loud it startled him, that he voiced his concerns to her.

"Tulah, I know you've had a rough time adjusting since being here, and I'm happy to know you've got a friend in Mabelle, but I don't think you ought to be hanging around her so much. You're starting ta pick up bad habits."

"Bad habits like what?"

"Well, you swore so loud last night I thought a sailor had come in. Honey, that's not you. You've always been a lady; pretty, perfect and lady-like."

"And now I'm not?"

"No. I didn't say that. All I'm sayin is Mabelle and Earl are good people, but they like to drink, smoke and play loud music and cards all night. Their life style is different from ours, except now you're doing the same thing."

"What's wrong with that?"

"What's wrong with drinking and swearing?"

"I only swore the one time, Louis."

"Only one time that you think I know about. That's right, I know you swear, and I know you be drinking."

"Nobody hear me, but Mabelle."

"Tulah, you have children, Earl and Mabelle don't. That kind of livin may be okay for someone without kids, but you have children and they watch you. They ask me what you be doing over there so late into the night. And the music play so loud the whole neighborhood can hear it. I know she's your friend, but you have an example to set."

"Whatchu sayin, Louis."

"I'm saying I don't want you over there drinking and playin cards all night. I want you home with us on Friday nights."

"I'm home all da time. I'm home when you ain't. At least you work, I'm here in dis house all day wit nothin ta do. Friday is da only day I get to do somethin fa ma'self and have some fun."

"You can have fun wit us. We're your family and we need you here."

Tulah took a seat on the edge of the bed and looked down at her hands. She twisted her gold band around her finger and thought about what Louis was asking her. She knew he was right. It wasn't as if she wasn't expecting it. She had actually expected him to say something a lot sooner than he did, but that was typical of Louis. He was always so patient with her, letting her have her way and trying to please her. It was for these reasons, in addition to the point he made about family that she agreed to stop hanging out at Mabelle's on Friday nights.

"Alright Louis, I'll stop hanging out down there, but can I get a job?"

"A job?" Louis laughed and that angered Tulah.

"What's funny about dat? Lots of womens got jobs. Mabelle said she could probably get me a job wit her. And you know we can use da money, Louis. For as long as we been here we still ain't got no furniture. We ain't never got enough food in dis house and you know these girls always needin somethin'."

Louis didn't answer; he just shook his head not willing to hear what she was saying or consider the possibility of what they could gain.

"Louis, why not?" He still didn't answer. "Just listen to me. They always need help…"

"No Tulah. It's out of the question. My wife ain't going to work. We have kids, and you gone stay home to raise them while I go to work. That the way it's gone be, Tulah. That's final."

The tone in which Louis spoke to her, she knew it was no point in trying to change his mind. She got up, walked to the bathroom and slammed the door. For the very first time, Louis did not come after her. Typically if they had an argument or a disagreement, Louis would always come after her and try to smooth things over or reach a compromise that they could both live with, but now, Louis made no effort to appease her. Tulah stayed in the bathroom for over twenty minutes before realizing that Louis would not be changing his mind about this. She recalled the conversation she'd overheard between Louis' mother and her friend Johnny Mae, on the day of the funeral, and how women have to make sacrifices for their husbands and familys. She also recalled making a promise that she would do what ever it took to make Louis happy in return for all he had given to her. Even now, she understood that Louis wanted to take care of her, and by asking him to let her work, was a way of undermining him as a man, implying that what he is doing is not enough. She never wanted to make Louis feel that way, so she got up went to him and told him that she would do things his way. She did ask, however, if it were possible to get a telephone so she could at least call her Aunt Cora, and keep up with how her brother, Aaron, was doing because she got so lonely, and Louis acquiesced.

The following Monday morning began like all the others. Packing lunches, getting the girls dressed, walking Gracie to school, and coming back to an already clean house. The only thing different was that Tulah didn't have Friday nights at Mabelle's to look forward to. She came up with a story about how she couldn't go over there because the Gracie had lots of homework over the weekend and needed help completing it before Monday. That story lasted for a couple of weeks, and then Mabelle persisted that she should come after helping Gracie, no matter what time it was. When Tulah still didn't come, Mabelle eventually stopped asking. Whenever Mabelle would see Tulah, she would speak kindly to her, but it wasn't with the same warmth like it used to be, and that saddened Tulah because she felt that she had lost her only friend.

Winter turned to spring, and spring to summer, and when summer turned to autumn, and the leaves had intermittently turned yellow, orange and brown, Lucille was old enough to go to Kindergarten, and join Gracie at school. The girls were familiar enough with the neighborhood that they were able to walk to school together without Tulah. One afternoon after the girls had left for school, and Jessie was down for a nap, Tulah walked to the store. As she walked back home, she noticed a moving van was parked on the sidewalk unloading a truck full of expensive and fancy looking furniture. She couldn't help but to stop and look, because all the beautiful furniture reminded her of the lovely home she used to have back in Marietta when Louis had a thriving photography business. She shook her head thinking how Louis doesn't even take pictures anymore. He completely lost interest in photography. And the thought of having a home like the one they used to have was such a far off conception that she wouldn't even allow herself to think about it. However, watching the movers unload the rich and elegant furniture, Tulah was transported back to a time when she was truly happy.

She thought about being in Georgia and remembered the richness of the earth, the freshness of the air, the openness of the land, and the fullness of their prosperity. She and Louis were so happy living there. She remembered how they would take long walks down the red dirt road, go fishing in the pond, and swim in the lake. She thought about how she would pack Louis a lunch and walk it over to the studio, and they would sit and eat lunch together. At night, they would sit on the porch, in that swinging chair Tulah loved so much, and talk for hours about their future as lightning bugs would light up the night. It was the best time of her life. Everything had taken a turn from how it used to be. She and Louis didn't even seem to be as happy. The time spent between them felt so routine, not natural or fun like it once was. Louis was always working trying to make ends meet, and when he was home, he was so tired that he would fall asleep right after supper. At that moment, she missed home more than she ever had before and wished she could be back there. She shrugged her shoulders at the thought, feeling helpless to change any of it, and started back towards her house.

"Hey there!" She heard a booming voice shouted out to her. Tulah looked around trying to find the voice that yelled in her direction. "Over here." The voice rang out again. Tulah peeked around the tall boxes trying to connect a face to the voice. Suddenly, a smooth looking gentleman with skin the color of dark coal stepped from behind the truck. He had deeply intense eyes, with thick, curly lashes and shiny, black hair that laid on his head in giant waves. He wore pin-stripped baggy pants and a white sleeveless tee shirt.

"Hey foxy Mama. You live around here?" He asked smoothing his already perfectly coiffed hair back in place while chewing on a toothpick. He looked Tulah up and down and licked his lips like he was prepared to sink his teeth into her. Tulah was so taken back by his assertiveness that she turned and looked around, thinking he had to be speaking to someone else.

"I'm talking to you." He assured her.

"Oh. Hi." Tulah stammered.

"You live around here, sweet thang?"

Tulah instinctively touched her chest and lightly rubbed her neck.

"Yeah. I live right down the street."

"It's gone be nice living near a pretty little thang like you. I'm Tyrone." He told her extending his hand. "What's yo name, sweetheart?"

"Tulah Belle."

"Too sweet." He responded, taking her hand and flashing a beautiful set of pearly white teeth. Something about his jet skin in contrast to his white teeth was very attractive to Tulah. His teeth were probably the straightest and whitest that Tulah had ever seen. As he took her hand he noticed the gold band on her finger.

"You married, Tulah?"

"Um hum. Yeah."

"All, that's too bad. I was shole looking forward to askin you out. What's yo man's name?"

"Louis Starks."

"Well, Tulah, you tell Louis that he is a lucky man. Alright?"

"Alright."

"Cool. Well, I gotta get back in here. It was nice meeting you, Tulah Belle."

"Thank you, me too." Tulah stammered again, but Tyrone was already out of sight. She watched a little longer as the movers hauled tables, lamps and sofas into the place where Tyrone would be living and wished that she could have some of the beautiful furniture delivered to her home. She started back towards her house and saw Mabelle walking towards her from the other direction. She felt happy to see her and picked up her pace to meet her. "Hey Mabelle, whatchu doing home from work so early?"

"I lost my job, Tulah." Mabelle told her.

"I'm sorry, Mabelle. What happened?"

"You got minute?"

"Jessie back at da house sleepin. I need ta check on her ta make sure she alright, then I can come back down if you want me to."

"Go on and check on your baby, I'll get us some coffee ready."

"Okay. I'll be right over."

Tulah went to the house and check on Jessie, who was still sleeping soundly, she put her groceries away and went back to Mabelle's. Before she could knock, Mabelle opened the door to receive her. "Come on in, baby." Tulah came in and turned to look at Mabelle.

"You been cryin?"

"Yeah, crying and laughing."

"What's wrong?"

"Girl, I been so tired these days, I didn't know what was wrong with me. I thought I was sick because I ain't never got no energy. I'm always feeling tired. Come on in and have a seat." Mabelle told her leading the way to the sofa. "Anyway, I fell asleep at work one day and my boss caught me and told me she bet not ever catch me sleeping again or that was it for me. Tulah, I'm telling you the truth, I don't know what came over me, but I got so sleepy that I couldn't stand it no more. I went and crawled my big self in dat lady's tub, pulled the shower curtain back, and went right to sleep."

"Naw you didn't."

"Yes I did. And when I woke up, she was standin right over me wit a pitcher of water in her hand."

"Did she po it on you?"

"She was about to, but I heard her saying 'look at dis fat heifer' and that's what woke me up."

"What happen afta dat?"

"She asked me if I was taking drugs. I told her no, I don't take no drugs. So then she sent me to the clinic." Mabelle got up and paced the floor. "Tulah, you not gone belive what the doctor told me."

"What Mabelle? You ain't sick is you?"

"Girl, no I aint sick, I'm pregnant!"

Tulah jumped up from her seat and ran over to Mabelle.

"Oh girl, congratulations! I'm so happy for you. Earl gone be so surprised."

Mabelle laughed.

"I know, can you believe it? Aint that something? Me pregnant."

"That's exciting, Mabelle. You gone love being a Mama."

"What I'm gone do wit a baby?"

"I'll help you, Mabelle. You gone make a good Mama."

Chapter 21

Louis stood outside of the steel mill smoking a cigarette. He was on a shift change and went outside to catch some fresh air from the blazing temperatures that surfaced from the searing heat of the melting steel. His dampened clothes clung to him as sweat was excreted from his forehead, neck and back from the stifling heat. Just as he was finishing his smoke, his friend, Martin, came out and joined him.

"Got a smoke?"

Louis reached inside his breast pocket and retrieved a pack of Camel Light, cigarettes. He hit the bottom of the pack to free one of the tightly packed cigarettes and handed one to Martin. Martin placed the cigarette between his lips, lit it and took a long drag, savoring the taste of the burning nicotine.

"It's hotter than hell in there."

Louis nodded, silently agreeing with Martin.

"You working tonight?" Louis looked at Martin, his eyes questioned his meaning.

"Overtime, man. They offering overtime for whoever want it. Not just for the white boys this time."

"Man, I just pulled a second shift." Louis told him, "I've been working sixteen straight hours."

"Oh hell, I forgot. They already think you a white boy. You probably get all the overtime you want, huh?"

Louis tilted his head to the side weighing Martin's question.

"No, I don't get as much as I want, and not nearly as much as I need."

"What you mean by that?"

"Tulah's been on my case about getting a job."

"She wanna work?"

"Whew, does she? She been asking me about going to work for nearly a year. First, she wanted a telephone, I got her that. Then she wanted some furniture, so I got her that. Then it was a sewing machine. Said she could make the girls clothes and save us some money, so I got her that, too. Then it was some new curtains. She just keep at it, won't stop asking. And when I tell her no, or that we can't' afford it, she'll start up with the wanting to go to work routine. Man, I think I may let her go if that what she wants to do."

"Man, you can't let your ole lady go to work! You got kids. She need to be home with your kids."

"Man, I don't know what else to do."

"Tell her no. Women need to know they place, man. I wouldn't let my ole lady go to work if I had kids at home."

"That's easy for you to say, you ain't got no ole lady."

"I know I don't. But if I did have one she wouldn't be going to work."

Later that day, as Louis took a seat on the bus, he looked out of the window and let the conversation he had with Martin replay in his head. He wanted to afford Tulah the kind of lifestyle that would make her happy enough to want to stay home and raise his children. He wanted to give her the same kind of lifestyle that his father gave his mother, but things were so different now. Women wanted their own independence and didn't care much for staying home. Now that the girls were at school all day and Jessie could go to a free day care with other children her age, Tulah was more determined than ever to go to work, and Louis had just about run out of excuses to make her stay home. The bus screeched to a stop, interrupting Louis' thoughts. He stood to exit the bus and slowly walked home hoping that he would'nt have to have yet another quarrel with Tulah about her going to work.

By the time he reached the stairs, the aroma of smoked neck bones and navy beans permeated the narrow hallway. He climbed the stairs, eagerly anticipating a hot meal. As soon as the key turned the lock and the door swung open, the girls ran to greet him.

"Daddy's home!"

"Daddy, Daddy." They cried in unison, all running to be the

first to give him a hug. This was the best part of Louis' day. As he greeted the girls, kissing and tickling them, he caught a glimpse of Tulah standing back watching. She had her arms folded and was smiling as she witnessed the girls fighting over their father. Seeing Tulah stand there with a modest smile on her face, reminded him of the first time he saw her. She was as beautiful today than she was then, even more so, Louis thought to himself. The love he felt for her as his wife and as the mother to his children was so incredibly overwhelming to him that he could'nt resist her. He walked away from the girls and walked right up to Tulah. As exhausted as he was from a sixteen hour shift, seeing Tulah gave him renewed strength. He picked her up in the air and swung her around. The girls squeeled with delight watching Louis spin Tulah around. Tulah giggled with pure enjoyment, surprised by Louis' unexpected gesture.

"Stop, Louis. You making dizzy."

Louis stopped spinning her, but contined to hold her suspended in the air, smiling at her. Tulah couldn't help blushing. "You so crazy, Louis. Put me down." Louis lowered Tulah to her feet and kissed her on the forehead.

"Where'd all that energry come from? I know you got to be tired."

"I am tired. But I'm happy to be home with my pretty wife and my sweet little girls. Is dinner ready? Cause I'm starving."

"It's almost ready, bout ten mo minutes to go."

"Good, I'm going to take a shower."

"It'll be ready when you get out."

Louis turned on the water and let it run until it became hot and the bathroom was humid and steamy. He lathered several times to be sure the smell of sweat and molten steel was completely washed away. He had been working sixteen hour days at least three to four times a week, and was perfectly exhausted. Wrapping a towel around his waist, he wiped away condensation that had built up on the mirror from the steam of the shower. Looking at his reflection he was not pleased at what he saw. He looked tired and pale, and there were dark circles under his eyes. He was at least 15 pounds thinner than his regular weight. He knew he couldn't go on this way, working himself half to death, but he made a vow after living such a humble existence, that he would never be broke again. The money at the factory wasn't great, but working overtime would get him by with what he needed. If it weren't for Tulah's constant requests, he could even manage to save a little money. He rubbed his hand over his face, feeling a slight stubble that was just beginning to grow on the surface, but decided to wait another day before shaving.

"Dinner's ready!" He heard Tulah yell on the other side of the door.

"Alright, darlin', I'll be right out."

After dinner, Louis cozied up in his chair and tuned the radio to his favorite station. The girls gathered around him and sat on his lap to listen in with him. Before long, Louis was fast asleep. Tulah got the girls ready for bed and cleaned the dishes. When she got ready to go to bed, she stood staring at Louis before she awakened him to join her. This evening, like all the others was so routine, that Tulah knew almost the exact time Louis would start dosing. If only he would let her work, even part time, she thought, he wouldn't have to work as hard. Where his stubbornness came from, she would never know. She wasn't angry with him because of it though, how could she be mad at a man that wanted to care for his family. She only wished he would listen to reason.

"Louis! Louis! Come on now, it's time to go to bed." Louis opened his eyes, mumbled something unintelligible and went back to sleep.

"Come on now, Louis. It's almost eleven o'clock. Come on." She said shaking him. He was so tired, Tulah could have blown a trumpet in his ear and he would've slept right through it. She went to the kitchen and stuck her hands in the ice box, getting them good and cold, and then she went back to Louis and put her icy hands on his cheeks. He jumped and his eyes popped open.

"It's bedtime." She told him.

After she got Louis to bed, she lay there staring at the ceiling. She wanted to wake him so they could talk, but she dared not interrupt his much needed sleep for that.

The following morning before the crack of dawn, Louis was off to work. A couple of hours after, the girls were gone, and Tulah was home alone. She planned to check on Mabelle, but figured she was probably sleeping in, so she decided to go down a little later. She cleared the breakfast dishes, did some lightweight housework and decided to walk to the market to get some butter beans for supper. Walking to the store, she saw her neighbor, Tyrone, standing on the grass yelling instructions at some workers he had at his house. She felt excited and giddy at the thought of encountering Tyrone. It was something very different and appealing about him to Tulah. It could have been his smooth, dark complexion, as if midnight had been poured over his flawless, silken skin. Maybe it was his bright teeth, dazzling smile and intense stare that penetrated her in one gaze. Perhaps it was his cool and confident demeanor that inexplicably pulled Tulah into him. Whichever attribute it was that intrigued Tulah most, she was open and receptive to meeting his acquiantence once again.

Anxious to say hello, she subdued her propensity to walk over to him for fear of looking forward. Casually walking by, Tulah went unnoticed by him, disappointed, she went into the store. After purchasing beans and a few other items, she left the store and walked back home, this time on Tyrone's side of the street. As she walked by, she looked for him, inconspicuously darting her eyes over to where he stood minutes before, but he was no where in sight. She stayed on the his side of the street until she was directly in front of her house, so it wasn't so obvious that she was hoping to see him. She laughed at her little stunt, and then scolded her self for being silly. Later that evening, Louis came home early.

"Hey! What are you doing home so early?"

"I couldn't work another shift today, I'm too tired."

"All poor baby. Come on and have a seat, you need me to get you anything?"

"Naw, I just want to sit here in my comfortable chair and go to sleep. I think I'm too tired to eat."

"You know, Louis, you wouldn't have to work so many hours if you let me work."

"Not today, Tulah."

"I'm just sayin. I could be at work when yall gone an back home before you get in." Louis didn't reply. He bent over to unloosen his work boots, but Tulah ran over to him and did it for him.

"Where are the girls?"

"Down at Ms. Minnie's house, playin in her yard." Louis eased back in his chair and closed his eyes.

"Louis it don't be nothing for me to do all day. Everybody be gone and I be here by myself doin nothing. I can't stand being in this house no mo."

"I thought you were going to help look after Mabelle."

"Mabelle be sleep all day. She don't want no company. Besides, I'm tired of looking after everybody, I want to do something for me. You wanted me to stop going over there on Friday nights so I did, and now I don't have nothin' to look forward to. Louis, I caint stay in this house all day, I'm gone go crazy in here."

"I know, Tulah, but I think it's important for you to be here for the girls. They need you to be home."

"Naw dey don't. Dey go to school all day, and when dey come home, dey be playing in Ms. Minnie's yard and runnig wit dey friends. You at work all day. Everybody got something ta do but me."

"All Tulah, it aint' that bad."

"Don't you tell me that! You don't know what it's like to be locked up in this house all day wit nothin ta do." Louis didn't respond. He wasn't asleep, but he closed his eyes pretending to be.

"Louis, you here me? I know you ain't sleep." Louis still didn't respond. Tulah walked over and took a seat on the sofa. She took in a deep breath and let it go slowly, trying to find a way to tell Louis what she had been thinking.

"I wanna go home." Louis opened his eyes, taken aback at what he'd just heard. "What do you mean you wanna go home? This is home."

"You know what I mean. I don't like it here, and I miss my aintie. I ain't seen nor heard from her since we been here, and I wanna go back home.

"But Tulah, this is home, honey."

"It aint home!" She screamed at him. "I hate living here. You and these girls the only ones happy, but aint nobody asked me how I feel. I gotta be locked in this house all day wit nothing to do, I aint got no money, no friends, and no family around me. I wanna go home, Louis. Caint you just send me, for a little while anyway?" Tears began to form in her eyes.

"Can't you just call Cora or send a letter?"

"I don't wanna write no letter, Louis."

"Well, how you know if she's got room to put you up? She had borders the last time we were there."

"Louis, dat was almost four years ago. Besides, I aint gotta stay wit her. We got our own place down there." When Louis saw tears streaming down Tulah's face he turned away and got quiet.

"I need to go and check on da house anyway. Ain't no telling what shape it's in. It's our place and we still responsible for the upkeep."

Louis shook his head.

"What Louis, why you shakin yo head?"

"Uh, that's not gone work."

"Yes it will. Dat way, I can go and check on yo Mama, I can see aint Cora, see about our place, and then come back here. Louis please, don't say no."

"No Tulah, that's not gone work." Tulah had gotten tired of begging and having Louis tell her no. "You tell me why?" She screamed. "Don't you care if I'm happy?"

"Of course I am."

"Then you tell me why I caint go. I got a place of my own, I don't have to stay here. I don't even have to ask you." Tulah became hysterical. "I'm packing my bags and I'm going."

"Tulah, wait a minute." He said, walking towards her. "How are you going to get there?"

"Same way I got here. Bus tickets is cheap, and I can afford it by myself."

"Wait Tulah, hold on."

"What?"

"Something I need to tell you."

"What?"

Louis took a deep breath. "Come here and sit by me, baby." He said taking a seat on the sofa. "Don't try to talk me out of it."

"Come on, sit down." Tulah complied, and took a seat next to Louis.

"It's something I need to tell you."

"You said dat already. What is it?"

Louis got up and walked away from her. He put his hands in his pockets, then pulled them out patting his breast pockets for his cigarettes.

"You stalling." She told him. Louis pulled out a cigarette, lit it and took in a long drag. Tulah stared intently at him, but refused to ask him again what he wanted to tell her. Louis blew out a thick cloud of smoke.

"It's gone."

"What's gone?"

"Our place."

"Whatchu mean our place is gone?"

"It's gone, Tulah, I sold it."

"You sold my house!" Tulah jumped off the sofa and asked again, almost pleading that she had misunderstood what she had just been told. "Not my house, Louis. You don't mean the house that Mama Lou gave me?"

"It's gone, Tulah. I had to sell it…"

Tulah ran towards Louis swinging. She had tears in her eyes and was flailing her arms with her fists bawled throwing punches and connecting. "You sold my house?" She screamed still swinging at him. Louis stepped back to avoid getting hit, but Tulah kept coming towards him. He grabbed her arms and held her.

"Stop it girl! You gone hurt yo'self." He said, holding her.

"Let me go, Louis. You let me go!" Tulah said struggling to get away from him.

Louis wrapped her in his arms to restrain her and talked quietly and calmly in her ear.

"I'll let you go, but you gotta calm down."

Tulah continued to squirm and pull away from him.

"Why Louis? That was mine. Mama Lou gave it to me. I ain't have nothing till she gave me that house. It was mine and you ain't have no right to sell it. It wasn't even yours to sell!" She cried, tears running down her face. "I caint believe you would do such a thang to me, Louis. Not you of all people." She said shaking her head in disbelief, backing away from him. "You ain't have no right. No right at all. I'll never forgive you fa this, Louis. Never!" She ran in her room and slammed the door behind her.

Louis ran behind her and grabbed the knob to open the door, but Tulah screamed from the other side of the door, "Don't come in here, Louis. I don't even wanna look atchu. Just leave me alone."

Louis stopped in his tracks and backed away from the door. He knew he was wrong to have sold her place, but he felt that it was the best thing to do at the time. Later that evening, the girls came in, had dinner, got prepared for bed, and Tulah was still locked in her room. Louis told them that mommy wasn't feeling well because of a stomach ache, when the girls asked why she was in bed so early. When the time came for Louis to go to bed, he was hesitant to go in the room with her, so he lightly knocked on the door and waited for a response. When there was no answer, he tentatively went in. He sat on the bed next to Tulah and asked her if she was awake.

"Yeah, I'm wake, but I don't want to talk to you."

Louis rose from the bed, respecting her wishes.

"Wait! I need to know something."

"Yeah?"

"When did you sell it?"

"Before I left. It was shortly after we went to live with Mama and Daddy."

"Is dat where all dat money come from the day you was leaving and you gave me some?"

"Yeah. That was the money I got from the house."

Tulah shook her head, still not believing what she was hearing and a single tear rolled down her cheek.

"Who'd you sell it to?"

"Tulah, would'nt you rather talk about this in the morning?"

"No. I wanna talk about it now. Don't you think you owe me dat?"

"It was a man from in town. You never met him. I only met him a couple of times myself."

"That was a low down dirty thang you did ta me. When was you planning on telling me?"

"I don't know."

"You don't know? Was you evva gone tell me?"

"I don't know. It's just that we were trying to save money to move up here, and I couldn't even find a job. I couldn't find nothing. We had gone through everything we had and there was nothing left, Tulah. Everything was gone. There was no work and things weren't getting any better."

"That was the meanest thang anybody evva did ta me, Louis. And I don't care how you try to fix it up, it ain't no excuse. Where's the rest of the money?"

"It's gone."

"All of it?"

"All of it. It's nothing left. I'm sorry, baby. I'm so sorry."

"I don't wanna hear no sorrys. I don't wanna hear nothing

you got to say. I don't want you in here wit me neither. And since I ain't got no house of my own, dis here is my room, and right now you aint welcome here."

"Tulah,"

"I don't wanna hear it, Louis, just leave." She said as tears rolled down her cheeks. Louis got up and closed the door behind him.

The following morning, Louis knocked on the door before going in.

"Tulah, I'm leaving for work." When she didn't reply, he told her, "I love you, Tulah, and I'm so sorry about what I did. I promise you I'm gone spend the rest of my life making it up to you. I just want you to know that I only used the money to get us here, to find a place and send for you and the girls, that's all. I know I was wrong, but please, just think about what I said, and know that I love you, okay?" Still there was no reply from Tulah, so Louis closed the door behind him and left for work.

Chapter 22

Tulah prepared homemade chocolate chip cookies with chopped walnuts and walked a plateful down to Mabelle's. She knocked on the door, and Mabelle yelled though the door, telling her to come in. When Tulah went in Mabelle was lying on the sofa with a pillow behind her head. She looked odd because she didn't have any make-up on and looked a lot bigger than before. Tulah hadn't seen her in a few weeks, but in that short time, Mabelle had really changed.

"How you feeling Mabelle?"

"Girl, where you been? I been sick."

"I been home. I asked about you, and Earl said you was doin fine. What's wrong?"

"I been put on bed rest."

"What dat mean?"

"I got a rare blood type, make it hard for me to carry babies. That's why I be so tired all the time. Anyway, the doctor say I need to stay off my feet and get plenty a rest. He say if I move around too much I could lose the baby." She explained while wiping tiny sweat beads off the bridge of her nose.

"That's awful."

"I know. That's why I'm laying up here getting so fat. All I do is eat and sleep. I'm gone be big as a whale by the time this baby come."

"Well dat ain't important, the important thang is dat you stay off your feet. And speaking of getting fat, I brought you some chocolate chip cookies."

"Oooh Tulah. Homemade?"

"Um hum. Dey good too. My grannie's recipe."

Mabelle giggled.

"Well bring em here."

Tulah walked over to her and handed her the plate. "Ooh, they're still warm."

"Yup, I brought em straight out da oven. Hey Mabelle, you got some of dat wine left?"

"You know I do. You gone have a drink this time of day?"

"Yeah, I need one."

"You need one? Uh oh, what's wrong?"

"I don't wanna talk about it, but trust me, I need a drink."

"It's in the kitchen, you know where I keep it."

Tulah walked to the kitchen and helped herself to a glassful of wine, pouring it in a jelly jar, she walked back to the living room with Mabelle, taking a seat on the chair.

"So what's going on, Tulah?" Mabelle asked chomping down on the cookies.

"Ooh girl, I'm so mad at Louis."

"What could that sweet man possibly do to make you mad?"

"I don't wanna talk about." She said sipping the wine. There was a noticeable silence in the room, and then Tulah spoke.

"He ain't as sweet as you might think. He ain't perfeck."

You sure you don't want to talk about it." Mabelle smiled at her.

Tulah laughed realizing she had already began talking about it.

"Yeah, I'm sure. I mean, I ain't goin into details, but I'll tell you what, me and Louis ain't evva went dis long without, you know."

"How long?"

"Almost two weeks."

"He musta really made you mad."

"He did. I'm just now starting to talk to him again."

"Well baby, you can't hold out on him for too long. He still a man, and men have needs. You know what I mean?"

"Yeah, I know dey do, cause I got needs of my own." They both laughed. Tulah stayed with Mabelle all morning and left for home close to one o'clock. She wanted to get an early start on preparing dinner, but needed to stop by the market. Walking to the store, she passed by Tyrone's house just as he was coming out.

"Hey, Sweet thang."

"Heeey." She said crossing over to his side of the street. She looked forward to seeing Tyrone and flirting with him.

"What you been up to? I ain't seen you around, you been hiding from me?"

Tulah couldn't help the excitement she felt when in his presence. She let her eyes slide easily over Tyrone's muscular body. As expected, Tyrone was sharply dressed in black baggy pants, a matching black, satin button up, with a red tie and red suspenders. His hair was coiffed in finger waves and he had on a cashmere coat with a fox fur collar. Tulah was impressed with his expensive clothes and aromatic cologne.

"Naw, I ain't been hiding. We just been missin' each other I guess."

Tyrone smiled seductively at her. He was confident in his magnetism with the ladies, and Tulah was no exception. He toyed with her, talking sweetly and flirtatiously to her.

"How your man treatin you?"

"Good."

"Is he?"

"Yeah."

"He treat you good all the time, or just some time?" He asked looking her up and down, while licking his lips. Tulah instinctively laid her hand on her chest and started rubbing her neck. Tyrone noticed and smiled more, knowing he had Tulah right where he wanted her.

"He treat me good all the time."

Tyrone tilted his head to the side, "Something tells me you not being completely honest with me."

"Yes I am."

Tyrone ran his hand over his slick hair, and leaned into to her, talking softly,

"I know you are, baby, cause you wouldn't lie to me would you?"

"Uhn uhn. I don't have no reason to."

He reached out and touched her face with the back of his hand.

"You so fine."

Tiny, sprikily hairs stood up on the back of her neck and goose bumps surfaced on her skin. Tulah blushed, and rubbed her chest and the back of her neck. She fidgeted nervously, not knowing what to do with her hands. She felt suddenly hot, like she would break into a sweat. Too much wine, she thought to herself.

"Thank you."

"So where's your man?"

"At work."

Tulah noticed her heart was racing and her voice tremored. She felt nervous and had to pee. She took in a deep breath trying to calm herself.

Tyroned looked around and leaned in closer to Tulah.

"Why don't you come on in for a minute?"

"Oh uhn uhn, I caint go in there." She said shaking her head and backing away, but he stopped her by grabbing her by her wrist. "It's okay, baby. I just wanna get out of this cold." Tulah looked down at his hand that was wrapped firmly around her wrist. Her eyes nearly popped out of her head when she saw the size and clarity of the diamond rings that adorned his hand.

"Oh, I'm sorry sweet thang. I don't mean no disrespect." Tyrone told her releasing his grip. "Aint you cold?"

"Yeah, a little."

"Where you from, down in the country somewhere?"

"Yup, Georgia."

Tyrone smiled that dazzling smile at Tulah, "I knew it- a country girl. I like that. Sweet Georgia peach." He said in a way that was both seductive and inviting.

Tulah felt like she would set ablaze at that very moment. It was something about the way Tyrone talked to her, looked at her, that got her aroused and it freightened her. She caught herself by following Tyrone's eyes, which were glued to her hand, as she went from rubbing her chest and neck, to practically fondling her cleavage. What is it about this man that sets such a fire in me, she thought to herself.

"I gotta go Tyrone."

"No you don't, come in for a minute. Let me talk to you." He asked again, this time gently pulling her towards his house. "I won't keep you long, I promise. Come on."

Tulah almost took him up on his offer, but her actions showed her that she no longer knew what she was capable of.

"No Tyrone, I gotta go." She said snatching her hand away and backing away from him.

"I thought you was going to the market?"

"Dat's okay, I don't need it." She said turning away from him and running back to her house. She ran all the way up the stairs and into the house. She slammed the door behind her and leaned against it, taking in long exaggerated breaths and slowly releasing them. She placed her hand on her heart noticing how quickly it was beating. Tulah closed her eyes and smiled thinking about how she felt when Tyrone touched her, looked at her. She shook her head, trying to shake off the memory of him, and then went into the kitchen to prepare dinner for her family.

When Louis came in from work, he tried to kiss Tulah, like he does everyday. To his surprise, she reciprocated and kissed him back. Louis smiled and felt relieved.

"Welcome back." He told her.

She looked at him but did not return the smile.

"I ain't been nowhere. It just took me some time to get past what you done to me."

"I'm glad you finally got past it."

"I'm not past it- not all ta'gether. A part of me will nevva fa'give you, Louis. And I know how mean dat might sound, but it's da troof."

"Yeah, that sounds pretty extreme."

"Well, ain't what you did ta me extreme?" She retorted.

"Yeah Tulah, it was. I was wrong, I know it. I'm just glad you talking to me. I hope we can move past this."

"It's gone take me some time to get over it. So you just gone hafta bear wit me."

"Okay."

"Louis, just don't evva lie to me. I can take a lot, but I caint take being lied to."

"I promise to always tell you the truth, about everything."

"Good." She told him, locking the door. "The girls down to Ms. Minnie's house listening to the radio."

"They're not going to be out too late are they? It's a school night."

"They know what time to be back."

"Okay."

Tulah looked at the clock. "So dat mean we got two hours." Louis looked at her and knew exactly what she meant.

Louis dealt with the fact that Tulah held a grudge, it was

justifiable. He was just happy that thet were speaking and back to making love. He knew he had some making up to do and was up for the challenge. And while Tulah's expedient forgiveness benefited them both, it was purely selfish in nature. There had been a great fire set in her and there was only one way to quench it. Her body burned with desire and ached with wantonness. With her body, she made love to Louis, but with her mind she stroked, kissed and caressed Tyrone. She despised herself for doing that to her beloved, but in her present state, she couldn't help it, because what she felt was bigger than Louis.

Chapter 23

"Mabelle tells me you're a good worker, and that's exactly what I'm gonna need. I need you to show up on time, everyday, no excuses. Can you cook? Because I'm gonna need you to prepare meals at least twice a week. Those will the days I'm in late, and will need Mr. Fortson's meals prepared and on the table once he arrives." Ursula Fortson, Tulah's new boss explained to her. Tulah was filling in as Mabelle's replacement since she was on bed rest and could no longer work.

"This house has been in shambles for the last few months. Since Mabelle left, we've gone through three housekeepers, and have had to get rid of everyone. Mabelle wasn't the best, but she was a far cry better than the others we've had. I guess it's true what they say about good workers being hard to find."

She turned and looked at Tulah. "Mabelle recommended you highly. That's the only reason we're giving you a chance. Coloreds are so irresponsible."

Tulah instinctively opened her mouth to give Mrs. Fortson and verbal lashing at for her comment about coloreds, but quelled her inclination because she badly wanted this job and was determined not to sabotage herself just to relegate herself to home and do nothing all day. Since Tulah had a vantage point with Louis, he finally gave in to her demands and let her go to work. The only stipulation was for her to be home in time to receive the girls from school and have dinner ready for them. But already Mrs. Fortson was asking her to stay late two nights a week to prepare dinner for her husband.

"I do cook, but I caint stay late to prepare dinner fo yo

husband, cause I got a husband of my own who'll be countin on dinner when he get in."

"Well, that poses a problem. Mabelle didn't apprise me of any certain conditions."

"I'm a good worker. I'll be here everyday and on time just like you askin, but I cain't stay late."

"And what am I supposed to do about dinner on my late days."

"Maybe you can hire yo'self a cook."

Mrs. Fortson's nostrils flaired and she turned red in the face.

"Excuse me? Young lady I won't stand for any insolence out of you."

"I'm not tryin to be… whatever it is you said, if dats a bad thang. I'm just makin a suggestion."

"Well, it sounded pretty sassy to me."

"No ma'am."

Mrs. Fortson looked at Tulah out of the corner of her eye, uncertain about her ingenuousness. She relaxed a bit and took in a long breath and let it out slowly, before continuing. "Alright, well, I'll take that into consideration. Follow me, I'll show you the rest of the house."

Tulah stayed at Mrs. Fortson's house until nearly three o'clock, way past the time she should've left in order to catch the bus back across to her side of town and be there on time. The bus screeched to a stop, letting her off right in front of the market. She decided to go in and get a few things for dinner and ended up coming out with two grocery bags. She rearraged the bags as she tried to exit the store lifting her knee to rest one of the bags, as she reached for the handle with her other hand. The door suddenly swung opened, and there stood Tyrone revealing his pearly whites at Tulah.

"Hey sweet thang, let me help you wit those." He said taking the bags from her. Tulah was both surprised and embarrassed that he spoke to her in a tone that everyone around them could hear.

"I can carry my own groceries." She snapped at him taking one of the bags back.

"Yeah, I'm sure you can, but you shole was struggling with that door." He laughed, while she stared at him angrily. "All come on sweet thang, why you being so mean? I'm just trying to be a gentleman." He opened the door and stood back to let her walk past him. Tulah walked out of the store and then turned and looked back to see if anyone was watching her.

"Whatchu looking at?"

"I'm tryin to see if you caused a scene with yo ole loud talking self."

"Ain't nobody stutten you. These people around her don't care nothing about who you talking to."

"Well, dey a lot different from da people where I come from."

"That's cause you in the city, baby. Here, everybody do they own thang. They mind they business and you mind yours."

"Is dat da way it work?"

"That's right."

"Well, that might be a good system yall got going here, but I'm still a married woman and I caint let you carry my groceries to my door."

"How you gone unlock the door and get em up the stairs by yo'self."

"I'll manage."

"You a feisty little thang ain't you?"

"It's what I been told."

"You ought to let me take you out sometime."

"I caint let you take me out!" Tulah answered, offended by his offer.

"Why not?

"Cause I cain't."

"You can do what ever you wanna do. You grown ain't you?"

"Me being grown is besides the point. I'm still married."

"So!"

"So? Tyrone you is terrible. Ain't you got no sense of doing the right thang?"

"This is the right thang." He stopped and grabbed her by the arm. His grip was so firm and urgent that Tulah immediately became aroused. Leaning in close to her, he told her.

"I'm tired of playing games witchu. I want you for myself and I know you want me too. I can feel it. I feel it everytime I get close to you. I feel it right now. Look at how you make my nature rise." He took a step back so she could see him. Tulah looked down, and saw a noticeable buldge in his pants. She was appalled by his assertiveness, but let her eyes roam over his groin area taking in the fullness that protruded out of his pants. He walked up close to Tulah and took her free hand and placed it on his buldge.

"That's how you do me everytime I see you." He whispered huskily in her ear. Tulah tried to snatch away, but he held firm to her wrist making her feel his rising nature.

Tulah wanted to back away, everything in her told her to back away. Yet when she looked at Tyrone and their eyes locked, she couldn't move. He moved her hand over the part of his pants that protruded making feel his manhood. She became so aroused, that it was difficult for her to breathe. An explosion took place within her and her underwear became whet. Tyrone leaned in close to her and pressed his lips against hers. Tulah closed her eyes and enjoyed the feel of his sweet lips that completely enveloped her mouth with his kiss. He pulled away from Tulah and handed the bag back to her.

"When you serious about getting together, you let me know." He rubbed his hands over his slick hair, straightened his pants, winked at Tulah and walked away. Tulah stood in place watching Tyrone walk away from her. A part of her wanted to run after him, tell him that she is serious and ready, but another part of her, the sensible, reasonable part of her told her to collect herself and go home. Tulah composed herself, looking around to see if anyone witnessed the kiss, shifted the bags in her arms and walked back to her house. Thoughts of Tyrone haunted her for the rest of the day and all that evening. She closed her eyes and replayed the encounter over and over again in her mind, and was amazed at the kind of power he had that she actually climaxed at his touch. She knew that this latest event surpassed the harmless flirting that she would normally engage in, and that she had surely crossed over to a leval of imminent peril. Nevertheless, her only thought was seeing him and working out a way to make it happen.

Everyday after that one, Tulah could not get Tyrone off her mind. He was different from any man she had ever known and loved his direct, forcefulness. She would often compare his smooth, charismatic swagger, to Louis' mild-mannered, easy going timidness. However, Louis was not naturally timid, it was just that he sensed something different in Tulah, and knowing that she resented him for selling her house, he was especially careful around her, making a concerted effort to please her and not to make her angry. Tulah couldn't wait to see Tyrone again to tell him that she was ready. One afternoon after getting off work, she went and knocked on his door. She waited on the porch nervous and excited about what she was about to do. She knocked and knocked, but no one answered. Just as she was turning to leave, the door came open and a woman stood there asking if she could help her. It was obvious that Tulah had awakened her because she kept yawning and she squinted her eyes, shielding them from the daylight. She was a pretty, light-skinned woman, small framed like Tulah, with big, bright eyes. She was wearing a pink silk house coat with a white satin gown underneath. Her hair was scattered all over her head like someone had raked their hands through it. Tulah stood there speechless looking at the woman and feeling like a fool. When she finally found words, she forced them out of her mouth forging something about being a neighbor and wanting to deliver a message to Tyrone. But the woman stumped Tulah again when she told her that she could deliver the message. Tulah told her that she would come back later and quickly walked away.

The next day as Tulah got off the bus, Tyrone was there waiting for her. Tulah saw him, but walked past him without saying a word. He ran and caught up with her asking what the problem was.

"I ain't got nothing to say to you."

"Then why did you come over?"

"How you know I came over?"

"I got the message."

"Is that right? And who delivered the message?"

Tyrone laughed. "Oh, is that what all the attitude is about?" He laughed again. "Man, I tell you. You women are too much." Tulah stopped and turned to face him. "If you seein somebody, what you askin me out fo?"

"I ain't gotta lie." When Tyrone said that, he got Tulah's attention. "I asked to take you out, cause that's what I wanna do. Lena is a friend of mine. I'm a single man, and yes, I have friends. But I ain't commited to nobody."

"Yeah, but I am."

"Okay, Ms. Commited, you the one came by, so you tell me what you wanted."

Tulah gave him a looked of disdain and started to walk away, but Tyrone stopped her.

"Look, ain't no reason to act like that. You came by cause you cant stop thinking about me." He said walking closer to her. He rubbed the back of his hand on her face and let it travel down her neck. Tulah instinctively closed her eyes and lifted her chin, as he continued to slowly caress her, stopping at her cleavage. Tulah got that feeling again, a throbbing urgency in her sweet spot as her nipples became firm and erect. Each time she got close to him, she would become lost in his touch. She wanted to resist him, but the feeling she got was so unique and unlike anything else she's ever experienced, she couldn't get enough.

"Let me take you out. It's a club down on Woodward I wanna take you to next Friday. It starts at eight o'clock. You work out the details, but I want you wit me next Friday. Come by around six thirty, alright?" Tyrone grabbed Tulah's hand. "You gone be there?"

"I'll see what I can do."

"Work it out. I'll see next Friday at six thirty."

Tulah found it difficult to walk away from him. She had gone from being afraid and shy, to eager and anxious. She wanted to be angry with him about Lena, but because he was so direct, not trying to hide behind a lie, it further intrigued her. Even though telling Tulah that he was single and had friends was not what she wanted to hear, she appreciated his honesty. She decided at that moment that she would definitely be there next Friday.

Tulah started going down to sit with Mabelle every evening after dinner. She would often take a plate down or offer to clean. Earl would sometimes be home, but many times he would leave when Tulah came over. Tulah was tempted to tell Mabelle about Tyrone, but didn't know what her friend would think of her, so she kept it to herself. However, going over to spend time with Mabelle gave Tulah an idea of how she could get away with Tyrone. She had planned everything. She told Louis that she was going to work late on Friday night and would be stopping to check in on Mabelle right after. She told him that if she got in late that he shouldn't wait up for her. Then she told Mabelle that she probably wouldn't be coming over on Friday because she had to work late.

When Friday morning arrived, Tulah was up early. She made

Louis' lunch, prepared breakfast, got the girls off to school, and went to work. After she got off work, she had three hours to spare before she was expected at Tyrone's house. If she waited until six thirty to go there, she would risk running into Louis as he is usually home between six and seven. If she went too early, she feared that she would look to eager, and she had too much pride for that. She ended up going to Woolworth's department store walking around and looking at all the pretty things they had. Walking around the store with nothing to buy, time moved especially slow. Deciding that she had no other recourse, she went to Tyrone's house, knocked on the door and hoped that he would answer. He opened the door wearing a white button down shirt that was open in the front revealing a perfectly chisled chest and tight abs. He flashed that million dollar smile at Tulah and opened the door to let her in.

"Hey sweet thang."

"I know I'm early, but my girls will be home soon and I didn't want them see me coming over here."

"It's cool, baby. You coulda came this morning if you wanted to. How you doing?" He walked up to her and kissed her on the cheek. His lips were moist, warm and soft. The smell of his aftershave was tantalizing, teasing her sensibilities. "Come on in." He grabbed Tulah's hand and led her through the narrow hallway. To the right was the livingroom. It was furnished so beautifully and lavishly that Tulah wanted to cry thinking about the home she once had that closely resembled this one. However, this home was much more elaborate. The furniture much more expensive and he had original paintings by real artists on his walls. The curtains were closed, and the room was dark, but Tulah took in every ounce of beauty the room had to offer. He led her to the kitchen that had a new, modern ice box and matching stove in it.

"Ever cook on a stove like this one?" Tyrone asked her. She shook her head as he continued to lead her through the house. "Well, you will be. I can't wait to get a taste of some real down home country food." When Tulah did'nt respond he turned and looked at her. "What? I know you can cook."

"Yeah, I can cook. But what makes you so sure I'm gone be cookin fa you?"

"You will." He replied and kept with his tour of the house.

Tulah snickered and shook her head at his cocky arrogance. He was so sure of himself, which was just another trait that further attracted her to him. After he had given her the grand tour, he took her into the living room and sat on the sofa. He pulled her arm so she could sit down next to him. As she sat, he scooted closer to her, looking her in the eyes.

"You are so pretty, Tulah. I like you." Tulah's heart quickened in pace. Her breath caught in her chest. "Do I make you nervous?"

"No." She lied. Then she laughed. "A little."

"Why?"

"Cause I aint nevva met nobody like you. You so demanding. Like you gotta have thangs yo way. Like it ain't no other way but how you want it."

"It ain't no other way. That's how I do thangs. If I want something, I go after it. How you gone know if you can have it or not if you don't at least try?"

"Even if what you want is a married woman?"

"You ain't satisfied, though."

"Whatchu mean? Louis is a good man."She defensively told him.

"I'm not saying that he ain't. I'm just saying that you ain't happy wit him no more. The fire burned out. You came up to the big city thinking everything was gone be different, better. And all you found out is that the city ain't did nothing but take your husband away from you. Your kids at school, your husband at work and you run back and forth to your girlfriend's house cause ain't nothing for you to do all day."

Tulah was offended that he thought he knew her so well, but she couldn't deny it, because it was as if he was looking right into her soul.

"It ain't like dat."

"I watch you. If you aint working, you sittin' on that porch. You run back and forth to the store, to your neighbor's house and then go sit on that porch again till its time for your kids to come home." Tulah shook her head, but couldn't find words to counter what he was saying. He placed his hand on the bottom of her chin and turned her face towards his.

"Hey, it's okay, I understand. Life ain't always what we expect it to be. It disappoints us sometime." His words struck Tulah in a way she wasn't expecting, and her eyes started to water. She tried to blink away her tears, but when Tyrone kissed her softly on the cheek, a single tear rolled down her face.

"Come here." He told her, standing and pulling her off the sofa. She followed him to a room opposite of the living room that had a small sofa, with end tables on each side. Standing next to the wall was an oblong, oval shaped mirror that stood on a wooden stand, reflecting the entire length of your body. Lying across the sofa wrapped in cleaners plastic was a peach colored dress with sequence beads on the front. Tyrone picked up the dress, held it up to Tulah, and nodded his head with approval.

"This is for you."

"For me! How you know if it's gone fit?"

"I know how to size up a woman pretty good. Try it on." He told her, as he walked out of the room and closed the door behind him.

Tulah quickly undressed and pulled the plastic off of the dress. As she pulled the pretty, peach dress over her head, she relished in the feel of the soft chiffon against her skin. As the dress slipped down past her waist and hips, it caressed her slendor body as it slid into place. Tulah smiled as she looked into the mirror. She turned from side to side admiring how it looked on her. She was further impressed that Tyrone picked a dress that fit her in size and color so perfectly. She stopped and stared at her reflection in the mirror. "What are you doin?" She asked herself, suddenly sobered by her actions. "I caint do this, what am I thinking?" She covered her mouth with her hand and felt shame for how she had behaved thus far. She thought about Louis and her children and how much she loved them- she couldn't betray them like this. Then another thought quickly followed the first. A thought reminding her that Louis had betrayed her, lied to her, and kept her money.

Every since they had been here, Louis tried to keep control over her by keeping her locked in the house, refusing to let her work, and stopping her from going to Mabelle's for cards on Friday nights. Tulah became angry and frustrated. She suddenly felt justified for what she was doing. She knew she loved Louis and would never leave him, so she had to be careful with how far to go with Tyrone. But tonight, she was going to have herself a good time. She felt that she deserved to have a little fun. She opened the door and yelled out to him. "Hey Tyrone, it's a perfect fit!"

Chapter 24

Tyrone and Tulah walked hand in hand into a club called Henderson's, on Woodward Avenue, in downtown Detroit. They were all decked out, semi-matching and turning heads. As soon as the doorman opened the big steel door, the sound of a live jazz band boomed in syncopation as a lively crowd swayed to the rhythm. The smoke filled club was dimly lit, and had red and blue lights that spotlighted the stage to showcase the talented musicians that played finger-popping beats that vibrated in their chests and excited their souls. A big, silver ball hung over the stage that bounced the reflection of the lights off the walls, casting beams of red and blue over the entire audience. Tyrone locked arms with Tulah as he led her down to a table in the front. As soon as they took their seats a waiter came over to take their orders. Tyrone stood to talk in the ear of the waiter over the loud music, and in a flash, he was back with fried chicken dinners and two whiskey filled glasses. Tulah took a sip from her glass, grabbed her chest, and blew hot air out of her mouth.

"It's whiskey. You gone need a chaser with that." He told her offering her a coke.

They ate and drank and enjoyed the show. After the jazz band played, a male singer came out with three female back up singers behind him. He had on a black tuxedo and they had on short, red, flashy dresses that shimmered in the light. Their long, shiny, black wigs swayed to the rhythm of the music. Tulah was in awe watching the singer belt out tunes as the women shoobeedeedooed, and doowapped behind him. She had never seen anything like it before in her life, and had never had so much fun. When it was time to leave, she had to go back to Tyrone's house to change her clothes, but was concerned with the smell of smoke that lingered on her. Tyrone offered her his shower, and surprisingly, she accepted. When she stepped out of the shower there was a big towel lying on the seat of the toilet. She dried herself, and quickly dressed in the clothes she came over in. As she prepared to leave, Tyrone walked over to her. She knew he would try to kiss her and the thought of it made her nervous. He came and stood right in front of her, and she responsively closed her eyes and lifted her head to meet his lips. When the kiss didn't come, she opened her eyes just as he was planting a gentlemanly kiss on her forehead. She looked at him, perplexed that he didn't kiss her in the way she expected. He smiled at her, took her by the hand and walked her to the door. He stood on the porch to watch her home safely and then retreated inside.

When Tulah went home, the house was quiet and everyone was asleep. She changed into her nightgown climbed into bed thinking about her night with Tyrone. She wondered, though, why he didn't kiss her when she finally decided not to refuse him. That was her single last thought before falling off to sleep. Early the next morning, Louis awakened her telling her to get the girls dressed and fed. Typically on Saturday mornings, they would sleep in and Tulah would prepare a big breakfast for them. But this particular morning, Louis was up and dressed and was urging her to get the kids dressed as well. After they were all dressed, they boarded a bus that let them out on Gratiot Avenue. The girl's eyes widened as they stepped off the bus and saw a sight that reminded them of being home. There were merchants with horse-drawn carriages, some with live chickens and rabbits, and some had fresh corn, tomatoes, cucumbers, and other colorful farm fresh fruits and vegetables. People stood shoulder to shoulder as they browsed and perused the stands buying and selling fresh spices, fish, poultry and meat.

"What is this place?" Tulah asked Louis.

"This is the Eastern Market. You can come here and get anything you want from fresh food to flowers to rabbits." Louis told her.

"Can we get a rabbit?" Lucille asked.

"Ooh yeah, please Daddy." Gracie added.

"Oh no. We came to get groceries and that's it."

"Pleeease Daddy." Lucille begged.

"We have a hamster at school, and my teacher let me feed it sometime. I don't think they're that different from rabbits, Daddy. So I can take care of it." Jessie offered.

"That's awfully nice of you sweetheart, but no pets, okay? Just food this time."

As they walked through the outdoor market, merchants continued unloading truckloads of fresh fruits and vegitables as customers rummaged through boxes of grapefruits, apples and pears. "This kinda reminds me of home." Tulah told Louis. He bought the girls their own bag of popcorn while he and Tulah shopped for groceries.

"Since you got off work late and we weren't able to do our regular weekly shopping, I figured I would bring you down here this morning. Do you like it?"

"I love this place."

"Martin told me about it. It sounded like something you would like."

"How can they carry on like dis everyday, wit all the hustle and bustle?"

"They're not open everyday, just on Saturday's."

After they shopped, they walked back to the bus stop carrying bags of fresh fruits and vegetables. As they got off the bus and walked home, Tulah saw Tyrone standing on his porch watching them. As they got closer to Tyrone's house, she tried to stay calm and not look at him. Her heart quickened, her breath became labored and she felt that she would pass out. She tried to pick up her pace, but Louis walked slowly, moseying on by, almost deliberately taking his time. As they walked past Tyrone, he and Louis caught eyes and Louis offered a casual greeting, while Tyrone offered a silent hello by simply nodding his head. Tulah's heart was beating so wildly, she thought that she would faint. Once she got the groceries put away, and prepared lunch for her family, she went out on the porch to see if Tyrone was still there. He wasn't. She smiled thinking about her night with him, and wondered again, why he didn't kiss her.

Days and even weeks had passed before Tulah saw Tyrone again, but when she finally did, she was with her girls and couldn't talk to him. She looked at him and he smiled and

nodded and kept about his business. She wondered what she had
done to make him act that way towards her. She wondered if the
other lady was back at his house and perhaps that was the reason
for his indifferentness. Whatever the reason he had to act that
way, she had every intention of finding out why. Tulah decided
that she was going to knock on his door when she got off work
that following afternoon to have a talk with him, but the next
morning, on her way to the bus stop, she couldn't take waiting
another whole day. She stormed up his stairs and banged on the
door. Tyrone opened the door, then stepped aside to let her
come in.

"What's wrong witchu? Why you treatin me like I don't exist
no mo?" When he didn't respond, she searched his eyes looking
for an answer. "Did I do something wrong? If I did, just tell me."

"Tulah, girl, go on home."

"Whatchu takin bout, Tyrone. Why you doing me like dis?
You got somebody else?"

"No, I aint got nobody else, but you do."

"Huh?"

"You got a family. I ain't messing with that."

"What about whatchu told me." She said almost pleadingly.
"You said you want me. Are you sayin you don't no mo?"

He chuckled, shook his head, and ran his hand over his tight
abs that was slightly revealed through his opened shirt, silk
pajamas. "No baby, I want you, but it wouldn't work."

"Why not? We got away with it last time, nobody knew."

"I aint the sneaky type, Tulah. Whatever I decide to do, I aint
gone be hiding from nobody. Can you handle something like
that?"

"Whatchu mean? You want me ta tell my husband?"

"I'm not askin you to do nothing. I'm just saying that I am a
grown man, and when I date a lady, I'm gone do it openly. I'm
not gone be sneakin around like some coward. And since you got
a husband, one that you ain't leaving no time soon, I can't get
down with you like that." Tulah stared at him, digesting what she
had just been told. For the past weeks, she thought of nothing
else but seeing him again, feeling his lips against hers, smelling his
cologne, and looking forward to that feeling she got when she
was in his presence. Now he was telling her to get lost, but she
wasn't about to let that happen.

"But Tyrone, I don't wanna stop seeing you."

"It won't work. My life is too different from yours. And besides, it's a lot of things about me that you don't know."

"Dat don't matter. Let's just try to work it out." She said, losing control as her voice tremored.

"Go on, Tulah." He said nodding towards the door. When she didn't move, he walked over to the door and held it open. She stood there staring at him, with her arms folded across her chest, but he remained fixed in his decision. Feeling defeated, she took in a deep breath and blew it out. Then she got angry and stormed over to the open door and slammed it shut.

"How you just gone do me like this? I'm tired of men thinking dey can do me any kinda way without for one minute considering how I feel."

"Whatchu talking about? Who doing you any kinda way?"

Tulah caught herself. "Forget it."

"No. Whatchu talking about?"

"I'm talking about you and Louis. Yall the only mens I know, and both a yall treat me like I don't matter."

"Girl, what are you talking about?"

"You telling me dat you caint see me no mo. What about how I feel? You kept on and kept on and finally when I say okay, now dat I'm ready, now you wanna stop."

Tyrone nodded. "And what else?"

"And Louis."

"What about Louis? What did he do?" She dropped her head, but Tyrone lifted her chin with his hand. "Tell me what happened?"

"He sold my house!" Tears filled her eyes and she cried grabbing Tyrone around the waist. He held her, rubbing her back.

"What house?"

"I had my own house back in Georgia. This old lady I used to take care of gave it to me free and clear when she died. Louis sold the house and spent the money to get us up here wit out me knowin about it."

"He sold your house, and didn't tell you?" Tulah sniffled and nodded her head. Tyrone held her in his arms. "It was the only thang in the world that I could call my own. I worked so hard to get it how I wanted it. I loved that house. It wasn't as nice as some, but it was mine." She cried in his chest. "And guess how I found out?"

"How?"

"He told me he sold it when I told him I wanted to go back home."

"Why were you going home?"

"Cause I hate it up here. You was right about whatchu said dat day. I thought thangs would be better. But it aint no better, if anything, it got worse. I aint even start likin it here till I met you." She confided. Tyrone cupped Tulah's face in his large, rough hands and kissed her. She kissed him back, passionately, hungrily. When Tyrone tried to pull back, Tulah held to him tighter, not allowing him to let her go. He took her hand and placed it on his rising nature. Tulah grabbed and squeezed it hard. He picked her up, carried her to his bedroom, and made love to her, enrapturing her with his touch. He loved Tulah in ways she didn't know were possible, causing multiple climactic eruptions, as her body convulsed from pleasure. Tulah knew she had to go to work, but nothing mattered to her at that moment, except lying in Tyrone's arms, waiting for him to love her again. She stayed with him the entire day. After passionate love making sessions, she submissively went to the kitchen and cooked for Tyrone, just as he predicted that she would.

The next morning, Tulah went to work like nothing happened. She went to the servant's quarters, put on her uniform and went about her business of cleaning the house. When she saw Mrs. Fortson, she nodded and smiled with no word of an explaination as to why she didn't show up and offered no apology.

"How dare you walk up in my house after that stunt you pulled yesterday?" She bellowed at Tulah. "You cant just not show up here, after what you did. What do you have to say for yourself."

"Oh. I'm sorry. Somethin came up." Was all that Tulah had to say.

"Well, that's not good enough."

"What do you want me to do?"

"I want you to take that uppity, arrogant attitude, and get outta my house!" Mrs. Fortson screamed. Tulah stopped dusting, layed the duster on the table, and headed back towards the servant's quarters. Mrs. Fortson followed her, still screaming.

"Where do you think you're going?"

"You just told me ta get outta yo house."

"That's right, you get outta here right now!" Although she had just been fired, Tulah didn't mind, because there was something else she'd much rather spend her time doing. She later told Louis that Mrs. Fortson let her go, because she found a live in housekeeper who would be taking over. When he asked what she would do now, she simply replied that she would just stay home.

Early one morning, close to three o'clock, there was a desperate knocking at their door. Louis jumped out of bed, went to the window and yelled out.

"Who is it?"

"Louis, it's Earl. I gotta get Mabelle to the hospital, I think she's about to have the baby."

"Hold on, Earl. I'll be right down."

"What is it, Louis?" Tulah asked getting out of bed and wrapping her housecoat around her.

"Mabelle's about to have the baby."

"It's too soon for her to have the baby. She got another month to go. Something must be wrong."

"Well get dressed, because he needs our help."

Louis went down and to talk to Earl and then ran back up the stairs. He explained that he was going to fetch a cab while Earl went to get Mabelle. Louis helped them get a cab, but Earl was afraid because Mabelle was not far along enough to deliver, and insisted that he ride to the hospital with them. The doctor took Mabelle to the back right away and Louis stayed and offered support to a nerve wrecked Earl. Two hours and twenty minutes later, the doctor came out and announced that Earl was the father of a four pound and 11 ounce baby boy. Earl was ecstatic. He went in to see Mabelle, who was so exhausted, that she slept the entire time he was in the room. Once Louis got the news that the baby was fine and Mabelle was resting comfortably, he left to go home.

By the time Louis returned home, it was after seven o'clock. He gave Tulah the news about Earl and Mabelle's brand new baby boy, then showered and left for work. Tulah had been up since Louis left, anxiously waiting to get word on Mabelle's condition, so when Louis went to work and the girls went to school Tulah layed down to take a nap. She had only been sleep for few minutes before she started to dream. She dreamed that she walking down the street carrying a new blanket to give to Mabelle's baby. The blanket was white and had gold circles on it. On her way there, she heard a whooshing noise behind her. She turned to see what the noise was and upon first glance, witnessed a beautiful white and gold horse drawn chariot descending from heaven. The chariot came down and stopped in front of Mabelle's house. Tulah ran to see what was going on, but couldn't get her legs to work. She tried and tried to run, but it felt like her feet were stuck in mud, keeping her glued to the spot where she stood. A tall man, whose face couldn't be seen because of a blinding glow around his head, came out of Mabelle's house carrying her baby wrapped in the blanket that Tulah was carrying. When she looked down and realized that she no longer had the blanket, the man stepped into the chariot and it ascended back into heaven carrying Mabelle's baby with him. Tulah woke up in a panick. She replayed the dream over in her head and came up with the same conclusion- Mabelle's baby is gone.

Chapter 25

Tulah couldn't get enough of Tyrone, she spent every moment of free time she had with him. When Louis would leave for work, and the girls got off to school, she would go right over to Tyrone's house, and stay there all day. On the days he couldn't be with her due to his line of work, he would give her large amounts of cash to go to Woolworth's Department store to buy herself something nice. After shopping she would go back to his house lounging around, cooking, or taking long bubble baths from the wide variety of fragrances she'd collected since she'd been there. Being at his house had become a home away from home. Tulah always hated when it was time to go home at the end of the day, even if Tyrone wasn't there. Love making with Louis had come to a complete hault. At first she would force herself out of obligation to him as his wife, which had come to be a complete and utter chore. But after a while she stopped forcing herself saying that she just didn't enjoy sex anymore. However, the truth was that she did enjoy sex, she just didn't enjoy it with Louis.

When Louis confronted her about where she was getting money to shop and buy fancy clothes and expensive perfume from she snapped, telling him not to worry about where she gets money from. She reminded him that he didn't tell her how he spent her money, so he doesn't have the right to ask her how she's getting hers. Louis had been patient with Tulah for months, putting up with her tantrums, random outbursts and disappearing acts. At first he attributed it to the resentment she harbored against him, but after a while, it was clear that it was something else that had Tulah so resistant towards him. She eventually stopped cooking dinner, and cleaning the house, leaving that for him or Gracie to do. Perplexed by her behavior, Louis uncharacteristically started leaving work and coming home early, trying catch her at something, but she was always ahead of him. After several weeks of the cat and mouse game, Louis snapped. He demanded that she tell him what's going on, but Tulah refused to talk to him. They screamed and yelled at each other, but Tulah never gave Louis any idea of what was going on. Then finally he asked her a question in which he feared the answer.

"Is there someone else?"

Tulah paused before answering. She weighed the consequences of her answer and decided that she was not going to be like him and tell a lie.

"Yeah, there is." Louis' heart sank. He knew it. In the back of his mind he knew all along, but was afraid of asking for fear if learning the truth.

"Are you in love?"

"Yeah."

Louis pounded his fist against the wall. "Why dammit?"

"Louis every since we been here, nothing mattered but what you wanted. You didn't even look at me anymore let alone ask me what I thought or wanted. You made me stop hanging out over Mabelle's, you wouldn't let me work, although I begged you for years, and on top of that, you sold my house and didn't even tell me."

"Tulah, I…"

"Hear me out, now. You only let me work because you felt guilty about what you did. You wouldn't buy me a ticket or send me home, no matter how many times I asked. Aint Cora is the only family I got, and you kept me from her. Maybe not purposely, but the fack of the matta is dat I haven't seen my aunt if over five years, Louis. I'm tired of living my life for everybody else, it's time I start living for me."

"Living your life for everybody else?"

"Yes. For everybody except me."

"Tulah, we are your family. It's what you're supposed to do."

"Well, I'm tired of it."

"What are you saying, girl. You ain't makin sense?"

"I'm saying I'm moving out."

"What? Where? With him?"

"Yeah, wit him. He know how to treat me and he buys me nice thangs and gives me all dat I need."

"Wait a minute, Tulah. Think about what your'e saying. We got a family here, what about the girls?"

"I have thought about it Louis. And the girls will be just fine wit dey Daddy. For once, you gone see what it's like havin to live for everybody else's happiness and puttin yours aside."

"Wait Tulah, let't talk about this."

"Aint nothing left to talk about, Louis." She said grabbing a bag and zealously throwing her things in it. "You get to figure it out on yo own."

"Where you going? To him? At least tell me who it is." Tulah stopped and faced Louis. She took a deep breath and told him it was Tyrone Baxter, who lived on the corner. Louis went ballistic.

"You mean that slick-headed, fast talking, switch blade carrying, hustler? Tulah that man don't care nothing about you, he's a womanizer. He got women all over town, and he put them in danger by carrying drugs for him. Is that the kind of life you want? I can't believe this." Louis screamed at her. "You know you're just a stupid little girl, who don't know nothing. That man is playing you." Tulah became infuriated and screamed as loud as she could. She charged him, swinging her arms furiously and hitting him as hard as she could. Louis grabbed her by both wrists and threw her to the bed. Tulah sobered, realizing that she had pushed Louis too far. He towered over her and pointed threatingly in her face.

"Don't you put your hands on me ever again, Tulah. If you want that black-faced, low-life, good for nothing pimp, go to him."

Tulah got up, wiped the tears from her eyes, grabbed her bags and stormed out of the house. Louis sat down on the bed and hung his head in defeat. Tears welled in his eyes as he put his hands over his face and wept.

"What am I gone tell my girls, dear Lord? What am I gone tell my babies?"

When the girls came home from school, Louis was sitting in the living room with tear stained eyes, looking straight ahead and smoking a cigarette. Gracie came in first and spoke to Louis.

"Hi Daddy." Gracie offered, but Louis didn't respond. She looked into his face and immediately started to cry.

"What's wrong, Daddy?" Louis grabbed Gracie and rocked

her in his arms. Lucille and Jessie came in shortly after and saw Louis holding Gracie, so they ran over to join in.

"What's wrong with Daddy?" Jessie cried.

"I don't know." Lucille answered.

"Daddy, what's wrong?"

Louis gathered himself and sat the girls down for a talk. All day he had practiced the speech he would give them about why their mother left. Sitting them down, he lit another cigarette and tried to explain to them, in a hypothetical way, what happens to people when they are unhappy. Looking into the intense and inquisitive little faces of his girls, he stood up, paced the floor and started over, this time telling them the truth. He explained that mommy had left because she wasn't happy living there anymore. He told them that it wasn't their fault, nor was it his, but just that she was no longer happy.

"Where did she go?" Gracie asked, "Is she coming back?" Lucille chimed in, "Is she mad at us? I want to see her." Jessie added. The girls had a barrage of questions about there mother's where abouts that Louis did not have the answers to. However, when asked about where she was, he weighed the consequences of telling the girls the truth, but then decided that he was not going to cover for her. He decided that telling the girls the truth was the best thing to do. After all, Tulah was living right down the street with her lover, and that was something he wouldn't be able to keep from them.

"She's down the street with that dark-skinned man, the one with the greasy hair."

"Down the street with a dark skinned man?" Gracie asked, searching her mind for who he couldn've meant. Then gasping, she asked, "You mean with Mr. Baxter?"

"Yeah, she moved in with him."

"Why would she move in with him?"

"Why don't you all go on down there and ask her?"

"You want us to go over there?"

"Yeah, go on down and knock on the door. Ask her why she left us and why she's living with Tyrone."

Jessie climbed on Louis' lap. "Daddy are you sad?"

"Yeah, I'm sad, baby. I'm sad and disappointed."

"What should we say?" Gracie asked. "What if Mr. Baxter comes to the door instead of mommy?"

"Then you tell him you're there to see your mother. No, don't say that. Tell him... no, better yet, ask him why is your mother living there with him. Ask him why did he take your mother away from her family."

"Did he take mommy away?" Jessie asked innocently.

"No. Mommy went on her own." Lucille answered for him.

"Don't say that, Lucille." Gracie scolded.

"It's the truth. Mommy is always talking to that man."

"What you mean, Lucille?" Louis asked.

"I always see mommy talking to him whenever we go to the store. Sometime I tell her that I'll go to the store for her, but she always wants to go herself. And everytime she would be down there talking to that ole, ugly man."

"Why didn't you tell me that before?"

"I don't know."

"Um hum, it's okay, baby. Come on. I want you all to go on down there."

"Do you really want us to go, Daddy?" Gracie asked.

"I wanna go." Lucille interjected. "I wanna hear what she has to say."

"Daddy, I don't think Jessie needs to go." Gracie reasoned, "She's still a baby and she wouldn't understand."

"I'm not a baby, I'm eight years old!"

"All of you go. Go on right now."

Louis made the girls go down and knock on Tyrone's door. He stood on the porch watching them as they marched down to his house and knocked on the door. He couldn't see who opened the door, but within moments the girls all went inside. While they were gone, Louis smoked incessantly; lighting one cigarette after another. Pacing the floor, he stressfully raked his hand over his head, and was even tempted to pray. He hadn't prayed in nearly six years. Because he'd experienced so many adversities in his life, he didn't think that God cared about him anymore, so he responded to that by completely shutting God out of his life. He often thought about God, though he wouldn't allow himself to trust God, because he didn't want to be let down again.

However, in this brutally unforeseeable and ambiguous interlude, he desperately needed God's help. There had been a vicious cruelty waged against him and his family and he felt helpless in terms of how to respond, because it was his beloved

Tulah, that was at the center of it. Yes, Louis had known for a while that Tulah had not been happy, but this selfish, unrivaled act of blatant adultery and premeditated betrayal was flagrantly mean, and according to Louis, beyond Tulah's volition. He completely blamed Tyrone for this detestable offense. Louis sat on the sofa and laid his head in his hands. He wondered what his neighbors, friends and family would say once they found out what's happened. What a scandal, he thought to himself. How could his girls live with this kind of embarrassment? Louis felt like he could die. He wanted to get out of there, disappear and never come back- and he considered doing it.

He thought about leaving while the girls were down the street with Tulah and Tyrone. He would just grab a few things, pack a bag and leave before they got back. Let Tyrone play Daddy for a week or two, and see how much he would want Tulah after that. He would toss Tulah out on her butt without a second thought and she would come running, begging for Louis to take her back. The thought danced in his head and his feet almost moved in that direction, but Louis was not willing to gamble with his daughters for the likes of that black-faced, back-stabbing, low-lifed pimp.

"How could she be so stupid?"

He paced the room, walking from one corner to the other, then he walked out on the porch, looking for the girls, and when he didn't see them, he would start pacing again. When the girls finally came returned, Jessie ran in her room and slammed the door behind her. Lucille came in with her arms folded across her chest and Gracie came and took a seat on the sofa. Louis jumped up to go after Jessie, but Gracie stopped him by grabbing his hand. "Let her go, Daddy. Let her have a minute alone."

"Well, what happened? What did she say?" Louis asked looking at the girls.

Lucille stood against the wall not saying a word and Gracie took in a long breath, exasperated, she blew it out before answering. "She says she's not coming back."

"Ever?"

"That's what she said."

"Tell me what she said, exactly." Louis quizzed.

"She didn't say nothing. All she kept doing was bringing out new clothes for us to see. 'Look at this dress and aint this pretty'. " Lucille mocked. "She never even asked us how we felt! She never said sorry, all she wanted us to do was see her fine new clothes. And poor little Jessie kept saying, 'that's pretty momma', but momma didn't even look at her for looking at them new clothes."

"Where was Tyrone?"

"I don't know."

"Was he there?"

"He was there, in the back somewhere. When we knocked on the door, he had us to wait on the porch, and then Mama came and let us in."

Lucille did all the talking, and Gracie kept her head down while holding Louis' hand.

"Come here." Louis told them, putting his arm around Gracie and reaching for Lucille with the other. "I know it's hard right now, but we're gonna get through this, okay? We are still a family, me, the both of you, and Jessie. And we have to be strong for one another. I don't know if your mother's going through a phase, or if something else is going on, but we can't fall apart because she's gone."

"Daddy, I don't know what's wrong with her." Gracie spoke up.

"I know baby, I don't either."

"Daddy, may I be excused?" Gracie asked. "I want to go and see about Jessie."

"Sure baby. That's right, go check on your sister."

Gracie got up and walked towards the back. She wanted to check on Jessie, but the real reason she asked to be excused was because her stomach had been bothering her after hearing the news about Tulah. But, after seeing her at Tyrone's house, it started cramping so bad, that she almost doubled over from the pain. She went to the bathroom and drank cold water out of the faucet by cupping it into her mouth. Then she washed her face, and sat on the edge of the tub rubbing her stomach. When the pain finally started to subside, she went to check on Jessie, who was already fast asleep. Gracie turned out the light, then climbed in bed and thought about the way her mother was ensconced in Tyrone Baxter's house so comfortable and so at ease, like it was her rightful place to be there. She agreed with Lucille' assessment of her mother, Tulah never acknowledged their feelings. Her only concern was the pretty clothes that Tyrone bought for her. That was Gracie's single last thought before falling off to sleep.

The following morning, Louis woke Gracie before leaving for work. He told her to get up and wake her sisters so they wouldn't be late for school. Gracie thought about what happened the night before, shook her head in disbelief, and then dragged herself out of bed. She went to the bathroom, undressed, and stepped into the shower. As she stepped out, she looked down at the clothes that she had dropped to the floor and saw that her panties were soiled. When she picked them up to get a closer look, she realized that through the night she had become a woman. She quickly turned on the faucet and let cold water run over her undergarments, hoping they weren't permanently stained. She woke Lucille and Jessie, made them breakfast, and saw them off to school, telling them that she was staying behind to clean up and would be there shortly after. She stood out on the sidewalk watching her sisters as they walked down the block, the same way Tulah would do when she saw them off to school. When they successfully made it across the street, Gracie walked down to Tyrone Baxter's house and knocked on the door. When Tulah came to the door, tears flooded Gracie's eyes as she told her that her period had come.

"What happened?" Tulah asked.

"I don't know. My stomach was hurting real bad last night and when I got up this morning it was blood in my panties."

"Yeah, you thirteen years old, that's about right, I guess. You a big girl now, so dat mean you can't be messin around wit no boys, cause you can get pregnant now."

"What am I supposed to do?"

"About what?"

"I'm bleeding, Mama! I could die. What if I bleed ta death?" Gracie cried.

"God. Aint I ever teach you nothing bout how your period work? Girl, you gone be alright, it's gone stop. It's gone last for about five days, then it's gone stop."

"For good?"

"Naw, not for good. It's gone stop until next month, then it's gone come back for about five days every month."

"For how long?"

"For the rest of yo life, or at least till you go through da change."

"Mama, I need you to come home." Gracie cried. "I don't know what to do. I'm scared."

"Scared of what, girl? Shoot, dats all a part of being a woman. What'd you use to catch it?"

"Toilet paper."

"You did da right thang. Come on in while I get dressed, and then we gone walk up here to da store and get you some feminine napkins. I guess Lucille will be startin' hers, too. She right behind you in everything you do."

Tulah got dressed and walked to the store with Gracie. She bought enough feminine napkins to last for two months. As they walked back, Tulah told Gracie that she loved her and that she needed her to look after her sisters and her Daddy. She told her to be a big girl and that she was proud of her. She kissed her, gave her two dollars, and went back to Tyrone's house. Gracie stuffed the two dollars in her pocket and walked back home alone.

Chapter 26

Over the next few months, Gracie and Jessie continued to run back and forth the Tyrone's house whenever they needed to talk to Tulah. Lucille on the other hand, refused to go anywhere near there. She would send messages through her sister's or would simply go without seeing or talking to her mother. When the weather started to break and spring arrived, Tyrone grew tired of the constant interruptions, so once again, he hired a moving truck, and he and Tulah moved to the other side of town. Tulah would come and visit the girls when she knew Louis wouldn't be home, and eventually showed them how to catch the bus so they could go visit her. Gracie and Jessie would catch the bus every Saturday to go and visit Tulah. Lucille would go sometimes, but many times she elected to stay home. Her inconsistency had become so predictable, that whenever she opted not to go visit Tulah, it was rarely questioned as to why.

Tulah and Tyrone settled into a small trailor home located just south of eight mile. It was a smaller home from where the couple moved from, but it was a newly constructed subdivision and much cleaner. Tyrone spoiled Tulah, buying her nice clothes and taking her to the swankiest supper clubs around town. Once he took her to the Paradise Theatre, a premier music center located in downtown Detroit to see Lady Day herself, Ms. Billie Holiday. The lengendary performer entertained them with sultry ballads and poignant lyrics, swaying and slurring through most of the songs. Tulah was awestruck by the ambiance, energy and elegance of the theatre, as she had never seen anything like it before. She enjoyed being on the arm of a well-known and respected man such as Tyrone. Everywhere they went, people knew him and wanted to pull him aside, whisper in his ear, and slap palms, many times leaving money in his hand. She even saw a man give Tyrone a big wad of money, and when she asked him about it, he told her to never ask him about his business, that way she couldn't incriminate herself. Tulah didn't understand his meaning, but she respected what he said enough to not ask.

More and more, people were coming to their house looking for Tyrone and either picking up or dropping off packages for him. If he wasn't there, they would reluctantly leave it with Tulah and tell her to make sure he gets it. One man in particular visited frequently and asked lots of questions. He would always come in looking around the house as if taking inventory, and he would always keep one eye on Tulah. She thought the man took a liking to her, but later decided that he was more interested in what belongings they had in their home. Tulah didn't get a good feeling from him, but dared not mention it to Tyrone because he had already told her that his business was his business and not hers. One evening, just after taking a bath, Tulah laid across the bed to polish her nails when she heard an urgent knock at the door. Before she could get up to see who it was, she heard a loud thud as if the door was being kicked in.

Tulah froze in place as policemen invaded her home, kicking in the bathroom and bedroom doors and ransacking her small, well-kept home. She was pushed against the wall as one officer handcuffed her and put her in the back of a squad car. An hour later, Tulah found herself in a dirty jail cell with a toilet, a bunk bed, and a haggered looking woman with a blond wig, who was picked up for soliciting. Tulah kept telling the officers that they had made a mistake by taking her to jail, but they wouldn't listen to her, telling her, to tell it to the judge.

Tulah became irate, crying and screaming at the officers while hanging onto the bars telling them that she needed to call Tyrone. A tall, white officer, with a big nose walked over to Tulah's cell and stared her down.

"If you don't pipe down and stop making all that noise, I'm gonna take you downstairs where all the murderers and rapists are and let them have their way with you."

The thought of what he threatened to do frightened Tulah so badly, that she slowly backed away, not taking her eyes off him until her back was against the wall. Then she slid down against the wall until her knees where touching her chest and cried helplessly in her hands. The officer turned and walked away laughing, obviously pleased with himself for scaring Tulah into submission. When the officer was out of sight, the blonde headed woman told Tulah that what he did was just a scare tactic to keep her quiet.

"How do you know?"

"I've been here more times than I care to remember. I know how the game is played" She told her.

"How you get outta here? Better yet, why did you come back?"

"I gotta live, honey."

"I don't know whatcu mean?"

The woman laughed. "I can see you inexperienced. Just as green as a blade of grass. What you in for, honey?"

"I don't know."

"Sure you do."

"I don't!" Tulah screamed. "I didn't do nothin'."

"Who's Tyrone?"

"How you know Tyrone?"

The woman laughed at Tulah.

"You only screamed his name twenty times. That your man?"

Tulah nodded. "What's he do?"

"Huh?"

"Your man, honey. I bet he's the reason you're here. What kind of work does he do?"

"I don't know. He wouldn't let me ask him about his work." Tulah answered. The woman laughed again. "Either you real smart, or real stupid. Which one are you?"

Tulah shook her head and tears began to fall. "I don't know." She answered ingenuously. "All hell, please don't start that crying again. Look, I can see you don't know shit from sugar, so I'm gone help you out. You tell that officer that you want your phone call. You're entitled to make one phone call. Now, you can try callin that man of yours if you want to, but I'm willing to bet, if they ain't already got him, he long gone by now. I would'nt waste my dime calling him. You call somebody who you know is gone come and get you." She told Tulah, while lighting a cigarette. "Since this is your first offence, meaning you ain't never been to jail before, they'll probably let you out. Anyway, after you get outta here, you stay away from men like Tyrone. Them slick, city boys can spot a sweet little country girl like you a mile away. They good to you, but ain't good for you." Walking over to the toilet, she placed the cigarette between her lips, hiked up her dress, and squatted over the toilet. She peed while letting the cigarette dangle in her mouth and continued with her instructions.

"You gotta stop all that crying, though. Ain't nobody gone listen to a sniffling, little cry baby. You gotta speak up and act like you know what you talking about. Tell them you need to speak to your lawyer."

"I ain't got no lawyer!"

"I know that." She answered, wiping herself and pulling her skirt back into place. "But they don't. Just tell em that, okay? Oh yeah, and keep with the stupid routine."

"What stupid routine?"

"That one." She said pointing in Tulah's direction. "Keep telling them you don't know nothing."

Tulah collected herself as much as she could and called the officer down to her cell. She told them that she knew her rights and wanted her one phone call. Surprisingly, they acquiesced, and let Tulah out of the cell to make her call. As Tulah walked away from the cell, she looked back at the blond woman and mouthed a thank you to her. The officer took Tulah to a small room in the back to use the phone. As she held the receiver in her hand, she momentarily didn't know who she would call. There was no chance of her calling Louis. Even though he would probably come, she couldn't ask that of him. There was only one other person who she could call, so she dialed the number and hoped for the best.

Mabelle didn't get down to the jail house until the next morning, but even after she posted bail, Tulah wasn't released until later that evening. Tulah hadn't seen her friend in close to a year, and was happy that Mabelle so willingly came to her rescue. Mabelle drove Tulah to her house, only to find that the house was left wide open and had been looted. The house was in disarray. Broken glass everywhere, furniture flipped over, doors kicked in, mattresses turned over, clothes thrown around and tables turned upside down. Mabelle stayed for a while helping Tulah clean up and get things back in order. It took Tulah two days to get the place back like it was.

Four days had passed before Tulah saw Tyrone again. It was at a preliminary hearing when he was indicted for selling and distributing drugs, along with other felonious charges. The same guy who would always come to their house asking questions was working as an informant to the police and had helped to bring Tyrone down. As it turned out, Tyrone was a big drug dealer, who ran numbers, and was rumored to have women working for him, although the courts couldn't prove it. Tyrone was sentenced to ten to fifteen years in prison with a possibility of parole in no less than eight years. Tulah thought she would die when she heard the judge read the verdict, because not only would she miss Tyrone, she didn't know how she would survive without him. She trembled as she nervously awaited her sentence, but the judge was lenient because it was her first offence. She was put probation for her involvement. She had to do eighty hours of community service and find a job by the time she went to her first probation meeting or do thirty days in jail. She got a job as a pants presser at the cleaners, making twelve dollars a week. It wasn't enough to keep the house that she and Tyrone lived in, so she rented a room with an older couple on the North West side of Detroit.

Tulah begged Mabelle not to say anything to her girls or Louis about what happened, but it was obvious that she did, because when she went to see the girls, they couldn't look at her. Gracie, always true to character, was gracious and polite. Jessie was Mama's baby, come what may, but Lucille stayed in the room and refused to come out. Tulah was tempted to go in the room and make Lucille talk to her, but her guilt wouldn't allow her to be so presumptuous. Besides, the girls were growing up. They had their own ideas about things, people, and just how the world works in general, and Tulah had to respect that. She understood that there were things she missed in the girls rearing, but the way she saw it, her mother wasn't around for her rearing, and she turned out fine, so she convinced herself that her girls would be fine as well. She was just grateful that they had a good father to look after them. Tulah looked at the clock and knew Louis would be coming in soon, so she gathered her things and prepared to leave before having to encounter him. Gracie walked Tulah to the door, and just before she walked away, she told her that Cora had been calling, because she hadn't heard from her and was wondering if everything was alright.

"Whatchu teller?"

"I told her that you were fine, and that I'd make sure you would call her."

"Good girl. Thanks Gracie. I"ll see you next time." She told her before walking away.

Chapter 27

As time moves forward at a steady pace, change will surely occur with the same consistency. Some changes however, bring about more change, turning bitter into sweet, darkness into daylight, and rain into sunshine. It was change that altered the neighborhood where Louis and his girls lived, as most of the white neighbors moved out, and blacks quickly moved in to take their place. There were changes in Louis job, when he stopped from working at the steel factory and moved to the automotive plant, earning sixty nine dollars a week; and it was change that transformed the girls from awkward looking, skinny girls, into beautiful, blossoming, young teens. They grew fast and developed early, achieving womanly curves and budding breasts by the time they reached their teens. Gracie and Lucille got equal attention from boys their age; however, it was Lucille who seemed to revel in engaging them in coquettish conversation.

Louis observed how the girls were growing and beginning to take an interest in boys, and it disturbed him because he knew there were limitations as to what he could do to prevent it. Watching Gracie and Lucille was like seeing Tulah at their age all over again. It both pleased and saddened him that they were so much like their mother. It bothered him mostly because it was at this tender age they needed Tulah to coach and guide them through their pubescent years. But because Tulah's behavior had been so unstable and sporadic, he thought that perhaps it was best that she wasn't. Since Louis had taken a job at the automotive plant, he had less time to spend with the girls because the job was so demanding, requiring that he work longer hours.

Gracie and Lucille would manage just fine adjusting to his new schedule; however, his concern was not being able to spend time with Jessie. Gracie, ever compassionate and mothering to her little sisters, picked up the slack and did all that she could to support the family, but there was simply no getting control over Lucille. She would leave the house right after school and stay gone all day, returning just before it was time for Louis to come home. Her breasts were beginning to form, filling out the small cups of her brazierre, and she stayed in the mirror admiring them, while sticking her chest out, accentuating their form. One of her class-mates, Barry Blackman, told her that she had pretty, fat legs, so she resolved to wearing skirts everyday. Lucille had gone boy-crazy.

One day after school, Gracie looked for Lucille so they could walk home together like they did everyday, except Lucille was nowhere to be found. Gracie looked everywhere and still couldn't find her. She found a group of Lucille's friends leaving the school, and asked them if they had seen her. One of the girls pointed to the stairwell and ran off laughing. Gracie shrugged off her frivolous behavior and headed for the stairs to find Lucille. When she got there, she found Lucille and Barry Blackman locked in an embrace, kissing, while his hands vigorously explored her bottom. Gracie was appalled.

"Barry Blackman!" She screamed. "Take your filthy hands off of my sister."

Barry instinctively jumped and backed away from Lucille, while she smoothed out her crumpled skirt that just a moment ago was pulled up over her backside.

"You scared me!" Lucille rebuked her.

"Why are you letting him put his hands on your butt like that, what's wrong with you?"

"Gracie, go home and mind your own business." Lucille responded nonchalantly.

"You are my business. Now you get your books and get home right now." Gracie reprimanded, pointing her finger.

"You're not my mother, Gracie. Just cause you think you are doesn't make it so." "You better get outta here right now, Lucille. And you!" She said, turning her rage to Barry. "Don't you ever put your hands on my little sister like that again."

"I'm sorry." Barry stammered.

"You don't have to apologize to her. Stay outta my business, Gracie."

"Your business? You got your business hanging all outta your pants, acting like some kind of tramp. Now you get your books and go home!"

"Who you calling a tramp?"

"You! For letting this boy put his dirty hands all over your butt. I can't wait to tell Daddy."

When Gracie said that, Lucille became enraged. No longer able to contain her mounting fury, she balled her fist and charged Gracie, sending her tumbling down the small landing and down five stairs. When Gracie felt herself being thrust down the stairs, she grabbed hold of Lucille's shirt and pulled her down with her, sending her buttons flying in every direction. Gracie and Lucille went blow for blow, rolling on the floor, pulling hair and ripping each others clothes. Barry tried to pull them apart, but the girl's faught feverishly, hitting and kicking him whenever he got too close. The commotion drew the attention of the math teacher, who, all the kids swore lived in the basement of the school because he wore wrinkled clothes and was always at the school, even after everyone else had left. He broke up the fight, took them to the office, and then sent them home with a suspension letter, advising that they would not be let back into school until after a parent teacher conference had been arranged.

"It's all your fault." Lucille admonished. "Barging in on me like you're my mother."

"Shut up, Lucille. Don't you get it? Daddy just got this job and he can't be taking time off work to get us back in school. If he takes time off, he could lose his job."

"Well, you didn't have no right,"

"I didn't have no right to do what? Come in and stop my little sister from acting fast and hot tail? You don't be letting that boy feel all over you like that. Do you know your friends laugh at you? They talk about you and laugh."

"No they don't."

"Oh yes they do. When I asked where you were, they couldn't even answer me for laughing so hard. They're the ones who told me where to find you. They think you're fast for letting that boy touch you like that, and I think you're stupid."

"Take it back, Gracie."

"I will not take it back. I mean it. I think you're stupid for letting that dumb boy put his stinking hands on your butt. You don't know where his hands been. You know how nasty boys are."

"Take it back, Gracie." Lucille warned.

"Or what? What are you gonna do? You've caused enough trouble. Now we're kicked outta school until Daddy takes us back." Gracie shook her head. "As hard as Daddy works, you go and pull something like this. You really disappoint me."

"Gracie, you don't have to be so mean." Gracie looked back at Lucille whose feelings were obviously hurt. Lucille stopped walking and put her head down. "I'm sorry Gracie. I didn't mean to put Daddy's job in jeopardy and I don't want to disappoint you." Gracie walked over to Lucille and put her arm around her shoulder. "I know. But you just gotta be smarter about these things. Don't worry, we'll work something out, okay?"

Lucille nodded and they walked down the street with their arms drapped around each other's shoulder. As they walked past Mabelle's house, Lucille looked at Gracie suddenly endowed with an idea.

"Gracie, do you think we can ask Mabelle to help us."

"How do you mean?"

"She ain't working, maybe she could come up to the school with us. That way we don't have to tell Daddy, and he won't have to take time off from his job."

"That just might work. But you gotta be the one to ask her."

"I will. If you promise to come with me."

"Okay."

Gracie and Lucille climbed Mabelle's stairs and knocked at the door. Mabelle opened the door and greeted them with a big smile.

"Hey girls. How yall doing?"

The girls stole guarded looks at each other before answering.

"We fine." Lucille spoke up.

"What brings yall down here to see me? You wanna come in?" She asked, stepping aside to let them in. Once inside, Lucille gave a watered down version of what happened between herself and Gracie. She told Mabelle that they had gotten into a shoving match over a disagreement about an assignment. As Lucille went on about what happened she stole fleeting looks at Gracie, hoping that she would not have a sudden attack of conscienciousness and tell Mabelle the real truth. After explaining what happened, she asked if she would take them back to the school, so that Louis wouldn't have to take time off work.

"So what you mean is that you don't want him to know about what happened at school today?

"No, that's not it at all."

"It isn't?"

"No."

"Okay, well then explain to me once again why you shouldn't tell him."

"We don't want him to take off of work."

"Well, yes, you made that clear. But what does that have to do with him not knowing about it. Don't you think he would want to know what's happening with his girls? Don't you think it's his right to know?"

Gracie put her head down thinking that asking Mabelle to go with them was a bad idea, but Lucille persisted in convincing Mabelle that it was out of concern for their father. Mabelle agreed to go to the school with them but only if they tell Louis about what happened. Later that evening when Louis got home, Gracie and Lucille held hands as they approached Louis.

"Daddy we need to talk to you about something." Gracie informed him.

"Can it wait? I'm tired."

"No Daddy, it can't wait." As Louis looked at them standing there holding hands, he realized the gravity of the situation. Louis' heart skipped a beat as he sucked in a breath and let it go slowly. He sat back in his chair, stressfully rubbed his hand over his face, and prepared for the worse. His eyes blinked intently as he gave them his undivided attention.

"What is it?"

Gracie handed Louis a folded piece of paper, crumpled from being stuffed in her pocket. "What is this?" Louis asked, taking the paper.

"Read it." Louis slowly unfolded the paper, afraid that it would reveal his most dreaded fears. He knew by letting the girls stay home unattended so often would surely prove to be disasterous. If only he could've found a way to preclude what he was about to learn from the letter, he thought to himself, his life would be so much better. As Louis read through the scribbled lines, he let out a sigh of relief and his heart resumed to its normal pace. He leaned back in his chair and breathed slow and heavy. Only then did he realize how fearful he was at learning that one of his girls could have gotten themselves into trouble with a boy.

"What happened that you girls would fight with one another at school?"

Lucille looked at Gracie and commenced to telling her diluted version of what happened. That evening as Louis lay in bed, he couldn't help but to extrapolate on what he feared most – the thought of one of his girls getting pregnant. This was a constant concern of his. Especially since he's been working so much and didn't have time to spend with them. Both girls had started their period, so getting pregnant was definitely a possibility. He didn't have to worry about Gracie so much, but Lucille had more than just a healthy curiosity for the opposite sex, she was receptive and flirty. Although he still viewed Jessie as baby, the reality was that she was only three years behind her sisters, and she studied them and tried to emulate everything they did. Raising three young girls on his own had become too much for him to handle. When they were younger, his major concerns were the basics – food, clothes and shelter. But now that they've reached sexual maturity, and were curious and attracted to boys, as boys were to them, Louis was never at peace about leaving them alone. He worried constantly. He knew Lucille had tweaked the truth when she told him about what happened at school. He could tell by the way she went on and on, over-expletive in the way she described the details while Gracie avoided looking directly at him. He knew it had something to do with a boy without it ever being said. Louis tossed and turned most of the night trying to figure out a better way to care for his girls. After deliberating for most of the night he concluded that there was only one viable solution to his dilemma, and he would go to work on carrying out his plan in the morning.

The following evening, the girls were on their best behavior. The house was clean, dinner was cooked and the girls were either studying or doing homework. When Louis came in, the girls greeted him in their usual sweet way and offered to make a plate for him. But tonight, it was Louis' turn to sit the girls down and have a discussion. As they were seated on the sofa attentively waiting to hear his announcement, it broke his heart to look into their sweet and innocent faces and deliver the news to them.

"I been the best father I know how to be to you girls, but you growing up now. You ain't little girls no more, you young women and you need somebody to look after you better than I can."

"Daddy, what are you saying?" Gracie asked.

"Let me finish Gracie. I'm getting to that. You at the age where you changing from girls to women and I know you interested in boys." Gracie looked over at Lucille and gave her the evil eye. "And that's okay, its normal, but I don't know how to look after you or teach you things you need to know about being a woman."

"Daddy?" Gracie said, standing.

"I know it's gone be hard for you, it's gone be hard for me too."

"Whatchu saying, Daddy?"

"I'm saying that I got three bus tickets. One for each of you."

"Where we going, Daddy?" Lucille asked, rising from the sofa. But Gracie put her hand on her shoulder and gently pushed her back down.

"You sending us away?" a teary-eyed Gracie asked.

"I'm not sending you away. I'm just gone let you go and live with my Mama for a while. She can teach you how to be a young ladies a lot better than I can. I already talked to her about it and she excited to have yall come."

"But Daddy, how could you?"

"Gracie, it's not that I want to, I just can't do it any more. I don't wanna see my girls ruined by some boy."

"Daddy, you don't want us no more?" Jessie asked. Louis went over, picked up Jessie and sat her on his lap. "I don't want you girls to think that I don't want you, because I do. You mean more to me than anything in this world."

"Then why we gotta go live down south?"

"Because I don't have time to raise you and I don't want to see you get into any trouble."

"How you know we won't get into trouble down there?"

"I'm sorry, but I've already made up my mind. It's all settled. You'll be leaving on next Saturday." He lifted Jessie off of his lap, got up, walked in his bedroom and closed the door behind him.

Gracie, Lucille and Jessie remained in the living room, looking at each other in disbelief. They had just been hit with the worse possible news they could ever have been given. First their mother abandoned them, leaving them for a greasy haired husler, who lived right down the street, and now their father, the one who they hoped would always be ther for them, was sending them away to a grandmother in the south who they didn't even know. Jessie was the first to allow tears to fall, then Gracie. But Lucille wouldn't give in to them, resisting them, she bawled her fists and dug her nails deep into the fleshy part of her hands.

"What are we gonna do?" Jessie asked.

"Don't worry sweetie, I'm gonna take care of you." Gracie assured her, wiping tears from her eyes.

"Whose gonna take care of Daddy?" Jessie asked again.

"Who cares?" Lucille spat. "I hate him."

"Don't say that, Lucille."

"I do. I hate em both. And ain't nobody's gonna make me go nowhere. I'm getting outta here."

"And going where?"

"I don't know, but I'm leaving. Yall with me, or you gone stay here and be sent away like some ole raggedy hand me down?"

"I'm going with you, Lucille." Jessie told her.

"No you're not, Jessie, and she's not going either. Lucille can't go running off in the streets with no destination, and stop making the baby think she can run off with you."

"I'm not a baby, Gracie, and I want to go." Jessie added.

"Gracie, you can stay if you want to, but I ain't going. Ain't nobody sending me nowhere."

"I wanna go with Lucille."

"Jessie, let me handle this. Think about what you're saying, Lucille. Daddy bought tickets and already called Grandmother, he don't mean no harm, he only trying to do what's best."

"So you agree with Daddy? You're okay with being sent away?"

"No, I'm not okay, with it. But Daddy tried the best he could, it's the only way he know how to show he care. And if it wasn't for you being so fast none of this would be happening anyway."

"Don't put it on me. Mama and Daddy are the ones keep pushing us away like we don't mean nothing, and I'm tired of it."

"Daddy didn't push us away." Jessie retorted.

"Well, what do you call it?"

"Lucille, stop filling her head with lies about Mama and Daddy. And please let's stop talking about running away. This is a lot to digest, so lets just go to bed, and see how we feel in the morning, okay? Maybe then, this will make better sense." When Lucille didn't respond, she asked again "Lucille please. Okay?"

"Okay."

"Good. Let's get some sleep."

Gracie climbed into bed, held onto her pillow, rocked herself back and forth, and cried. She cried for her mother leaving her, for her father sending her away, for always hiding her feelings and trying to be strong. She cried for being tired, but mostly she cried because she felt so utterly alone. She didn't have anyone to talk to, express her feelings to, or anyone who could tell her that things will get better. She held on to her pillow and stuffed the corner of it in her mouth to muffle the sound, and cried herself to sleep. After everyone had gone to sleep, Lucille got up through the night and threw some clothes in a bag. She woke Jessie, told her she was leaving and instructed her to quietly get dressed. Jessie did as she was told and the two of them quietly sneaked down the stairs and out of the house.

They ran down the street and turned on the corner heading north to an unknown destination. The night air was cold and crisp and the sky was dark. Their only light was offered by a half moon that hung low in the sky creating shadows that followed them through desolate streets. After an hour of running to nowhere in particular, sobered Lucille of her impulsive actions, causing her to realize her err. However, her anger and resentment from the rejection she felt compelled her to keep running even though everything else that was reasonable and practical told her to go home. She carried Jessie on her back hoping to find shelter and take refuge from the night. She crossed streets, climbed fences, ducked behind trees and crawled under hedges. She ran until her calves throbbed with pain and her back ached from the weight of her little sister, who, oblivious to the danger Lucille put them in, slept intermittently, completely trusting her sister's decision. Lucille stopped when reaching a six foot fence that had barbed wire at the top with metal spokes sticking out of it. Surveying the fence, she surmised that it had to be at least two blocks in length; therefore, the only sensible thing to do was to climb it. She figured the wire part wasn't that tall, so she should be able to get over it relatively easy. She lowered Jessie until her dangling feet touched the ground waking her from her slumber.

"Where are we?" She asked sleepily.

"We gotta climb this fence. Do you think you can make it?"

"Where are we going?"

"I haven't figured that out yet."

"Then why do we have to climb this fence. What's on the other side?"

"I don't know, Jessie. Look, do you think you can get over those wires at the top?"

Jessie looked up at the tall fence with the spikey wires on top and then looked at the length of it.

"I don't want to climb over those wires, we could get all scratched up."

"I know, Jess, but there's no other way."

"I wanna go home."

"Too late for that."

"But you don't even know where we're going. It's cold, and it could be strangers out here."

"Jessie, stop whining. Nobody forced you to leave. We're here now, so let's just keep moving. You gotta climb as close to the top as possible, so you can put one leg over the wires to get to the other side. Do you think you can do that?"

"I don't know."

"I'll go first. Just watch me, and then I'll help you over."

"Okay."

Lucilled climbed as close to the barbed wire as she could without touching it. As she approached the top, she realized that getting over was not going to be as easy as she first thought. She remained in one spot trying to figure out how to get over, when bright lights suddenly shone on her. She looked down at the car responsible for the high beamed lights and saw two figures jump out.

"Lucille, don't move!"

It was Louis, still dressed in his pajamas and his old beat up work boots, being chauffeured by his co-worker, Martin. Both men carefully approached the fence trying to coax Lucille down.

"No Daddy, I'm not coming back."

"Lucille, if you touch that wire you'll be electrocuted."

Lucilled looked at the wire and became frozen in place with fear. She wanted to move, but her body refused to cooperate, rendering her powerless to help herself down. She looked down at Louis and called out to him.

"Daddy, help me."

"I'm coming, baby. Just whatever you do, don't touch that wire."

Louis took off his coat, handed it to Martin and started up the fence after Lucille. Once he reached her, she reached out to him.

"Sweetheart, I need you to put both hands on the fence and slowly climb down. Don't look down, but feel your way. Daddy's right here with you, I won't let you fall."

"I'm scared, Daddy."

"It's okay, Daddy's right here."

Lucille slowly climbed down to safety and upon reaching the bottom she hugged Louis around his waist and cried.

"Daddy, I don't wanna go to Georgia. Let me stay here with you, I'll be good. I won't get into any trouble. Daddy, please. Just don't send me away."

Chapter 28

A week after the night Lucille tried to run away, she sat quietly on a bus bound for Georgia. Gracie and Jessie sat in the seat behind her, because she insisted on sitting alone. In the days that followed, Lucille became more withdrawn and introverted, isolating herself from her Louis and her sisters. Contrary to the belief that Lucille was going through a period of adjustment, finding a way to embrace the inevidable, she was secretly trying to figure out a way to forever escape the rejection and uncertainties of her life that she had become all too familiar with.

At the end of a long and taxing bus ride, they girls arrived in Marietta. When the bus pulled to a halt, Lucille spied a petite older woman with her white hair pulled back into a bun, accompanied by two robust and brawny looking men. I bet that's grandmother, she thought to herself. And I know that can't be Joseph and Joshua, so big and burly like that, she said of the two men who stood beside her.

"There's Grandmother! And oh my God, look at how big Joseph and Joshua have gotten." Gracie exclaimed, referring to her two cousins.

"Where's grandmother?" Jessie asked stretching her neck to get a better look.

"Right there." Gracie said pointing, then knocking on the window and waving.

"That's Daddy's Mama?"

"Yup, that's her alright. I would recognize her anywhere. You were so little when we moved from here, I'm sure you don't remember her. Come on, let's get our bags." Gracie instructed while moving swiftly towards the exit.

Even though neither of the girls was there by choice, they all felt some excitement when seeing their estranged grandmother and cousins. As the girls filed off the bus, Sarah greeted them with a big smile and a warm embrace.

"Oh my Lord, look how you girls have grown."

"Hi grandmother." Each one recited when receiving a hug. Joseph and Joshua stood back smiling as they watched their grandmother reacquaint herself with her granddaughters.

"My Lord, I just can't believe how big you girls are. How old are you all now?"

"I'm fourteen." Gracie answered. "Lucille's thirteen and Jessie's almost eleven."

"The last time I seen you, you was little bitty girls, bout five and six. And Jessie, you was just a baby. Ooh you sure are some pretty girls. You all are a lot like your mother. Have you seen her lately?"

Gracie put her head down before answering, "No ma'am."

"Well that's alright. She's gotta find her way. You know your mother loves you, though. Don't you?"

Gracie kept looking down, and Lucille looked away uninterested, but Jessie spoke up.

"Yes grandmother, I know know she does. And she's gonna send for us when she finds a place of her own."

"That's right, baby. Hey, say hello to your cousins. You all remember Joe and Josh? Joe, yall say hello to your cousins."

Joshua, now seventeen and Joseph nineteen, greeted their cousins with an awkward hug, and then offered to take their bags. Joe loaded their things in the car and climbed behind the driver's seat. Gracie sat up front with the two boys, while Sarah squeezed in the back with Lucille and Jessie. As they drove along the country side, the beauty of the south became more evident to each of them. The grandiose sycamore trees stretched towards heaven, tickling the sky with its budded branches, the gentle breeze caressed the skin, and the sweetness of the air, like fresh nectur gave them a feeling of security. The clean ponds reflected the heavens, showcasing its beauty while accommodating lazy geese that swam carelessly thereon.

Little bare foot boys sat on the edge of the pier with big,

straw hats that fell over their eyes, casting their fishing rods into the lake. The dirt roads were comparable to that of clay, and were as red as a ripened pomegranate. Miles and miles of corn fields stretched across the terrain, and wheat fields and fields of sugar cane stood in place of once empty land. Big billowy, puffs of clouds hung low and heavy in the sky, shadowing the earth from the radiant, hot sun, while rows of clean, dampened laundry blew freely in the wind, carrying a clean fresh scent. There was a different feel to the south. It was calmer, freer and more relaxed. People moved at a slower pace and didn't appear as rushed as people in the city. Jessie closed her eyes and took in a deep cleansing breath. She had already begun to feel at peace with her surroundings.

"Addie's got to be, what, sixteen?" Gracie asked.

"Yup, dats right." Joe answered with a thick southern accent.

"Who's Addie?"

"Dats my little sister." He answered, turning to look at Jessie.

"You all talk funny."

"Jessie! Mind your manners." Gracie scolded.

"That's okay, she's just speaking her mind." Sarah defended.

"Yeah, but she knows better." Lucille added.

Driving up to the large, white framed house, the girls were enamoured at its beauty. The towering columns of the colonial home beckoned them, welcoming them home. There was a perfectly manicured landscape of flowers, trees and shrubs.

"Grandmother, your house is beautiful."

"Thank you, Jessie. It took me a long while to get it like this. Maybe I can get you to help me in the yard sometime."

"Sure, grandmother. I'll help." As soon as they piled out of the car, Jessie placed a big, floppy hat on her head and further inspected the yard. Her lavender dress blended in perfectly with the beautiful and colorful landscape of lilacs, lilies and azaleas. She ran to the porch and sat on the swing.

Sarah took the other girls inside to get them settled in. Sarah explained that two of them could share a room and the other could sleep on the sofa in the back room, because Joshua and Joseph shared the other room. Once the economy came out of a slump, Henry and Etta moved out to get their own home and took Addie with them, but they left the boys behind with Sarah, because she was old and alone, and Henry thought it was best that they stay and help to look after her. Sarah enjoyed having Josh and Joe live with her because they reminded her so much of when Henry and Louis were boys. She cooked for them and fussed over them the same way she did when her boys were growing up.

Josh and Joe had been in some trouble with the law when they were younger, Joe more so than Josh, but after their grandpa died and they moved in with Sarah, they've made an effort to stay on track and have been doing much better. Sarah had a huge dinner prepared for the girls, with home made apple turnovers for desert. After they had eaten, Josh offered to drive the girls over to Cora's house, who has been dying to see them every since she got the news that they were coming. Lucille, of course, opted not to go, saying that she was tired and wanted to get some sleep. She also volunteered to sleep in the back room, because there, she knew she could have some privacy without the interruption of being asked 'so what do you think?' She didn't want to embrace her grandmother, her cousins, Aunt Cora, or the south. She was dead set on finding her way back to the city.

After the Gracie and Jessie got back from Aunt Cora's, Sarah was waiting up for them. She hugged and kissed Jessie, and told her to go get washed up so she could go to bed, but she asked Gracie to stay and talk.

"How are you doing, baby?"

"I'm fine, grandmother."

"That's the proper and polite answer, but I want to know how you are really doing."

Gracie closed her eyes, took a deep breath, and then told her grandmother all the things that were locked away in her heart, things that she vowed she would never let out. Sarah comforted Gracie and told her that all things worked together for the good.

"That's one of your Daddy's favorite Bible verses." She told her.

"I never see Daddy reading the Bible."

"Never?"

Gracie shook her head. "Hum, that's odd. Because your Daddy would sit right out there on that swing every morning, and take this big, Bible right here." She said lifting the Bible off the table, "And he would hold it on his lap and read chapter after chapter."

Gracie enjoyed hearing stories about her dad and what he was like as a boy.

"Gracie, how's Lucille doing?" Sarah asked.

"She's not doing to well, grandmother. She hated that we had to come here, and she says just as soon as she can, she's going back to Detroit."

Sarah chuckled a bit. "You know she's a lot like your Mama."

"Is that a bad thing?" Gracie asked tentively.

"Oh no baby, that's not a bad thing at all. She got your Mama's feistiness and spunk. Your momma's got a lot of determination and will power, and those are good qualities. See your Mama lost her Mama when she was real young, so she didn't have nobody to teach her certain things. A lot of things she had to figure out on her own and she just got a little confused about what she really wanted. That's why your Daddy sent you to me, because he knew he couldn't teach you things you need to know about being a becoming a lady and he didn't want you to have to go through the same thing. So you see? It'll all works out. Everything is going to be just fine."

Those were the words that Gracie longed to hear. And as her grandmother spoke them, she held on to them, comforted by the promise they offered. She kissed her grandmother before going to bed and felt a sense of peace.

The following morning, Josh drove the girls to the local school that was right down the road. Gracie and Jessie headed towards the door, but Lucille walked in the opposite direction.

"Lucille." Gracie said, exasperated. "Where are you going now?"

"I got other plans. Just don't say nothing, act like you don't see me." She said walking away. "I'll catch up with you before we're expected home."

Gracie stood there watching Lucille walk away, knowing there was nothing she could do to stop her. She took Jessie by the hand and led her into the school. Lucille walked away from the school and down the long dirt road. Because the town was so small, her presence was detected right away, and everyone greeted her with a nod or a smile, letting her know that they acknowledged her as a newbie in town. She passed a section in town where there seemed to be a small community within the community, as the homes were spaced just a few feet apart, unlike the rest of the homes, where woods, trees and a small man-made ponds separated them. An old woman sat on the porch watching Lucille as she passed by and offered a standard greeting.

"Hey."

"Hey." Lucille replied.

"Which family you belong to?"

"Excuse me?"

"It's only three of us here, the Hills, the Starks and the Zacharies. I'm a Zachary, so I know you don't belong to us."

"Oh, I see what you mean. I'm a Starks."

"Is that right? Come on over here lemme git a look atcha."

Lucille walked over to the porch and climbed the first two stairs. The woman stared at her momentarily before announcing that she looked like her Daddy.

"You must be Louis' girl."

"Yes, ma'am."

"Um hum, I thought so. How's he doing? Move to Detroit didn't he?"

"Yes, that's right."

"What you doing here? You visiting yo grandma?"

"For a while." Lucille responded. The old woman continued to stare at Lucille then shouted for someone inside to come out. "Hey Memphis, come on out heh. I want you ta see Sarah's granddaughter." Lucille shook her head and rolled her eyes. She didn't feel like meeting anyone new and certainly didn't feel like being polite. Her patience had already begun to thin out, but before she could announce that she had to get going, Memphis appeared through the rickety door.

"Hey!" He offered.

"Hey!" Lucille repeated mockingly. Oh God, she said to herself, noticing the rough and slick patches of hair that was badly in need of a touch up and the shiny gold teeth that bejeweled his over-exaggerated mouth.

"Nice ta meetchu." He said extending his hand. Lucille reached out to meet his hand, and he shook it so hard, she thought he would shake her arm out of its socket.

"She shole is pretty, aint she?" He asked the old woman. "She light, just like the rest of dem Starks. How long you gone be here?"

"Not long." Lucille answered. "I'm going to be getting back to Detroit real soon."

"Dats where you from?" He asked, still grinning.

"Yeah."

"Shole nuff? I'm gone be moving to Detroit wit some of my kinfolks in just a few weeks. Maybe we kin keep in touch wit each other when I get there."

Lucilled perked up when she heard that. Ideas danced in her head at lightning speed. All she had to do was to cozy up to the wide-grinned, gold toothed man, and hitch a ride back to the city with him. But where would she live after she got there, she thought. Then another idea entered her mind.

"You're going to live there permanently?"

"Shole is."

"I bet your wife is excited about moving, huh?"

"Girl, whatchu talking bout, I aint married. Is you?"

Lucille smiled upon hearing his answer. "Hum? Oh no, I'm not married either." She answered sweetly.

"Whatchu doing up heh in da middle of da school year."

"Oh, me and my sisters were gonna finish out the school year here, but I don't think I'm liking it too much. I just wanna hurry and get back home."

"Oh. Where you headed now?"

"Just taking a walk and admiring how lovely the country is. I haven't been here since I was four. I bet you could show me some pretty places around here."

"Yeah, I kin show you some. I'll be back, Big Mama." He said to the old woman who sat with feet crossed at the ankles, while nervously shaking her over abundant thighs.

"Alright. Tell yo grandma I said hey."

"I shole will." Lucille answered in a southern drawl.

Memphis took Lucille all over the country side showing her all the places that the town people admired as their jewels of the south. The picturesque mountainside, the rolling green hills, crytal clear ponds and lavish landscapes. Memphis would show Lucille all the beauty of the south, and then in some corny, country way, he would compare it to her beauty.

"These mountains so pretty, I kin stare at em all day long. But then you so pretty, I kin stare at you all day and all night." Lucille didn't want to say too much too soon, but she knew she had to make her move quickly, because she only had a few weeks. Judging him by virtue of the way he wore his hair, his gold teeth

- 269 -

and thick southern drawl, she was confident that she could easily persuade him with her swift, city girl cleverness that would engulf his country, backwood, dull intellect.

"Is that your real name, Memphis? Like the city?"

"Shoot naw. Dats what everybody call me, though. I went to visit some of my kin folks up there, and when I got back I talked about it all da time, so my uncle started calling me Memphis and it stuck. I shole love it there, all them pretty mountains. My real name is Walter."

"I like Walter better. It sounds more sophisticated. You gotta girlfriend, Walter?"

"Naw. I had a girl, but when she found out I was moving, she got mad and quit me."

"Why would she do something like that?"

"Well, she knew we couldn't be together no more cause I'd be living up north, and she'd never wanna to leave here."

"Oh that's too bad. Now what is a handsome man like you gonna do without a girl?" Walter blushed. "I don't know."

"Well, that's okay Walter, I don't have a boyfriend either."

"I don't believe dat. You tryin jive me."

"No I'm not. I really don't have one."

"Dem boys up in the city must be crazy."

"Really, why do you say that?"

"Cause. Shoot I'd do almost anything to have a girl as pretty as you. How old are you?" Lucille silently rejoiced, as that was the response she was counting on.

"How old do you think I am?" She stood back, placed her hands on her hips, arched her back, and jutted out her perky, developing breasts, while pirouetting.

Walter surveyed Lucille from head to toe, careful not to look at her private areas for too long. He looked at her bright eyes, warm smile, and then he went on to her figure that complimented her good looks. She wasn't too full up top, but had a small waist, curvaceous hips, and big legs. He could tell by looking at her face that she was relatively young, but by judging by her figure she appeared much older.

"I don't know, maybe about seventeen."

"I look seventeen to you?"

"Yeah, I guess."

"Walter, I'm only thirteen."

"Naw." He grinned. "No way."

"Yeah, I'm thirteen."

"Wow, you shole don't look like it."

"You ever kissed a thirteen year old?"

Walter turned away from Lucille looking in the other direction. "No."

"Do you want to?" He looked back at Lucille to see if she was serious, then he quickly looked away. "Why you ask something like dat?"

"Because I want you to kiss me. Besides age don't mean nothing if you married."

"Who said anything about getting married?"

"Well, do you think I would let you look at me and kiss me if we weren't getting married?"

"I don't know."

"Sure you do, Walter. A proper lady does'nt allow just any man to kiss her. He would have to be special. And if we were to get married, you can do a lot more than just look at me." She said, smiling demurely at him. "But if you don't want to, that's fine with me." Quickly changing her tone and demeanor. "I guess I should be getting back home then, instead of wasting my time here."

"Well, wait a minute, Lucille." He said, reaching for her hand. "Don't be so quick to leave."

"Why not?"

"Just wait a minute. Why you in such a hurry, girl?"

"Well, why should I stay?"

"Cause I wanna kiss you, if that's okay."

Several weeks after Memphis met Lucille on that old dirt road, he packed up his automobile and headed for Detroit with Lucille accompanying him as his new bride. Lucille hugged Gracie, kissed Jessie and even shed a few tears, but after they said their goodbyes. She climbed into Memphis' car and waved goodbye as they disappeared down the road.

Chapter 29

With Lucille gone and married, Gracie and Jessie settled into Sarah's home feeling the void of losing their sister. Jessie took it especially hard. She missed Lucille terribly, and was down in the dumps for a week after. Sarah, Gracie, even Josh and Joe did everything they could to cheer her up, but Jessie's pain was incurable. Joe had a friend who lived up the road, whose dog had just had puppies. They were little black and white mixed breeds with spotted tails, white paws, and just as cute as can be. Joe asked Sarah if he could bring one home for Jessie, to try and cheer her up, and Sarah agreed. Just as soon as the pups were old enough to be separated from their mother, Joe brought one home to Jessie. She was sitting on the porch when a little, speckled puppy came running around the front of the yard. Jessie jumped up, ran over to him and scooped it up in her arms.

"You like em?" Joe asked.

"I sure do. It's the cutest little thing." She said hugging it close to her chest.

"It's yours."

"Really?"

"Yup. I got im from a friend of mine and grandma said you can keep em."

"Is it a boy or girl?"

"Girl."

"Well, in that case, I'm gonna call her Belle. Hey there, Belle girl. Grandmother, look at what I got!" She said running into the house with Belle in her arms. Belle became Jessie's constant companion. She was with her all the time, except when she went to school. Having Belle made Lucille's absence quite bearable. In the days and weeks to come, Jessie would still miss her, but took comfort in writing, and telling Lucille all about her new pup.

The school year was just about over and spring was in full effect. Everything on Earth was alive again, blossoming and budding, promising a summer full of fun filled, crazy and lazy days. Gracie had become good friends with her cousin, Addie, who was only a year older. They had many of the same classes at school and spent lots of time together. They went to the soda shop together, did each others hair, and on occasion, they would dress alike. Gracie felt bad about leaving Jessie out many times when she and Addie were together, so she would invite her to come along. Jessie however, declined saying that she didn't want to leave Belle, who was never welcomed by Addie, because of her allergies. Jessie spent most of the summer alone. She kept busy by either helping Sarah in the yard, or going to her Aunt Cora's house. Between the two of them, Jessie had become quite a cook and would prepare dinner on her own at least twice a week.

Jessie also learned to swim that year, and would frequent the pond just down the road to keep in good practice. One afternoon, while she was swimming in the pond, her cousin, Joe, came over and watched her as she practiced her breast stroke.

"You're not doing it right." He called out to her.

Jessie looked over her shoulder, and saw Joe standing on the bank, smiling down at her.

"That's why I'm practicing."

Joe looked around, not seeing anyone in sight, he told her.

"I can show you how- if you want me to."

"Okay, but you don't have any trunks."

"Oh, dat don't matter, we swim in da pond all da time without trunks." He told her as he pulled his shirt over his head.

"Well, what are you gonna swim in?"

Joe answered by pulling his pants down until they fell around his ankles. Then stepping out of them, he kicked them to the side. Jessie's eyes widened in disbelief as she watched her cousin undress in front of her. Standing there in just his briefs, he dove into the water and disappeared below the surface.

"You swimming in your underwear?" But Joe didn't answer because he was still submerged underneath the water. Jessie looked around trying to find him. Just as she spotted his form floating nearby, he popped up right beside her.

"Did I scare you?"

"No. You didn't scare me. But I'll tell you what, you people in the south have some strange ways."

"Why you say dat?"

"Cause you swimming in your underwear."

"Oh, dat aint nothing. We do it all da time. Sometime, when aint nobody around, we swim wit nothin' on."

"You mean you swim naked?"

"Come on, let me show you how to posture yo'self." He said grabbing Jessie around the waist. He had her to lay face down with her body flat like a board, and then he placed his arms underneath her.

"Good job. Now turn over on your back." Jessie was trying to do just as he asked, but became doubtful of his intentions when he rubbed his hand over her buttocks, cupping and holding it. She jumped so hard, that she fell out of his arms and into the water creating a big splash. Catching herself, she looked at him with contempt.

"What you do that for?"

"Do what?"

"You know what you did." She told him, backing away.

"Come on Jess. I'm sorry. I was just playing with you."

"No." She said shaking her head and backing away.

"Come on Jess. Look, you're my little cousin. I was just messin around. I won't do it no more. Come on, you was doing so good."Jessie stood there looking at him, not certain as to believe him or not. "Come on silly. It's okay. I won't do it again." Jessie apprehensively walked back over to Joe. "Promise not to do it again." He kissed his two fingers and held them up in the air. "Promise. Now come on." Jessie walked back over to Joe and let him place his arms under her body to help her float. Just as she had begun to relax, he placed his hand between her legs and firmly gripped her vagina, wiggling his fingers against her private area. Just briefly, Jessie felt a sensation that she had never experienced before, but she pushed away, freeing herself from his firm hold and then jumped out of the water.

"Don't be touching me like that, boy. You nasty!" Joe stayed in the water laughing at her. "You know you like it."

"I don't. I'm telling grandmother." Joe's face turned serious. "You better not tell. If you do, I'll lie and tell her you wanted me to."

"You wouldn't."

"Yes I would." Then he pointed his finger at her. "You just bet not tell, or you'll be sorry."

Jessie became frightened. She gathered her clothes and ran away before putting them on. When she got home, she went into her room, closed the door and fell across her bed. Grabbing a pillow, she clutched it to her chest. Jessie was afraid of what just happened. She was afraid of Joe, of what he did, and of the feeling in her vagina when he wiggled his fingers against her. She hated him for doing that to her. Jessie heard the clicking of the door knob as it slowly turned. Frantic, she sat up and stared at the door, hoping that the intruder wasn't Joe.

"Why do you have the door closed?" Gracie asked.

Jessie breathed a sigh of relief when she saw her sister enter the room. "What's wrong?"

Jessie opened her mouth, anxious to tell Gracie what Joe did to her, but then she closed her mouth, remembering the threat that she'd be sorry if she did. She put her head down and answered, "Nothing, I'm just tired."

"You been swimming?"

Jessie thought it was a trick question to get her to admit to what had just occurred with Joe.

"No." She answered nervously. "Why?"

"Cause your hair's all wet and crinkly, and I saw wet clothes by the back door. If you haven't been swimming then you're gonna have to explain to Aunt Cora why your hair is messed up after she just pressed it."

"Oh. Well, I did stop by the pond on my way home."

"I figured as much. You need to just let me plat your hair, then you can go swimming all you want."

Gracie went on about platting Jessie's hair and going to a dance with Addie, while Jessie's thoughts drifted back to the funny sensation she got when Joe touched her. After Gracie changed her clothes and brushed her hair in place, she left just as quickly as she had come. Jessie got up from the bed, securely closed the door, and then laid back on the bed. She took her hand and placed it on the same area of her vagina that Joe intrusively wiggled his fingers against her and imitated his movement. Initially, there was no special feeling she got from her iratic hand motion. Just as she was about to give up, she felt it again, sending an excitable surge through her body. She located the spot that gave her the greatest sensation and concentrated on rubbing firmly and quickly against it. She closed her eyes, enjoying the feeling, rubbing, gripping, and rotating, until the feeling intensified and her small body jerked with pleasure. When she stopped, she opened her eyes and noticed that her fingers were wet. Just then, she heard a knocking on the door.

"Yes?" She answered nervously.

"Can I come in?" Sarah asked.

Jessie grabbed the pillow close to her stomach and curled in a fetal position.

"Yes grandmother, you can come in."

Sarah opened the door, walked over to Jessie and took a seat on the edge of the bed. "Are you alright?"

"Yes."

"I left some pastries out on the table for you. Aren't you hungry?"

Jessie wanted to get Sarah out of her room as quickly as possible so she could further investigate the new and wonderful feeling she discovered in her body.

"No I'm not hungry, just a little sleepy." She answered, feigning a yawn. "Aren't you feeling well?" She asked, reaching over and touching her forehead with the back of her hand. "I'm fine, grandmother." Sarah surveyed Jessied curled up and clutching onto her pillow. "Well, why are you hunched over like that?" She asked pulling the pillow away from her. She looked down at Jessie and saw that her pants were wet. "Baby, are you okay? I think you had an accident, your pants are wet." Jessie looked down at the bed and noticed a small wet circle beneath her. She became nervous and her brain clicked at a rapid pace trying to think of a reason why her bed and clothes were soiled. "I'm okay, I was swimming at the pond, but I got all tired out so I came home to take a nap."

"You still wearing your bathing suit?"

"Yeah." Jessie answered peeling back the collar of her shirt to reveal the strap of her swim suit. "Well, you gone be sick for sure laying in those wet clothes. Come on, let's get you out of those clothes."

"Grandmother," Jessie stopped her. "I can do it myself."

"You sure?"

"Yes grandmother, I'm sure." Sarah smiled at Jessie and resplied, "I guess my little Jessie is growing up. You let me know if you need anything, alright?"

"Alright."

Rising from the bed, she walked over to the door. "You want me to shut your door."

"Yes, please."

Sarah smiled again, and closed the door behind her.

Jessie sat staring at the door making sure Sarah was gone before getting up. She moved the pillow out of her way and examined the small circle. Placing her hand over the soiled area, she lifted it to her nose. She looked down at herself and was amazed at the feeling she got from tickling her fingers over her privates. Jessie got up from the bed and removed the sheets. She balled them up and took them out on the back porch to be washed with the rest of the laundry.

Later that evening, Jessie finished washing the dinner dishes and was putting them away when Gracie and Joe came in. "You all missed dinner again." Sarah yelled to them from the living room. "Sorry grandma." Joe responded. "Yeah, sorry. I had dinner at Aunt Cora's."

"You all need to tell somebody when you not gone be home for dinner. You have me prepare all that food and then nobody's here to eat it except for me and Jessie."

"Grandma, you cook enough food to feed half of Qwinneth County, whether we show up or not." Joe teased. He walked over to Jessie and grabbed her on the top of her head and playfully shook it. "Hey shrimp," He said. Walking over to the ice box, he pulled out a plate of neck bones and fried okra. "You wanna snack?" He asked Gracie.

"No, I've had enough to eat. I'm going to bed."

"Wait for me." Jessie told her, placing the last dish in the cupboard. She walked past Joe as he ate from the plate, not once looking up at her.

As they prepared for bed, Jessie sat on Gracie's side wathching her as she tied her hair in a scarf. "Gracie, you ever get a funny feeling down there?"

"A funny feeling down where?"

"You know. Down here." She asked, pointing to her vagina.

"Um mm. Why do you ask?"

"No reason."

Gracie turned and looked at Jessie, giving her, her undivided attention. "Why do you ask?"

"I was just curious."

"Why?"

Jessie knew she was trapped. "I heard some girls talking about a feeling they got down there."

"Oh." Gracie went back to tying up her hair. "Well, I guess I do sometimes."

"What's it feel like?"

"You sure it was some girls you heard talking about it?"

"Um hum." Jessie answered, innocently.

Gracie walked over and sat on the bed. "Well, I'm sure you're too young to quite understand, but as you get older, your body is going to go through some phenomenal changes."

"Like what?"

"Well, for example. Out of nowhere, you're going to feel a pulsating and throbbing urgency in your p-hole."

"My what?" Jessie asked, giggling at her sister's description of the vagina.

"Your p-hole. You have two holes, see? One is the hole your pee comes out of and the other p-hole is the hole you have sex with."

"You ever have sex?"

"No. I think about it sometimes, and Addie talks about it all the time, but she's older, so I guess she would."

"Is it a good feeling?"

"I think it is, because some of the girls who had it, seem to really like it."

"You think Lucille's having sex?"

"She's married, so I'm sure she is."

"I wonder if she likes it." Jessie said contemplatively. "Tell me more about that feeling. The one in your p-hole."

"That's it. It throbs. No, it's more like a heartbeat."

"What do you do about it?"

"Nothing you can do. Just wait till it stops."

"I heard those girls say that they rub on it."

"That's called masturbating."

"Who?"

"Not who, but what. It's called masturbating. I learned about it in phys ed."

"What does that do?"

"I guess it's supposed to make that urgent feeling go away. Releases the sexual tension that's built up inside."

"Will it hurt you?"

"It's not supposed to. You know Jessie, I'm real comfortable having this conversation with you."

"I'm sorry."

"This is the kind of stuff girls my age talk about. Not the kind of talk one would have with their baby sister. So enough talk about sex, okay?"

"Okay."

"So you just tell those girls, if you hear them talking about it, that you're not quite ready to listen in on that kind of conversation."

"Okay."

"Now let's get some shut eye."

Jessie lay in bed thinking about how her body jerked and water came out of her when she touched herself. She wanted to ask Gracie about that part, but didn't want to let on that she knew so much about it. She also thought about how Joe touched her in just the right spot that gave her that pleasurable sensation. He must know a lot about it to be able to go right to it, she thought to herself. Jessie wondered if boys got the same feeling when they are touched. She presumed that Joe probably masturbates all the time, and then she fell asleep.

Chapter 30

A year had come and gone since that day at the pond when Joe fondled Jessie, and unbeknownst to him, taught her something new and exciting about how her body worked. Since then, Jessie had become a pro at masturbating. Whenever she felt stress or pressure of any kind, she would go to the bathroom, pull her panties down, and rock, pump and rotate her fingers in a circular motion while gyrating her hips until her body exploded, sending her into a frenzy of involuntary jerking motions that would leave her feeling weak. She could complete masturbation in four minutes flat. She knew that because she timed herself one day to see how quickly she could make it happen. Jessie loved to come home and find that she was the only one there, so she could release herself of the tension that had built up since her last session.

One day, Jessie came home from school and no one else was there. A note left on the table from Sarah suggested that she eat leftovers because she and Gracie had gone into town. Instead of going to the bathroom, where her regular rituals took place, Jessie went into her bedroom so she could lie down and be more comfortable. She removed her undergarments, stretched out across the bed, and went into motion. She took her time since no one was there, careful to guide her hand slowly over her genitalia, prolonging the growing pleasure. When her body finally went into spasms from her quick hand motion, she opened her eyes to find Joe standing in the doorway watching her. She sat up hurriedly and snatched the blanket over her naked bottom half, trying to cover herself. Embarrassed and afraid, tears quickly flooded her eyes as a silent exchange of thought passed between them. Joe backed away and shut the door leaving Jessie in the room alone.

Jessie stayed in her room for over an hour before she could bring herself to come out. She carefully tipped around the creeky house, but there was no sign of Joe. Not having much of an appetite, she went on the porch to the old wooden swing and rocked herself. Shortly after, Josh pulled into the long driveway chauffering Sarah and Gracie. They all jumped out of the car unloading packages, bags and big brown boxes.

"Hey Jess. We got a package for you from your Daddy." Sarah told her.

Jessie rose from the swing and walked out to meet them, "Where yall been?"

"In town, and to the post office. We got lots of good stuff today. Packages from Daddy, and a letter from Mama and one from Lucille."

They brought all the packages inside and plopped them down on the kitchen table. Every one stood around anxiously waiting to see what was inside. Joe came in and stood behind Sarah peeking over her shoulder. "What's all this?" He asked. "Louis sent some packages for the girls." Sarah answered. Jessie stole a glance at Joe and quickly looked away. "Can I open it in my room?"

"Don't be silly. Just open it, Jess." Gracie told her. Jessie took her package and cut the seal with a knife, freeing the contents onto the table. A yellow dress, three undershirts, one training bra, two pair of panties and two pair of socks fell onto the table. Surveying the contents, Jessie instinctively looked at Joe who raised his brows and walked away. She snatched up the garments and held them in her arm. "These are private things."

"I know they are. I wonder how Daddy knew to get stuff like that." Gracie quipped. "I know I'll be opening mine in my room."

"Open the letters." Sarah reminded.

"Oh. I almost forgot." Gracie took a seat at the table and opened Tulah's envelope first. She read to them how Tulah was working as a housekeeper and was taking night classes at an adult education center on the west side of town to get her high school diploma. She said that Lucille and Memphis had been over to her house for dinner and that Lucille had a surprise. "No wonder we got letters from the both of them. I can't wait to read Lucille's to see what it says."

"I bet I know." Sarah offered.

"I bet you're right." Gracie agreed.

"What?" Jessie asked. Gracie ripped open the letter excitedly and read through the first few lines that was in concurrence to what Tulah's letter said. Then she got to the lines that announced that she and Jessie were going to be aunties.

"I knew it. That's gone make me a great grandmother." Sarah said crossing her hands over her chest. "The Lord took your grandDaddy too soon. I wish he was here to know he would've been a great grandDaddy."

"I'm gonna be an auntie? Ooh I'm so excited!" Gracie hit Jessie for her insensitivity. "I know what you mean, grandmother. I wish he could've been here, too." She said eyeing Jessie. "Oh grandmother, I'm sorry."

"It's okay, baby. I know you excited about the new baby."

"Hey look." Jessie said grabbing the envelope. "They sent pictures."

There was a picture of Memphis standing behind Lucille with his arms wrapped around her waist holding her stomach. Lucille looked so pretty. She was leaning her head back against Memphis and smiling. The other picture was a picture of Tulah with her housekeeping uniform on. She had a scarf on her head and was wearing a pair of cat-eyed glasses.

"I sure miss everybody."

"Me too."

"Daddy said we didn't have to be here that long and it's been almost two years. Is he ever gonna send for us?"

"I don't know, Jess. I don't know."

During the night, there was an urgent knocking on the door. Josh got up to answer the door and then lights came on and voices could be heard. He knocked on Gracie and Jessie's door before entering. He told them that their Aunt Cora had a stroke. Gracie jumped out of bed hysterically.

"I gotta go see about her."

"Okay, you get dressed and I'll take you." Josh told her.

"I'm going, too."

"No Jess, you stay here with grandmother. Don't wake her.

But if she wakes up on her own, tell her what happened, and tell her Josh is taking me over there."

"But I want to see about Aunt Cora, too."

"I know. But sweetie I need you to stay here. It's not going to be anything you can do tonight anyway. Please Jess, just do as I ask."

"Okay."

Gracie got dressed and left hastily. Jessie stayed up front looking out of the window until she saw Josh's lights disapate in the darkness. She closed the curtains and turned around. Joe was coming out of the back, bare chested and wearing only sleep shorts.

"What's all da commotion?"

"My Aunt Cora had a stroke."

"What? Just now?"

"Not long ago. One of her boarders came by and told us."

"I'm sorry to hear dat. You okay?" He said touching her shoulder.

"I think so."

"Can I get you something?"

"No thank you." Jessie answered, wondering why he was pretending that he didn't see what he saw the day before. Joe was always like that, though. When he touched her before, giving her that funny feeling, he later acted like it never happened. And then when he spied her masturbating, he closed the door and never once mentioned it or gave her a knowing look. Why, Jessie wondered, does he act that way? She couldn't figure him out. Joe would always be a mystery to her.

After things quieted down a bit, Jessie went back to bed. Concerned about Aunt Cora's condition, Jessie tossed and turned not able to fall asleep. She was tempted to release herself, as she would normally do when she felt stressed, but she was reluctant to do so since it was Aunt Cora who was at the center of her distress. She resisted the urge and continued to toss and turn until she slowly dozed off. Now sleeping soundly, Jessie felt a hand grip her by the waist, and roll her onto her back. Still half asleep, Jessie allowed herself to be turned. She felt the hand rub her stomach and then slowly move toward her private area. In the darkened room, Jessie could only make out a shadowy figure, but automatically knew that it was Joe. Startled, she reflexively pulled away from him, but he pushed her back down and placed a finger over her mouth quieting her. Jessie wanted to push him away, but his fingers had already found their way to her vagina and had begun methodically massaging it. Jessie submissively layed back, letting Joe fondle her clitoris until her wetness dampened his fingers. Jessie thought it was over, but he continued to probe the folds of her vagina, pushing his finger deep inside her. She tried to sit up, but once again, he pushed her back down, this time silencing her with a kiss. He pressed his moistened lips into hers, and seductively licked at her lips, before invading her mouth with his stiff tongue. His finger slid in and out of her while his tongue became familiar with her mouth. Up until then, Jessie stiffened her body, only half-heartedly obliging his gestures. But after feeling his finger slide in and out of her, she completely gave in, and gently pumped her hips in unison to his hand motion. Joe pulled away from her, but Jessie wanted more, this time sitting up, and placing his hand back on her throbbing spot. Joe bent over and kissed her once more before quietly leaving the room.

The next morning, Jessie awakened to the aroma of fried ham, grits, scrambled eggs and oven fresh biscuits. Gracie's side of the bed didn't look slept in, so she sent up a silent prayer that everything was okay. She slipped on her housecoat and went into the kitchen. Sarah, Josh, Joe, Addie and Gracie were sitting at the table already having breakfast.

"Why didn't somebody wake me?"

"There's plenty left. Grab a plate and dig in." Josh told her.

"How's Aunt Cora?"

"She's resting comfortably. Doesn't seem to be any long term damage, but I'm gonna stay with her for a while. Just until she able to get around again."

"Who's with her now?"

"Her boarder."

"Can I go see her?"

"Of course you can. Right after you eat and get dressed, Josh is gonna take us back over there."

"My my, look how the shrimp is getting big." Addie offered.

"She growing up fast isnt' she?" Sarah agreed.

"Yeah she is. Looking all womanly." Jessie felt exposed. She pulled her housecoat closed and tied it at the waist as if that would some how hide her indiscretion.

"Oh don't tell her that, she thinks she grown as it is." Gracie added.

There was a knock at the door, before a loud voice bellowed through the house.

"Where's everybody?"

"Back here!" Sarah responded. "That's Henry and Etta."

Henry walked into the kitchen, his large frame dominating the room, and Etta, just as fat as she was pretty, followed close behind.

"Morning', how's everybody doin?" Henry greeted.

"We heard about Cora. We came to see how she gettin' along."

"Thanks, Aunt Etta. She's doing better now. She's resting." Gracie told her.

"That's good." Henry added. "What caused it?"

"Nobody knows. I think she gone need medication. But who can afford it?"

"Ain't it da truth." Etta agreed.

"Momma, you got enough food for me?"

"Henry you just ate before we left da house." Etta scolded.

"That was an hour ago."

"You know she got enough, Daddy. She always cook more than enough." Josh teased.

Sarah grabbed a plate for Henry and began piling it up high. "You all get up and let your Mama and Daddy have a seat, she told the others.

"You can have my seat, Aunt Etta, I gotta get packed anyway."

"Where you going?" Henry asked.

"I'm gone be staying with Aunt Cora for a while."

"That's real good of you, Gracie. Mama you gone be alright, or should I make Addie stay in Gracie's place?"

"Oh no, I'll be fine."

"I can help grandmother." Jessie added. "I cook two meals a week all by myself as it is. Don't I grandmother."

"Yes she does. Jessie's a big help around the house."

Josh took Gracie and Jessie over to Cora's house and then brought Jessie back to Sarah's afterwards. Sarah had settled in for the evening and was getting ready for bed when Jessie came in and gave her an update on Cora's condition. Bidding Sarah good night, Jessie went out on the porch and sat in the swing. The night air blew cool against her skin causing her to shiver at its breeze, so she decided to go in and have a snack before going to bed. As she went into the kitchen and saw Joe sitting at the table, her heart quickened in pace, thumping so loudly against her chest, she thought he would hear it.

"Hey."

"Hey." Joe responded.

"Where's Josh?"

"He left."

"Oh. Is grandmother already gone to bed?" She quizzed.

"Sleeping soundly."

Jessie went to the ice box, retrieved a bottle of milk, poured herself a glass and sat at the table with Joe. She was prepared to talk to him about what happened the night before, but true to character, he got up from the table, washed his plate, put it away and then walked out of the room. Jessie was appaled at his behavior. All day long, she thought of nothing else but what happened the night before, and then for him to waltz past her like nothing happened was more than she could stand. She started after him, and then stopped herself thinking that perhaps he thought of her as too fast. That was a nasty thing I let him do, she thought to herself. "Oooh, sometimes I hate myself for being so stupid."

She finished her glass of milk and then somberly walked through the dark house towards her room. She dressed for bed, tied her hair back and climbed into bed. Laying in the dark, she realized that she needed to relieve herself. Getting up from her bed, she walked down the hall to the bathroom. As she came out, Joe was at the opposite end of the hallway waiting for her.

"Come here." He whispered. She obediently followed him through the kitchen, past the living room, and to the back room where he often slept on the broken in sofa. He stopped in front of her and then turning to face her, he lifted her chin and tried to kiss her. She slapped his hand away. "No."

"Why not? You liked it last night."

"That was wrong. We should'nt have done that."

"Why not?"

"We related."

"So."

"So? Are you crazy?"

"No I'm not crazy. Keep your voice down." He whispered.

"I'm not doing this." Jessie said pushing past him. Joe grabbed her arm and stopped her. Her heart skipped a beat and she immediately became aroused at his touch. "Just sit down for a minute." He whispered. Jessie obliged, taking a seat on the sofa. "Why you be acting so strange?" She asked him.

"Shhh." He reminded her to keep her voice down. Whatchu talking about?"

"You be acting like nothing happened." She whispered.

"How should I act, like we did something and now you my girlfriend?" Jessie took a moment to consider what he was saying. "Well, you don't have to act like that when it's just me around."

"Let me make it up to you." He said rubbing his hand over her breasts, thumbing her nipple until it became erect. "You like dat, don't you?" He whispered. Jessie answered by closing her eyes and releasing a slight moan. He gently pushed her into a lying position and pulled her nightgown up over her hips. Jessie was still wearing panties, so he gently rubbed on her through her underwear. Not able to locate her spot, he pulled at them, sliding them past her hips and down her legs. Jessie lifted her hips up so he could take them off, but he only moved them past one leg, leaving them wrapped around the other leg. His suckled her breast while his fingers went to work on her clitoris. So overcome with desire, she breathed heavily, as her heart pounded quickly against her chest. Jessie parted her legs, making herself more accessible to him. She closed her eyes and enjoyed the feeling of his warm, wet mouth over her breast, while his hand probed and fondled her until his finger penetrated her opening. Joe stopped and stood quickly, unfastening his pants. He let his pants drop around his ankles and held his erect manhood in his hand, gently rubbing and pulling at it. He slowly approached Jessie, but she stopped him.

"No."

"Why not?"

"Because. What if grandmother hears us?

"She won't hear us. You know how hard she sleeps."

"Um um, I don't wanna do that."

"You want me to give you all the pleasure, but what is dat doin fa me?"

"No." Jessie contended.

"Alright get out, then." He said pulling his pants up and zipping them.

"You puttin me out?"

"Whatchu wanna stick around fo? Get me all revved up, then you go and act all scared. You a teaser."

"No I'm not." Jessie didn't fully understand what a teaser was, but she didn't like the sound of it. "Get on outta here." Joe repeated. Jessie got up, disappointed because she had not yet reached her climax, snatched her panties from around her leg and balled them up in her hand. She walked towards the door, but then stopped just before reaching it. She turned to him and asked,

"What if you hurt me?"

"I'm not gone hurt you. I'll be real gentle, I promise. Come here."

Jessie walked back over to the sofa and took a seat next to him.

"Just relax, okay. Don't tense up, stay loose."

"Okay." And Jessie gave in.

Chapter 31

Tulah grunted and moaned loudly, while she violently tossed and turned. She was immersed in a terribly disturbing dream. Enveloped in a mysterious darkness, she heard a shrill cry for help. She couldn't see the face, but in her heart she knew it was Jessie. Wandering aimlessly through dark, obscure paths, she pushed past hanging branches and mirey muck, hoping that the loud sobs would lead her to Jessie. The cries started out loud and strong, but then regressed, sounding like a young child and then eventually like a baby. It baffled Tulah because she didn't know if she should look for Jessie or the crying baby. Even though she was sleeping, Tulah felt a heaviness that oppressed her, making her feel burdened and distressed. She screamed out to Jessie asking her where she was, but Jessie stayed hidden in the darkness. 'Where are you?' Tulah screamed, but the cries of the baby overwhelmed Jessie's cries and the whole forest went dark. Tulah awakened to her own voice calling out to Jessie.

"Come on, baby. You gone need a new suit." Pearl told Louis. "We need to find you a nice grey one to match those dreamy eyes. We gone be the best looking bride and groom ever." Louis smiled weakly and walked fast to keep up with Pearl's fast pace. She was excited about marrying Louis; the only problem was that Louis never really told her that he wanted to get married. Pearl asked Louis if he ever wanted to remarry, and when he said 'sure, why not,' Pearl took it as an unoffical proposal.

"My uncle, the one that lives in Ohio, is a reverend, and I'm sure he'd be happy to marry us in his church. Now I know you wasn't expecting to be out here looking for a suit today, but I figured we might as well look since we already downtown."

Louis followed Pearl as she marched him up and down Grand River, trying to find him a suit. He liked Pearl, but she was too forward and awfully pushy. She was instrumental in helping him buy nice things for his girls and she helped him to send them off, but she has since tried to be his overseer, managing every aspect of his life.

"You know if we get married in the fall, Jessica can wear that yellow dress we sent her."

"You mean Jessie."

"Yeah, of course I do. Well, anyway, she can wear that dress."

Pearl drug Louis through the downtown area all afternoon, until he finally told her that he was meeting his daughter for a late lunch.

"Well, let me stop at this one other shop and we can be on our way."

"No Pearl. We are not meeting my daughter for lunch, I am."

"Louis, I don't know what that's supposed to mean, but you know I'm going with you. It's high time I met your daughter anyway. I been hearing about her all this time and ain't met her yet."

Louis knew it was pointless to argue with Pearl, because once she got her mind made up about something there was no changing it. Therefore, Louis allowed her to drag him to three other stores before she was ready to meet Lucille for lunch. There was a little black owned coffee shop in the area where he had planned to meet Lucille to discuss an important matter with her. When Louis and Pearl finally arrived, with Pearl's bags in tow, they were forty five minutes late.

"Hi baby." Louis said walking over to kiss Lucille on the forehead. "Sorry we're late."

Lucille looked at Pearl, then back to Louis awaiting an explanation for the unexpected guest. With his eyes, he apologized for the intrusion.

"This is my friend, Pearl. Pearl, this is my daughter Lucille."

Pearl reached out to shake Lucille's hand. "Oh, you're expecting. How precious. But you're so young. How old are you, if you don't mind me asking?" Lucille glanced over at Louis before answering. "I'm sixteen."

"Sixteen! Wow! You married?"

Lucille looked at the woman, taken aback by her forwardness.

"Anyway, Daddy. How have you been?" She said, ignoring Pearl.

"I'm fine, baby. Look at you." He said reaching for her hand. "You look beautiful."

"Thank you, Daddy."

"How's country?" Lucille laughed. "Daddy, you know his name is Memphis, why do you do him like that?"

"Oh, I'm just teasing." Louis laughed.

"Memphis, is that your husband?" Pearl asked.

Lucille nodded her head without looking at her. "That's sweet. Did your father tell you that we're getting married?"

Lucille looked at her father, her face became serious. Louis closed his eyes and discreetly shook his head, letting Lucille know that Pearl was in a fantasy of her own. Lucille gave him a subtle nod, letting him know that she understood.

"No. I hadn't heard."

"Louis, why haven't you told her?"

"We'll talk aout that later, Pearl. Why don't we order, I've kept my grandbaby waiting long enough."

"Oh um, Daddy. Your grandbaby's fine. I got tired of waiting so I order my lunch before you got here."

Louis and Pearl ordered their lunch and ate, while Lucille had dessert. Lucille had to sit through Pearl talk about her dress, her parents, and the money they were planning to spend on her wedding. At the end of an agonizing lunch, Pearl excused herself to use the restroom. When she got up to leave, Lucille scooted her chair closer to Louis and pulled a letter out of her purse. She told Louis that Jessie had sent her a letter that had her concerned.

"Something's not right, Daddy. I think you need to check on her."

"She's there with Mama, Gracie, Cora, not mention Etta. She's got more people there to look after her than she had here."

"I know, Daddy, but something's not right."

"What did she say?"

"It's what she didn't say." She said looking at the letter. "I know how strange that sounds, but you gotta trust me on this."

"Well, Lucille you still not giving me nothing to go on."

"Okay, this part here." She said pointing to the letter. *'I wish that I could express to you how I feel. I've made some mistakes and some bad decisions and I wish I could take them back, but I can't. I guess I'll have to hold them in my heart and hope God will forgive me.'* What do you think that means?"

"I don't know, but it doesn't sound like she's in no real trouble."

"But there's something else, too."

"What?"

"Mama's been having those dreams again. You know the kind she has that's warning and revealing?"

"Oh Lucille, I don't wanna hear about your Mama's dreams."

"Daddy, how can you say that?"

"Well, what do you want me to do?"

"I don't know, Daddy. Maybe I shouldn't have said anything." She said folding the letter and stuffing it back in her purse.

"Oh, here comes your friend." She said rising from the table. "I've had enough of her for one day, so I'm just gonna excuse myself."

"Wait Lucille. Don't be cross with me. I just don't see a need for concern."

"Forget it, Daddy. I'll see you later." She said walking away.

Lucille waddled out of the restaurant and down to the bus stop. She took a seat on the bench and pulled the letter out of her purse, and read it again. "Dear Lord, look after my little sister."

Jessie wasn't too concerned when she missed her period the first month. But when it didn't come after second month, she became afraid. After that one forbidden night with Joe, she would let him come into her room or she would visit his two and even three times a week. They would plan to meet in covert places like down at Critter's Creek, or back at home when no one was there, so they could indulge themselves in the rapture of lustful and passionate sex sessions. Jessie was sequacious when it came to Joe, obliging his every sexual whim. So when she told him that she missed her period for two months in a row, the last thing was she was expecting was for him to turn against her.

"Don't come to me wit dat garbage, cause I don't wanna hear it."

"What am I supposed to do?"

"I don't know and I don't care. Like I got something to do wit dat. You better get outta my face."

"But Joe!" Jessie cried. "I'm scared. What am I supposed to tell grandmother?"

"Aye, dats not my problem. You gone hafta figure it out on yo own."

"Joe. Don't do me like this."

"What the hell you expect me to do? Be a Daddy? You so stupid. Just a stupid little girl."

"How can you treat me like this?" Tears rolled down her cheeks and fell off the ends of her face. "What am I supposed to tell my Daddy?"

"Tell him whatever you like, just keep my name out of it."

"I'm not gone be stuck in this by myself. I'm telling the truth. I'm gone tell everything, even how you touched me that day at the pond." She threatened.

Joe jumped up and pushed her into the wall, knocking a picture off the wall and breaking its frame. He pressed the back of his arm into her neck and whispered in her ear. "You think about telling yo Daddy or anybody else anything about me, I'll kill you. You hear me?" He asked, pressing harder against neck. "I'll kill you and nobody will ever find you. Now get out!"

Jessie cried so hard, she felt sick to her stomach. She ran to the bathroom, kneeled over the toilet gave up the contents of her lunch. Distraught, she walked down to the river where she could be alone and figure out her next move. Her own flesh and blood had seduced her, took her virginity and then treated her with the same cruelty, disgrace and dishonor of a common whore, she thought to herself. "He threatened to kill me." She cried harder, reliving the dreaded conversation with Joe. She sat on the riverbed, and stared into the water thinking that she should just jump in and drown herself. That way no one will ever have to know that she had shamed herself with her cousin, who was seven years her senior. Jessie stayed at the riverbed until it was dark and cold and she could finally control her tears and stop them from falling. She pulled herself together and started back in the direction of home. Not able to see two feet in front of her, she tripped on something that sent her crashing to the ground. Focusing her eyes, she saw a sleeping man that was so drunk that she didn't even wake him. He grunted a little and turned over, as his drunken breath permeated the air. She wanted to ask if he was okay, but he never knew she was there. She grabbed his grungy old hat and placed it next to his head and started home.

After that day at the river, Jessie went home and fell into a depression. She became withdrawn and isolated herself from the rest of the family. She wouldn't eat anything and nobody could get her to talk about what was bothering her. They were all terribly concerned. Jessie sent a letter to Lucille, because she missed her and finally understood her urgency in wanting to go home. She wanted so badly, to confide in her and tell her what happened, but she understood that, this was a secret that would forever be locked in her heart. As time when on, Jessie's belly grew at a rapid pace. She refused to eat hoping that she could some how prevent her stomach from growing. When that didn't work, she wore baggy clothes to further conceal her expanding belly.

One morning, Jessie was in the bathroom dressing when Gracie mistakenly busted in on her. Jessie tried grabbing her dress to cover her swollen abdomen, but Gracie had already seen all that she needed to.

"Jessie! Oh my God, are you pregnant?" Placing her hand over her mouth that nearly dropped to the floor. She came in, closed the door behind her and snatched the dress away from Jessie. "Oh my God, you are pregnant."

"No I'm not." Jessie defended.

"Yes you are. Look at you. How far are gone are you?"

Tears flooded Jessie's eyes and fell in big drops.

"I don't know."

"No wonder you've been acting so strange. Why didn't you tell somebody, why didn't you tell me?"

Jessie sobbed. She sat on the toilet, covered her face and cried.

"Whose is it?"

This was the question that Jessie dreaded. She wanted to confess all to Gracie, and tell her how afraid she'd been from the discovery of her pregnancy, but mostly because how she was threatened by Joe. She was tired of hiding the secret of her illicit affair with her cousin and wanted to finally get it out of her system. However, she didn't want her family to learn that she voluntarily partook in an act that was both incestual and immoral.

"Jessie! Whose is it?" Gracie demanded.

"I don't know." Jessie cried.

"What do you mean you don't know? You know who you were with." She said grabbing her arms, looking her right in the eyes. "Who are you trying to protect?"

"Nobody."

"Then you tell me whose it is."

"I can't." Jessie managed to say between sobs.

"Why not, Jessie? Why can't you tell me?"

"Because." She said covering her face again.

"Because what?"

Jessie shook her head relentlessly.

"Was this done against your will?"

Jessie paused for a moment considering that thought as a way out of her dilemma. She tentively nodded as an idea slowly formed in her head.

"It was against your will? Are you suggesting…"

Jessie looked at her with tearstained eyes and confessed, "I was raped."

Gracie ran out of the bathroom and hysterically called for Sarah.

"Grandmother! Grandmother, come quick!" Gracie cried and screamed as loud as she could. Sarah ran as quickly as her old legs would carry her.

"What is it child? What's wrong?"

"It's Jessie." Gracie was crying so hard she was out of breath.

"What's wrong with Jessie, where is she?"

"Jessie's pregnant! She was raped and now she's pregnant."

Sarah covered her mouth and tears came to her eyes. "My Lord, child. What is this you telling me?"

"She's been raped!"

"Where is she?"

"She's in the bathroom. Grandmother, she's pregnant."

Sarah grabbed her heart and held onto the table. Thoughts ran together in her mind of the violent intrusion that forceably tore away her grandchild's innocence. Spontaneous pictures flashed in her mind of the ferocious and savage attack. This wasn't supposed to happen. Jessie was sent to be under her care and it was her job to protect her. Where did it all go wrong? Sarah wondered. Tears forced themselves from her sad and over-burdened eyes and her heart ached.

"Dear God, no. Oh my poor baby. Jessie! Jessie baby, come

here." Tears fell down Sarah's face and Gracie screamed towards heaven. "Lord why did this happen to my sister?" Jessie apprehensively came into the living room where both her grandmother and sister cried for her stolen innocence as well as the unwanted and forbidden seed that was forced upon her by a cold-blooded, merciless predator. When Jessie walked into the room, Sarah turned her head not able to look at her. Jessie took a seat on the sofa and Gracie pulled the material of her dress back so her stomach was clearly visible. Tears slid down Jessie's face and fell onto her protruding belly.

Sarah shook her head, not willing to believe that she'd missed something so obvious. Gracie kneeled in front of Jessie and took her hands in her own.

"Sweetie, I'm so sorry this happened to you."

Jessie nodded her head as tears continued to fall. Sarah walked over to Jessie and sat on the sofa next to her. "Baby, who did this to you?" Jessie shook her head, reluctant to give the name of the culprit. Her initial thought was to say that Joe had forced himself on her, but she knew that would cause more trouble than what she was already in. Her brain was clicking, searching for something to tell them, but no reasonable answer came to mind.

She covered her face with both hands and shook her head.

"Jessie talk to us?"

"I can't."

"Jessie, please."

She remembered the fire in his eyes and the conviction in his voice when he told her that he would kill her if she told.

"No! I can't tell you."

"Jessie, we're trying to help you, but you gotta tell us who did this."

"He said he'll kill me."

"Oh Lord, Jesus." Sarah cried.

"Jessie, nobody's gonna hurt you. If you tell us who did it, we won't let him hurt you anymore. Understand? Just say his name." Gracie pleaded.

Jessie covered her face with her hands and shook her head not willing to divulge anymore information. "Okay, then tell me where this happened."

Jessie became catatonic, staring at the wall in front of her as if watching it on an invisible screen. "I was at the river. There was a drunken man sleeping and I tripped over him."

"He did this to you?"

Jessie nodded her head and looked at Gracie. "Yes, he did this to me.

Chapter 32

Jessie never expected that one lie would turn into something so destructive and damaging, forever changing the lives of the good and decent people who lived in that town. The Sheriff and the deputy had personally come to Sarah's home to question her, and the entire town coalesced, as scores of people volunteered to help in the manhunt to find the rapist. Jessie had to be seen by a woman's doctor, one who knew about the female body and babies to see if she and the baby were doing ok. Etta stayed with Jessie through the examination and explained that her doctor was called a mid-wife, but she knew as much about babies than any man doctor. Everyone came by to express condolences and say how sorry they were. However, when Joe came around, he just looked at her and shook his head as if she was something pitiful and pathetic. "Forbidden fruit" is what he would say to her when no one was around, "forbidden fruit, gone bad." Jessie hated Joe. She would get a sickening feeling at just the sight of him- such a contrast from how it used to be.

When Louis got word about what happened to Jessie, he cried and snatched the phone off the wall, sending it crashing to the floor, and then he hopped on the next train to be with her. Tulah wanted to come, but didn't have enough money to make the trip, so Louis told her he would go first, and if need be, he would send for her. Jessie was elated to see Louis when he arrived. She ran to him like she was still his little girl, the only difference now, was that she was a lot bigger. Louis held Jessie in his arms and rocked her. "I'm sorry, sweetheart." He whispered as he kissed her on her forehead. Jessie told Louis that she wanted to go home with him and he was fully prepared to take her. He kept his anger in check, though, careful to remain calm for Jessie's sake. When she was not around Louis banged his fist into the wall and tears welled up in his eyes. He thought that he was sending her away to a place where she would be safe, and yet somehow the opposite had happened. He kept a hanky in his back pocket, making it easily accessible if he needed to wipe away tears that he tried to keep hidden. He consulted with the sheriff and other people around town looking for any leads he could find.

It was early on a Tuesday morning that the sheriff knocked on Sarah's door, telling her that they had found the offender. They told Louis that since Jessie was still a minor, he had to bring her down to the station to identify him as a suspect. Louis was overjoyed when he got the news. He ran to Jessie's room, yelling through the door that they had found the guy.

"Jessie! Jessie come out here! They caught the guy, baby. They got the man who did this too you. Praise God! Jessie? You hear me? They got him." Louis said shaking his fists in the air excitedly. Sarah heard Louis yelling through the house and ran to him.   "What's this you saying?"

"They got him, Mama. The sheriff want Jessie to come to the station and identify him, but they got him."

"Thank you, Jesus. Jessie, I'm coming in." Sarah told her, knocking before opening the door. When she went in, she didn't see Jessie anywhere in sight. She looked around the room thinking that perhaps she wasn't there until she heard faint sniffling sounds coming from below the bed. Jessie was laying on the floor, curled in a fetal position. She had been crying so much that her eyes where puffy and swollen and she could barely catch her breath. Sarah looked back at Louis, whose face was red and distressed at the sight of Jessie crying like that.

"Let me talk to her." She told Louis in a quiet, concerned voice. Sarah nodded reassuringly, letting him know that she could handle the situation. Closing the door, she walked over to Jessie and got down on her knees. She lovingly rubbed her back and gently stroked her hair.

"Baby, I can't imagine what you going through, so I'm not even gone try. But I just want you to know that we love you, baby, and were here for you. There ain't nothing or nobody that can change that. I know it's been hard for you, keeping this a secret for so long and feeling scared and alone. But it's over now. The sheriff got the man responsible for this and they gone lock him away for a long time."

Jessie kept her eyes down, refusing to look at Sarah. She didn't feel worthy to look straight at her. All while Sarah went on about how things would get better, Jessie knew that they wouldn't. Things just continued to get worse. First, her indiscretion with Joe, then finding out that she was pregnant, and then the lie saying she was raped. And just when she thought it couldn't get any worse, the sheriff snatches up an innocent man who they've pinned this horrible injustice to, and is threatening to put him in jail. Things spiraled out of control and she had no way of stopping it. If she told them that their guy didn't do it, they would think she was lying because she was afraid of the threat she told them about. The only way she could get out of this was to tell the truth about what happened, expose herself, Joe and their incestuous relationship, and she was not about to do that. So she convinced herself that she had no other recourse and had to stick to her story.

"Grandmother, if I go down and identify the guy can I go home with my Daddy?"

"Of course you can. All you gotta do is go one down there and tell the sheriff that this is the man who did that to you, and you can leave." Jessie remained on the floor trying to prepare herself for what she knew she had to do. She finally willed herself off the floor and pulled herself to her feet. Sarah held her hand to console as she prepared to go to the sheriff's office. As they entered the living room, Louis was sitting on the sofa talking to Joe and a young lady who Jessie didn't recognize.

"Jessie, this is Marleen, Joe's girlfriend. She wanted to come by and see how you are doing." Louis told her.

Jessie looked at Joe, who looked at her and then casually looked in the other direction.

"I'm awfully sorry about what happened." Marleen told her. Jessie nodded her head and walked away. When she and Louis made it to the Sheriff's office they asked Jessie lots of questions. "Where were you, what were you doing there, what time was it, what were you wearing, what did he say, and did he have a weapon?" All while Jessie talked to them and answered their questions, a lady nearby took notes. After the inquisition, they took her in the back where all the prisoners were kept. The deputy took her to the very back of the building where they held a single prisoner in the cell. He yelled at him and told him to stand up.

"All you gotta do is say whether this is the guy or not and we'll take care of the rest." The deputy told her.

Jessie glanced at the man and quickly averted her eyes. She didn't want to look at him for too long or else he would have become human to her. She turned away, nodded her head and quickly walked away.

"What does that mean?" The man yelled from inside the jail cell. "What are you doing to me? Hey! Come back here and tell them the truth. Tell them I didn't do it." He screamed after her. When Jessie made it back to the front, Louis took her in his arms comforting her. The deputy told her that the man's name was Willie Purfoy. He was a drunken old hobo who had been wandering around homeless ever since his wife put him out.

"Why did she put him out?" Louis asked.

"Lost his job for drinking. Spent all his money on moonshine and women. Yeah, this is our guy. I'm just glad he's off the street."

"That makes two of us. I'm not a violent man, but I don't know what I would've done if I had found him first." Louis confessed.

"I understand. I got a daughter myself." The deputy told him.

"Daddy, I wanna leave as soon as possible. Can we go tomorrow?" Jessie asked.

"Sure baby."

"Wait, hold on." The deputy interrupted. "You can't leave just yet young lady."

"Why not?"

"You just identified this man as a rapist. This is going to trial."

"Trial?" Louis asked.

"Oh yeah. This'll be the biggest trial this town has ever seen. I'm afraid you won't be able to leave till this is over."

Jessie burst into tears and ran out of the building. When she got home, she went straight to bed and Gracie went in after her trying to console her.

"Are you alright, sweetie?"

Jessie answered by shaking her head. "I feel so bad that this has happened to you. I should've been around more instead of running with Addie so much. I guess I'm part to blame."

"Don't say that, Gracie. It's not your fault."

"I know it's not my fault, but you're my little sister. It was my responsibility to make sure you were okay. I should've kept a better eye on you."

"Gracie, please don't feel like that. I feel bad enough with out you trying to take responsibility for this. I can't take you trying to carry the burden."

"Oh sweetheart, I'm sorry. I didn't mean to make this about me."

"I just wish..."

"What Jessie? What do you wish?"

"I wish I could die."

"Jessie, you mustn't say things like that."

"I do. I wish I were dead, and then I wouldn't have to go through this."

"But you don't have to go through it alone. Me and Daddy, grandmother and all the rest of the family are here for you, and we're gonna get through this together."

"I hate him, Gracie. I hate him for what he did to me." Jessie said crying.

"I know sweetie, I hate him too."

While Gracie stayed with Jessie trying to comfort her, Louis and Sarah were in the next room discussing what they were going to do about the baby.

"Mama, I don't know what to do. She's only thirteen; she can't take care of a baby. And even if she could, I don't want her to keep a baby by the man who raped her. It'll be a constant reminder of the most traumatizing thing that's ever happened to her."

"I know it, Louis. I don't even know how to advise you on something like this. I done prayed and prayed, asking the Lord to give us direction."

Louis put his head down. "I think I'm gone call Tulah. See what she got to say about this."

"Well, Louis you've been the only parent for the past few years, maybe you should decide what to do about it."

"I know, Mama. But Tulah is still Jessie's mother, and she has a say. She wanted to come, too. I told her that I'd come and see about her first, and that I would send for her if need be."

Sarah nodded her head not wanting to comment too much on the subject.

"I know Tulah left, but she aint never stop caring about these girls. She's smart, too. I know she'll help us figure out what to do."

The following morning, Louis woke up at the crack of dawn. Everyone was still sleeping and the sun was just peeking over the horizon creating a reddish, orange glow across a cerulean sky. Louis put on his housecoat and went out on the porch and sat on the swing. He looked around at the dawning day and smiled remembering the days he used to spend on this porch with God. He saw how much things had changed since he was last there, then observing the trees, the redness of the earth, the grass and the flowers, he realized how much things had actually stayed the same. The circumstances that affected his family in the last few months were more than enough reason to get reacquainted with God. He went inside and got his Mama's Bible from off the living room table and took it out on the porch with him. He layed it on his lap and rubbed the finely textured paper between his fingers, took in a long cleansing breath, exhaled, and then said good morning to God.

The next few weeks were daunting for Jessie. The court assigned attorney sat down with Jessie to take a report and document what happened. Preston Jackson, a hard nosed, no-nonsense, white man with a generous belly, receding hairline and fat fingers, was sent to represent Jessie. He sweated profusely, constantly wiping his forehead with an open palm then wiping it on his pants. He appeared nervous and agitated, uncomfortably fidgeting in his chair, and nursing a smoker's cough. He sat across the table from Jessie and Louis and proceeded to thumb through her file, his eyes quickly scanning over the report that the sheriff had taken. The room was silent, disturbed only by a faint wheezing sound coming from Preston's slightly parted mouth, and a fly buzzing deliriously around the room. Underneath the table, Jessie's felt her legs began to tremble. She tried to stop them, but had no control over the involuntary tremors. Preston took in a breath and blew it out loudly, sounding like a deflating ballon. When he peered over his file and stared into Jessie's eyes, it was as though he could see straight through her, weakening her and unveiling the lie that she had told.

"Is this what happened? Uh, right here you said…uh, 'he pinned you down so you couldn't move'. Wuz that the way of it?"

Jessie nodded her head. "You gone hafta speak up, girl."

"Yes, that's how it went." Jessie answered nervously. Sensing her apprehension, Louis reached over and grabbed her hand giving it a reassuring squeeze.

"You said he wuz drunk, so much so, that he staggered when he walked. If that wuz the case, why couldn't you get away from em'? Did you try to fight?"

Jessie looked at Louis before answering. He encouraged her by nodding his head.

"Yeah, I tried, but he was just too strong."

"Well, why in God's name didn't you tell somebody what happened sooner?"

Jessie felt trapped. She wanted to flee. She wanted to run out of the room, away from his gazing stare, his skeptical inquisition and his accusatory tone. Her eyes began to water.

"Oh you gone hafta do betteran' dat. You caint go to crying everytime somebody asks you a question. I'm on yo side. I'm trying to get down what happened so I kin defen you." Preston glared at Jessie. His dark, beady eyes, accusing her each time he looked at her. "Look, I know you ain't probably never been to court before, but you gone hafta speak up and tell what happened. Your story caint change either. The other attorney gone be beatin you up, badgerin you about what Willie did and you caint go to cryin."

Jessie nodded trying to be strong, but she knew that Preston didn't believe her, that's why he was being so stern. She tried answer him, but when she opened her mouth, she bursted out in tears. Louis put his hand out towards Preston and then turned to comfort Jessie.

"Oh go on and take her home." Preston admonished. " Let her get some rest and we kin start over tomorrow." Louis helped Jessie to her feet, gave her a hug, and then took her home.

Both attorneys had to interview the town's people for jurors, which turned out to be a trying experience. Because the town was so small, most everybody interviewed knew Jessie or her family, which disqualified them as possible jurors. It was considered a conflict of interest. Interviews for jurors extended beyond Marietta in search of people who didn't know the Starks family. The news of what happened traveled throughout all the surrounding cities. People whispered when they saw Jessie some even pointed. Reporters from other townships came in talking to neighbors, asking questions and hanging around the court house, while others took pictures of Sarah's house. Jessie had no idea that this would turn such a monstrosity of sorts. When the search had finally been narrowed down and jurors were selected, the trial was set to begin. Jessie was already jaded with the whole ordeal. Each time she walked into the court room her breath became labored, her heart skipped a beat, and the palms of her hands became clammy.

Jessie had to be in the court room day in and day out listening to Preston Jackson debate, argue rebuttals, and try to persuade the jury, while the defendant's attorney faught to prove who was telling the truth and who the real victim was. During the trial Jessie learned a lot about Willie Purfoy- more than she actually cared to know. She found out that he was married to Viola Purfoy, who had five of his children. He was a man who had dropped out of school in the third grade to work and take care of his family after his father ran off. After he was married, he continued working to support his wife and children until one day, about seven years ago, a tragic accident claimed the life of his youngest son.

Willie took to drinking, finding consolation in the excessive indulgence of cheap, Georgia moonshine. Drinking became his only way of coping with the accident, and after a while it grew out of control. After continuous warnings, Willie showed up at work one day after a drunken binge and was fired on the spot. Willie and his wife separated shortly after. One afternoon while visiting his family, he and Viola had a terrible argument and Willie left hurriedly. He went down to the river where he finished off a bottle of liquor and then fell asleep.

"The State is trying to create an impression that Willie is an evil, distorted and twisted individual. Yes, Willie Purfoy is a drunkered and a wine bibbler." His attorney defended. "But a rapist he is not." There was a crescendo of voices in the court room and the judge's gavel pounded relentlessly on stand to control the turbulent crowd. Jessie stole a glance at Viola whose sad eyes were tearstained and grief stricken. She coddled her children close to her, careful not to let Jessie catch her staring, wondering if there was any truth in what she claimed. Jessie studied each one of Willie's children as they embraced one another, holding hands and trying to be strong. Day after day, Jessie was forced to listen to how much Willie and his family had been through, and through it all, what a good man he was. When they brought Willie on the stand, he looked at Jessie and pleaded with her to tell them the truth.

"We've been through enough, damn you! If you do this to me, you might as well put a gun to my head." The unruly crowd exploded with contemptuous remarks and jeers. The judge's gavel pounded against the wooden and brass block, the sound echoing in Jessie's ears.

Jessie jumped up and ran out of the court room. Louis, Gracie and Sarah ran after her, but she refused to return to the court room. Preston asked for a recess, and then took her inside the judge's chambers to talk to her privately.

"You've got to pull yourself together. I told you it wouldn't be easy, but you can do this. Hell, you got the whole town out there backin' you up. Just stick to what happened."

"No, I can't." Jessie cried. "I won't do it!"

Preston became enraged. "Whathchu mean you can't do it?"

"I wanna get outta here. I want to go home!" Jessie screamed at him.

"Jessie, calm down."

"I won't calm down. I can't do this, don't you understand? I want to go home."

Preston sent for Louis to try to reason with her, while every one else anxiously awaited in the court room. When Louis came in, Preston ran to meet him.

"She's hysterical. I can't get her to calm down. She says she's not gone testify."

Louis went to Jessie. "What's wrong, baby? Tell me what it is."

"I can't do this, Daddy. This is too much for me."

"Tell her if she doesn't testify, he could go free." Preston advised.

When Jessie heard that, she knew that she would not testify against Willie. She had already created a mess and made so many mistakes, but she would not be responsible for taking this man's freedom, keeping him away from his wife and children. Perhaps this was the way out, she thought.

"I'm not going through with it." She told Louis.

"Why, Jessie?"

"I can't be sure it was him, Daddy. It was dark and I, I...I didn't get a good look at his face."

"He admitted to being down at the river that night. He said with his own mouth that he was so drunk he didn't even remember seeing you. It's him, Jessie. He did it."

"I don't want to accuse the wrong man."

"If you don't testify, he will be set free. And if that happens, there's no turning back."

"I know, Daddy. But I can't go through with it."

"Do you understand that he will be released and back out on the streets?" Preston asked her. "Is that what you want?"

"Yes. That's what I want."

"She doesn't know what she's saying. You have to talk to her, make her change her mind."

Jessie looked at Louis and told him in her most sincere and heartfelt voice, "Daddy, this is not the man responsible. I will not testisfy against him and I will not change my mind." She rubbed her hand over her belly and then looked back a Louis. "Daddy, please take me away from here. I want to go home. I wanna go back to Detroit."

Because Jessie did not testify against Willie, he was acquitted and immediately released. The sheriff had to disperse the crowd because they refused to leave, not satisfied with the ruling, they demanded justice. Some of them heckled Jessie as she walked out of the courtroom, while others pitied her, thinking she was too afraid to tell the truth. "That's okay, baby. 'Venges is mine saith the Lord'. God will work it out." A lady in the crowd encouraged. "Keep yo head up, honey. You ain't did nothing wrong." Another one yelled out. "Don't let that whiskey drinkin fool go. Where he at, we'll take care of him." The crowd jeered. Jessie kept her head down trying to avoid the stares of the unruly crowd.

A few days later she was all packed and ready to leave with

Louis. Louis was expecting to take Gracie home as well, but she decided that it was best that she stay behind to look after Aunt Cora and Sarah. Sarah prepared a big home going dinner for Jessie and invited all their family and friends. Gracie, Addie and Aunt Etta all brought gifts for Jessie. Everyone was there, Uncle Henry, Josh, even Aunt Cora made her way over. Needless to say, Joe was the only one who didn't show up, and that was fine by Jessie. They all ate, laughed and cried and said their goodbyes, before seeing Louis and Jessie off. The next morning, after Louis spent time on the porch holding the Bible and communing with God, he boarded a train bound for Detroit and took his baby girl home.

Chapter 33

Tulah, Lucille and Memphis were at the train station by a quarter of one, anxiously waiting for Louis and Jessie's train to arrive. When Tulah last saw Jessie, she was she was a bright-eyed, little innocent ten year old, who believed that the whole world was harmless and good. Three years later, Jessie returns a thirteen-year-old mother to be, impregnated in the the most vile, mean, intrusive manner that one human being could inflict on another. Tulah was nervous about seeing Jessie, after so much has happened, and felt largely responsible for the devastation that her family has endured. She didn't know how well her presence would be received, however, she was prepared submit to whatever resentment that was harbored in the hearts of her loved ones. She understood that she was wrong for abandoning them for her own selfish needs at a time when they needed her most. Sorry for her misdeeds, she was willing to do anything to redeem herself and be reconciled to her family. Tulah experienced a barrage of emotions as she paced nervously throughout the train station wringing her hands in anticipation. She felt nervous and anxious, nauseous and fidgety, hot and cold, restless and fearful while her heart dipped and dived causing her to feel light-headed and wanting to flee.

The wheels of the steam locomotive slowed to a stop and let off a loud, steamy whistle to announce its arrival. Lucille held firmly to Memphis for support and anxiously patted his chest. Tulah stood alone with no one to offer her support. She tried to be strong, but her legs betrayed her, trembling uneasily as though they would give out. When the doors on the train were opened, passengers eagerly unloaded and moved about hastily. Tulah wondered if she would recognize her, if she still looked the same, or if she had been transformed by calamitous circumstances, into someone whom she could not identify. Her eyes darted from one passenger to the next, trying to locate her estranged daughter. She saw Louis first. Actually it was his hat that got her attention. It was tilted down in the front and stopped just above his brow. When she was finally able to see his face, it was intense and serious looking, but he was just as handsome as he was the first day she met him. He was holding Jessie's hand, but with all the traffic, Tulah only saw half of her arm. She pushed through the crowd making her way closer to them when Louis looked up and he and Tulah made eye contact. When their eyes met, her breath caught in her chest and tears welled in her eyes. She tried to hold them back and was winning the battle until a path was opened and Jessie appeared through the crowd. Her tears fell fast and easy clouding her eyes so that she could barely see. When she saw Jessie's sweet face and swollen belly she fell to her knees and wept. Jessie dropped Louis' hand and ran to her. Tulah, still on her knees, hugged Jessie around her waist and cried. It was then that Tulah understood that old adage about wishing she could turn back the hands of time.

Louis went over and helped Tulah to her feet. Allowing him to assist her, she turned her attention to him, wrapped her arms around him and cried in his arms.

"Come on, let's get outta here, we can have our reunion at home."

Lucille hugged Jessie and they giggled with excitement patting each others expectant bellies. Lucille and Jessie walked arm in arm to Memphis' car that was parked right outside, while Tulah walked behind them with Louis by her side. After loading the bags in the car, Memphis sat up front with Lucille, while Louis, Tulah and Jessie all squeezed in the back seat. Louis wanted to go home, but Tulah insisted that they come to her house where she had dinner prepared for them. Crowded around the small table, Tulah brought out milk crates in place of chairs to accommodate her guests. As they ate, there was an awkward silence the hovered over the room as each stole fleeting glances from one another in between bites, all wanting to ask questions, but too afraid to speak up. After dinner, Lucille and Memphis prepared to leave and offered to drop Louis and Jessie home.

"Please, don't go. Not yet anyway. I need ta talk ta yall."

Jessie acquiesced, but Louis appeared hesitant. "Louis, please. It's some thangs I need ta say ta you, too." Louis agreed, so Lucille and Memphis left. They adjourned to the living room where Tulah went into her spiel.

"I promised ma'self dat I wusn't gone cry no mo. Ain't no sense in me feeling sorry fo ma'self, but I am sorry for da thangs dat I did. I know all this is ma fault. If I had been there fa yall, none of dis woulda happened."

"Mama," Jessie interrupted.

"Hold on, baby, let me get it out. I been holdin on ta this fo a long time and it needs ta be said. I was wrong. I was wrong fa what I did ta yall girls and to yo Daddy." Louis looked at her, and then looked away. "I wish I had da power to change thangs and take back every bad thang yall ever went through. I was selfish and stupid and I'm sorry. I know that don't change thangs nor make thangs any betta, but I do apologize to you from the bottom of my heart." Tulah said placing her hand over her heart, blinking back tears.

Jessie fault hard not to cry as well. She loathed herself for creating a lie that continued to grow and devastate everyone around her. It was difficult for her to watch Willie Purfoy and his family catch the brunt of its destruction, but then Gracie felt it, Louis felt it, Sarah, and now Tulah. Incidentally, the one who took advantage of her, betrayed her, threatened her, and then rubbed it in her face by bringing his girlfriend around; the one who was responsible for most of the damage, is the only one who hadn't suffered any consequences, and it was Jessie who protected him. She silently reprimanded herself for her stupidity, but yet, offered no confession as Tulah went on and on pouring her heart out and begging for their forgiveness.

"I know I don't deserve it, but I would really like it if you would give me a chance to make it up to you by helping you to get through this. Louis, I say this to you as much as I say it to Jessie. I'm sorry and I really wanna help."

"What can you do now, Tulah?"

"I can start by being here. I can go to the doctor with Jessie, cook meals, and find out about getting the baby adopted."

"No." Jessie interrupted.

"What did you say?" Louis asked.

"No. I don't wanna give my baby up." Louis and Tulah looked at each other, trying to make sense of what they had just heard.

"You mean you want to keep the baby?"

Jessie looked down and nodded her head. Louis went over to her, got down on one knee and lifted her chin.

"Jessie, you don't have to. Under the circumstances it's perfectly understandable, and no one would hold it against you.

Jessie kept her head down refusing to look at Louis. Louis looked at Tulah silently asking her to support him. Tulah walked over to Jessie and placed her hand on her shoulder.

"Jess. I know all this may feel a little confusing and overwhelming, it's a lot for a young girl to handle, but keeping the baby is not the right answer."

"Well, what is the right answer, mother? For me to leave my baby, abandon it like you did me? Well, I'm not gonna do that. I've already thought about it and I've decided that I'm keeping it." Jessie got up and walked to the door. "I'm ready to go, Daddy. Can we leave now?"

Louis got up and started towards the door, but Tulah pressed her small hand on Louis' chest to stop him.

"Hold on, Louis." She said never taking her eyes off Jessie. "Now you wait a minute, young lady. I will not have you thinking you got the right to come in here and disrespect me and say whatever you want to me. I made my mistakes, I have. And I'm right here willing to do what I have to, to make up for em. God will judge me for what I did wrong." Tulah pointed towards the ceiling. "God will, not you! Now I ain't always right, but I'm always yo Mama, and you will not disrespect me like that ever again. Do you understand me?"

Jessie looked in the other direction avoiding Tulah's penetrating stare. "I said do you understand me?" Tulah asked walking closer.

"Yes, I understand. I'm sorry, mother."

"Good. Now if you wanna go home now, that's fine. But you need to think about how a young girl like you is gone raise a baby alone with no means of taking care of it. You got a place ta live. You can always stay wit yo Daddy, or wit me, but it's a lot more to caring for a baby then to put a roof over its head. You think about how you gone do dat. And if you think welfare gone do it all, then you need to think again."

Tulah walked over to the sofa and took a seat. She shook her head before speaking.

"Louis, I'm sorry for all this. Maybe you should take Jessie on home you and me can talk later."

"Okay Tulah, goodnight."

Jessie thought about everything Tulah said to her and knew that she was right. The truth was that she had already thought about giving the baby up. Jessie despised what she did, she despised Joe, and she especially despised the way she was cornered into protecting him. She no longer wanted any part of him or his child to remind her of the dreadful mistakes she'd made in disgracing herself with him. Jessie had every intention of giving the baby up until she felt a faint flutter in her stomach, reminding her that there was a tiny life was growing inside of her- a life that depended on her for love and protection, feeding off her own body in order to survive. Each time the small fetus tickled the inside of Jessie's womb, she grew more in love with it. Joe no longer mattered. In her mind he didn't even exist. The only thing that mattered was that the baby was a part of her, and was helpless to any of the scandalous deeds that got it here. Jessie wanted to redeem herself of all of the lustful and dirty things she did with Joe and felt that she could accomplish that by keeping the baby. As she gave more thought to her dilemma, weighing the consequences of either decision, she was certain she was doing the right thing. She got on her knees and prayed before going to bed. She asked the Lord to give her direction and strength to move forward in a new life with her baby.

The next morning Jessie awakened to an urgent knocking on the door. She called for Louis, but when he didn't answer she got up to see who it was. Jessie went to the porch and looked down. She saw a woman walking around the house peering through each of the windows.

"May I help you?" Jessie yelled down from the porch.

"Who are you?" The woman quizzed.

"Who are you?" Jessie countered.

"I'm Pearl Stevens, Louis' fiancée."

Jessie raised her brow and turned her ear to the woman. "Louis' what?"

"His fiancée. Is he here?"

"Um, no. I don't think he is." Jessie answered.

"Well, can I come in and wait? I came all the way over here from the other side of town."

"Uhh, sure. I guess so. Give me a minute."

Jessie put on a housecoat and walked down the stairs to let her in. As she opened the door, Pearl pushed past her and made her way up the stairs. Once inside, she looked around the house as if Louis may have been hiding from her.

"Who are you?"

"I'm Jessie."

"Not his daughter, Jessie?" Pearl asked eyeing Jessie's swollen belly.

"Yeah. I'm his daughter."

"Well honey, you look like you done got yo'self in a fix." She said with obvious disdain. "I met your sister. She's quite young to be having a baby, but a least she's married. Are you?"

Jessie looked down, momentarily shamed by her circumstances, and then she put her head up and answered defiantly.

"No I'm not."

"Are you getting married?"

"Not any time soon."

"Humph. Louis said he had to go check on his daughter who had gotten into some trouble, but he didn't say it was this kind of trouble. How long are you gone be here?"

Before Jessie could answer, there was a sound of keys jingling in the door, then footsteps on the stairs. Jessie breathed a sigh of relief, tired of the inquisition by the stranger claiming to be her father's future bride. Jessie and Pearl stared at the door in anticipation. When the door swung open, Louis came in with a bag of groceries and was accompanied by Tulah. Louis' befuddled look told them that he wasn't expecting Pearl.

"Hey Pearl. What are you doing here?"

"I was expecting you back two days ago. When I didn't hear from you I decided to come over and see what was going on. I met Jessica, but who's this?" She said eyeing Tulah.

"My daughter's name is Jessie, and this is her mother, Tulah."

"Nice to meet you." Tulah said, extending her hand. Pearl ignored Tulah's gesture and turned to Louis.

"Had I known you were having a family reunion, I would've stayed home."

"Tulah, Jessie, can you all excuse us for a moment?"

"Okay, I'll get the groceries put away." Tulah said taking the bag from Louis. Before they could leave the room, Pearl put her hand on her hip demanding answers.

"Why haven't you called?"

"Why did you show up without calling?"

"Since when do I have to call before coming to my fiancée's house? Oh, wait. I guess since you have your ex-wife and daughter here, there's no room for me. Is that it Louis?"

Louis looked at her and shook his head. He knew this was a conversation he needed to have with Pearl, but have been putting off hoping things would work itself out. But now that she was here causing trouble and demanding answers he knew that the inevitable had come. "As a matter of fact, Pearl, that is it. I don't have room for you in my life."

Taken back by his candor, Pearl adjusted and quickly changed her tone. "Well Louis, if you need time to work things out I'll understand. I see Jessica done got herself into a fix..."

"You see Pearl, here's the thing." Louis said interrupting her. "This is my family and they need me. This is not something that's gonna work itself out in a few days or in a few months, this is gonna take time, and I wouldn't think of making you wait."

"I don't mind, Louis."

"But I do. Tulah and Jessie gone be staying here with me till we can work through this and I'm willing to put in as much time as its gone take."

"What? You mean they gone be living here?"

"Yes."

"Your daughter is one thing, but why does your ex-wife have to stay?"

"Cause I asked her to. Jessie is both our daughter and she needs us both, so I asked her to move in with us."

"Oh no, Louis. I won't stand for that."

"And I don't expect you to. Thanks for all your help, Pearl. I'll always think fondly of you."

Pearl couldn't believe what she was hearing. She searched Louis' eyes looking for some sign of allegiance to her, for all that she's done for him, but all she saw was a vacancy there, and the loyalty he had for them. She nodded her head understanding that she had been outranked, kissed him on the cheek and walked away.

Louis had gone to Tulah's house earlier that morning to privately discuss what they would do about Jessie's condition. Tulah had been up all night wondering the same thing, so when Louis showed up she was happy and relieved that they could figure it out together. It was Louis' idea that Tulah give up her apartment and come back to live with them. Initially, she was hesitant, not knowing what to expect or what was expected of her, but then she decided that she owed it to her family to at least give it a try. Besides, she wanted to be there for Jessie. After dinner, Louis and Tulah sat down with Jessie to talk about the baby. Jessie explained that the baby was just as much hers as it was the absent father's and that she was going to love and care for the baby on her own. Louis accepted her stance, but Tulah was not as easily convinced. Even though she had not been around her daughter, she still knew her well enough to know that there was a major element missing from her story. Tulah probed Jessie with a barrage of questions in an effort to get closer to the truth, but Jessie held fast, not divulging anything.

Later that evening, Louis sat on the porch smoking a cigarette while Jessie sat in the living room reading. Tulah had cleaned the dishes and went to check on Jessie.

"Can I get you anything?"

"No thank you, I'm fine."

"You know, when I was pregnant I used to really enjoy a cup of tea. Would you like a cup?" Tulah offered.

"Yes mother, that sounds delightful."

"I'll get some started." Tulah went into the kitchen to prepare a cup of tea for herself and for Jessie. She brought the cups into the living room, handed one to Jessie and took a seat right next to her. Jessie took a sip from the cup and it felt warm and soothing to her stomach.

"This is really good. Thank you."

"You're welcome. It's a special blend. I made it with real tea leaves." She told her. They drank their tea, talked about names for the baby and how Tulah and Louis would be grandparents twice in just one year. Tulah collected Jessie's cup before she had a chance to finish. Remembering what she learned from Mama

Lou, Tulah walked into the kitchen and swirled the remaining tea around three times before draining the cup. She stared into the cup and then looked towards the living room where Jessie sat contently reading her book. Even though the reading was sketchy, Tulah knew that the truth about what happened in Georgia would forever be kept a secret and safely tucked away in Jessie's heart.